Praise for Sara Fawkes

"A titillating story that was enjoyable and very hot . . . suspenseful and full of intrigue."—*The Romance Reader*

"Steaming hot, scandalicious to the nth degree . . ."
—*Scandalicious Book Reviews*

"Smoking HOT! Full of intrigue, secrets, hidden agendas, back stabbing, lust, domination, romance, danger, and of course, action. There is so much to like!" —*Crazy Four Books*

"A crazy, erotic trip into the world of money and sexual submission on a billionaire scale. With a lot of sex, a bit of romance, plenty of toys, and lots of guns, this story doesn't have a dull moment."
—*The Season for Romance*

"*Castaway* leaves readers hankering for more. Fawkes is finding her stride as an established author." —*Under the Covers*

"Dripping with lust and passion. There's passion, drama, danger, and if that wasn't enough, there's a dash of naughty sex to spice things up!" —*My Two Cents*

"HOT! I mean REALLY hot! Nothing short of amazing. Superbly written and impossible not to go on to the rest of the series."
—*Reviewing Romance*

"One of those awesome books that grabs your attention in the first few pages, hooks you with the emotions of the character, and pulls you into their world." —*Codi Gary's Books*

"Filled with true passion, great sex, and danger—what's not to love!" —*Shh Moms Reading*

"A wonderful mix of lust, love, betrayal, and action. The perfect book that held my attention through to the end." —*Nightly Reading*

anything
he wants
– & –
castaway

sara fawkes

ST. MARTIN'S GRIFFIN 〰 NEW YORK

ANYTHING HE WANTS & CASTAWAY. Copyright © 2014 by Sarah Pearson. All rights reserved. Printed in the United States of America. For information, address St. Martin's Press, 175 Fifth Avenue, New York, N.Y. 10010.

www.stmartins.com

The Library of Congress Cataloging-in-Publication Data is available upon request.

ISBN 978-1-250-05495-1 (trade paperback)
ISBN 978-1-4668-5794-0 (e-book)

St. Martin's Griffin books may be purchased for educational, business, or promotional use. For information on bulk purchases, please contact Macmillan Corporate and Premium Sales Department at 1-800-221-7945, extension 5442, or write specialmarkets@macmillan.com.

Anything He Wants was first published as a five-part e-book series in 2012 by St. Martin's Griffin.
Castaway was first published as a four-part e-book series in 2013 under the title *Anything He Wants: Castaway* by St. Martin's Griffin.

First Edition: October 2014

10 9 8 7 6 5 4 3 2 1

anything he wants

1

The high point of my workdays lately was seeing the gorgeous stranger every morning.

I hurried through the lobby toward the elevators as fast as decorum and my heels would allow, passing ladders and service crews working on the old building's antiquated electrical systems. The dark-haired stranger arrived at the elevator like clockwork, at 8:20 A.M. every day, and this morning proved no exception. I jockeyed my way through the crowd until I stood close, but not conspicuously so, to the stranger and stared at the elevator doors while pretending to ignore him. It wasn't a game, although it sometimes felt that way. Men that handsome always stayed several steps outside my sphere of influence and this man was no different.

Didn't mean a girl couldn't dream.

The doors opened and I moved with the small crowd onto the elevator, making sure my floor was pressed. The old—or "historic," as some liked to say—building was in the midst of a full renovation. Everything was being upgraded to new, more modern settings, but for now they still had the older-style elevators. Smaller and slower than current models, the metal box nevertheless did its job as it chugged up to the floors above.

I rearranged the large satchel in my arm, sliding a glance sideways and catching his eye. Does he know I watch him? Flushing, I turned my gaze forward once again as the elevator opened to let another string of people off to their floors. My stop was still eleven floors away; I did data entry as temp work for Hamilton Industries. The company spanned most of the upper levels but my small cubicle was tucked away in a forgotten corner near the middle.

I loved the clean-cut, suited look, and the dark-haired man was always impeccably dressed in suits and ties that probably cost more than what I made in a month. Everything about him screamed high society, far out of my league, but that never stopped my fantasy life from including him. The handsome stranger was part of my dreams, the face I saw when I closed my eyes for bed. As I'd had nothing between my legs not run by batteries in well over a year, my fantasies were getting pretty kinky. I took a moment to think about them now and a slow smile spread across my face. It didn't take much to get me going, but the image in my mind of being pushed against a wall and ravaged . . . Oh yeah.

Passengers continued to disembark and as the elevator doors shut, I pulled myself out of my reverie as I realized that, for the first time, I was actually alone with the stranger. Clearing my throat nervously, I smoothed down my pencil skirt with my free hand as the old elevator continued its trek up to my workplace. Breathe, Lucy, just breathe. Desire curled in my belly, fueled by thoughts of all sorts of naughty things in elevators. I wonder if this one has cameras. . . .

I heard a faint rustle behind me, then a thick arm appeared beside me and pressed a red button on the panel. Immediately the elevator ground to a halt and before I could say anything, arms appeared on either side of my head and a low voice next to my ear murmured, "I see you on this elevator every morning. Your doing, I take it?"

Shocked into silence, I could only blink in wide-eyed confusion. Should I pinch myself? Is this really happening?

As I was pressed against the elevator doors by a hard body behind me, the cool metal against my suddenly hard and sensitive nipples elicited a breathy moan. "What—" I started, immediately forgetting whatever I was going to say as I felt his hard length press against my hip.

"I can smell your arousal," he growled, that low sexy voice making my stomach tighten. "Every morning you get on this elevator and I can smell your need." One hand moved down and entwined with mine as he dipped his head toward my neck. "What's your name?"

My mind went blank for a moment, forgetting the simplest of answers. Oh God, that voice is pure sex, I thought wildly, lifting my hands to brace myself against the hard surface before me. His voice was low and had a lilt I couldn't place, and my chest grew tight with need. "Lucy," I finally managed, hoping my brain was done short-circuiting.

"Lucy," he repeated, and I drew in a shaky breath at hearing my name said in that too-sexy voice. "I need to see if you taste as good as you smell."

There was no request for permission in his voice, only an implacable demand, and I rolled my head sideways to allow him access. His lips slid across the soft skin behind my ear, tongue flicking out to touch me; his teeth nipped the lobe and I moaned, pressing back against him. He rotated his hips and my breathing sped up, needy pants a staccato in the silence.

"God, you're so fucking hot." His hand trailed down the side of my body, across my hip and down my thigh until he found the hem of my skirt. His hand then retraced its steps back up, skimming lightly across the smooth skin of my inner thigh, pulling the material of my skirt up toward my hips. Unthinking, I spread my legs to give him access and gasped loudly as fingers slid along the outside of my soaked panties, pressing against my aching core.

Was this really happening? My body bucked, trapped between the metal doors and the hot body behind me. It was like every fantasy I'd ever had was being played out in person, and I was helpless to stop my conditioned response.

His fingers pulsed, sliding across my clit with increasing frequency, and my hips moved of their own volition, craving more of his touch. I cried out when his teeth sank into my shoulder, then his fingers slid beneath the thin cotton and lace and stroked my wet skin, pulling at my tender opening in a way that had me moaning loudly inside the elevator.

"Come for me," he murmured in his low Vin Diesel voice,

lips and teeth running along the exposed line of my neck and shoulder. His fingers pushed deep inside, thumb flicking my hard nub, and with a strangled cry I came hard. My forehead rested against the hard steel of the door as I shuddered, suddenly boneless.

Below the numbered panel to my right, a telephone rang out.

I stiffened in shock, the blaring tones cutting through my murky haze. Lust gave way to mortification and I pushed against the door to free myself. The dark stranger stepped back, allowing me space, and pressed the red button again. I hastily rearranged my clothing as the elevator chugged back up the shaft; a few seconds later the telephone stopped ringing.

"You taste even better than I imagined."

I turned, helpless against that voice, to see him licking his fingers. The look he gave me made my knees weak but the ringing phone had woken me up and I fumbled blindly for the floor buttons, pressing every button within my reach. This only seemed to amuse him, but when the doors opened to an empty hallway two floors below mine, I stumbled out. No people were in sight on this floor, to my relief—I wasn't sure I could take more attention right then.

A quick whistle behind me drew my attention and I turned to see the stranger pick up my satchel and hold it out to me. It had slid out of my arms, forgotten, to the floor while we were . . . I cleared my throat and took it with as much dignity as I could muster.

He smiled, the simple expression changing his entire

countenance. I stared, dumbstruck at his utter gorgeousness, as he winked at me. "I'll see you again," he said as the elevator doors shut, stranding me temporarily on the lower floor.

I took a deep breath and fumbled with my clothing, tucking my blouse into my waistband with shaky fingers. My panties were a lost cause—I'd have a wet spot on my dress all day if I continued to wear them. Focusing on that and not the growing embarrassment of my actions, I searched and found a bathroom nearby in which to clean myself up.

A few minutes later, clean but vulnerable without any underwear, I took the stairs up two flights to my floor. The halls leading to my area were packed with last-minute arrivals, and I made it to my cubicle without any problems. I was a minute late clocking in on the computer but nobody seemed to care as I got right to work, drowning myself in my job to try and forget my shocking display earlier.

2

The day passed in a mental jumble. No matter how I tried to focus on my work, I couldn't make myself concentrate. I found it necessary to double-, then triple-check my work to make sure I'd done it right. The temp data entry assignments I was given were tedious and brainless, but nevertheless I kept messing them up. My mind would flash back to the elevator, the handsome stranger and the first semipublic orgasm I ever had, and when I got back on track I couldn't remember what lines I'd entered in the computer.

This was so unlike me. I'd always been a sexual creature but never was the type who knew what to do about it. The boys never asked me out; I wasn't invited to parties or the like even in college. The few boyfriends I'd had, if they could be called that, hadn't stayed around long. My life at the moment was boring, mostly out of necessity—college loans didn't pay themselves, and living near the city made things even tighter—but I couldn't find much connection with most men. They wanted to go party, I wanted to read; they were *Sports Illustrated*, I was *National Geographic*.

Dating, while the least of my worries at the moment, was definitely not a strong point.

Despite my attempts to forget the whole situation in the elevator, by lunch I desperately wanted my vibrator and a swift kick in the rear. My actions and instant response to the stranger were troublesome, regardless of my fantasy life. It couldn't happen again no matter how much I may want a repeat. I needed this job, even if it was monotonous, and I couldn't afford any more distractions. But my job didn't require much brainpower to begin with and I couldn't stop remembering how soft his lips were, and how his teeth across the skin of my neck sent shivers down my spine. His large hands had held a dual promise of strength and tenderness that my body refused to forget.

It was a long day.

Barely managing to get my quota of files archived and turned in by the end of the day, I contemplated taking the stairs down fourteen flights but finally opted for the elevator, which I made sure was stranger-free. I cut through the underground parking garage while the bulk of the crowd headed for the taxis out front. Few people were able to park under the building; certainly not a new temp, even if I did have a car. But cutting through the garage was a much faster route to the subway station two streets away, and nobody had told me the shortcut was off limits.

I headed down the single flight of steps and out into the chilly afternoon air of the underground garage. The squeal of tires came from somewhere in the multilevel complex but I saw nobody else, just lines of cars. Rubbing my arms, the bite in the air promising cold temperatures as soon as the sun set, I turned toward the guard shack, wishing I'd brought something to slip over my arms. It was late spring but the weather had taken a colder turn over the last few days and I wasn't dressed appropriately.

Someone grabbed my arm and jerked me sideways into the shadows beside me. Before I could make a sound, a hand clapped over my mouth, and I was dragged back into a small alcove half hidden from the rest of the garage reserved for motorcycles. I struggled but the arms holding me were implacable, like iron across my body.

"I did tell you I would see you soon." The voice was familiar and deep, and I recognized it immediately. It had been running through my head all day long in fantasies I'd tried in vain to stamp out.

As soon as I heard his voice a wave of relief washed over me, followed quickly by confused anger. Why on earth do I trust him? Frustrated by my own apparent stupidity, I stomped down as hard as I could on the instep of the stranger's foot. He grunted but didn't release me, instead spinning me and pressing me up against the cold concrete wall. His body molded itself to my back, hands holding my wrists against the concrete. "You can fight," he murmured, running his lips along the back of my ear. "I like that."

His casual dismissal annoyed me. I threw my head back, trying to hit him in the face, but he ducked out of the way with a chuckle. Another attempt to stomp his foot with my pump was foiled when his leg snaked between mine, leaving me unable to struggle that way. The fingers around my wrists, softer than iron manacles but no less firm, set fire to my skin without giving me any room to move.

"Let me go or I'll scream," I said in an even voice, trying to turn my head to catch his eye. It frustrated the hell out of me that I was neither afraid nor as angry as I knew I should be; the man was once again prompting the wrong feelings for the situation. I had to be brain damaged if I thought I could trust the man when I didn't even know his name!

He leaned forward, pressing his face against my hair and taking a deep breath. The appreciative rumble deep in his throat reverberated through my body. "I couldn't stop thinking about you all day," he murmured, not acknowledging my threat. His thumbs made light circles on my wrists and my body clenched at the almost tender motion. "How quickly you responded to me, your smell, your taste."

I swallowed, trying to ignore the sudden flutter in my belly. No, I thought desperately, I can't be turned on by this. The sight of him looming over me, however—his hard hot body pressing against my back—was making my head whirl and limbs ache to wrap around him. Dammit. "Let me go," I said between gritted teeth, trying to ignore my body's traitorous reactions. "This is wrong, I don't want . . ."

He laid a soft kiss on the skin behind my ear as I trailed off, a stark contrast to the unbreakable grip he held on my wrists. My breath caught in my throat as lips and teeth dragged down my neck as his hips rolled against my backside, his hard length sliding along the crease of my backside.

"I would never take a woman who doesn't want me," he murmured, moving to whisper in my other ear. "Say 'no' and I will leave you alone forever." He ran his lips down the side of my throat, giving my shoulder a gentle bite as he waited for my answer.

By now I was shaking, but not in any kind of fear or distress. When one of his hands left my wrist and skimmed along the underside of my arm I didn't move, reveling in the sensations his touch produced. His hand moved up the back of my thigh under my skirt, fingernails raking the skin, and a finger slid between the firm lobes of my backside. He gave a growl, squeezing my butt with both hands and spreading the cheeks, then pressed between them with the hard bulge still locked behind his pants. A moan slipped from my mouth as I arched my hips back, using the wall as leverage to get closer.

The hands left my backside and I was flipped around to face him. I had a brief close-up glimpse of a familiar handsome face and green eyes, then his lips crashed against mine in the hottest kiss of my life. I responded, arching closer so I was flush against his body. I slid my hands across his torso, moving them up and through his hair, but he grabbed my hands and stretched them high above my head. A leg between my thighs pushed me higher and I ground my hips, rubbing myself against the rock-hard thigh. Breathy moans escaped my lips as he moved his mouth lower, sucking and nibbling on the sensitive skin of my neck.

"I want to feel your mouth on me," he murmured, gliding his lips up my neck and jaw line. "I want to see you on your knees, that perfect mouth around my cock . . ."

This time when I tried to free myself he didn't stop me, instead he stepped back and set me on my feet. My hands went immediately to his waistband, sliding down the zipper. He reached down to help me, and as he pulled his member free of the pants I sank down on my heels and flicked the tip with my tongue. He tasted clean, and the sharp intake of breath above told me he liked what I was doing. His need was my own; I felt a fresh wave of heat between my legs as I moved my head forward, sucking the head deep.

"God!" His body shuddered and, suddenly bolder, I wrapped a hand around the thick base and pulled him farther into my mouth. My tongue rolled along the base and flicked the tip, then I started bobbing my head over the thick member. His hips jerked, thrusting in time with my mouth; a hand came to rest behind my head, pulling insistently, but I controlled the pace. I undid the button of his pants and reached inside, cupping his balls with my free hand. He shook above me, dick jumping in appreciation, then both hands dug into my skull, pulling me closer and silently demanding more, deeper. This time I obliged, releasing the base and pulling him as far in as I could, bobbing and weaving my head and tongue. My free hand slid down between my legs, gliding through my wet folds and pressing against the throbbing nub.

"Are you touching yourself?" I heard him grit out above me. The thrust into my mouth grew more frenzied as I sped up my own ministrations, the hard length in my mouth muffling my cries. The stranger was silent for the most part, but the few moans he did let free when I swirled my tongue or massaged the tip with the back of my throat were gratifying to hear.

Part of my brain, a very small part, wondered what on earth I was doing, but I tuned it out. I had gone far too long without anyone noticing me; even my coworkers ignored me. So for a man this beautiful to see me, let alone approach me in any fashion, was a heady notion. I didn't allow myself to wonder why he chose me or what would happen next—right now I only wanted to feel. Fingers dug into my scalp and my own orgasm rushed to meet me even as his balls contracted, close to their own finale.

Hands pushed me away, back against the concrete wall, and I disengaged with a surprised pop. The man before me bent down and wound his arms around my torso; I was lifted into the air and thrust back against the wall, a hard body settling between my legs. I turned startled eyes to the handsome stranger's face, now only inches from mine, then I felt his member probing my entrance. He pressed inside and I bit back a cry from the intense pleasure. Muscles that hadn't seen action in too long were stretched, my own juices giving him an easy entrance. His lips crushed mine, swallowing my cries as he pounded me back into the concrete wall.

The orgasm I'd been coaxing along with my fingers rocketed to the surface with the rubbing and stretching and grinding. My scream was caught by the stranger's lips as I came hard, waves of pleasure rolling through my body. I kissed him wildly, nipping at his lips and raking my fingernails down the jacket arms of his suit. My response brought out a similar wildness in him and he pounded into me, releasing my mouth and latching onto my shoulder with his teeth. My cries, fainter now after the orgasm, still echoed off the walls in the small alcove.

He gasped against my skin, then he pulled out and came on the ground beneath me, his free hand rubbing out the last of his orgasm. Sandwiched between his hot body and the hard concrete, I finally noticed the chill of the cold stone and the sound of cars deep inside the complex making their way toward the exit. The chill against my wet thighs served as a wake-up call to what I had allowed to happen; I pressed feebly against the hard shoulders, my body still limp from my orgasm.

The stranger stepped back, still supporting my weight with large hands beneath my backside, then slowly lowered me to the floor. I wobbled in my heels, gripping his arm for support before stepping away. The enormity of what I had just done—again—sent my mind reeling. I shivered, only partly from the cold, then jumped as something warm and heavy covered my shoulders. I glanced up briefly at the now jacket-less stranger but was unable to utter any words of thanks. He helped hold it for me as I slowly pulled the dress coat over my arms. While not a cold-weather jacket, it remained warm from his body and cut the worst of the chill, which helped immensely.

"Let me take you home."

The moment I heard the words I shook my head, stepping away from him. My body burned with shame and I couldn't bear to look at him. "I need to catch the train," I mumbled.

A finger came under my chin and tilted my head up until

I was looking into the strong lines of that handsome face. Even after riding the elevator with him so long, I'd never been this close, and the sight took my breath away. Dark skin, whether through genetics or being kissed by the sun, only served to accent deep green eyes framed by black lashes and dark brows. His thick hair was nearly as black, falling in strands across his brow, tousled now thanks to my handiwork. A light shadow along his jaw, the skin prickly to the touch, seemed to complete the picture and made my heart skip a beat. His stony expression didn't quite match the concern in his beautiful eyes as he peered down at me, thumb caressing my chin. "Please," he said softly.

My body still responded to his touch; I wanted to lay my cheek against the rough skin of his hand. Tears pricked my eyes at the silly sentiment—was I really so desperate?—and I stepped back again, pulling from his grip. Clearing my throat and forcing myself not to act like a simpering twit, I looked him in the eye. "I need to catch the train." Keeping my head high even as shame made me want to crawl away and hide, I started walking away then faltered. "Your jacket," I murmured, and started to shrug out of it.

He held up a hand to stop me. "Keep it." A bemused smile flickered across his lips and it seemed for a moment I had his full attention . . . and approval. "You need it more than I do right now."

The air was chilly and I knew I looked a mess; the coat hung on me but at that moment I needed the cover. Murmuring my thanks I walked quickly out of the alcove and started toward the exit. I lifted a shaky hand to my head; my hair was loose but seemed to be in order. I'd need to find a mirror quickly as I was certain I looked a fright.

I heard the sound of a car pulling up behind me and stopping. Against my better judgment I glanced back to see a chauffeur step out of a long black limousine and open the passenger door, then the handsome stranger ducked inside. I stood there, staring like an idiot, as the driver closed the door and pulled out toward the exit. The windows of the car were tinted so I couldn't see inside as it passed by me, and I watched as my erstwhile ride pulled past the guards and out into the loud traffic outside. Who on earth was this man? I wondered, then shut off that line of thought and headed out of the empty garage.

I ducked inside a nearby café and locked myself inside the bathroom to clean up. My skirt and blouse fared well enough, flattening back to some semblance of order. Smoothing down my hair proved impossible, the dark blond strands refusing to cooperate after being so deliciously manhandled, so I dug around inside my bag for a hair tie and did a loose ponytail. I didn't bother reapplying my makeup, but did clean up the smudges around my blue eyes so I at least looked presentable. Fifteen minutes later I ducked back out, my satchel hanging by its strap over a bare arm and the dress coat draped over the bag; despite the chill, I felt strange wearing it. I caught a later train than usual but most of that time was a haze, my brain repeating one thought over and over again.

What the hell was I doing?

3

The next morning, I arrived at work half an hour early and made sure the elevator I took did not contain the stranger. Nervous as I was that someone might comment on my actions the previous day, it was a relief to be ignored as usual by the people around me. The building at that hour held a fraction of its usual occupants, and I hurried to my desk to avoid any unwanted confrontations with certain green-eyed individuals.

I'd spent most of my evening and night trying to figure out whether or not I should go to work the next morning. The recklessness and downright stupidity of my actions haunted me all night, making me go so far as to question my sanity. This isn't who I am. I'd never been so thoughtless about my actions, and a desperate libido wasn't enough of an answer for me.

I'd started searching out job opportunities, something I could turn to if my present situation went sour, but the market was as tough as ever. The proper half of my brain demanded

I quit this job, but the logical portion maintained I needed the money. My bills were coming due and I had no savings that would allow me time to search out a better employment situation.

Oh, Lucy, how far you've fallen.

Once I got to my desk I spent my time on work that avoided me having to log in to the computer as I didn't want my early arrival noticed by management. My coworkers arrived, chatting among themselves as they passed by my tiny cubicle, but I stayed in my little corner for most of the day, content to be ignored. The day went by uneventfully until almost four in the afternoon when my boss poked her head around the walls of my desk. "Follow me please, Ms. Delacourt."

My manager's presence startled me. I saw her almost every day but, after my initial interview, she had all but ignored my presence in the office. That she chose now to talk to me had the world spinning and my stomach curling into knots. Her tone brooked no argument, however, and with a hurried "Yes, ma'am," and a brief pause to get myself together, I pulled myself up on trembling legs and followed after her.

She bypassed her office door and strode out the door of our office section to the hall outside. I followed after her silently, afraid to ask what this was about for fear of learning the whole building knew about my sexcapades the day before. I could think of no other reason I'd be called out, and I doubted they'd take me out of my section simply to fire me.

We rode the elevator silently up, and my apprehension

grew as we neared the top of the building. My manager never once spoke to me and was impossible to read—not that I tried too hard, afraid of what I'd find. The moment the elevator doors opened I knew I was in an entirely different world. Gone were the lifeless narrow corridors as I stepped into a wide passage lined with dark wood paneling that had the company name HAMILTON in bold letters across the wall. The wide entryway led toward a reception desk in the opening of a large open room. Office doors lined the walls and two large glass-encased conference rooms on either corner of the large area. There was a rich old-world sense about everything, dark woods and gold accents mixing with modern lighting and artwork.

"Mr. Hamilton is expecting us," my boss said to the lady at the desk, who nodded and picked up a phone as we passed.

I stumbled at her words, my legs suddenly refusing to work. Why are we in the corporate section of the building? I'd never read up on the company; it was a temp job, meant only to be a short-term employment gig, but I knew this wasn't just any floor. It has a Donald Trump feel, more a reception area than an office. There was no way, however, that they'd send me here if they knew what I'd done.

Confusion and trepidation continued to climb as I followed my supervisor at a cautious distance. She headed toward one of the offices and knocked before poking her head inside. "Mr. Hamilton will see you now," she said, motioning for me to enter.

I stood there, staring mutely at my manager for a moment, then slowly moved toward the door. I gave her one last confused glance as I walked through, then came to a halt inside as renewed horror washed over me. Oh no, no no no . . .

"Thank you, Agatha, that will be all for now."

Nodding once, my supervisor pulled the door closed as I stood, aghast, inside the large office. My mouth worked soundlessly as I stared at the familiar figure sitting behind the desk. My eyes fell to the name plate on the desk. "Jeremiah Hamilton," I said, my body numb with shock.

The dark-haired man behind the desk raised cool eyes to appraise me. "Ms. Delacourt," he said in reply, gesturing to a chair in front of his desk. "Please take a seat."

My heartbeat sped up as I heard his voice, confirming my worst fears. Unable to speak, I moved to the chair he'd motioned me toward, movements jerky and hesitant, and sat down. He ignored me, running through something on the tablet in his hand. As we sat in strained silence I glanced around the large office. Windows covered the wall behind the CEO's desk from ceiling to floor, giving a panoramic view of the streets below. The desk was a dark wood and sturdy, covered sparsely with a laptop computer, the name plate, and a Newton's cradle, the steel balls unmoving. The chair I sat in was plush and thick with rolling castors at the bottom.

"Ms. Lucille Delacourt," the stranger said, startling me. Jeremiah Hamilton, I reminded myself, still unable to get my brain around my current situation. "Currently a temp data clerk out of the Executive Management Solutions employment agency, hired one month ago by Agatha Crabtree. Correct so far?" At my jerky nod he continued. "I see you used your passport as identification." He glanced up at me. "Passport?"

Talking was difficult with a suddenly dry mouth, but I still tried. "I always carry them with me."

He raised an eyebrow. "Them?" the CEO asked, his expression probing for more information, but I only shrugged, words failing me.

There was a moment of silence before he resumed speaking. "Grew up in upstate New York, attended Cornell University for three years before dropping out. Menial jobs since then and you moved to the city three months ago. Why did you drop out?"

The summary of my life was cold and brief, the words piercing through me. The question at the end sailed right past me; it was the generous pause that made me look up into his expectant face. "What?" I asked, cursing inwardly for not listening.

"Why," he repeated, "did you drop out of college, Ms. Delacourt?"

His tone demanded an answer but it was complicated and personal, bringing up memories I still struggled with nearly three years later. The question was an invasion of my privacy and I knew I didn't legally have to answer, but I found my lips moving anyway. "My parents died."

There was a long pause this time as I stared at my hands, trying not to cry—a difficult task, given the nerve-wracking situation I'd gotten myself into. *Would they be ashamed of where I was now?* I wondered, swallowing back tears. They had sacrificed so much to let me get ahead, most of which I hadn't discovered until after their death. Losing the house I'd grown up in, the one that had been in the family for two generations, because of the huge mortgage they'd taken out to pay my tuition, had been a sickening blow. I'd tried so hard to keep it from falling into the bank's hands, but . . . Swallowing the lump in my throat, I struggled to regain my composure.

"I'm sorry for your loss," Jeremiah said after a long moment of silence. He cleared his throat, and I heard him lean back in his leather chair. "What brought you down to New York City?"

I thought I detected a note of concern in his voice but still couldn't bring myself to look at him. Even though the question was personal and none of his business, I still answered. "I lost my family's house and had to move; an old college friend in Jersey City said I could live with her."

"I see." Jeremiah scratched his chin for a moment. "Do you know why I've asked you to come, Ms. Delacourt?"

It was the question I dreaded and couldn't possibly answer. Swallowing, I raised my head to meet his green eyes but my courage failed me. "No?" I replied, more a question than an answer.

He opened his mouth to say something, paused, then tried again. "Let me tell you how your day would have gone today prior to our meeting." He folded his arms on the desk before continuing. "You would have worked until half an hour before closing, when you would have been called into your supervisor's office. She would have explained that your temp work contract was terminated and today was your last day.

You would have been given your last paycheck and escorted out of the building."

For the second time that morning, the bottom dropped out from under my feet. "You're firing me?" I asked in a faint voice, unable to believe my own words. Anger bubbled up at the unfairness of my life. "Is this because we . . ."

Jeremiah held up a hand to stop my words and shook his head. "The decision on the layoffs has been planned for a month now. We no longer need most of the temps in your department." His eyes narrowed as he added, more to himself, "I signed the directive earlier this week before I knew who you were."

"Nobody's hiring right now," I whispered, forgetting my looking for another job was supposed to be secret. No reason to hide that now. The anger was difficult to sustain as I realized I'd have to weather another blow after so many in my life recently.

"I looked at your file and you did good work," Jeremiah continued as I stared, numb, at the top of his desk. "We would give you an excellent recommendation for any future job inquiries."

At a loss for words, unable to think of what to say, I looked up and stared at the CEO. "Why did you tell me this?" I mumbled. "Why bring me up here?"

"Because I have another offer for you, a job, if you're interested. I'm in need of a personal assistant."

I blinked several times, taken by surprise at the offer. I peered into his face but it was like granite; I couldn't tell at all what he was thinking. Suspicion curled in my belly as I asked, "What kind of personal assistance?"

"Anything I want."

I took a deep breath at the words, my mind taking me to all sorts of places within that phrase. He couldn't mean . . . surely he's not implying what I think. But something in his eyes, despite the relaxed business demeanor, implied it was exactly what I was imagining. His gaze promised all sorts of wicked things—or maybe it was my mind trying to make my fantasies a reality. I needed to be sure. "About yesterday, when we, um . . ."

Jeremiah leaned forward and rested a strong chin on his fingers. "Yes," he said simply, the one word answering all my questions.

I tried to get indignant at the proposition, tried to find some way to protest and maintain some shred of dignity, but I was too practical. Right now I desperately needed a job and here was an offer, and I couldn't afford to let it pass not knowing when I might get another. My heart constricted as I remember how, for nearly two years, I'd poured every dime I earned into keeping my family's house, only to lose it and wind up with nothing anyway. Without any immediate family willing or able to help, if it hadn't been for a former classmate offering to let me stay with her, I would have been on the streets. What was meant as a temporary solution, though, had progressed longer than either of us had planned; between the creditors constantly calling and the high price of living in the big city, I never seemed to have a penny to my name.

That didn't mean, however, that I was just going to say

yes. "What are you offering?" I demanded, raising my chin and hoping he didn't see the flush that suffused my body. *I can't believe I'm actually considering this!*

A slow smile tipped one corner of his mouth. "Full benefits, a raise in pay, and all travel expenses paid." He wrote something on a small Post-it note and passed it over to me. "This should be sufficient for a starting salary."

The sum on the note made me faint—I could have my student loans paid off in only a few months, and have more than enough money to go back to college within a year. My jaw wouldn't work as I fumbled for words, unable to think of what to say. *It's an opportunity*, part of me insisted while another part, the one that usually sounded like my parents, screamed at me to RUN! I sat in silence a moment, pondering my options, then drew in a shaky breath. "I want this in writing."

Something told me that hadn't been the answer he was expecting; he cocked his head sideways and his eyes crinkled, the only sign I saw of humor. That gorgeous face remained otherwise stoic as he nodded. "Very well," he said, "but first I need to interview you further for this position." He leaned forward and set his chin on steepled fingers. "Stand up, bend down, and put your elbows on the desk."

4

I froze, the earlier phrase, "anything I want," echoing through my head. After a tense moment where I warred with myself and lost, I rose to my feet and moved toward the desk, bending down to place my elbows along the edge of the dark wood. Nervously, I watched Jeremiah as he stood and came around the desk. "Stay like this until I tell you to move again. How many words can you type a minute?"

The question surprised me, but I'd been drilling myself lately on questions for job-hunting and knew the answer. "Eighty."

"What strengths would you bring to this position?"

He disappeared behind me, breaking my concentration. I could turn my head to see him but kept my gaze on the desk as I answered the commonplace interview question. "Attention to detail, and dedication to get a job done no matter what."

A chuckle came from behind me at the obviously rehearsed answer. "Where do you see yourself in five years?"

I started to reply but was startled into silence as a hand slid up my thigh, sneaking beneath my skirt and over my ass before pulling away. I swallowed, my breath ragged, but still managed to respond. "Finishing law school preferably, or in a job I love."

That got me a low "Hmm," but silence otherwise. My pulse increased and I closed my eyes, trying to keep myself under control. It was just like on the elevator—one touch and I was lost, my body craving his contact.

"What would you consider your dream job?"

Fingers slid between my thighs, running along the thin cotton of my panties, and a moan escaped my mouth. My hips pressed down, seeking more contact, but again the hand disappeared, and I bit back a groan. The respite allowed me to gather my thoughts to answer, although it was difficult. "Someplace where I matter, and can help people."

"Good answer," he murmured, then the hand was back, pressing at the soft flesh between my legs, turning me into a writhing mess. My palms pressed down on the desk, nails digging into the cool wood as I felt a rush of heat in my belly. A hand smoothed over my back and down one hip as the fingers continued to tease and torment me. I kept my trembling arms on the desk as something hard pressed against my backside. The fingers finally moved beneath the panties and pressed inside me, sliding easily along the wet folds. I choked on another cry, trying and failing for silence.

"My office is soundproof and the door is locked," he murmured, answering a question I hadn't thought to ask. Fingers penetrated deep inside me, causing my body to quake.

"Before we go any further, however, we need to get rid of these."

The thin cotton panties I wore were pulled down my legs and, without thinking, I stepped out of them as they hit the floor. A shoe pressed against the inside of my foot, widening my stance as his hips pushed against my backside. The fingers between my legs never let up their exploration; my breathing was rough as Jeremiah lifted the skirt to bunch at my waist, his bulge thrusting against my backside.

His thumb, which had previously been massaging the hard bud between my legs, slid back to my rear opening. I surged forward in shock, the desk and his hips holding me prisoner as the thumb eased around the tight hole. The idea of a man being interested back there had never occurred to me; I wasn't so naïve as to be ignorant of the idea, but it had never come up before. Thinking proved difficult, however, as he continued to manipulate my body until I was trembling with need.

Lips pressed against my neck. "Eventually," he purred in that deep voice, the word a promise, as he caressed the opening once more, then moved his thumb back to my clit. By now nearly every breath was a moan as I tilted my hips up, desperately needing to be filled. His fingers teased and tormented but never let me fall over into orgasm.

Something shifted behind me; Jeremiah lowered his body along my bare bottom, then teeth grazed the skin over one buttock as hands spread my cheeks. Before I could even comprehend what was coming, I felt for the first time in my life a tongue against my most intimate of places, licking up the crease, then pushing inside my weeping opening. I surged forward against the desk with another loud cry, and couldn't stop myself from making another as he controlled my body's responses with his tongue and fingers. The unfamiliar and exotic feel, unlike anything I'd ever experienced before with my limited activities, pushed me over the edge. I came loudly, my nails scratching against the hard surface of the desk and my body bucking uncontrollably.

I laid my head on my hands as I heard the crinkle of the condom wrapper, then a moment later the hard length of his cock slid between my ass cheeks. The fingers were pulled out only to be replaced by a thick presence that forced its way inside my tight opening. I moaned again as he pushed inside, while one thick arm reached around my waist and pulled me tight against his body. He pressed me down against the desk as he slid out then in, stretching and electrifying the tender skin. Still riding the wave of my orgasm, his movements left me panting and frantic, pushing back against him wildly.

"Fuck, you're so hot," he murmured in my ear as he thrust hard, earning another cry from me. I braced myself against the edge of the dark wood as he pounded into me, his thrusts shaking my entire body. One hand lifted to my neck, tilting my head back against his shoulder and partially restricting my breathing; it didn't stop the breathy moans I made as another wave washed over me and my body shuddered for the second time in as many minutes.

My head fell to the side and teeth grazed my neck, running along the line of my shoulder as his hand pulled away the material of my blouse. The soft feel of his lips across my skin was a direct contrast to the hard pumps of his hips, but I reveled in the experience, allowing him to set and control the pace. Two orgasms left my body limp, drained from the experience, but Jeremiah held me up easily in his strong arms. I arched myself back against him even though my skin was almost too sensitive for his thrusts, the pleasure too much.

Like before, his teeth sank into my shoulder as he shuddered, his hard thrusts almost lifting me from the floor. He let out a ragged grunt and with one last stab, he shook against my back, coming inside me. The hand around my neck released and blood rushed to my head again, making me dizzy. He laid me carefully atop the desk, resting his hard body atop mine as we both struggled to catch our breath.

After a moment he pulled out and stepped away, leaving me alone against the cool wood. It took a moment before I finally became aware of how exposed I was, but I still spent another minute catching my breath before I lowered my skirt. I was wet enough that sitting in the chair would stain my skirt so I wobbled in my heeled pumps, using the desk as a brace.

"That wraps up this interview. By the way, you're hired."

Still breathing hard, I turned my head to look over at Jeremiah Hamilton standing at a small coffee bar on one side of the office. His suit and dress pants were back in place, as impeccable as if nothing had just happened. The look on his face was probing and inquisitive, but I couldn't tell what he thought to discover. I tried to feel shame, anger, outrage at my wanton actions and his taking advantage of my situation, but all I could come up with was a deep exhaustion and a sense of security.

I am so screwed.

A hand at my elbow turned me gently, and a glass of water was pressed into my hands. "Go clean yourself up," Jeremiah said as I took a sip of the cool liquid, his voice as soft as I'd yet heard. "I'll make arrangements and we can leave once you've come back."

My brain wasn't firing on all cylinders so I thought perhaps I had missed something. "Arrangements for what?"

"You said you carry your passport with you?"

I blinked, back to being confused. An odd question. "Um, yes, I do?"

He nodded as if that answered everything. "Perfect. Then you'll come with me today and can serve as my escort."

I took another sip of the water, still baffled by the direction of this conversation. "Your escort where?"

"Paris. We leave in an hour."

5

Limousines were roomier than I remembered. Of course, the last time I'd been inside one was high school prom and it had been packed to the gills with friends and their dates.

I snuck a glance at the handsome man near me in the backseat of the limo. He ignored me for the moment, focused on the tablet in his lap and leaving me to my own devices. My leather handbag sat in my lap and I hugged it close, still reeling over the day's events. Was I really on my way to Paris?

The last two days had been crazy. I still couldn't believe that Jeremiah Hamilton, CEO of Hamilton Industries, a multinational business conglomerate that rivaled anything Trump ever produced, sat across from me in the dark limo. It still hadn't fully sunk in that I was heading to the airport to fly with him to Paris. As his personal assistant. With a forthcoming contract whose stipulations revolved around the phrase "anything he wants."

As far as ranking in the Worst Days Ever, this was in the

top five. Definitely a tie for first on Most Mindboggling Day Ever.

Manhattan rush-hour traffic being the normal tangle of pedestrians and vehicles, I didn't pay much attention to our route, too caught up in my thoughts. I noticed traffic decrease, however, as we left Manhattan, and belatedly realized we were heading toward New Jersey. It wasn't until the limo began passing planes behind a tall fence that I looked out the window and saw with some surprise the sign for Teterboro Airport. The New Jersey airport wasn't as big as its New York City counterpart and while I'd never flown through there, I knew it served a large number of private flights and airplanes. I'd only ever been through JFK so the smaller airport was something new. I saw a number of small charter planes parked along the asphalt, the kind taken by tours and the very rich.

Well, I suppose today that's us. The thought sent a wave of chills up my spine and I shivered, rubbing my arms. Oh God, what was I getting myself into?

"You're sure I won't need clothes?" I asked for the third time as we pulled into the airport terminal. I hadn't been allowed to bring anything with me aside from personal effects already in the office—namely, what was in my purse and the work clothes I was still wearing. The skirt and blouse were clean but hardly enough for any kind of overseas trip.

"They will be provided for you," Jeremiah assured me. "Your contract will go over all of this."

It was the same answer I got anytime I asked him a question about this surprise trip. At this rate, my contract will be longer than Tolstoy. The flippant thought did nothing to settle my nerves. I haven't signed anything yet. I can still leave, find another job.

The sudden image of me flipping burgers for a living made me shudder and a wave of sorrow washed over me. Is that where I'll end up? Could this really be my last chance? I looked up to see Jeremiah watching me. There was no emotion on his stoic face, yet his penetrating gaze made me feel like he could read my mind. Frustrated, unwilling to let him see my indecision, I clenched my jaw and refused to look away first.

The door opened, breaking our staring contest. I grabbed my bag and climbed out past him, but thought I saw humor on his face as I passed. *So he likes conflict,* I thought as we were hustled into the building. *Good, because I'm not going to crawl and beg for respect.*

An image popped into my head of me on my knees in front of him, looking up into that gorgeous face, and I felt a flutter in my belly. Aw, dammit.

The speed by which we passed through security was a novel experience. The most grueling part of the process was security poking through my purse and finding the underwear from yesterday I'd forgotten was still there. My whole body heated at that discovery but they remained professional. Once security cleared us, we moved through the small waiting area and were taxied across the tarmac to our waiting flight.

Long and sleek yet a great deal smaller than what I was used to flying in, the airplane wasn't anything like a commercial jet. There was no other way I'd ever get to travel in something like this; normal girls like me never so much as saw the inside of one of these planes unless they were flight attendants or pilots. The interior was as posh as the outside promised, with leather seats twice as wide as anything I'd ever seen. The pilot allowed us to take our seats before closing the door and retreating into the cockpit. Impressed by my surroundings, I started playing with the various gadgets and implements attached to my seat. It even had its own private phone under one thick arm rest, which I found amusing.

A thin tablet slid onto the table I'd unfolded, the same one I'd seen Jeremiah working with earlier. Startled, I glanced over to see Jeremiah seated in a nearby chair. "What's this?" I managed, my earlier amusement dimming.

"I drew up your contract in the limo, but you'll need to sign it before we take off." When I hesitated, he leaned in to catch my gaze. "You knew this was coming."

"No joke." The sarcastic reply belied my nervous tension. Was I signing my life away?

"A car will take you home if you wish to leave." He pulled a silver stylus from his jacket pocket and held it out to me. "The choice is yours."

I snatched the stylus from his fingers, clenching it in my fist so I wouldn't betray my shaking as I scanned the document. I'd grown adept at deciphering legalese during college but the wording was fairly straightforward. The paper put a more legal spin on the phrase "anything he wants" but the message was the same, even including a nondisclosure agreement. On coming close to the end, however, I did trip over one stipulation we hadn't discussed. "Fifty thousand dollars?" I squeaked, looking up in surprise.

He nodded. "If you are still in my employ in six months, you're entitled to a bonus," he said, quoting the contract almost verbatim. "It, along with any weekly paychecks due, won't be taken from you should you terminate the contract after that time."

So even if I quit, I'll still get something out of this. Seeing it in writing helped my mind come to terms with this absurd choice. The contract, while vague on my specific duties, gave a professional vibe to the whole situation and made me feel, well, less slutty. Who knows? . . . Maybe this is a standard contract with the rich and famous. I'd hardly know otherwise.

Still, I hesitated. *I can still leave,* I thought, staring at the stylus in my hand. *I can end this silly charade, take a taxi back to my apartment.* . . .

. . . and then what?

One of the biggest worries I'd had since moving from my hometown to live with an old college acquaintance was the sudden high cost of living so close to New York City. The foreclosure of my family's home had left me all but destitute; I had no options to live anywhere else, and saving money, despite my best efforts, had proven ineffectual. My current living arrangements had been meant to be temporary, and I knew from my friend's recent attitude that I was quickly using up what welcome I had left. My only hope was to pay down a little more of my student loan debt, and then I'd be in the position to begin paying rent. Until then, I was perilously close to living in a shelter, a thought that made my blood run cold.

Jeremiah regarded me patiently, his pitiless stare almost a welcome change. Since my parents died, I'd struggled not only to pay the bills but also with people's views of my situation, and I was tired of being "that poor orphan girl" in the eyes of others. The CEO had made it abundantly clear what this contract entailed—my "interview" had been me splayed across his desk as he took liberties with my body that left me a moaning, panting mess. The memory made me want to cringe and hide; I'd never been that kind of girl and yet a stranger had seduced me not once but three times in a twenty-four-hour span. The contract in front of me represented financial independence, but only in exchange for another, more personal form of freedom.

I have no other choice.

I read through the contract twice, the enormity of my decision weighing on me, then with shaky fingers I signed my name digitally across the bottom and handed back the tablet. Jeremiah reached up and pressed the attendant button. Immediately the engines began gearing up, and I made sure I was buckled in. I gripped the chair tight and tried to ignore my own unease about the flight and the man seated across from me.

"You don't like flying?"

I kept my eyes closed and feigned sleep as the engines geared up and propelled us down the runway. The process was smooth and not as loud as I'd imagined for such a small plane, but I didn't breathe easy until we were in the air.

We were still climbing when Jeremiah took off his belt and stood, heading to the main area behind me. I kept my eyes straight ahead, determined to ignore his presence, until a hand carrying a glass of clear liquid appeared before me. "I don't drink," I said.

"Not even water?"

I didn't find his amusement charming but took the drink from his hand with a mumbled, "Thank you."

"There's food in the bar if you need something more substantial."

"I'm not hungry, thank you."

My stomach chose that moment to growl loudly, exposing my outright lie. "Okay, fine, maybe a little."

His lips compressed and I had the feeling he was trying to keep from smiling. "You really had no idea who I was, did you?"

Suddenly not in the mood for conversation, I huffed out a breath and shrugged. "Apparently, you're not as popular as you seem to think."

He took my sarcastic words in good humor. "And how popular am I?"

Squirming in my chair, I looked up to see amusement crinkling the edges of his eyes. He does stoic really well, except his eyes. They were the most beautiful green I could remember seeing on a man, vibrant against the olive complexion and dark hair. Realizing I was staring, I cleared my throat and struggled for an answer to his question. Witty rebuttals escaped me, however, and I shrugged, taking a quick sip of my water.

I ignored his chuckling. "You may want to rest," he said, "this is going to be a long flight."

As he went to the rear of the airplane I stayed in my seat, reclining and snuggling into the large chair. Unfortunately my stomach, now aware of food nearby, wouldn't let me rest. I managed to stall maybe half an hour, busying myself with the various gadgets around me, before finally getting up and heading back to see what was available.

When I passed my boss he was sitting in one of the wide chairs, a glass of dark liquid in his hand. I could feel his eyes on me as I went into the kitchen alcove and poured myself some orange juice before peeking at what food was available. I snagged a premade chicken sandwich with ingredients that made it sound like fine dining, and ate in the small room.

The man made me nervous; I couldn't trust myself around him. Whenever he was nearby I kept imagining erotic scenes I only read about in romance novels and saw in my fantasies. That had been fine when he was a stranger on an elevator I saw once a day. Now I needed to get him out of my head, but easier said than done; he had become a prominent fixture in my fantasy life and my body wouldn't allow me to forget him. Even the hopelessness of my current situation couldn't stop my reaction to his presence, the same reactions that had gotten me into this mess in the first place.

Grabbing a bottle of water, I turned to leave the little kitchen area and ground to a halt when I saw him standing beside the opening. He moved toward me and I backed up a step, only to bump into the countertop. "I, um," I stammered, "I should get back to my seat. . . ."

His fingers were toying with a button on his shirt. "Could you help me with this?" he asked, indicating his shirt and ignoring my statement. "It seems to be stuck."

I blew out a disbelieving breath. Seriously? His words came across as a lame line, almost absurd given the situation, but another line I'd heard earlier that afternoon popped into my head. *Anything I want.*

I snorted. So now I'm dressing him, too? This wasn't what I thought I'd signed up for but with a small huff, I reached out and took the button. His fingers brushed mine and I tried to ignore them along with the tightening in my belly.

Surprisingly, the button really was caught but it took only a few seconds to untangle. I released his shirt when I finished, leaving the button open, but he captured my hands before I could step away. "Check the others, perhaps?"

I glanced up into his eyes then quickly down again. *This is stupid,* I thought, trying for anger as my hands were pulled back to his shirt. I was supposed to be a lawyer, someone who stood up for the little guy; this isn't what I took out massive college loans for, to be a glorified seamstress. . . .

Jeremiah stared down at me and I tried hard to ignore his gaze—easier said than done. Giving him a brief glare that was mostly bravado on my part, I started unbuttoning his shirt. The material was thin but strong, not silk but something similarly expensive. I didn't make it to the third button before my hands began to tremble, not from fear but from his proximity. It didn't take me long to realize there was nothing beneath the shirt but skin. The more buttons I released the more torso was revealed, dark skin against a white shirt that refused to stay closed on its own. He took a step closer, looming above me, and my whole body began to quake. *Oh my God.*

My life up to that point hadn't involved many men outside of family and a few study buddies. High school, then college, had been all about academics; I had always been more interested in books and studying than forming any relationships with the opposite sex even if they had been interested. Life after my parents died had been a blur; there was never time to do more than work at various jobs and worry about my future. If anyone had been interested I certainly never noticed, but I definitely noticed the man in front of me now.

Fighting the urge not to touch the smooth skin beneath my fingers was a losing battle. He took a small step sideways and I unconsciously moved, too, turning slowly with him as he pulled off the shirt and threw it over the chair beside us. I was breathless as my eyes roamed the body his shirt had previously covered, then the flutter in my belly became full-blown sparks when his fingers skimmed up my arms. I didn't even realize we were moving, too caught up in his proximity and touch, until my back pushed up against something hard—a wall. My hands tightened against the firm muscles of his abdomen as I looked up to see him watching me with an intensity that left my knees weak. There was no thought of resistance as he pressed his body against mine and lowered his head to take my lips.

What started out soft, barely a brush of our mouths, morphed quickly into something much more passionate. Helpless against his assault, I moaned into his mouth and skimmed my fingernails down his taut body, responding to his kiss with a fire I didn't know I had. My touch served only to enflame him as he pressed closer, his tongue coming out to briefly flick my lip and tease my mouth open. His large hands roamed down my body, settling on my waist, his fingers digging into my hips and backside, pulling me closer against his wide frame.

My hands came up around his neck, tangling in thick dark hair, as desperate for his touch as he seemed to be for mine. One leg wedged itself firmly between my legs and I gasped as it pressed against parts of my body that were swollen and begging for more. The hands clutching my hips tightened and I was suddenly lifted, pressed against the wall and supported only by his body and grip. My hips wrapped around his waist as his lips left mine, teeth skimming down along the soft skin of my throat as he thrust his hips against me. A small cry burst from my throat, then again as his teeth latched on loosely to my shoulder through my blouse and he rolled his hips again.

My hands fumbled for his face and I kissed him again, making panting moans into his mouth as he continued to rub himself against me. My skirt was almost up to my waist and his fingers crept toward the apex of my legs, pressing against the thin barrier of my panties toward my aching core. I moaned into his mouth, nipping his lip and arching my hips down against his hand, desperate for more.

"Perhaps you can help with my pants button, too?"

The low words took me a moment to process but managed to cut through the haze of lust. I broke off the kiss, realizing what I'd almost allowed to happen—again—and looked into his eyes. The hot need there still made my insides melt, but when I pushed weakly at his shoulders he stepped back, lowering me gently to the floor. My skirt was bunched around my hips, and I hurried to correct it as I skittered sideways out of his reach.

"You should get some rest, it's a long flight to Paris."

I looked back at him. He stood there looking good enough to eat, seemingly as comfortable naked as he was wearing those buttoned-up expensive suits. Why am I walking away from him again?

Principles. Morals. Oh yeah. Dammit.

Giving him a jerky nod, I forced myself to turn around and walk back to my seat. Grabbing a pillow from a nearby cubby, I sat down in my seat and pushed the chair so it was reclining backward. I didn't think I'd be able to sleep but managed to finally fall into a fitful slumber as the sun passed the horizon, the orange glow extinguished by the earth below.

At some point I awoke to find it was dark outside the windows and a blanket had been laid over me, the edges tucked in around my body. I frowned, certain it hadn't been there when I sat down, and looked behind my seat to see Jeremiah fast asleep in another chair nearby. His shirt was once again buttoned, the suit jacket folded neatly in the chair beside him. He took up more space in the chair so wasn't able to tuck himself up like me, but seemed comfortable reclining back. Sleep had softened the hard expression on his face; he looked different, younger, more relaxed.

I wish I could hate him, I mused, but there was no anger in the thought. The man in that chair had all but blackmailed me into signing a contract that allowed him whatever liberties he wanted to take, yet there had been moments of tenderness that shone through. He never did anything I didn't want, I thought, fingering the blanket around me. I wonder which is the real man: the hard CEO who interviewed me bent over his desk, or the man who covered me with this blanket.

I shelved that conversation for another day, exhaustion making my eyes heavy. Yawning quietly, I pulled the blanket up to my chin, nestling in the comfortable chair, and slid back into a sound slumber.

6

D o you have anything to claim?"
Considering I wasn't allowed to bring anything with
me. . . . "No."

The man checked my passport again, then handed it back
to me, motioning for the next person as I walked past the
desk. Bold letters displayed above me told my location in several languages and I stopped and stared. *I'm really in France.*

Jeremiah stood nearby and as I drew abreast, he laid a
hand on the small of my back and steered me through the
small crowd. I saw a line of people waiting for the new arrivals as we made our way out to the main terminal. A large
bald man with a blond goatee stood next to a far wall, and
strode forward to meet us halfway to the doors. "Lucy," Jeremiah said, "this is Ethan my chief of security. He'll take you
to the hotel."

We shook hands but it was clear my presence wasn't the
man's priority; his eyes remained fixed on Jeremiah. "Celeste

is still here." Ethan's voice had a Southern twang, light but noticeable. "She won't leave for another three hours."

Jeremiah nodded. "Perfect. See to it that Ms. Delacourt here gets to the hotel."

"What about you?" I asked as he started to walk away.

"I have to deal with the vultures." To Ethan he added, "Try not to be seen."

I watched him walk away toward the glass doors leading out. *That's it?* I thought, confused. *I'm being given over to the chauffeur and secreted out of the airport?* It occurred to me I should be happy to be out of his presence but, suddenly alone with another stranger in a strange country, I found I missed the stoic man.

"Okay, let's go."

I followed Ethan silently, sneaking glances back toward my boss. As Jeremiah exited the glass doors I saw a commotion outside as several people rushed toward him. Flashes of cameras and the garbled din of voices flowed to me as we exited farther down from the action, ignored by the crowd. "What's that about?" I asked, struggling to keep up with Ethan's long strides.

"Paparazzi." Ethan held the door open for me as we exited the terminal a ways beyond the throng. "His attendance at the gala this weekend is high profile enough to earn press coverage."

Gala? I got into the back of the large SUV waiting at the curb. Another man who had been waiting behind the wheel exited the vehicle so Ethan could take his place, and we pulled out. "Is he going to be okay?" I asked, looking through the rear window at the swarm of reporters.

Ethan snorted. "This is nothing, and he did it mostly to divert attention so we could leave unmolested. He won't be far behind us."

Indeed, I saw him move through the crowd as a limo pulled up and breathed a small sigh of relief. *I could never do that*, I thought, thankful in hindsight for the reprieve. The thought of all those cameras in my face, following me everywhere. . . . I shuddered just thinking about it.

There were a million questions running through my mind but the man driving didn't seem the talkative type so I kept them to myself, instead enjoying my first real view of Paris. The European city had always been someplace I longed to visit; my parents had been history buffs and that had rubbed off on me as well. Paris had always seemed so far off and exotic, a totally different world in which I could immerse myself. While still in high school, I had secured a promise from my parents that, when I graduated and got my bachelor's degree, they would pay my way to the French city. That wish had never materialized—their deaths my junior year of college had derailed my planned life, forcing me on a radically different path than I'd always imagined—but my love for the city remained. The glimpses of the Eiffel Tower through the buildings made me smile, some of the stress of the last couple days draining away.

I'd been so young back then, unable to see just how stretched thin my parents were on finances. Reluctant to look a gift horse in the mouth, it never occurred to me to ask where they found the money for my Ivy League college education. Not until they died suddenly, leaving me to pick up the pieces, had I finally realized how much was on the line. There had been life insurance but barely enough to cover funeral expenses and lawyer fees; after that, every penny I made went into trying to save the house, only to lose it anyway. The memories were an aching hole in my heart, but seeing Paris finally served as a balm for some of that pain. *I wish you guys were here to see this with me.*

I had no idea where we were going, but when we finally stopped and a valet opened the door for me, my jaw dropped as I stared in shock at the hotel. "We're staying here?"

I didn't get an answer and, honestly, the question was rhetorical anyway. I stared up at the magnificent Paris Ritz, finding it incomprehensible that I would be sleeping there. Another Parisian establishment I'd only seen online and in magazines, pictures hadn't done the structure justice. While not as big as I'd thought, it was as grand and stately as I'd always dreamed and I was itching to see the inside.

A redhead in a pale fitted dress suit made her way toward us, heels clacking on the stone ground. She seemed pleased to see Ethan but paused when she saw me. The big driver gave her hand a kiss, a romantic gesture that seemed at odds with his gruff demeanor. "Celeste, this is Lucy Delacourt, Mr. Hamilton's new personal assistant."

The confusion immediately cleared from the woman's face, although she still seemed surprised by the news. "Pleased to meet you," she said with a warm smile, extending her hand in greeting. "I'm Celeste Taylor, the head of operations for Hamilton Industries." Her handshake was firm and business-like, her smile a welcome relief after the stoicism I'd seen so far. "It's been a while since Remi has taken another assistant."

Remi? "Yes, well, I'm new." It was difficult to know how much I should talk about so I decided to keep it professional. "I was hired yesterday afternoon."

Celeste's eyebrows rose almost to her hairline. "Well, he certainly moved quickly this time." Her gaze softened. "This must all be so strange to you."

This first bit of genuine sympathy almost made me cry. I wanted to thank her but managed to refrain from throwing my arms around her shoulders, and instead swallowed back my gratitude. "Yesterday I was a temp barely getting by. Now I'm, well . . ."—I gestured to the hotel around me— "It's a bit overwhelming."

"Yes, I imagine so." She looked around the car. "Do you have any luggage with you?"

"Uh . . ." I couldn't figure out how to explain that bit of detail. Who flies across the Atlantic without bringing any clothes or luggage for the trip? Me apparently, but I didn't know what to say without bringing up embarrassing details.

Celeste cocked her head to the side at my uncomfortable silence, eyes narrowing. She took a step back, examining me from head to toe, then nodded. "Ah, I see why," she said with a knowing smile.

I looked down at my clothing, not understanding her

meaning. They were still clean, although rumpled a bit from the trip and my sleeping in the chair. "Why, what's wrong with what I'm wearing?"

This got a laugh from Celeste. "Oh, it's not my opinion you should be worrying about," she said, shaking her head and grinning. "If Remi doesn't like something, he'll do everything in his power to change it. He's a steamroller, used to getting his own way in matters. You don't have to say anything, I can already see it happened to you." She motioned toward the door of the hotel. "Come inside, it's chilly out here."

I followed her up the walkway while Ethan stayed out by the curb, fielding a call on his cell phone. "When did you meet Mr. Hamilton?" I asked.

Celeste gave me an amused look at the use of the man's formal title. "We went to school together years ago, although I moved out west almost immediately after graduation. Got a divorce, moved back to start anew, couldn't find anything. Almost gave up hope, then Remi found me." She shrugged. "I started out as a manager, then when he restructured the entire company after his father died I was given a choice: take the COO position or I was fired. Like I said," she added, rolling her eyes at me, "a steamroller."

"Sounds familiar." The doors were opened for us by hotel employees and I stared in wonder around the entryway. "This place is even better than I imagined."

"Wait until you see the suites." She glanced at her watch. "My plane doesn't leave for almost three hours. Want me to show you around?" When I grinned at her, she took my arm. "You have to see the pool first. Always takes my breath away."

"So are you and Ethan . . . ?" I trailed off, not wanting to imply anything, but Celeste nodded.

"I was already working as COO when Jeremiah part-nered with Ethan to run the fledgling security company. I was used to a bit of freedom, so when suddenly there were more hoops to jump through just to get inside the building, I resented it. All the protection seemed like overkill, and I was probably the most vocal detractor." Celeste smiled. "Then there was the fact that Ethan was always underfoot, asking if I needed help or an escort. When the new head of security insisted on walking me to my car anytime I needed to so much as get my purse, I tried to put my foot down but was overruled."

"Sounds like he was stalking you," I commented, voice dry.

"No no, it wasn't like that. Ethan kept everything on a strictly professional level and, well, I never really thought anything more about his actions. This job keeps me busy twenty-four seven and I didn't think I had time for a rela-tionship, so it never even occur to me. . . ." The redhead rolled her eyes. "Honestly, I probably never would've noticed him beyond an annoying security detail had he not saved my life."

My eyes grew big. "Really?"

Celeste nodded. "I bucked tradition somewhat by pre-ferring to drive the business car myself, rather than have a chauffeur. So I was walking out of the office one night and was jumped by a group that tried to throw me into a van. It was late and I was sure nobody was there to help me, then suddenly this big bald guy is there, beating my attackers to a pulp—that was the first time I really and truly noticed him." She shrugged, a rueful smile tilting her lips. "He then assigned himself as my permanent driver and the rest is history."

"Wow," I murmured, "how romantic!"

"Yeah, maybe," the redhead demurred, then slanted a look at me. "So, how did you land the most coveted job in the country? Anytime Hamilton Industries puts out calls for interns, we have applicants coming out our ears."

By that point we had reached the indoor pool, an extravagant sight surrounded by pillars and a recessed ceiling. "This is gorgeous," I breathed, momentarily ignoring the question and sharing a grin with Celeste. "The rest of the hotel is like this?"

"Yup," she replied, grinning. "The rooms are even better, no two are alike. Wait until you try the food, it's outstanding!"

What did I do to deserve this? I wondered, staring at the over-the-top opulence. The lavish surroundings only served to accentuate my situation as a fish out of water. I couldn't believe my luck, or that I was even here, yet staring at the lavish displays and ornate fixtures brought out my own insecurities. The world had been so different only a few years ago, then everything I'd loved and taken for granted had disappeared. Staring at the opulence surrounding me, I felt a similar fear creep over my heart. Will this chance be pulled away just as quickly?

Celeste glanced at her watch. "I need to get going," she said, a note of regret tingeing her words. "Even private planes have a schedule to keep."

My shoulders slumped at the words. I barely knew the woman, but was nevertheless disappointed to see her go. The last two days had been hectic and stressful, and Celeste's presence, however brief, had been a welcome balm. Extending my hand, I said, "Have a safe flight."

She took my hand in a steady grip, then leaned in close. "Look, be nice to Jeremiah okay? He can seem like a jerk sometimes but he has a big heart for those he cares about or decides to protect."

Her words startled me. Be nice to him? "He's my boss," I said stiffly, not sure how to respond without sounding petulant. "I have to respect him."

She started to shake her head, paused to think for a moment, then nodded ruefully. "That's close enough, I guess." Leaning close, Celeste added in a lower voice, "It's been almost two years since he had a personal assistant; the last one, hmm, left on bad terms. As his assistant, however, you'll be accompanying him to functions and serving as his escort. Most of the press are used to these arrangements and should leave you alone but be aware you may get some attention. It's inevitable."

Did he treat them all like me? I was surprised to find that the mention of previous assistants irritated me. Then Celeste's warning about unwanted attention sank in and I remembered the swarm of paparazzi outside the airport. My skin crawled at the thought of being surrounded by the photographers, and suddenly this whole venture seemed like a very bad idea. Then again, when had I ever thought the whole situation was anything but a strange trick of fate?

"Ah, speak of the devil."

I turned to see the tall figure of Jeremiah enter the hotel. He had a small wrapped box under one arm and was speaking privately with Ethan near the entrance. They had a similar vibe I found interesting and I mentioned it to Celeste.

"Well, they were both in the military together . . . maybe it's that."

"Military?" I never would have pegged him for a soldier. It seemed there was a great deal I didn't know about the man I was now working for.

Celeste nodded. "They were both Army Rangers until Remi's dad died and left him in charge of the family business. Nasty business, that. I came in right afterward and helped with the fallout."

I wanted to ask more but both men made their way toward us and the moment was lost. Celeste smiled and stepped forward, taking Jeremiah's outstretched hand. "Looks like I'm no longer needed for this little soirée tonight."

Jeremiah raised Celeste's hand for a brief kiss before letting go, but beside him I saw Ethan flinch at the gesture. The redhead stepped back, then looked up at the tall bald man beside her. "Ready to go, babe?"

I blinked as Ethan's stolid face softened into a smile. Celeste gave me a wave and they walked off, the big man's hand at the small of the COO's back. Only then did I notice the gold band on his left hand.

"They've been married almost a year now." At my startled glance, Jeremiah quirked an eyebrow. "The question was written all over your face."

I ducked my head at his sardonic tone, clearing my throat. "What now?" I asked, slipping one last glance at the retreating couple. The stress was back as I realized I had no idea what he wanted.

"Celeste showed you around the hotel?"

"A bit, yes." I couldn't stop the smile that lit my face. "It's absolutely incredible. Pictures never did it justice."

He gave an amused chuckle. "Wait until you see the rooms."

7

I sank into the warm water, gripping the sides of the huge porcelain bathtub so I wouldn't slide under the surface. Foaming hills of bubbles tickled my nose as I settled into a comfortable position and I grinned, blowing them so they danced in little puffs through the air. The deep tub was surprisingly comfortable and I settled in, breathing a sigh of relief and fiddling with the water knobs with my toes.

Jeremiah had sent me upstairs to the room, saying he had to take care of a few things before joining me. I had followed the hotel worker who showed me to my room and when he'd open the doors, I'd been rendered speechless. The interior of the suite was the most over-the-top, gaudy place I had ever seen, with its gilded mirrors and paintings, white panels trimmed with gold, crystal chandeliers and lamps, and Rococo moldings and filigree along each corner and open panel. Tapestries lined the walls and every inch of the room screamed *Look at me, I'm expensive*, hitting you over the head with its overstated elegance and extravagant, lurid design.

I absolutely adored it.

While the hotel host had been showing me around I'd barely been listening, too busy exploring on my own. The suite included several sitting rooms with furniture that looked expensive but very uncomfortable. Every amenity I could think of, and several I'd never have considered, was provided free of charge. I thought I'd died and gone to heaven when I saw the bathroom with its tall ceilings and mirrors, marble countertops and floors, and a tub almost as big as a hot tub sitting in the middle. My host had time to point out the closet of linens and robes before I shooed him out as politely as possible and drew myself a bubble bath. My mother used to collect old-fashioned perfume bottles, and it delighted me to see the hotel used these for bath oils. I chose a lavender scent before stripping out of my work clothes, grabbing a robe, and locking the door.

I allowed myself to enjoy the warmth and mellow scent of the water for a while before setting about with actual bathing. Using my toes to fiddle with the hot water knob kept the bath water warm as I thoroughly scrubbed my skin. I took my time but eventually my wrinkled hands convinced me to leave the bath, the bubbles only a white film atop the water. Slipping into the robe and wrapping my hair in a towel, I poked around the countertops and drawers to see what other treasures were hidden in the bathroom.

Three sharps raps against the locked door made me jump in surprise. "I'd like to see you out here." Jeremiah's deep voice carried through the thick wooden door, his words a command that was expected to be obeyed.

I froze, the tension I'd managed to wash away earlier now back with a vengeance. A quick glance around the ornate room made me realize with dawning horror that I had no clothes besides the robe and towel; I'd left them in the bedroom now occupied by my boss.

Swallowing, I took a look at myself in the mirror. My face was scrubbed of all makeup, shiny and clean but naked without my usual mask. Underneath the towel wrapped haphazardly around my head, my hair was a mess and still too wet to brush.

I can't let him see me like this, he'll kick me out of this hotel!

I hastily pulled the towel off my head and called out, "Just a minute," so he wouldn't think I was ignoring him. *Why do you care what he thinks?* a rational side of my brain tried to ask as I fumbled with my wet hair and smoothed out eyebrows that desperately needed a brow pencil. *Don't you want to stay away from him anyway?*

Maybe, but I'd at least like to look decent when I'm walking away.

Tousling my longish hair into some semblance of order and straightening my robe, making sure the belt was tied snug, I walked over to the door. Pausing for a moment, I gave myself one last look in the mirror—*seriously, you're never this vain!*—before unlocking the door and striding out.

Jeremiah stood across the bedroom beside a small silver cart with domed dishes. The faint aroma of food wafted to my nose, making my mouth water. He looked up as I approached, his eyes taking in my robe and wet hair. "How did you like your bath?"

I resisted the sudden urge to gush, shrugging one shoulder. "Not quite what I'm used to."

His steady gaze made me want to fidget as though caught in a lie and it took a great deal of self-control to keep myself still. He turned to push the cart toward the table and suddenly I could breathe again. *Stop letting him get to you like that.* My responses to him were silly but I couldn't help feeling threatened, as if I were the prey to his predator.

"I have something for you."

That got my attention. "Breakfast?" I asked, my eyes falling to the dishes beside him. My tummy rumbled in anticipation.

"In a moment, perhaps." He straightened and looked me dead in the eye. "Take off your robe and come here."

Everything inside me went cold. I hugged the robe around me, trying to stave off the inevitable. "Why?"

He said nothing, and I looked up to see him watching me. There was no emotion in his gaze; as far as he was concerned, I was to disrobe and go to him merely because he said so. Because I'd signed a document saying I would do what he said. At the time it felt like he'd given me a choice, but now, I felt like I'd been pushed into a carefully orchestrated ruse. The glittery trappings around me did nothing to disguise what they were: a cage, designed to keep me off balance and at his mercy.

Finally, finally, I got mad. "Why me?" I gestured around the room. "Why all of this?"

He cocked his head to the side. "Why not you?"

He was turning my questions back around at me and that

pissed me off. "I was nothing in your life, hands to type data, then be tossed to the streets when I was no longer useful. So why am I here?"

His lips thinned but he said nothing. Moving across the room to a large marble table, he picked up a crystal carafe and poured himself a glass of the amber liquid it held. "My career consists of me looking for potential," he said, swirling the liquor around as he regarded me dispassionately. "It's my job to find businesses that I can buy or sponsor, fix up, then sell for a profit."

"So what am I, a project?"

A tip of his head sideways confirmed my suspicions. "You were ambitious, clever as a college student, used to a certain kind of existence. Life dealt you a hard hand, brought you lower than you thought possible." He saluted me with the glass before taking a sip. "You would never have turned down a chance to get back on your feet, no matter what the cost."

"So give me a job," I said, the sarcasm dripping off my tongue. "You didn't need to strip me of my dignity, make me . . . The elevator, the garage—"

The thump of the glass on the serving tray shocked me out of my anger. "You rode that elevator every morning," Jeremiah said in a low voice, staring at the crystal carafe, "giving me those little glances, getting close but not too close." His eyes met mine, and I sucked in a breath at the fire I saw there. "I knew your scent, knew when that need rolled across you. Those secret little smiles, not knowing what was going through your head. . . ."

My breath caught as he trailed off, the fingers clenching

the top of the glass white with strain. *I don't believe you.* "I'm nobody," I said, my own words driving daggers through my heart.

His free hand clenched into a fist against a hard thigh as his jaw tightened, then his body relaxed. He strode up to me and I fell back a step, trying in vain to hold the last of my anger as a shield. Being so close to him was intimidating; my heart thudded in my chest as I looked to the side, unable to be strong any longer.

A finger came under my chin and lifted my head until I was staring up at him. His face was as implacable as ever but his voice was mild as he repeated his earlier request. Demand. "Take off your robe."

The words reverberated through my body, his proximity doing strange things to my mind, and I found my hands untying the belt to my robe. The soft material slid back off my arms and onto the floor, pooling at my heels. Fully exposed to him for the first time ever, I closed my eyes against his perusal, a tear squeezing out between my eyelashes.

When he put his arms around me I stiffened, but his hands stayed on my shoulders as he turned me around. "Look at something," he said, and when I didn't immediately open my eyes he repeated, "Look."

A large oval mirror stood in front of me, and I cringed at my reflection. "What do you see?" he prompted.

Flabby tummy and thighs, big hips, boobs that need a bra to look good. "Me." I'd always been my own worst critic: my blond hair looked limp from the long flight overseas, and my pale skin was in stark contrast to his darker complexion.

Never in my life had I felt comfortable naked, and now was certainly no exception. Looking in the mirror proved difficult as the comparison between his dark, masculine beauty and my normalcy left me miserable.

I saw him frown in the mirror. "Do you know what I see?" he said, tilting his head to study my reflection. "I see a beautiful face," he murmured, running a finger down my cheek and along the side of my neck. "Soft skin, the right curves." He leaned in close to the side of my head and breathed deep. "You also smell good enough to eat," he added, his words almost a growl.

My breath caught, his words making my belly tighten. One large hand covered my breast, fingers tweaking one nipple, and this time I gasped aloud. His grip on my shoulder tightened as the hand circling my breast dipped lower, skimming across my belly and leaving a trail of fire in its wake. "So beautiful," he murmured, and my head fell back onto his shoulder as the hand splayed over my hip, fingers digging deep into my skin. I watched him in the mirror, my heartbeat loud in my ears, as that hand smoothed over my mound, not sliding lower but feeling its shape.

Abruptly he stepped away and let me go, leaving me confused and off balance. "Don't move," he said, his voice a whip, and I froze. My instinctive obedience disturbed me but I stayed standing as Jeremiah picked up the box I'd seen him carrying in the lobby and handed it to me. "I was going to save this for later but now is a better time."

Suspicious, I took the package and opened it, pulling back the tissue paper. My eyes widened as I ran a finger along a pair of nylon leggings and beneath them, the satin straps of a sheer white bustier. Speechless, I looked up at my boss then back down to the contents of the box, not sure how to respond.

Jeremiah took the box out of my hands gently when I didn't do anything for several seconds. "Turn around."

As I did what he said, he pulled out the skimpy articles and then, to my further surprise, began dressing me. First the white bustier, which he laced up behind me; it covered my breasts and belly, with straps that hung down to my thighs. I stepped into the tiny panties, then the thigh-high stockings to which he connected the straps from the bustier. There was something incredibly sensual about the whole affair despite how professional he went about it. I'd never in my life worn lingerie like this, certainly not for a man, and it was an interesting experience. *I'm too fair to wear white,* a cynical part of me thought, but I kept that observation to myself.

When he finished, he took me by the shoulders and turned me around so I was facing the mirror again. "Now what do you see?" he asked, leaning close to my ear.

I blinked. Wow, so this is what you get with high-end lingerie. The white fabric managed to hide what I'd always hated and accentuate what I never realized I had. My hands ran down my waist, modestly cinched by the strings along my spine, and over my hips to finger the satin straps running down my legs to the stockings. The whole ensemble wasn't overly restrictive but tight enough to pull parts in and push certain things up—namely my chest, which I'd never considered particularly impressive. *Looking good now,* I thought, gliding my fingers across the firm tops of each breast.

Suddenly remembering he'd asked a question, I cleared my throat to answer but didn't know what to say. I locked eyes with him in the mirror and he nodded, obviously seeing my answer there. "Glad we see eye to eye," he murmured, running his hands up my arms and across my shoulders. "Now that we have that squared away . . ."

A hand twisted in my hair and my head was wrenched back. I gave a small cry, my hand covering his in surprise as I looked back at him. His face had grown cold as granite, green eyes intense, but his voice was smooth as silk. "I don't like being contradicted. When I tell you to do something, I expect it done immediately or there will be consequences." The hand in my hair tightened. "On your knees."

8

Iknelt quickly to the ground, the added pressure of the hand on my head forcing me to my knees. The garter straps against my back thighs and butt pulled tight, an interesting feeling but still eclipsed by the discomfort of the hand twisted in my hair. My head was tilted back and I watched as Jeremiah examined me from high above. "You enjoy this, don't you?" he murmured.

God yes! That traitorous part of my soul was on fire again, reveling in the forced submission even as I wondered what I'd gotten myself into. His hand left my hair and traveled down my cheek. "So beautiful, on your knees before me. You must see why I'm hard thinking of your mouth around my cock."

I shivered at the crude word, watching as his fingers skimmed over the bulge in his pants only inches from my face. Rolling my head sideways, I looked at our reflection in the large oval mirror. We weren't even doing anything—yet—but the way he stood over me, chin high and body straight as I knelt at his feet . . . My insides were melting, pooling between my legs to make me ready to take him. Craving his touch, I pushed against his hand like a cat, and was rewarded by his thumb stroking my forehead.

"I dreamed of you on your knees, that gorgeous mouth sucking me off." A finger ran across my forehead again, smoothing back the damp hair. "Would you like to help me come, little cat?"

"Yes," I breathed, then grunted in shock as he grabbed my hair again.

"Yes, what?"

"Yes . . ." I wracked my brain for an appropriate response. "Sir?"

He made an approving noise then his hands left me, moving to unfasten his pants and pull himself free. "I won't promise to be gentle," he grit out, his voice harsh with need, "as I've been thinking too much about this, but I do promise to finish whatever I start."

I wrapped both hands around his hard length, sliding them down to the base then back up experimentally. His hips jerked so I did it again with similar results before leaning forward and flicking my tongue over the head. I traced the ridge where it met the shaft before sucking him into my mouth, rolling the head with my tongue. I pumped my fist again, skimming the bulbous tip with my tongue and sucking at the soft knob, then removed my top hand and pulled him deeper.

He laid his hands on my head, not forcing me into anything but as a reminder of his presence. I bobbed my head over him, my hand stroking his shaft as I drew him deeper and deeper. The sounds coming from above me, low grunts and truncated breaths, were gratifying to hear. *I can make him lose control,* I thought, the idea giving me motivation to double my efforts. When I thought I had a handle on my movements, I released the base of his shaft and pulled him in as far as he could go.

A choked cry came from above, fingers digging into my skull. The thick head tickled the back of my throat, forcing me to withdraw or risk gagging. Wrapping my hand around the base, I began my efforts again but the hands on either side of my head pulled at me, his hips thrusting into my hot mouth.

"Hands behind your back." The words were a rough order. I paused only a moment before complying, twisting my arms behind me and locking my wrists. I prayed he would be gentle with me.

I should have known better.

His first thrust hit the back of my throat and my eyes watered immediately. "Hands behind your back," he barked again when I instinctively reached back around, "or I'll give you no choice and tie them."

It took every ounce of willpower I possessed but I forced my hands back into position, interlocking my fingers and hanging on for dear life. He repeated his thrust, this time not as deep, allowing me room to breathe. He continued like this, pushing himself in and out of my mouth, and I slowly began to get used to the movement. Indeed, pretty soon I was able to improvise, growing used to the tempo enough to use my tongue. I pressed against the base as they passed over; his plunging grew shallow, allowing me more space to maneuver and play. The small sounds coming from above, bitten-off groans and sharp intakes of breath, were sexy as hell and a good indicator that I was doing something right. When I flicked his tip with my tongue, forming a tight seal and sucking him deep, the gasp I heard above me made the corners of my mouth turn up.

His fingers dug into my skull, directing my head as his hips thrust him deep in my mouth. Any time I felt like gagging or had difficulty breathing he slowed down the pace, and I thanked him as best I could. My eyes flicked sideways to watch us in the mirror and the raw need I saw on his face—*I'm doing that*—was a powerful aphrodisiac. The throbbing between my legs increased, my tiny panties no match for the slickness running down my inner thighs. I need him inside me soon or this is going to be too much.

Apparently he thought the same because he pulled out and stepped back. My saliva glistened on the taut skin in front of my face. "Stand up."

Not sure whether he meant I could move my hands, I maneuvered myself upright until I was standing, arms still locked behind my back. There may have been approval on his face but he grabbed the back of my neck, his grip firm but not tight, and marched me to a round marble table with a thick wood base. "Lay across and grab on to the sides until I say you can let go."

I eyed the large table dubiously. It looked solid enough but the stone had to be cold and I wasn't wearing much. From somewhere deep inside my soul a small voice cried out, *You can still say no, it's not too late.* Body suffused with raw desire, I made my choice, however, and leaned down, grabbing the far edges firmly, and was relieved when it didn't move an inch. Jeremiah's hand left my neck, trailing down my back and across my bottom, giving one cheek a firm squeeze. "Spread your legs."

I did as he said and his hand trailed lower, following the line of the thong between my buttocks. I shivered as his fingers caressed the thin panties and me beneath them, and tilted up my hips for more contact.

"Are you on birth control?"

The unexpected question pulled me out of the haze of lust for a moment and I nodded. Irregular periods more than any kind of sex life were why I got the shots; I'd never really needed them for any other reason than medically.

In reward for my answer his fingers slid beneath the band of the small panties, pressing against my damp skin, and I moaned. He circled my entrance with deft fingers, then up toward the hard bud that throbbed with every beat of my heart. My breaths came in pants but he didn't go further, his hand merely exploring. "Would you like me to make you come, little cat?"

I nodded vigorously, his fingers making my breath catch. A chuckle came from behind me and lips pressed against the small of my back, just below the bustier. "You'll have to work for it . . . are you willing to do that?"

Before I could make any response, his thumb slid back through my folds and pressed firmly against my rear opening.

I surged forward in shock but the table prevented any escape from the foreign invasion. I trembled as his hand caressed both my entrances, the alien sensation a puzzle my body couldn't quite figure out.

"Many women enjoy backdoor play," Jeremiah murmured behind me, his fingers continuing their surface explorations. "Some actually prefer it as the forbidden gets them off." He leaned in close, his body molding to mine. "Some men also prefer this entrance, the tight fit and taboo as much of a turn-on as the sex itself." His lips were behind my ear as he added, "Guess which kind of man I am?"

I moaned helplessly, trapped between the cold marble table and his hot body. His fingers kept working on the hard nub between my folds, causing my hips to jerk and breathy pants to escape my lips. The two sensations at once made it difficult to differentiate which was the turn-on; his thumb would rub over both and I'd crave more. Confusion was difficult to sustain as the sensations threatened to overwhelm me. So when Jeremiah's thumb pushed inside, stretching the tight muscles in a way I never would have remotely considered sexy, I moaned and tilted my hips back against his hand.

His laugh was deep and sexy, washing over me and making my skin tingle. Those fingers redoubled their pace, finding places inside myself that left me shaking and bucking against him, my moans loud and unabashed. "You are so fucking hot," he whispered in my ear, rolling his hips against my backside. Still naked from the waist down, he slid his hard member between my thighs alongside his hand before repeating the motion. The inside of my legs were moist with my own juices and the roll of his hips against my backside was sexy as hell; my grip on the edge of the table tightened until my knuckles were white. My cries were long wails, the sensations and growing urgency making my body tense in anticipation.

"You'll come when I say, only when I say."

I whined, this time in protest, and his hand fell away. The sudden absence was like a cold bucket of water—an unwelcomed interruption no doubt punishment for my complaint. To my delight, however, the space was quickly filled by another sway of his hips as he slid his hard shaft slid between my thighs and a hand came up to clamp behind my neck. He didn't push inside, merely sliding along the wet folds. "Please," I moaned, lifting my hips to grant him better access.

"Please, what?"

His voice held amusement although I couldn't see his face, but this time I was sure I knew the answer. "Please, sir."

"What would you like, little cat? Do you want me inside you, that gorgeous ass of yours spread to take me deep? Should I ride you hard, force you to come with my cock pounding deep?"

That deep voice, gravelly and rich and right next to my ear, could melt stone. He slid across the hard bud between my legs and everything rushed back; I was so close, it wouldn't take much. . . .

I felt his bulbous tip nudge at my aching entrance at the same time hands spread my butt cheeks, fingers running along the puckered skin. He pushed inside both openings at once and I almost sobbed, the pressure and stretching a welcome relief. He wasted little time, his hips picking up a steady tempo even as his fingers worked my back hole. Within a minute I was moaning with each thrust, my cries echoing off the marble table and ornate mirrors in the room.

As his thrusts grew more forceful, banging the tops of my thighs repeatedly against the edge of the marble slab, I looked up into the large wall mirror above the mahogany dresser in front of me. It gave a clear view of the man behind me, and although I heard very little from him, I saw the raw need on his face. His mouth opened in muted gasps, the long arms reaching to my neck straining against the white shirt material. The corset back of the bustier with its strings and white lace was hot; it was impossible to believe it was my body reflected in the mirror.

Very quickly, however, it became all about the various sensations, the building explosion I desperately sought. He was pounding into me now, each thrust slamming me into the table, which, for all the abuse, remained steady. I wailed, my orgasm rushing to meet me. "Please, I can't stop. Sir, please!"

The hand between our bodies disappeared and Jeremiah increased his strokes, jerking hard inside me. Fingers on the back of my neck squeezed, throaty cries and guttural groans coming from close behind my head as fingers slid around the front of me, gliding over the beating core between my legs. "Come then, I want to feel your body's reaction around me."

There was no way I could have stopped myself. My orgasm flooded over me like a wave of light; I cried out, my hands gripping the table like a vise, body shaking. Jeremiah's thrusts hit places inside me that had the waves rolling on and on, but then I heard a guttural, hoarse cry from above and he jerked over me with only a couple of last erratic thrusts. I lay there for a moment, panting and thankful for the cool surface of the marble beneath my too-hot body. Jeremiah lay his forehead against my shoulder blades and we stayed that way for a moment, struggling to catch our collective breaths.

Finally he pushed himself off me and pulled out, running a hand along my spine as he stepped back. "You can let go of the table now."

Easier said than done. My hands were stiff and difficult to free and as I tilted upright I flexed them to return feeling. Leaning against the table for support, I gave myself time to catch my breath as Jeremiah rearranged his clothing, then walked over to a nearby seat. He picked up a small paper bag with some big swirly name I didn't recognize and brought it over, setting it gently on the table beside me. Leaning in close, he placed a surprisingly soft kiss to my forehead, then nudged me gently toward the bathroom. "Go, clean up and put these on. Keep the lingerie on underneath, I want to know it's there beneath the clothing."

My legs were like jelly but I took the bag and wobbled to the bathroom, remembering to grab my purse before locking myself inside. Setting the bags on the floor, I stood in front of the sink mirror and stared at my reflection in the tall mirrors. My blond hair was a mess, still damp from the shower, but the tousled look seemed to fit the rest of my outfit. I ran my hands down the stiff white fabric, turning so I could see the corset strings across my back. I'd never before worn lingerie this fine—heck, I'd never really worn proper lingerie ever—but staring at the flare of my bottom beneath the white lacy contraption, the strings barely covering the tiny thong that hadn't been much protection . . .

I looked good. It was a novel concept for me and I admired my reflection in the mirror. Then I sobered. I'm not going to end this farce, am I? Whatever games Jeremiah Hamilton was playing had gone too far; I'd allowed myself too many liberties to play the innocent in this game any longer. So what does that make me, a well-paid office assistant, or a glorified mistress?

The question disturbed me and I tried to block it from my mind. Taking a few minutes to clean myself up thoroughly, I discarded the tiny panties before turning to see what was inside the bag he had given me. A trendy pair of pants, simple yet silky blouse, and a pair of red flat shoes made up the clothing portion, while a brush and other toiletries lined the bottom. The clothes, as far as I could tell, were the right size even though I knew my curvy figure wasn't exactly the norm in Europe. He's obviously done this before, to know exactly what is needed. I didn't care to explore why that thought annoyed me. The revelation brought up more questions I didn't want to ask right now, so I pushed them aside and hurried to make myself presentable.

Twenty minutes later I emerged, fully clothed and refreshed, to see him waiting beside the table with the domed dishes I'd seen earlier. They contained a simple selection of fruits and crepes, with real whipped cream in a chilled metal dish. Looking at the clock I saw it was still morning and I thanked the powers that be I had managed to sleep on the plane. "What's the plan for today?" I asked, remembering Ethan mentioning something about a gala.

He took my hand and lifted it to his lips before popping a handful of grapes into his mouth. "Eat while you can," he said, watching me pile the fruit onto the thin crepe wrap. "Today, your work really begins."

9

Paris was as dazzling at night as in daylight, but I was too nervous to notice.

I smoothed the expensive dress with my hands, watching through the limousine windows as the city flashed past. The flutter in my belly at that moment had more to do with fear of what I was getting myself into and less to do with the man seated next to me, one large hand maintaining a possessive grip on my thigh.

Only forty-eight hours ago I'd been struggling to get by, worrying how homelessness was only a single paycheck away. Now decked out in a dress and shoes that cost three months of my previous salary, and on my way to a charity gala alongside one of the richest men in the world, that person seemed light-years away.

I'd pinch myself to see if I was dreaming but, after doing that all day, I was pretty sure this was real.

"You look nervous."

The softly spoken words made me swallow. I stared at the

hand on my leg, watching a thick thumb lazily caress the material, but couldn't bring myself to raise my gaze further. "I'm terrified," I admitted, but couldn't say more as my emotions jumbled all the thoughts in my head.

Jeremiah made a low murmur, acknowledging my answer, and we fell back into silence. The Eiffel Tower glittered on the dark horizon, a bright beacon over the still-busy city, but even that sight couldn't shake me out of my current doldrums.

"Where would you most like to visit in France?"

The question surprised me. I looked up to see him watching me, green eyes thoughtful. "Excuse me?" I asked.

Jeremiah pointed out the window at the passing city. "Most people want to see the Eiffel Tower, or visit the wineries, or any other number of activities. What is one thing you'd like to do?"

I didn't consider the question relevant to this particular moment, but I knew the answer anyway. I'd known it since childhood. "See the beaches of Normandy."

He blinked slowly, and I got the impression I'd managed to surprise him this time. "Really?"

I smiled at the bemused question in his eyes. "My great-grandfather was an RAF fighter pilot, and my dad always loved World War II stuff; I grew up watching movies and documentaries, anything about the subject. Guess his love rubbed off."

"RAF?" Jeremiah asked, interest sparking in his beautiful eyes. "Was your great-grandfather British?"

I shook my head. "Canadian. He died before I was born,

but my father always said he told the best stories." I found talking about my father painful, but strangely cathartic. I'd avoided even thinking about my parents for nearly three years, but now the memories allowed me to smile and relax. "He loved watching war documentary marathons on the history channels during military anniversaries. Mom always called him a useless lump those weekends, but she let him have his shows. He had a picture on our mantel of him on Utah Beach long before I was born, posing next to some of the old wreckage still on the sands."

I looked up to see him watching me with a strange expression, almost yearning. His face closed off immediately, settling into its normal neutral mask, leaving me to ponder what exactly I'd seen. Why would a billionaire envy me my piddly little life? "What about you?" I asked, praying I wasn't prying. "Did any of your family fight in that war?"

Jeremiah shook his head. "My father was too young and I doubt he would have gone anyway. Our family made their first million from the war movement, however."

I cocked my head, detecting a hint of bitterness in the statement. "They built ships and weapons?"

"No, they sold the necessary raw materials to the government at a huge profit. When the war was over, my family was richer than ever."

The anger in his voice confused me. Was he ashamed of his family's conduct? "Not everyone could fight in the war," I said. "My paternal grandfather was a fighter pilot but my other grandpa failed the entrance physical and had to stay behind. He ended up assembling ships and torpedo boats."

Something flickered in his eyes. "I didn't mean . . ."

I put a hand on his thigh. "I know. I just meant that your family helped in the war, too, no matter what the motivation. That is nothing to feel guilty about."

Something told me the CEO had never considered the situation like that. How hard it must be to be ashamed of your own family, I mused, because that was the impression I got from the conversation. I glanced up to see Jeremiah staring silently at me, his eyes probing. Suddenly self-conscious, I cleared my throat and fiddled with the purse in my lap. The hand on my knee crept up my leg and around my waist. Then he suddenly hauled me sideways until I sat face-to-face with him. I swallowed at the penetrating look he gave me as his fingers pushed an artfully curled strand of blond hair from my neck. "You look beautiful tonight."

That deep voice rumbled through me, setting my body on fire. I flushed and cast my eyes sideways, only to have him take my chin and gently pull my head back so I again faced him. His eyes searched my face then his hand followed, lightly tracing the edge of my brow line and jaw. "I'll be the envy of every man in there."

I swallowed, breath stuttering in my throat at his passionate gaze. The hand behind me dipped lower, cupping my backside through the green fabric as his fingers and eyes traveled down my body to the low neckline of the dress. I sighed, body yielding to his unspoken demands, reveling in the moment.

The day had flown by like a crazy, impossible dream. My boss had taken me to some of the trendiest (and most expensive!) shops in the city to look for a gown. It had taken three stores before we found what I thought was the perfect dress; apparently Jeremiah thought so, too, because he bought it on the spot when I stepped out of the dressing room. The green sleeveless number made me feel sexy, accentuating my curves in ways I'd never imagined possible. He then whisked me away to a salon for the rest of the transformation. Attendants used an airbrush for applying the makeup, something I'd never experienced before. Though I would have loved to see the process, they denied me the wall mirror, facing me away from it during the whole procedure. Afterward, however, they twirled me around and, even though I never really cared much for makeup, the result impressed me. They'd lightened my long blond hair several shades, and the makeup made my skin appear flawless.

The hand at my back crept up to my neck, grasping tight. He pulled me close in what I thought would be a kiss, but he stopped just short. "Tell me," he said, his other hand sliding beneath the high slit in the side of the gown, "are you already wet for me?"

Always. I swallowed, heart racing as his fingers crept toward my inner thigh. He played with the top of my thigh-high stockings, then up again toward the apex of my legs.

The dark green dress had necessitated different lingerie than the white set Jeremiah had gifted me earlier that morning. He had picked the ensemble out, then, when we returned to the hotel room later in the afternoon, had insisted on stripping me out of my clothing and dressing me in the new underwear. The whole thing had felt incredibly erotic, but Jeremiah made no demands on me despite the erection I'd seen tenting his pants. His approval, however, had warmed other parts of me; it felt good to be seen as desirable.

The memory itself made me hotter, and I gave a panting moan, opening my legs to his questing touch. His fingers slid along my panties, pressing against me without actually touching, and I shuddered. I heard his deep chuckle as he did it again, then raised his chin to kiss my forehead. "Looks like we'll have to wait," he murmured, and I gave a mewl of disappointment as he set me again firmly beside him. "Tonight, however, you're mine." The promise in his voice made me shiver in anticipation.

We turned off the street, heading toward a well-lit building. A throng of people milled about the entrance, and I tensed again. Jeremiah squeezed my leg, and I forced myself to relax, grabbing my purse beside my feet. The car pulled to the entrance of the building, and slowed to a stop, then I heard the chauffeur get out.

Showtime, I thought, hands wringing my purse. While there were not as many people as I feared—some had already entered the building—more than enough remained to set my heart racing.

The door opened, and Jeremiah emerged first, holding out his hand as I scooted toward the car door. Lights flashed as I stepped out, very conscious of the clingy dress and high heels. Jeremiah's arm was solid as he guided me effortlessly through the line of people, giving me firm ballast to which I clung. While I knew how to walk in heels, the attention we received had me feeling like a bumbling idiot. I focused on not falling or otherwise making a fool of myself, and breathed a relieved sigh when we reached the entrance and the cameras and babbling press faded into the background.

Jeremiah had given me little information—maybe deliberately—with regards to the gala. I knew only that it took place at the Port de Versailles and would benefit charity. The sheer number of people already there, and the way they moved, gave me the impression that we had not arrived anywhere near the start of the festivities. A quick peek at the events schedule pressed into my hands confirmed my suspicion, and also that there was much more going on than what I saw. Scanning the scheduled events, I pointed at one name. "You didn't tell me you were a guest of honor."

Jeremiah lifted one shoulder in casual dismissal as he guided us into the central area. A classical band played music at the far end next to the stage, and a few people swept across the dance floor, but most clustered in groups spread throughout the room.

"Ah, my friend, I'm glad you could make our little soirée." A short balding man stepped toward us, and grasped Jeremiah's hand in a vigorous handshake. He was wearing a tuxedo, complete with bow tie, and had a strong French accent. "I trust you only just arrived?"

"Hello, Gaspard," Jeremiah said in the way of greeting, a small smile playing over his lips. His approval seemed genuine; he obviously had a fondness for the Frenchman. "Thank you for the honor of the invite."

Gaspard laughed. "Forever modest, when so often it is you who funds these little endeavors."

I blinked and slanted a look at my boss. He seemed unperturbed by the praise, and I realized it was likely the truth. I didn't know he gave to charities. Indeed, there was a lot I didn't know about the man standing beside me, and my own ignorance was beginning to frustrate me.

"Who is your lovely companion tonight?" Gaspard asked, drawing my attention back to the present.

"May I introduce Miss Lucille Delacourt, my newest assistant. Gaspard Montrose is the man responsible for this whole affair."

"Enchantée, mademoiselle." Gaspard took my offered hand and laid a light kiss on the knuckles. I felt Jeremiah's hand on the small of my back clench, fingers digging into the fabric of my dress.

"Enchanté, monsieur," I greeted in return, then gestured to the large room. *"Cette salle est merveilleuse."* This place looks marvelous.

Gaspard's face lit up. *"Ah, mais vous parlez en français!"* Ah, you speak French!

"Un peu; je suis née au Québec avant de déménager à New York." Only a little, I was born in Quebec before moving to New York.

"Ah, French-Canadian." Gaspard beamed at me, obviously pleased, and I returned his smile. "Welcome to Paris, *mademoiselle.*"

I could feel the weight of Jeremiah's gaze, but ignored him, scanning the schedule. The booklet listed various charity presentations during the day but it was winding down for the evening, leaving only dinner and the final ceremonies.

"Ah, before you go in, Jeremiah, there's one thing you should know." Gaspard leaned in close to the taller man, and said in a low voice, "Lucas is here tonight."

Jeremiah stiffened, and when I looked up his face was like stone. Gaspard looked apologetic about the news. "I don't know how he received an invitation, but it was legitimate and he was allowed attendance."

I busied myself with my dress, curious as to who they were talking about but trying not to seem nosy. Jeremiah's jaw clenched, a muscle ticking in his cheek, then his face smoothed out. "Thank you for the news, Gaspard."

The Frenchman nodded, and turned to another arriving couple as we swept past. Now that we were no longer in front of the press, I felt much more comfortable walking normally but still had to work to keep up with Jeremiah. His long strides carried us into the hall, and I suddenly felt the weight of eyes on us. I clenched my teeth and tried to ignore the intrusive stares.

"You never told me you spoke French."

I'd been expecting a comment on my exchange with Gaspard and, despite a nervous flutter in my belly, managed a small smile of triumph. "You never asked."

My reply was cheeky, but I looked up to see him contemplating me, a bemused look on his face. "So during your interview when you said you had passports, plural . . ."

I nodded. "I have two: one Canadian and the other American. My mother is American but she moved up there after marrying my father. I grew up in Quebec, then moved back to New York when my grandma, my mom's mom, died. I was fourteen."

"You live an interesting life, Ms. Delacourt." Again I saw the approval on his face, and it warmed me to the tip of my toes. Surprising him was likely both a difficult and a risky proposition, but this time I came away unscathed.

I felt eyes watching our movement through the room, but nobody approached us, which I found odd. Jeremiah seemed to know exactly where he was going, and I tried to keep up. Our pace didn't allow much time for anyone to approach, and I wondered what was so important.

Unfortunately, I wasn't given the chance to find out. We stopped near the dance floor, surrounded by groups talking and laughing among themselves. He took my hand, the same as Gaspard only moments before, and laid a soft kiss across my knuckles. Unlike the Frenchman, however, this one sent tingles through my body; his eyes captured mine, and I knew he was aware of my reaction.

"I need to speak to someone in private," he murmured, his voice barely audible above the ambient noise. "I won't be more than a minute; stay here until I get back."

Then without another word he turned and walked away, disappearing through the cluster of guests.

10

When in fifth grade, I received my first, and last, major role in a school play. I practiced my lines at home and with the other students until I knew them forward and back. Even the dress rehearsals in the large gymnasium went without incident, the empty area safe from critics. I'd been proud to get my part, small but crucial, right up until the night of the first performance. Faced with a gym full of strangers, I froze, my lines disappearing from my head, unable to move or speak under what felt like a condemning tide.

Suddenly alone in that great exposition hall, in a foreign land not knowing another soul, that same freezing terror turned me to stone.

The beautiful hall, with its well-dressed patrons and high-class atmosphere, took on an almost sinister quality now that I was left to my own devices. The schedule crumpled in my hands as I peered about, trying to decide where to go. Staying put as Jeremiah said wasn't an option; I needed to get out of that sudden crush of bodies the same way I'd needed to leave that stage all those years ago.

"Lucy Delacourt?"

Hearing my name startled me out of my turbulent thoughts. Looking around to see who had spoken, I saw a dark-haired woman in a long yellow gown approach me. She seemed familiar, then a surprised smile tilted my lips as I recognized her. "Cherise?"

"Oh my God, it *is* you!" The smaller girl clapped her hands together in delight, beaming at me. "I thought I saw you come through the doors, but couldn't be sure until I got closer."

Still amazed to see someone I actually knew, I threw decorum to the wind and pulled the girl into a quick hug. Cherise had shared dorms with me for our first two years of college at Cornell, and while we hadn't seen much of each other during classes—she was premed and I was prelaw—we'd still hung out on weekends with the other students. I didn't question what providence brought her here, I just thanked whoever was watching over me for a familiar face.

"What are you doing here?" I exclaimed as we parted.

"I'm here with David actually." Her big smile widened in pride. "We help run a clinic down in Borneo and he's here trying to raise donations."

"You two finally got married?" When she nodded I just grinned. Cherise and David had been high school sweethearts when I'd met them in college. Both had big dreams of saving the world, and they seemed to be on their way. "So you're both doctors now?"

"No, I actually switched to business when David went into med school. It worked out well as I now help him run the business side of the whole operation. I get to be out in the field with him anyway, so it works great for me!"

Cherise brought with her the upbeat, infectious joy her friends had always luxuriated in. Her obvious pleasure in seeing me lifted my somber mood from moments earlier, and I finally relaxed. The bubbly brunette got an impish look to her eyes. "So spill: Was that really Jeremiah Hamilton with you at the door?"

I flushed at the question. *There's no reason this needs to be awkward,* I admonished myself. "He's my boss," I replied, shrugging my shoulder as if it were nothing.

"So are you two . . . ?"

"No," I replied, shaking my head emphatically. "I'm his new personal assistant, which I only just found out means I have to accompany him to these functions. This is all so new though." I didn't lie, but I still felt bad leaving everything else out, especially when I saw Cherise's disappointment at the news.

"Weren't you going to be a lawyer?" she asked, looking puzzled.

The question was a sore spot, but not something she would have known about. When my parents died, we were both college juniors and rarely saw one another. I'd inadvertently cut ties with most of my college acquaintances while I tried to get my life together, something that was still an ongoing process. "It didn't work out," I said, then in an effort to change the subject I looked around behind her. "Where's David?"

"Out in the crowd, mingling with the rich folks and trying to get more donations. Our presentation didn't net as much as we needed, so he's trying to get a few more sponsors." She rolled her eyes. "He's so much better at that than I am. It's weird walking up to a stranger and just asking for money."

"Funny," a heavily accented voice said nearby, "as this is what I see in front of me."

I looked over to see a tall, slim, blond woman standing beside me, eyeing Cherise with smug superiority. I had no idea how long she'd been standing there, but when Cherise's face fell my hands curled into fists. "Excuse me," I said bluntly, indignant at her treatment of my friend, "who are you?"

She turned her cool gaze to me, blue eyes giving me a quick once over. "I am Anya Petrovski. I understand you are Mr. Hamilton's new personal assistant." She studied her nails. "It is a position with which I am well acquainted."

The woman didn't offer her hand, and I wouldn't have taken it anyway. I neither liked the emphasis she put on the word "position," nor did I appreciate her knowing smirk. Annoyed at having my "business relationship" with my boss mocked by this woman, I used my anger as a shield. "If you'll excuse me, Ms. Petrovski, I was already talking with—"

"You will find that when you work for wealthy men, people will selfishly approach you only for your contact." Anya gave Cherise a condescending glance. "You must guard yourself against even such clumsy attempts."

Beside me, Cherise stiffened at the veiled insult. "This is a charity function, if you haven't noticed," I countered, coming to Cherise's defense. "If she wants me to help her raise money, it's my choice to do so."

Anya lifted a shoulder. "The venue only legitimizes the petty begging attempts."

My whole body tensed in outrage, and I was set to go off on the haughty, blond woman when Cherise backed away from us. "If you two will excuse me," she said stiffly, "I need to get back to my husband."

As she turned to leave I reached for her arm. "Cherise . . ."

"It's okay, Lucy, I'm happy to see you but . . ." The smaller girl gave the haughty Russian beauty an uncharacteristic glare. "When your business is done with this, this woman, come find us," she said before walking off, head held high.

"Why did you do that?" I said, rounding on the beautiful blond woman. "She was a friend."

Anya shrugged, but her cool eyes seem amused by my anger. "She means nothing to me. I have only been sent to collect you."

My hands clenched again. Surrounded by strangers, and in a foreign environment, I didn't want to draw any undue attention to myself. But I found it hard. The fact that my struggle obviously amused the Russian woman made my decision to keep calm, at least on the outside, even more difficult. "By whom?"

Her smirk widened. "My employer."

I bit my cheek to keep from saying the first words that came to mind. "Please tell your employer I'm indisposed for the rest of the evening."

"I really must insist." Anya linked her arm through mine

and steered me around. "Mr. Hamilton does not appreciate tardiness."

"What?" Her words surprised me, shock making me take a few steps before digging in my heels. "Jeremiah sent you?"

She responded with a jerk of her chin behind me, and I swiveled my head to see Jeremiah's profile between the guests. He sent this harpy to collect me? My lips pursed in annoyance as I grudgingly allowed myself to be led through the crowd, loathe to make a scene but really wanting free of the sanctimonious blond woman's grasp.

Several military figures surrounded our target, the uniforms a similar dark green but decorated differently to denote varying ranks. As we drew nearer I realized I'd made a grave error: this was not Jeremiah, but now there was no way to get free. A familiar yet foreign dark head turned in our direction and a set of cool blue-green eyes lit up as they saw us approach. Long slicked-back hair framed a familiar-yet-not face, olive skin bisected by a small white scar across his nose and one cheek. Dressed in all black and holding a wineglass loosely through his fingers, the familiar face lacked the cool rigidity to which I'd grown accustomed.

What have I gotten myself into?

"Gentlemen, if you'll please excuse me. We can discuss our business further tomorrow."

Even his voice sounded similar, but he had a slick quality and cynical air about him, much different than Jeremiah's stiff control. The stranger's carefree expression as he gave me a quick once-over disconcerted me, as I'd grown used to the stoicism I associated with the familiar face.

"And who do we have here?" he asked, lifting my hand
to his lips. The way he kissed my fingers was different than
Gaspard earlier. Whereas the older Frenchman had been
gallant, this was more personal than I'd prefer. His eyes held
mine, his lips lingering perhaps a bit too long across my
knuckles, and despite my best intentions I felt a flutter in
my belly. Annoyed with myself and my response, I snatched
my hand away, and watched as amusement flash in his eyes.

"This is Lucy Delacourt, the new assistant to Jeremiah."
Anya's accented voice held the same snide tone as before, but
her demeanor seemed more deferential. She sidled next to
the man, and wormed her arm through his—almost possessively. "Meet Lucas Hamilton, the true heir to the Hamilton
business." I couldn't miss the air of entitlement in her statement, and Lucas didn't deny the claim.

So this was the Lucas that Gaspard warned Jeremiah about
earlier? I frowned between the two gorgeous people. The
predatory nature of their gaze had part of me wanting to flee,
but I stayed, crossing my arms instead. A kernel of anger
smoldered in my belly at being thrown into this unaware,
without backup.

Lucas ignored the gorgeous woman hanging on his arm,
cocking his head to the side and studying me. "You seem
tense, love," he said, addressing me in a smooth voice. "I
don't want a beautiful woman such as yourself disappointed
by my company."

Beside him, Anya tensed, and the angry look she gave me
spoke volumes as to her jealousy. While it felt good to watch
her come down a peg, I had no desire to continue this con-

versation. Something told me I was way out of my league here. However this went, I doubted I'd come out ahead. "I thought you were someone else," I said stiffly, not bothering to mention that I was dragged to see him. "If you'll excuse me . . ."

As I stepped back to leave, the band behind me struck up a new tune, a livelier number that had several couples walking to the dance floor. Lucas stepped forward, shaking off Anya's grip on his arm. "Would you care to dance?" he asked, holding out a hand toward me.

Anya stepped forward, obviously having something to say about the offer. A sharp look in her direction by the man before me, however, and Anya stopped, simmering in place as she glared at me. *Why am I suddenly the bad guy?* I wondered, irritated by the entire game. "No, I'm sorry," I said stiffly, trying to maintain my poise, "but I really need to find my—"

"Really, I must insist." Before I knew it he had a hand around my waist, and was leading me out onto the floor. I balked immediately, digging in my heels. *Why is everyone insisting I do what they want tonight?* I thought, annoyance bubbling to the surface.

"We're quite visible here," he murmured, leaning in close. "You don't want to cause a scene now, do you?"

I hesitated, suddenly mindful of the strangers around us, and that momentary hesitation gave him all the time he needed. He swept me out onto the floor and into his arms before I could think to say no again, gliding us across the dance floor as smooth as silk. I tried to pull away, but his vise-like grip allowed me no escape. "Let me go," I said, my rising anger bleeding into my voice.

"And ruin a perfectly fine opportunity to dance with a beautiful woman? I think not." He seemed amused at my resistance; I danced stiffly in his arms, but my gracelessness didn't faze him a bit. He pulled me close to his hard body, arms like iron; my feet barely touched the ground, my weight supported almost entirely by his arms.

"We seem to have gotten off on the wrong foot. Tell me why: do I smell bad?"

The absurd comment caught me off guard, and I struggled not to be amused. Involuntarily, I breathed in his scent: spicy and sweet like cinnamon, and I couldn't tell if it was cologne or his natural fragrance. Annoyed at my reaction, I retorted, "I don't appreciate watching my friends get belittled, then being dragged to meet someone under false pretenses."

Lucas tipped his head to the side, acknowledging my blunt comments. "Anya can be tempestuous; indeed, it was once part of her charm. Perhaps we can begin again. I am Lucas Hamilton and you are . . . ?"

I frowned at his collar, refusing to meet his eyes in defiance. "You already know who I am."

A finger under my chin lifted my gaze. "But I'd like to hear it from your lips," he said softly, sweeping me in a big arc across the dance floor.

Butterflies exploded in my stomach, and my jaw clenched. Damn my body and its silly reactions. His hands were burning coals against my skin, eyes like magnets. Just like his brother.

Reminding myself of Jeremiah allowed me some measure

of control over myself—I didn't need another man to make me go weak in the knees and lose all willpower. One is quite more than enough. "What do you want?" I asked firmly.

Instead of disappointment at his seduction attempts being ignored, his gaze sparked with renewed interest and no small bit of amusement. "Besides a dance with a beautiful woman?" He shrugged a shoulder. "To make my stick-in-the-mud little brother jealous."

I pursed my lips, gut tightening. At least he's finally being honest. I think. "I'm not interested in playing games, Mr. Hamilton." I struggled slightly in his grip, jostling a nearby couple. "I'd rather not make a scene, but if you won't let me—"

"What if I answered any questions you might have about my brother?" At my startled look, Lucas gave a wry smile that almost seemed genuine. "My brother is one who keeps his secrets close." He swayed me closer, mouth dipping close to my ear. "Aren't there some things about your boss you were dying to know?"

I ground my heel into the toe of his wingtip shoes. Lucas winced and pulled away but didn't let go, continuing to twirl me across the wood floor. That infuriating mouth tipped up in the corners as I scowled at him. He knew he had me.

I was curious.

There was so much I didn't know about my new employer, and it kept me feeling off-balance when I was around him. The way Jeremiah watched me, his gaze piercing through my mind, I constantly felt like he could read my very thoughts. The idea of knowing something, anything, about him that could tip those dizzying scales in my favor, was as tantalizing as water to a man dying of thirst. Still, I didn't appreciate the smirk on Lucas's face. "Anya used to work for Mr. Hamilton? Um," I stuttered, "the other one. My boss."

His lazy smile grew. "She was his last personal assistant," he drawled, eyes watching me intently.

I struggled in vain to keep my reaction from showing. That harpy? What did he see in her?

I didn't realize I'd said the words aloud until Lucas threw back his head and laughed. The sound startled me, and I flushed. We drew a few glances from the couples around us, but the dancing continued. "She wasn't always this way," he said, humor lacing his voice. "Actually, she used to be a very sweet girl, much like yourself."

"What happened, then?" I asked, determined not to fall prey to any more of his lines.

He lifted a shoulder. "I seduced her away from him, then turned her into my spy. When he discovered this and threw her out, she came to work for me."

The arrogance in his voice was a bitter gall, and I tried again to free myself. Surprisingly, he loosened his grip as if to let me go, twirling me under his arm. He remained impervious to my glare, an infuriating smile fixed on his face, but I still held his attention. "Next question?"

I was dancing with a snake, but I couldn't see any way out at the moment. A quick scan of the room showed no relief coming to my aid, so I forged ahead. "What did Anya mean about the rightful heir business? You and Jeremiah are brothers, right?"

"Ah, straight to the heart of things." He twirled me again,

blue-green eyes deep in thought. "What do you know so far?"

Not much, aside from what Celeste had revealed earlier. "The Wikipedia version. He was in the military, got out, and took over the company . . . had a rough go in the beginning."

Lucas dipped his head. "A decent summary, if lacking in the pertinent details."

I paused, thinking. "What exactly does Hamilton Industries do? How does your family make money?"

He quirked an eyebrow but still answered my question. "Investment mainly, usually in other companies that then give us a large portion of their profits. The corporation at this point serves to maintain and grow the money that's already there, but there are many companies and people under its proverbial umbrella. We always . . ." He faltered, trailing off, then continued. "Tell me, how was your relationship with your father growing up?"

The bizarre question blindsided me. My mouth tightened, and I searched his face for any ulterior motives, but the question seemed genuine if more personal than I preferred. "Good," I said cautiously, "why?"

"Ours wasn't." Lucas's previously jovial expression shadowed. "Rufus Hamilton was impossible to please, especially if you were in any way related to him. Of course, we didn't realize this until we were much older and his demands had already warped our sensibilities. I'll give you the short version: I went the route expected of me, to take over the family business, while Remi rebelled the only way he knew how and joined the military without my father's consent. It was the one time he managed to thwart our father's plans, and that success ate away at the old man."

He paused, and the silence in the conversation stretched. "Obviously something happened," I said, prompting for more information.

Lucas snorted, his gaze far away and cynical again. "Yeah. The old man died." He looked down at me, and his lips tightened; another twirl, which I began to realize was how he gave himself time to think. "Rufus really couldn't have timed it better if he'd tried; heart attack took him out in the middle of a board meeting, and only days before Jeremiah was set to re-enlist. He surprised me by turning up at the reading of the will—my little brother hadn't left on good terms—but I was even more shocked when our beloved father left the bulk of his estate to his youngest son Jeremiah."

The controlled fury in Lucas's eyes as he spoke warred with the sneer that twisted his lips. He was looking off in the distance again, lost in memories he obviously didn't like. "Jeremiah got everything, including majority shares in the company, with the stipulation that if he refused to take over, the entire company and all its holdings would be liquidated and scattered. That would have meant the loss of thousands of jobs, and the collapse of a carefully built infrastructure spanning decades, all to get back at the son who had managed to outmaneuver him."

The callousness of the whole affair boggled my mind. "So willing Jeremiah the entire company was meant to be a punishment?" I asked.

I felt a brief shiver, as my voice jolted Lucas out of his memories. The dark expression disappeared, replaced by the smug amusement I began to understand was a mask. "Our dear Remi was always looking out for the common man," Lucas remarked, twirling us spiritedly around the dance floor. "It's why he joined the army, you know; he wanted to help others. So, when the executor read the will, lawyers and board members surrounded Remi, impressing on him the gravity of the situation, how many lives he would ruin if he turned it down, et cetera, et cetera. Given my little brother's predilection for being the hero, it was a no-brainer what he would choose."

"What about you?" I asked, genuinely curious. If Lucas told the truth at all, then his father had cheated him out of his inheritance through no fault of his own. While it didn't erase all my dislike for the man, it did put it into perspective.

"I survived." His gaze traveled over my shoulder, and a wicked smile curved his lips as the song came to an end. "Doesn't mean I don't enjoy my bits of fun when they come along."

I squeaked as he shifted me around, one arm looping behind my back, then bent me over until I was horizontal to the ground. Grabbing his shoulders, I stared wide-eyed up at his beautiful face only inches from my own. "Let's give them a show, shall we?" he murmured, then brought his lips down onto mine.

I stiffened, fingers digging into his dark suit. His mouth took full advantage of my shock, tongue and teeth playing with my bottom lip. The kiss was brief and, while it still brought butterflies to my stomach, I managed to keep my wits about me. As he pulled me upright, my arm was already in motion. My hand cracked along his cheek, momentum giving the slap strength. The blow stunned us both—I couldn't believe I'd done it and apparently neither could he. I saw open surprise in his gaze, and perhaps a smattering of respect enter his eyes as he released me.

"What's going on here?"

11

I breathed a sigh of relief at Jeremiah's familiar voice, but the look on his face when I turned wasn't the least bit comforting. I tried to move toward him, but Lucas gripped my hand tight, pulling me up short.

"Brother," his voice boomed, unnaturally loud now that the band had concluded their song. "Fancy meeting you here. Care to join me and my lovely companion for a drink?"

I tried again to wrench my hand from his grip, but Lucas held fast. Turning an apologetic gaze to Jeremiah, I was disappointed by the accusatory look I received in return. *Why is this suddenly my fault?* I thought, indignation bubbling up. *You left me to fend for myself!*

The confrontation attracted the attention of nearby attendees. Their prying eyes watched the drama unfold, but not a one moved a muscle to intervene . . . leaving me stuck smack in the middle. The two men seemed more intent on each other than myself although neither allowed me my freedom. Lucas still held my hand, and Jeremiah blocked any avenue of escape.

Together like this, I found it much easier to tell the two brothers apart, and I couldn't believe I'd mistaken one for the other. Jeremiah looked a caged bull, his broad frame hunched over and ready to charge. His impassive mask had slipped, and now his eyes blazed like the sun. In stark contrast, the leaner and slightly shorter Lucas sat back on his heels, a patronizing smirk on his face. There was a malicious twinkle in his eyes; he was obviously well versed in taunting his younger brother.

"What are you doing here?" Jeremiah all but growled, his eyes darting between his brother's face and our still-entwined hands.

"Perhaps I wanted to help the less fortunate, or to visit with my long lost brother. After all, our last meeting was so dramatic."

"You stole thirty million dollars!"

Lucas waved a hand in the air. "So I have been told," he remarked blithely, then looked at me. "Come, my dear, drinks are on me."

He pulled me forward a resistant step, and then Jeremiah stepped in the way, blocking his brother's escape. "I could have you arrested in two minutes," his low voice rumbled, faint enough that only those close by could hear the words. "Even in France they wouldn't hesitate to extradite you, Loki."

"Ah, little brother has been checking up on me!" Lucas

smirked and opened his arms wide, but there was a mocking gleam in his eyes. "You do miss me."

Following the conversation between the two siblings was difficult, causing more frustration to well up inside me. Both men seemed to have forgotten I was there while whatever problems lay between them were playing out in front of those around us. Along the edge of the dance floor I saw Anya watching us, a triumphant smile on her hard face, and wondered if she had been the one to point out my location in Lucas's arms to my boss.

Beside me, Jeremiah seemed to grow bigger, his expression darkening. "If you weren't my brother . . ."

"You'd what? Beat me to a pulp? Ruin my life?" The taunt in Lucas's voice was clear, and loud enough to be heard by those watching. "Too late, brother, someone beat you to it. Oh wait, no, that was you."

Jeremiah took a small step forward, and his brother held his ground. "Loki . . ."

"Enough!"

My voice cracked like a whip, the word piercing the tension. Both men started, then turned their furious stares on me. I myself was too angry to back down, however, and looked first at Lucas, raising my captured hand to almost eye level. "Let. Go."

There was a barely perceptible relaxing of his grip, and I snatched my hand back, stepping away. Jeremiah reached for my arm and I sidestepped him as well, much to his surprise. "Don't," I said, glaring at him.

He scowled back, clearly disliking my sudden defiance. "Ms. Delacourt," he started but I shook my head, meeting his angry expression with my own.

"You left me to fend for myself, and that's exactly what I intend to do." I spared a glance for Lucas, who was watching me with amusement, then back to Jeremiah. "It seems you two have some things to discuss, so I'll leave you alone."

My boss clearly didn't approve of my sudden independence, but right then I couldn't have cared less. I felt the weight of several onlookers' gazes, but stiffened my spine and walked away. The stupefied looks of the two men followed my exit; I could feel their gazes burning holes into my back. Unfortunately, I was not at all in the mood to appreciate the dubious victory I'd no doubt pay for later.

Few women at the function wore yellow dresses; so it didn't take me long to locate Cherise. She looked surprised at my presence, but before she could greet me I spoke up. "I want to help you."

David stood beside her, and he squinted at me. "Lucy?" he said in surprise, and I realized Cherise hadn't told him yet about seeing me.

"Tell me everything you can about your operation." Fire burned through my veins; I hadn't felt this alive in years. "I'm going to get you your funding."

When at college, one of my professors once mentioned in passing that I'd make a good lobbyist. Though never my goal, I recognized the accuracy of his observation. I found taking up the burdens and issues of others easier than dealing with my own; I never had problems approaching strangers on another's behalf. Years had passed since I'd last done anything like this, but my frustration needed an outlet and I threw myself into campaigning for my friends.

Over the next hour I charmed and cajoled my way through the crowds, translating when necessary and doing everything I could to help them. The process was surprisingly simple— the very nature of the event had already primed the attendees to write checks, and I had only to convince them why a little clinic in Borneo deserved their largesse. I dredged up every rusty social skill I'd ever learned, and flitted through the assembled group, sending them to David and Cherise before moving on to the next possible donor. Although I'd always been someone who was more comfortable as a wallflower than a social butterfly, I threw all caution to the wind and somehow managed to make people listen to me.

I caught glimpses of Jeremiah through the crowd, and could feel the weight of his gaze, but I ignored him as best I could. Easier said than done—even from a distance the man had the uncanny ability to throw me off balance. Still, I continued my crusade, and he didn't approach, giving me space—for which I was grateful. Neither Lucas nor Anya made another appearance, either, which also pleased me.

After an hour of moving from group to group, Cherise approached me and pulled me to the side. Grinning from ear to ear, her body all but vibrating with excitement, she said, "I don't believe it, but we've made nearly one hundred thousand so far!"

My mouth dropped open, and I had to stop myself from giving her a big hug. "Will that be enough to last you guys a while?"

"Enough?" She looked incredulous. "We could continue for several years with this at our current location—and not charge the locals a dime. Oh, thank you!" Cherise didn't seem to care about decorum, either, because she threw her arms around me in a quick but fierce hug. "You're incredible!"

"I would have to agree with that assessment."

Swallowing, I turned to see Jeremiah standing behind me, regarding us with a curious expression. He only had eyes for me, and when Cherise released me from her hug he held out a hand in my direction. "May I have the honor of a dance?"

My mouth worked silently, and I glanced at Cherise. Her grin had a knowing look about it, and when I hesitated she all but pushed me into my boss's arms. "The man asked you to dance," she said, eyes twinkling. "I think we can handle it from here."

No longer having an excuse, I stared at Jeremiah's offered hand. He had requested, not demanded, and he seemed content to wait me out. Looking into his green eyes, I realized I'd forgiven him some time ago for abandoning me, but I didn't feel like he should get off lightly. "You won't leave me alone on the dance floor, will you?" I teased, taking his hand.

Rather than the annoyance I feared I'd see, Jeremiah seemed almost amused by my question. "I promise not to let you out of my sight for the rest of the evening."

A promise in his tone sent chills across my skin as he led me to the center of the room. His touch was light as he gathered me into his arms on the dance floor, a stark contrast to his brother's earlier rigid grip. "I apologize for my conduct tonight," he murmured.

My eyebrows shot up. He apologized? To me? "Apology accepted," I replied, then let out a quick breath. "Your family is a bit dysfunctional, I see?"

A wry smile tipped one corner of his mouth but he didn't reply to the question. "You two were talking earlier," he said instead, the question in his voice.

"He answered some of my questions about you." When he tensed, I hurried to explain. "He said your father essentially forced you to take over the company. Is that true?"

"Essentially," he finally said after a long pause, but didn't elaborate.

"Celeste said you used to be an Army Ranger," I said after another moment of silence. His lips thinned, but I persisted. "What was it like?"

"Best thing I've ever done with my life." He slipped into silence again, but I could tell that he was thinking. "Originally, the military was meant only as a way to get away from my family, specifically my father. Once I got in, though, every aspect of that life fit me perfectly. I would have gone career if . . ."

If the choice hadn't been stolen away from you. As bitter as the argument had been between the two brothers earlier, I knew Lucas told the truth. Jeremiah's own nobility had forced him to leave behind a life he loved to save his family's company and all the lives of those connected to it. I leaned forward and laid my head on his shoulder; he stiffened in my arms, and I wondered briefly if I'd be pushed away, then his body relaxed and he pulled me closer. He smelled divine, like chocolate and cherries; the skin of his neck was close enough that I only had to turn my head to see if he tasted as good as he smelled. . . .

Forcibly reminding myself that I was in a room full of people, several of whom probably watched us, I lifted my head off his shoulder but didn't back away. Jeremiah must have somehow read my intentions; he pressed against me, a hard bump poking my belly. A dull ache filled my belly, body tingling from my heels to fingertips, and I swallowed a small sigh. His reaction to me acted as a drug all by itself, a powerful aphrodisiac that made me want to pull him someplace private to do naughty things. I saw the same desire reflected in his eyes as our gazes locked; his grip on my lower back tightened, pulling me in closer to rub against the hard shaft, and I felt a rush of heat between my thighs.

Someone tapped a microphone, then a familiar French voice came over the speakers. "We would like to take the opportunity to thank some members of our audience for their contributions tonight."

"I think they mean you," I murmured. There were definitely eyes on us now as the band ended the song, but Jeremiah didn't release me for several more seconds. Finally he stepped away but didn't let go, raising my hand to his lips.

I swallowed, heart skipping a beat. Celeste had told me that the press and general public believed he only took his assistants as platonic companions, but it would be hard to convince any onlookers of that tonight. Heck, I was getting confused, with too many mixed signals bouncing around my head. *One day at a time,* I thought as he released my hand and headed to the front of the gathering crowd. *This can all end in an instant, and I'll be back in a crappy Jersey apartment.*

Even with as much power as he wielded in our relationship, both business and personal, I knew I could walk away at any moment. While perhaps not enough to put us on even footing, the option gave me some stable ground in my suddenly topsy-turvy life, but the thought made my heart ache. Jeremiah wasn't the type to play games, but he was difficult to read sometimes.

"You're thinking too hard, my sweet."

I started, body tensing at Lucas's voice only inches from my ear. "Go away," I muttered, not taking my eyes off Jeremiah. He continued moving toward Gaspard, who began giving an introductory speech in French, and I was nervous what Jeremiah would do if he saw Lucas beside me.

"All in good time. I just thought it rude to leave without bidding farewell to such a beautiful lady."

I snorted in disbelief. "Go bother Anya, I'm sure she's used to it by now," I snapped, careful to keep my voice low, and heard a low chuckle in return. Most of the guests were ignoring us, for which I was grateful. "If you want to get back at your brother," I hissed in a low voice, "leave me out of it."

"Oh, but it's so much more fun this way."

Fingers grazed my hip, and I immediately lashed out, kicking backward with my heel, and grazing a shin. The hand quickly disappeared, and I had a moment of triumph until I heard him chuckle again.

Jeremiah had taken the stage by then, and I prayed he wouldn't look this way. "You're going to get me in trouble," I said.

"Oh, you'll probably enjoy it," Lucas all but purred, and I shot him a dark look. A self-satisfied smirk sat on his lips as he regarded me with unabashed interest. I rolled my eyes, determined to ignore him, and turned back to the stage . . . only to have Jeremiah's intense gaze rivet me in place. Damn it.

"Oh dear, looks like he's spotted our little tête-à-tête." Fingers brushed the hair back from my neck, and I flinched sideways. "I wonder what's going through his mind right now."

Judging by the look on his face, my boss and erstwhile lover was not amused, and I found myself in a quandary. My hand curled into a fist but I knew doing anything at this point would only bring me unwanted attention, and further amuse the snake at my shoulder. Jeremiah continued to glare in our direction, and Lucas, while no longer touching me, seemed determined to stand as close as he could manage. I could only guess what was going through Jeremiah's mind.

Up on stage, Gaspard came partially to the rescue. Noticing his guest's inattention and my current situation, the Frenchman clapped an arm across the billionaire's shoulders and managed to briefly distract him. I breathed a sigh of relief, one weight momentarily lifted. The two men shook hands for the cameras, signaling the end of the segment.

"Ah, there's my cue to exit." Lucas leaned in close, chest brushing my shoulders, and planted a quick kiss on my cheek. I jerked away but knew from the cloud covering Jeremiah's face that he'd seen. *"Au revoir, chérie,"* Lucas murmured before disappearing, leaving me to face the advancing bull all by myself. It was useless to try and plead my case, so I stayed silent as Jeremiah came up beside me.

"Let's go."

His low tone brooked no argument; his hand on my lower back steered me effortlessly through the crowd. I turned back to see Gaspard already held the audience's attention; few bothered watching our escape, for which I was grateful. Our exit from the large hall gave me the relief I'd been craving. I no longer had to worry whether I would trip or otherwise make a fool of myself in front of a crowd. The earlier euphoria from helping Cherise and David had worn off, and I felt exhaustion nipping at the edges of my consciousness.

Jeremiah fixed his flinty gaze on the doors leading out of the building, and I had the impression he deliberately ignored me. That made me nervous, as I didn't know what it ultimately meant. The ease we'd shared while dancing had vanished, so I stayed quiet, vowing to e-mail my good-bye and best regards to my friends as soon as I had the chance.

The limo was waiting for us outside the main exit. We dodged the few remaining paparazzi, and climbed inside the dark vehicle, the driver closing the door behind us. I took the edge of the bench seats on one side of the vehicle across from Jeremiah as we pulled out, heading back to the hotel. I watched nervously as he shut the dark glass partition between us and the driver.

I glanced toward the shrouded front of the long car, and in my moment of inattention he moved suddenly, pushing me back onto the long bench. Squeaking in surprise, I clamped my lips tight as he towered over me, one hand on my right shoulder keeping me pressed against the leather seat. His eyes trailed down my torso, then up to my face, and I swallowed at the fire I saw in his eyes.

"Open your legs to me."

My lips parted in shock. Breathing became difficult as he skimmed his free hand down the side of my body, running his palm along the thin material. The dress parted along the high slit and his fingers slid beneath, stroking my inner thigh.

"About your brother," I said in a shaky voice, sudden nervousness making me desperate to explain myself, "nothing happened; I thought he was you and . . ."

"No."

I fell silent at the word. Jeremiah paused, body tense. "I don't want to hear about my brother again tonight. Please," he added, the word ground out. When I nodded my understanding he relaxed a hair. "Now, where were we?"

His palm slid between my knees, prying them apart in increments as he pushed his way up my leg. My breath caught, belly tightening, as his fingers tugged at the garter strap along my thigh, smoothing beneath it to the belt around my hips. My legs pressed together involuntarily, and his hand stopped. "Open your legs."

The words surrounded me, a sensual net, and I swallowed. My body had already begun vibrating, breath coming in pants. Part of me almost feared what he would do to me—not that I expected anything painful or demeaning, but that I'd lose all control of my body. Perhaps that was the point. With a shuddering sigh, I forced the muscles of my thighs to relax and let my knees fall apart.

"More."

Swallowing, again I complied, opening myself to him. He shifted above me, removing his hand from my shoulder to brace against the couch. I gasped when a finger pressed through the thin line of panties against my core, and arched my body into the contact. He gripped my hair, holding me steady as his hand rubbed and prodded. My breath came in shuddering gasps as he leaned over me, his face pressed close.

"You're mine," he murmured, eyes ablaze. He sped up his ministrations until I was moaning, the grip on my hair tightening. "I want to hear you say it."

"I'm yours." I struggled to get the words out; my body quaked and pulsed like a heartbeat. Eyes fluttering closed, my whole being focused on the sensations his hands provoked. The ache between my legs spread; I slipped out of my heels for traction, tilting my hips toward his hand.

"Again."

"I'm yours, sir."

The grip on my hair tightened, and my eyes sprang open, my breath coming in gasps. His eyes searched mine, for what I couldn't tell, but I couldn't think to hide anything. All I wanted was him, and I tried to let him see my desperation. The walls of my opening pulsed, demanding attention, and I silently begged him for more.

His grip on my hair eased, and he shifted again, his gaze

no longer as intense but just as demanding. "I want to see you come," he murmured, lowering his face close to mine.

The words made me melt, his deep voice surging through my body. The deft fingers down there moved effortlessly underneath the panties, and I moaned loudly as they slipped through my folds and caressed my weeping opening. The car beneath me rocked slightly, reminding me where I was, but its movement only added to the sensations. A thick finger dipping inside, while his thumb flicked my aching bud, forced breathy moans from me.

"Only I am allowed to do this." Jeremiah accentuated his words by teasing a spot inside me with pinpoint accuracy; my hips shot off the seat, and I groaned. "No other man gets to touch you unless it is with my permission. Is that clear?"

I choked on my answer, waves of pleasure coursing through my body. I was rocketing toward an orgasm, and couldn't think straight. The hand in my hair tightened, and I managed to reply, "Y-yes."

"I can't hear you."

I cried out, the sensations almost too much. "Yes! Please, sir!"

"Eyes on me." I locked gazes with him, the power of his stare pinning me to the seat. His thumb rubbed harder as his finger hooked me from inside, rubbing my opening with expert precision. "Now, come," he said, and with a wail I joyously dove off the edge. Body shuddering uncontrollably, I clutched at his dress jacket, everything in me exploding. The last ounce of strength fled my body, and I melted into the leather beneath me, trying in vain to catch my breath.

Jeremiah released my hair, and sat back in his seat, leaving me sprawled along the bench seat. I managed to close my legs, but couldn't do anything more; pulses still rocked me, and my limbs felt like jelly. The car slowed and turned, pressing me back against the seat, and I started as a hand came to rest on my knee. Swallowing, I looked out the tinted window to see the bright façade of our hotel looming above.

12

We made the short trip up to our suite in silence, tension thick in the air between us. I had barely kicked off my uncomfortable heels, enjoying the freedom to wiggle my toes, before a thick arm snaked around my waist. He pressed his hard body to me, trapping me against the wall; a thigh wedged itself between my legs and, before I knew what was happening, Jeremiah's mouth covered my own in a scorching kiss. Still reeling from the limo ride, I wrapped my arms around his neck, fingers digging through his thick hair as I moaned against his lips.

Hands cupped my backside, and he lifted me high, and once more wedged me tightly between his body and the wall; I gripped his shoulders to steady myself, but he held me secure, lowering his mouth to run lips and teeth down my neck. He ran hands down my thighs, then wrapped my legs around his waist. I moaned as I felt his hard length press against my already throbbing core.

"Mine," he murmured, the low rumble moving through

me like a flood. Capturing both of my wrists in one large
hand, he pinned them above my head as his lips again found
mine, sucking and nibbling. His free hand kneaded the soft
flesh of my breast, thumbing the nipple, and I pushed into
his touch.

His need and unabashed passion set me aflame. I moaned
against his mouth, arching my body against his, trying desperately to get closer. He rolled his hips, pressing them against
me, and I gave a small cry. His teeth played with my ear and
dragged down the side of my throat, and I was lost to all else.

Belatedly, I noticed we were moving, but it didn't sink in
until the world tilted and I landed on my back in the huge
bed. Jeremiah wasted no time in covering me; he didn't seem
to care about the expensive dress, slipping a rough hand down
the front. The fervor of his passion made me hotter as well.
I wanted, needed, more. I tried to touch him but he grabbed
my wrists again, holding them beside my head as he sucked
and nibbled my neck.

"Roll over."

I quickly obliged, and felt the zipper of the dress glide down
my back and over my bottom. He peeled the layer from my
skin, then trailed his lips down along my spine. I arched up
like a cat, desperate for the soft touch, and heard the jangle
of his belt. Excited by the sound and what it represented, I
pushed my backside up to rub against his crotch, and to my
immense satisfaction heard his small indrawn breath.

Hands wrapped around my wrists again, pulling them up
toward the headboard. Cool leather wrapped around them
as Jeremiah deftly secured me to the brass railings with the

belt, effectively trapping me. Thus secured, he began to remove my dress; I lifted my hips to help as he peeled the material from my body before tossing it to the ground beside the tall bed. His hands kneaded my buttocks as he moved behind me, straddling my legs. I lifted myself up onto my knees, desperate for more contact. The position left me exposed, and his growl of approval made me shiver.

His hand splayed across my upper back, pressing my chest into the mattress, then he bent over me and lips trailed up along my spine. My exhalations were panting bursts, hands gripping the leather restraints tightly. His teeth scraped over the taut skin of my backside, and I couldn't stop the moan that forced its way through my lips. My body quivered, wanting more, but Jeremiah took his time. Hands caressed my hips, kneading the globes of my backside, then his thumbs ran down along the cleft of my backside toward my weeping entrance.

I surged forward when he parted the tender flesh, my frantic panting a staccato in the quiet suite. He breathed on me, a hint of what was to come, then lips and a hot tongue unerringly found my throbbing opening. I keened, my cry bouncing off the wall behind the bed, as he ran his tongue along the tight ring before pushing in further. One hand stroked through my folds and my entire body quaked uncontrollably.

He stayed there for a while as I moaned and thrashed. "Please," I begged repeatedly, although for what I didn't know. Perhaps release from the delicious torture, perhaps for more. Probably both.

His only reply was to chuckle and to continue the onslaught of pleasure.

When he finally inserted a finger, I pressed against it, desperate for more. He controlled everything, but where he rubbed inside only served to heighten the sensation. Fluid flowed down my thighs, and I was almost crying from the unrelenting intensity.

He pulled away suddenly, then twisted me around so I was laying on my back. I stared up at a savage face as he forced my knees apart, looped his arm under one knee, then slid his hard length deep inside me with one sure stroke. I arched my body and closed my eyes, breath stuttering in my throat at the sudden invasion. The belt kept my arms restrained as he pounded me into the bed, allowing no retreat from his passion.

"Look at me."

I opened my eyes and stared up into his beautiful, intense face. A hand snaked up my body, winding itself around my throat as his face pressed in close. His hips kept up their thrusting, and the continual flashes of pleasure made it hard to think. "Say my name."

"Jeremiah," I breathed, brushing my breasts against his body. Behind the green lingerie, my nipples ached for his touch. I drew my free leg up to his waist, twisting it across his body and locking my ankles behind his back. His eyes widened, and the thrusting grew stronger.

"Say it again!"

"Jeremiah!" I cried out desperately, the word almost a sob. "Please!"

The hand around my throat tightened, not enough to choke me but enough to cause a rushing in my head. His other hand settled on my breast, pushing the stiff material aside and kneading the tissue, pinching the nipple between his fingers. My hips fell into a rhythm, moving with him, our thrusts taking me higher and higher, almost there but not quite enough. . . .

Jeremiah's hand tightened again, constricting my breathing enough for anxiety to cut through the haze of lust. My eyes shot to his passionate green ones, and I read the same need coursing through my veins. I gave myself over to the sensations, trusting him in this even as my lungs began to burn.

Then he released my throat, and thrust hard, tweaking my nipple. The sudden rush of oxygen and blood flowing through my body overwhelmed me, and with a cry and a shudder I came for the second time that evening. I thrashed beneath him, twisting the leather belt above my head and riding the wave of pleasure.

I wasn't sure how long it took my brain to settle back into the present, but eventually I came back to myself and saw Jeremiah still looming above me. His eyes recorded my every reaction; a hand traced down the side of my face in the first honestly tender contact I could remember. A thumb ran over my lips, and I opened my mouth, pulling it inside and tugging it with my teeth.

It was then, when I saw the answering fire in his eyes, that I realized he was still hard inside me.

He reached above me and released the belt, unwinding it

from my wrists. My pinkies were numb and my wrists ached, but I didn't care. Keeping my gaze on his, I reached up and pushed on one shoulder, turning him over to lie on the bed. To my amazement, he allowed me to do so, and I followed him over until I was the one crouched over his large body. He had shed his dress jacket and slacks at some point, but still had his white shirt on with only the top two buttons undone. I straddled his hips, feeling his hardness pressing against my backside, as one by one I unfastened the remaining loops.

I had never yet seen him naked and, despite the languor making my limbs heavy, I was eager to search his body as he'd done mine. I could feel his scrutiny but he did nothing to stop me as I peeled back the white cloth and ran my hand along his hard torso. There wasn't an ounce of extra fat; lines of muscle stood out in prominent display, olive skin, and small dark nipples. However, scars marred the perfection: one small white irregular star on one shoulder and smaller lines across his chest and belly. I smoothed my hand over them one by one and saw him flinch but again, he didn't stop me.

Mine. The possessive thought surprised me. I skimmed my fingers up the line of his abdomen, across his pectorals, then leaned down to study his face. He watched me impassively as I traced the curve of his cheek, down past a strong chin with skin that, while clean shaven, still had a slight sandpaper bite. So very beautiful. Cupping his jaw, I levered myself up using his shoulder, then lowered my hips onto his hard member as I bent down toward his face.

A large hand clamped on my shoulder, and I stopped only inches from his lips. The look in his eyes was difficult to read, a guarded yearning I didn't understand. His hand stopped me from bending down, but nothing halted my hips, which continued their downward travel, taking him inside me. Jeremiah swallowed, his throat moving. I undulated my hips, pulling up then pressing him deeper, and he let out a stuttering breath. The hand on my shoulder loosened, and I continued down, pressing my mouth against his neck, then trailing down toward the star-shaped scar on his chest as I rolled my hips again.

I traced the white tissue with my lips, drawing a finger over one small dark nipple. Up close the scar was larger than I'd thought; the skin around it wasn't as discolored but still puckered from the past trauma. I looked up to see him watching me with that incomprehensible look; his full lips were open, and I desperately wanted to see what they tasted like. Rising over him again, I traced my fingers again down the side of his face. "You're so beautiful," I breathed, my eyes roaming over him.

The longing in his eyes deepened as my eyes fell again to his mouth, then he lifted a hand to tangle in my hair, and brought my mouth to his. Our lips clashed in a sudden hunger; his other hand dug into my hip as I rode him hard, hands stroking his torso.

Somewhere beside us a cell phone vibrated, a persistent distraction. "Sounds like someone really wants to talk to you," I purred, grinning down at him.

"They can call back later," he growled, then thrust his

hips up, pressing his hardness up deep inside me. I gasped, all thoughts of the caller flying from my head. He rolled me over onto my back and, teeth finding my neck, he hammered me into the mattress. I gripped him with my thighs, moaning, as he pierced me again and again. My fingernails dug into his shoulders, using his hard body for leverage as I met his thrusts with my own. He tugged my hair, wrenching my head back to look at his face. Desperate need shone bright in his eyes and I felt a moment's triumph when he grunted, surging inside me one last time as he came.

I closed my eyes, and held on to his shuddering body. His weight atop me held me secure and I sighed in contentment. "I . . ."

Love you.

My eyes popped open at the unbidden thought. Horrified at what I'd been about to say, I stared at the ceiling as Jeremiah stirred in my arms, finally rolling off me and onto his feet beside the bed. I swallowed, suddenly breathless—had I really been about to say that?

Silently I moved to the other side of the bed and then fled to the hallway bathroom, bypassing the open area linked to the master bedroom. Locking the door behind me, I stared at my reflection in the mirror, still horrified by my own thought processes.

I've known the man for, what, two days? Certainly not long enough to declare any kind of affection. Yet those three words had almost popped out, and that shook me up. My hands trembled as I turned on the warm water in the sink and grabbed a wash cloth to clean myself.

I'd never had any real relationships where "the words" had been exchanged. Even as a teen, I'd been too pragmatic to say it in reference to anyone but family. The fact that I'd been poised to let them slip out of my mouth caused more than a little distress.

It's silly to think about that this early, I admonished myself, then remembered my father had always said he'd fallen for my mother the moment he saw her. I swallowed at the memory; my dad had been the romantic of the family, my mom the more practical partner. I'd taken after my mom; I was always one more inclined to look before I leaped, but this whole situation was foreign territory.

There came the sound of knocking, startling me out of my reverie. Poking my head out the door, I heard it again coming from the entrance to the suite. Glad for the distraction, I grabbed a robe off the nearby hook. Slipping it over my body, I padded to the door, peering through the small peephole. A uniformed hotel worker stood there, holding something in his hands I couldn't quite make out. Curious, I opened the door a crack. "Yes?"

The man gave a small bow. "A gift for Mr. Hamilton and guest," he said in flawless English, presenting a bottle and two champagne flutes.

My eyebrows went up and, not knowing what else to do, I took them from the servant's hands. He gave another little bow, then backed up a step as I closed the door. I turned into the suite, paused, then opened the door again. "Do I owe you anything for . . . ?" The man had already disappeared however, so with a shrug I shut and locked the door again, carrying the bottle and glasses into the bedroom.

Jeremiah sprawled in a tall chair, frowning at the phone in his hand. When he saw me, his expression cleared and, to my surprise, a small smile spread across his lips. My heart skipped a beat; he was so beautiful, it was hard to believe he was all mine.

For now. I frowned at the pessimistic thought. Reality always intruded at the worst times.

He extended his hand. "Come here." When I padded over and took his hand, he said, "Kneel."

I did as he said without thinking, lowering myself to the floor. His hand stroked my hair as I settled to my knees. A part of me wondered why I obeyed him so readily; I wasn't a card-carrying feminist but I did have my pride. Somehow though, allowing him control gave me a measure of peace I hadn't felt in a long time. I'd been so burdened with my life that, in a way, this felt like a vacation. Seeing the approval in his eyes also made it worthwhile, although the practical side of me refused to delve too deep as to why. "Who called you?" I asked.

"Nobody important, or they would have left a message," he answered, then gestured to what I held in my hands. "What's this?"

"A gift, apparently."

He reached down and took the bottle and glasses. "Good champagne," he said, examining the bottle. "Must be from one of the patrons tonight."

I stared at the bottle, wondering how he knew it was a good vintage. "I've never had champagne before."

Jeremiah gave me a surprised look. "Never?"

I shook my head. "I only ever had sparkling cider as a youngster, and when I was old enough I never got invited to functions that served it."

"Well, then." Taking the flutes and bottle in one hand, he helped me to my feet, then steered me with a hand on my back toward the suite's kitchenette. "At least your first taste will be an expensive bottle."

I watched in amusement as he unwound the wire cage from the lip, then he pointed the bottle toward the wall and popped the cork. Taking the two flutes, he filled them just below halfway before handing me a stem. "Drink."

The pale yellow liquid fizzed in the glass, looking no different than the sparkling fluid I'd always grown up with as a kid and young adult. Curious, I took a sip then wrinkled my nose at the bitterness, the liquid making bubbles on my tongue. A second sip did little to endear me to the expensive drink. "Ugh, I'm not cut out to be a lush."

Jeremiah laughed, and the sound startled me. He seemed more relaxed and open, and for the life of me I couldn't understand what had happened. The look he gave me of almost boyish amusement had my heart doing flip-flops. Does the man realize how gorgeous he is when he looks at a girl like that?

"Perhaps it is a bit of an acquired taste." He swirled the liquid lightly in the glass but continued to watch me.

I flushed at his perusal, then kicked myself. Take some

initiative, girl, I chided myself. "Have you ever had a body shot?"

It was his turn to look startled; his eyebrows shot nearly to his hairline. "Have you?" he countered, and seemed unsurprised when I shook my head. Amusement lit his face and I watched him in wonder. His mood had turned almost playful, not at all the brooding, domineering man I'd seen so far. The challenge in his eye, however, stirred the rebel in me because I met his gaze with an eyebrow quirk of my own. Holding his eyes, I leaned my head back and tipped my glass over my chest, the fluid splashing onto the robe and down between my breasts.

My audacity had the desired effect. Jeremiah's eyes darkened and he reached out, pulling me back into his arms. "You are quite the tease," he said, plucking the glass from my hand and lowering his lips to my neck.

My belly cramped, and I flinched, but tried not to think much about it. Jeremiah's lips trailed down my neck toward the expensive liquid coating my breasts, but when my stomach twisted a second time, I gave a little gasp, my body bowing forward. The amusement vanished from Jeremiah's face as he pulled me upright. "What's wrong?"

His harsh voice demanded an answer, but I had none to give. "Don't . . . feel good," I managed, then stumbled toward the kitchen sink. I barely made it there before retching, unloading the meager contents of my stomach into the basin. My legs were turning to jelly and I was having difficulty keeping myself upright, even while bracing myself against the marble countertop.

I heard the sound of breaking glass behind me, and I looked to see a dark stain on one wall, the remnants of the champagne flute and its previous contents drifting to the floor. Jeremiah grabbed a nearby phone as I retched again. "I need a doctor in this suite immediately," he barked, then my legs gave out and he dropped the phone on the counter to catch me as I fell. "Lucy, stay with me."

My stomach heaved, clenching and twisting, and I cried out. A hand smoothed my suddenly damp hair back from my face as I shuddered, moaning, no longer in control of my body. I felt myself being lowered to the ground, and Jeremiah's blurry silhouette came across my field of vision.

"I need a doctor now!" A rushing sound filled my ears. Jeremiah's voice was dulled as if coming through water, but I could hear the frantic note in his words. Then my body stiffened, muscles constricting almost painfully, and the world went dark.

13

I was eight years old the first time I got the flu. It was so bad I had to be rushed to the hospital. While I couldn't remember much, I did remember vividly the aches and pains as my body struggled to rid itself of every last vestige of the foul disease.

Waking up in that hospital room felt similar, like waking from a painful dream. Eyes still closed, I turned my head to the side, the simple movement making me dizzy and nauseous. At my moan there was a commotion next to me, then a strangely familiar man's voice said, "Get the doctor."

Why was that voice familiar? Who . . . Thinking made my head hurt so I gave up for a while, trying to keep as still as possible. After a moment the nausea subsided and I cracked open one eye, then the other.

I was in a well-lit room, the bright fluorescent lights above like knives in my skull. Figuring for the time being it would be better to keep my eyes closed, I listened as several people filed into the room.

"Ms. Delacourt, my name is Doctor Montague. I'm going to need you to open your eyes."

"Hurts," I mumbled, my tongue sticking to the roof of a dry mouth. I tried opening my eyes again and it was a little better this time. The room and its occupants were fuzzy. The tall figure beside my bed leaned in close and shined a light in my eyes. I flinched but the pain from before was already subsiding and he only did a few sweeps before pulling the pin light away.

"How do you feel?" The doctor spoke very good English but I could hear the slight French accent beneath his words.

"Like I've been hit by a bus," I said softly. "Am I still in Paris?"

"*Oui*, you were brought here soon after your little incident."

"Where's Jeremiah?" I struggled to pull myself upright, ignoring the explosion in my head and the doctor's restraining hand. "Is he okay?"

"He's been coordinating with French officials on investigating what happened," a different voice stated. "Discreetly."

It took me a moment to recognize the familiar form beside the bed. I barely made out Ethan's bald head through blurry vision. "So he wasn't . . . ?"

"No, he wasn't poisoned," he replied, correctly guessing my unspoken question, and I let out the breath I was holding. "He's been going through various channels to try and find the culprit. I sent word that you're awake; he should be here any moment."

Hearing that Jeremiah was okay and on his way eased a

burden inside my chest. The doctor handed me a glass of water as I glanced toward the clock, then the dark window. "How long was I out?"

"Three days," Ethan replied, and I coughed on the water I'd just swallowed. The big man shifted. "We didn't know how it would end up. Lucky for you, Jeremiah has some medic training."

"I almost died?" My words were a whisper and I found it difficult to come to grips with the idea.

"You were a very sick woman, Ms. Delacourt." The doctor took my cup and set it on the table beside me. I finally saw clearly. "If not for the resourcefulness of Mr. Hamilton, we might not be having this conversation."

I stared at my hands for a long moment, emotions all jumbled together in my head. "I'm tired," I murmured, sliding back down the bed.

"Before you sleep," Ethan said, stepping toward me, "I'd really like to ask you a few questions about the man who brought the bottle to your room."

Everything in me went cold. "You think he was the one who . . . ?"

"That's what we're trying to find out."

The familiar deep voice made my heart leap. Jeremiah peered at me from the doorway, face inscrutable. He walked into the room and stood at the foot of the bed, and I thought I saw relief in his eyes before he glanced at the doctor. "How is she?"

"Awake, and that is a good sign. I'd like to keep her a little longer for observation."

Jeremiah nodded at the doctor, who returned the gesture and silently left the room. Fear settled over me like an oppressive blanket and I blindly reached for Jeremiah's hand when he took the empty spot beside me, not caring who saw the action. Someone tried to kill me. The very thought made my heart race.

"What do you remember about the man who delivered the champagne?" Ethan asked as I clung to Jeremiah's hand.

"He was ordinary," I said, then winced at the phrase. Way to be unhelpful. "He was white, dressed like a hotel employee, and had medium-brown hair and brown eyes I think."

"Hair and eye color can be changed," Jeremiah interjected. "What about facial features? Any scars or moles?"

Thinking made my head ache but I closed my eyes anyway, trying to recall the brief glimpse I'd had of his face. A few moments later, a picture emerged in my mind. "He had kind of deep set eyes, thin lips, and was a couple inches taller than me. Um, I think he had a mole on his left temple and a scar on his chin, but I don't know how much of that might be makeup."

Jeremiah and Ethan's gazes met briefly and my heart sank. I probably just described half the country.

"What did he sound like?" Ethan asked after scribbling notes on a small notepad.

"He spoke English really well. I thought he sounded American." Frustrated, I thumped my hand on the mattress. "I don't know. He seemed like a normal hotel employee and I didn't think to look that hard." A thought occurred to me. "What about the security cameras? There has to be something on them."

Both men shook their heads. "We already checked," Jeremiah said. "Whoever it was knew exactly where even hidden cameras pointed. We never got a face shot."

I slumped in the bed. "Is there anything I can do to help?"

Jeremiah's phone went off, and he pulled it out to check the screen. "I need to take this," he said, pulling his hand free from my grasp. "Ethan, see if you can find an artist to draw what she remembers. I'll be back."

Tears pricked my eyes as I watched him leave the room. *Silly girl,* I chided myself, blinking hard, *he still has to do his job.* It still hurt to have him gone, however; there was security in his presence that I didn't feel with a simple bodyguard.

"You know, this whole deal hit him pretty hard."

I looked over at Ethan, wiping my leaking eyes. The bald man wasn't looking at me, too busy typing into his phone, but I could still sense his attention. "What do you mean?"

He didn't answer for a moment, intent on his phone, then clipped it to his belt and looked at me. "How long have you two known one another again?"

The question felt like an interrogation and I frowned. "A few days, why?"

Ethan grunted. "He's pulled out all the stops trying to find out who did this. I haven't seen him this motivated in a long time. Even when we were in the military, or there were threats on his life now as CEO, he wasn't this driven for answers."

My mouth dropped open. "Really?"

Ethan shrugged one shoulder like it was nothing. "When we were in the army, we were involved in some dangerous missions, but to hear him talk, such things were par for the course. Even now, given the cutthroat business he does, he's received a lot of threats from all quarters. In fact, just after he agreed to sponsor my company, someone tried to shoot him outside his building." Ethan snorted. "Jeremiah had already broken the man's wrist and taken the gun by the time I got close."

"What happened next?" I asked when Ethan lapsed off, looking at his phone again.

"Nothing. He told me to find out who was behind it and let him know, then got on a plane for Dubai. Didn't seem worried in the slightest." Ethan peered at me. "Maybe it's because you got hurt on his behalf, he tends to be rather protective of people in his employ or care. Either way, Celeste has taken over business operations while he focuses on this manhunt and tries to keep the press from getting wind."

"So, the person on the phone just now . . . ?"

"Was probably one of his contacts. If he didn't want us to listen in, it was probably one that I don't approve of. Either way, he's gone to extremes on this one."

Jeremiah chose then to come back inside, stowing his phone in his pocket. I got my first glimpse outside the hallway and saw two men dressed in black, standing on either side of the entryway before the door closed again. Even has guards posted at the entrance. How much trouble are we in?

"I have the boys looking for an artist now," Ethan said. "Hopefully we can get someone up here within the next few hours."

"Good." Jeremiah moved to my bed then frowned down at me. "You should be resting."

"Who was that on the phone?" I asked bluntly. When his eyes narrowed, clearly annoyed with the question, I persisted. "If it has something to do with me then I should know. Who tried to kill us?"

Jeremiah glared at Ethan but the big security expert once again had his eyes fixed on his phone, deliberately ignoring our conversation. "I'm not sure yet," Jeremiah finally said. "I gave them the description you provided and they're hopeful. Now, rest."

My body demanded I follow the order—I'd been fighting to stay awake anyway, but I still struggled to keep awake. "You won't leave?" I asked, pushing myself deeper under the sheets.

His eyes softened a bit. "I'll be nearby," he promised, and at his words I finally closed my eyes, letting my exhaustion overtake me.

I stayed in the hospital for three more days under observation. The doctor seemed optimistic about my recovery, but I felt weaker than a baby. Needing help to do simple things like walk proved frustrating and I was determined to do it on my own. After I slipped and nearly fell trying to get myself to the attached bathroom however, Jeremiah ordered that I have constant help available, whether by nurses or bodyguards.

Most of my days were spent sleeping, but it quickly grew boring staying in the hospital bed. When I mentioned this to Ethan, the hulking bodyguard who was an ever-present fixture in my room, a brand-new tablet, still in the box, appeared beside my bed soon afterward. The device gave me something to do with my spare time, and I spent most of it researching my new boss.

I'd joked before that I knew the Wikipedia version of his life, and as it turned out so did the rest of the world. There were articles on him that mentioned his time as an Army Ranger, talked about his charity work, and went into detail on his business ventures, but I knew all this already. The media threw out words like "mysterious" and "enigmatic" when they described him, and the words seemed appropriate given the lack of any in-depth information through nearly all channels. Articles on the corporate changeover after his father's death were similarly shallow, mainly analyst predictions on where the company would go under new management, on whether a man who had minimal business education could really take over for the tycoon Rufus Hamilton, and so on.

By day three of my stay I was walking on my own again, just in time to leave the hospital. Our exit felt like an espionage movie: I was shuffled to the basement garage by the bodyguards and carefully packed into a waiting limo that I assumed would take us to the airport. Jeremiah watched over everything, never leaving my side, even maintaining a possessive grip around my shoulders as we drove out of the parking garage.

I dozed through most of the trip, using Jeremiah's shoulder as a pillow. I awoke once an indeterminate amount of time later to see we were no longer in the city but didn't think anything of it, nodding back to sleep until the car finally stopped.

Jeremiah shifted under me and I lifted my head, gazing blearily out the window. Grasslands surrounded us, the tall weeds waving in the wind. *This definitely isn't the airport*, I thought, rubbing my eyes. "Where are we?"

Jeremiah didn't answer the question, merely edged toward the door as it was opened from the outside. "Come find out," he said, taking my arm to help me out of the car. Nearby stood a building that looked vaguely familiar, and below the wind I thought I heard the rhythmic wash of ocean waves. There were other cars parked nearby and a few tourists milled about in the chill air, but the grassy hills seemed barren of much else. Sleep still fogging my brain, I struggled to identify where I was, the whole area familiar to me somehow.

Several men in dark suits were scattered around the area and one black man came jogging up to us. "The place is secure, sir," he said, and Jeremiah nodded. I peered curiously along the rolling hills, seeing a few memorial stones jutting from the earth but nothing that jogged my memory. It wasn't until I saw both the French and American flags waving high above the building's entrance, however, that I finally realized where I was.

"You brought me to Utah Beach," I whispered in stunned surprise. The historical site, only one of numerous coastlines used for the World War II Normandy invasion, was something I'd only seen before in pictures or on television with my father. The smell of the water unmistakable, the ocean, difficult to see through the winter haze, was directly behind the building. Speechless, I looked over at Jeremiah, my eyes filling with unshed tears. I'd only mentioned the location once, and had been certain he'd forgotten our conversation, but this was proof he actually had been listening to me.

Jeremiah took off his jacket and slipped it around my shoulders when I shivered. "You mentioned this was someplace you wanted to visit." He looked uncomfortable and edgy, and I wondered if it was my tears. "They have a museum with artifacts from the invasion itself. We can also go down to the water if you're up for it."

His voice was gruff and his demeanor short, but I'd grown used to it and didn't care. Happiness suffused me at the sight of a place I'd always dreamed of visiting. The wind off the water was chilly, cooling the already frosty winter air; the sky was overcast and looked like it might spit snow at any moment. The small photo my father had kept on the mantel didn't do it justice; the site was massive and sprawling, perhaps too much for my current state but, oh, I wanted to see it all!

Emotion choked me up suddenly, and I slipped my hand around Jeremiah's fingers. He stiffened and I saw him swallow, then his fingers relaxed into mine. "Help me inside?" I asked, burrowing myself deep inside his coat.

His gaze softened as he peered down at me, then he lifted my hand to his lips. "I'd be honored."

Looking around at a place I'd only seen in pictures online, I found myself inexplicably tearing up.

14

We didn't stay at Utah Beach nearly as long as I would have liked. Jeremiah never left my side as I pulled him from one exhibit to the next. I felt myself weakening after less than an hour so asked to go down to the beaches before I faded completely. He obliged me but cut the trip short after I stumbled twice and was shivering uncontrollably from the chill air despite the multiple layers of clothing I wore.

Jeremiah promised me I could come back again when I wasn't as sick or it wasn't so cold, and I believed him.

I slept nearly the entire plane trip back to New York, waking only when we touched down at the airport. True to his word, Jeremiah never left my side as we moved quickly through airport security to the waiting limo, which pulled out to parts unknown, at least to me. I rested my head on Jeremiah's shoulder as his hand moved around to my inner thigh, holding fast. There was nothing overtly sexual but I could feel the possession in his grip and didn't mind at all.

When I saw the beautiful large homes through the windows of the limo, I lifted my head to stare at the passing scenery. Partial sunlight from the overcast day reflected off the water nearby, and we passed a marina with large sailboats and more than a few yachts. "Where are we going?" I finally asked.

"The Manhattan loft is too public to keep secure. My family home in the Hamptons allows much more security until we get to the bottom of this mess."

Jeremiah growled the last part of his reply and I swallowed, reminded what was at stake. Turning my attention to the passing houses—no, mansions or estates were better descriptions—I tried not to think about how weird my life had become.

Few of the palatial homes we passed had any similarities to one another besides their size, not in terms or architecture, property, or grandeur. I'd never been to this section of Long Island or any of the more affluent sections of New York, but had heard it described by friends growing up and had seen pictures on TV and the Internet. Many homes along the coastline had piers leading out into the water with large entertainment areas that looked like parks, with green well-manicured lawns dotted with tables and chairs. Despite the obvious wealth in the area, many of the older estates along the water had a homey and well-worn feel to them, light and happy—so different from the big city only a couple of hours away.

The property our limo turned toward, however, was no less grand yet more forbidding than its neighbors. The small army of guards at the gate who made us roll down the window didn't make me feel any better, but Jeremiah seemed content with the security. "Is it always like this?" I asked as the big gates drew open.

"I had Ethan bring in nonessential personnel from his security business to watch the premises. Most of them are ex-soldiers so they know what to watch for."

"Oh," I said faintly, unsure how to respond. So he does have an army. "That's, um, great."

The driveway, while not long, was lined with hedges and trees that obscured the estate. It curved to the right and I sucked in a breath at the sight. My family had been middle class, and our home had been nice if not large. So the fact that my old house was a quarter the size of the building before me took my breath away. I could feel Jeremiah's gaze on me and felt I should say something, but I couldn't think of what. The house reminded me of an English castle, all heavy stone and ivy. The residence was blocked off from neighbors by trees and thick brush, but the grounds extended past the house down toward the water. Behind and to the side of the house, I could see a few smaller structures that I assumed housed the army surrounding us. The ground dipped sharply toward the water, and a boathouse jutted horizontally from the small hillside out over the water.

An expensive red car was already parked near the main entrance, and beside me I heard Jeremiah give an annoyed sigh. The limo stopped behind the car and as our driver moved around to open our door I saw a slim, blond woman step out of the other vehicle. "Who's that?" I asked.

"Family."

The grumbled word held a wealth of meaning but Jeremiah was already exiting the car before I could ask for more details. He helped me out of the vehicle as the blond woman made her way toward us. She was older than I'd first thought, although it was hard to tell her exact age; her lips looked too full and the skin of her face looked artificially tight and stretched. Only the semiloose skin on her neck and prominent collarbones, courtesy of a superthin frame, gave away her maturity.

"Darling, it's so lovely to see you." The woman opened her arms and embraced a stiff Jeremiah, who didn't return the favor. "The men up front said you were on your way so I waited. Would you believe they wouldn't let the Dashwoods in? They were so looking forward to a tour of the estate."

"The Dashwoods are not on the approved guest list." Jeremiah's voice was polite but strained, as if he was reining back his temper. "What are you doing here?"

The chilly reception didn't seem to faze the woman at all. "I told you, darling, I was merely giving the Dashwoods a brief tour of the estate. They were so looking forward to it and I think you hurt their feelings by turning them away. Perhaps now we can call them back?"

My presence hadn't yet been noticed, which was a relief. The woman was dressed to the nines in a tailored blouse and skirt that matched her shoes and small purse perfectly. I, on the other hand, wore wrinkled and travel-worn clothing, and I'd lost enough weight in the hospital for them to sag on my frame. I hadn't cared how I looked until this moment, so I tried to keep myself as invisible as possible. I'd grown very adept at the skill; our move from Canada to upstate New York my freshman year of high school had been tough, leaving me struggling to rid myself of an accent I never knew I had. I'd always been more of a loner anyway; blending in with large groups was just easier since I never had a flair for being in the spotlight.

Jeremiah sighed at the other woman's statement. "This isn't your house anymore."

The argument sounded old, and the woman shrugged it off. "Nonsense, darling, I'm still allowed to visit the old place from time to time." Her gaze turned to me, taking in my haggard and travel-worn appearance, and her eyes chilled. "Really, Jeremiah, must you bring your bits on the side to the family home? What if the press were to see her?"

My jaw dropped open at her words and my hands curled into fists, indignation spreading through my body. That bitch! I was so angry my mind couldn't think of anything to say that wasn't cursing or didn't lead to some kind of physical altercation.

Even Jeremiah was annoyed by the implication, stepping forward as if to shield us from one another while I fumed, my body tense. "That's enough, Mother," he snapped.

His words sent a jolt through me, and I stared between the two, incredulous. This shrew is his mom?

The woman sniffed in irritation, rolling her eyes at the reprimand. "Well, then?" she asked after a brief pause, looking annoyed. "Aren't you going to introduce us?"

Jeremiah looked like he'd just bitten into a lemon but his

manners prevailed, even if he didn't like it. "May I present Miss Lucille Delacourt, my new assistant. Lucy, this is my mother, Georgia Hamilton."

"Back to this charade again?" The condescension in his mother's tone was palpable.

Jeremiah didn't seem inclined to belabor the point, but I was suddenly unafraid to give the woman a piece of my mind. I opened my mouth to defend myself as the woman in front of us rolled her eyes, then inspiration struck and I plastered a smile on my face. "Hello," I said sweetly in French, laying on the false charm. "You should know that your lips and boobs look like they were done by the same doctor, except he got them backward."

Georgia blinked, obviously surprised. "Ah, you're from France?"

My grin widened as I realized she had no idea what I was saying. "I can see why your sons both have issues," I gushed, gesturing toward her immaculately matching ensemble. "It's a wonder you're still allowed here if this is what he has to put up with every visit."

"Lucy will be helping with the French segments of the business," Jeremiah interjected smoothly as his mother's eyes narrowed in suspicion. He slanted me a look but I couldn't keep the self-satisfied grin off my face. "I've hired translators too long and need someone in-house that speaks it fluently."

I kept the smile on my face but glanced at Jeremiah. *Could he be serious?* I wondered, then discarded the thought. It's probably another ploy to derail his mother. That would, however, be the kind of job I'd love to do. Perhaps we really can mix business with pleasure.

"Ah, well." Georgia smoothed her already impeccable clothes with thin hands. "I still think you had a total peach with that Russian girl, Anya. Started out a bit naïve perhaps, but she cleaned up nicely with a little help from yours truly. Such a shame when you let her go."

Naïve? I snorted. That's not a word I'd use to describe Ms. Petrovski. Jeremiah, however, seemed to disapprove of the conversation's new direction; a line formed between his brows as he frowned at his mother. Georgia merely shrugged, seemingly oblivious to her son's displeasure at the change of topic. "A pleasure to meet you, my dear," she said, but her face didn't seem too pleased. "Perhaps we can do lunch?"

Not on your life. I gritted my teeth, somehow keeping the smile in place as Jeremiah wound his arm through mine. "If you'll excuse us, I must show Lucy to her room."

"Won't you call the Dashwoods first and apologize? They were quite put out."

"Good day, Mother." Jeremiah ushered me toward the door, no more interested in staying with the woman than I was. There was a frustrated sound behind us, then I heard the car door slam as we entered the huge wooden doors leading into the building.

When I stepped inside the house I wasn't sure what to expect. The walls were lined with wood paneling and the sparse pieces of furniture were similarly dark, but the high ceilings and pale walls kept the atmosphere from being too dour. A large staircase twisted up on both sides of the entrance, and light streamed in from the opening beneath the balcony, leading into the rest of the house. Past the stairs and through the opening was a huge kitchen with dark wood cabinets and a large island in the center. The living room was set off by a large television, easily taller than Jeremiah, along the far wall. The back wall was almost entirely lined with glass, leading out onto a large patio overlooking the ocean.

The view took my breath away, but beside me Jeremiah growled in annoyance. "Why is that glass clear?" he said, holding my arm to keep me from entering the room.

"Sorry, sir," one of the men behind us said. "Your mother requested it this way."

"This is no longer my mother's house. Turn it on."

A second later, the view to the ocean disappeared, the glass fogging suddenly. Startled by the change I tensed, but Jeremiah harrumphed and led me into the room. "Smart glass," he said, answering my silent question. "It uses electricity to make the windows opaque. I had it installed throughout the house for privacy."

I'd never seen anything like it before. While I missed the view, the light still scattered through and lit up the room. Across from the TV room was a dining area with a giant dinner table and chairs; beside the table was a fireplace with a large mantel. The tall wall above it looked empty and I wondered what used to hang there.

"Anything else, sir?" Ethan asked, and when Jeremiah shook his head the security detail faded back toward the front door, leaving the two of us alone.

"It's beautiful here," I breathed, looking up at Jeremiah. "This is where you grew up?"

"One of the places." Jeremiah stepped into the kitchen as I looked around the open living space. "Do I want to know what you said to my mother?" he asked after a moment.

I smiled at the question. "I made a few keen observations, nothing more," I replied, slanting him an amused glance. When he didn't return my smile, merely nodding in response, some of my pleasure diminished. "I promise, I didn't say anything too rude," I added more soberly, not wanting to offend him. This was his mother, after all.

"She can be difficult at times, but it wasn't always like this." He stared off in the distance, lost momentarily in thought. "Keeping house for my father, having to live with his tyrannical dictatorship . . . I think that's why she took to Anya so much; the Russian girl reminded her of who she used to be." Abruptly he switched gears. "Are you hungry?"

Thrown off balance by the sudden subject change, I thought for a moment and then shook my head. "Do you cook? With a place like this, I'd think you would have your own chef."

"My parents did employ a chef when I was growing up, but I found it a waste." He checked inside the refrigerator and the pantry, grunting in approval, then looked back at me. "How do you feel?"

I yawned and stretched. "Tired." I'd slept a lot on the plane but it still didn't seem like enough. Watching Jeremiah and thinking about bed, however, made a shiver go through my body that had nothing to do with the poison. *Hmm, perhaps*

I'm not as tired as I thought. He had changed out of the suit and dress attire I normally saw him in sometime during the flight, and now wore a pair of expensive jeans and a white button-down shirt. When I saw him in the ensemble for the first time, the change had been a shock but a pleasant one; the way his body filled out the denim made my mouth water, and my hands itch to touch.

"Let me show you up to your room then." He laid a hand on my back and escorted me out of the room toward the staircase. I leaned against his body as we went up the stairs, winding my arm around his waist. He felt stiff beneath my touch, unresponsive, and I looked up to see him staring straight ahead, a frown deepening his brow. Confused, I pulled my hand back and was disappointed to see him relax. *What's going on?* I wondered, baffled by his response. I thought I'd finally started to understand him, but now he was like a stranger again.

The bedroom he led me into was large by any standard, with a king-size bed and attached bathroom. All the windows had the same opaqueness and I realized the smart glass I'd seen earlier ran the entirety of the house. Something gave me the impression this wasn't the master bedroom; while spacious, the room lacked the grandeur I expected for the penultimate suite. It was on the tip of my tongue to ask what my status was during my stay—was I a guest, or would our arrangement be an open secret?—but as he settled me into the bed, something told me I'd be sleeping alone. Reaching out spontaneously, I grabbed his hand and brought it to my lips, laying a kiss on one thick knuckle.

He stiffened at my touch, freezing for a moment; I thought I saw a flash of yearning race across his face but if I did, the moment was fleeting. Gently pulling his hand from my grasp, he pressed me back onto the bed. "You need rest," he murmured.

I need you. The thought made my mouth turn down in disappointment. He seemed reluctant to touch me, which hurt more than I thought, but I was tired. Perhaps this was his way of making sure I sleep?

Taking a deep breath to relax, I snuggled beneath the covers and closed my eyes, hoping my worries about Jeremiah's actions wouldn't keep me awake. As it turned out, my body did need more rest and before Jeremiah even left the room, I was out like a light.

15

The sun shone through the nearby window, and I woke feeling more refreshed than I had since my disastrous run-in with the poison-laced champagne. I stretched under the covers before pulling them aside to stand on the carpet. At the end of my bed lay a towel and robe as well as a sleek gray suitcase I assumed was mine, but my stomach rumbled, reminding me I'd turned down a meal before bed. Deciding to skip the bath for now, I padded down the stairs, hoping to find Jeremiah.

Unfortunately it was Ethan who sat at the foot of the stairs, perched atop a barstool that looked out of place in the entryway. He stood as I made my way to the bottom floor. "Good morning."

"Good morning," I replied cautiously. Unsure of what to do, I made my way around him and headed for the kitchen, but didn't see Jeremiah there, either. Sunlight shown in through the clouded glass and I frowned. "What time is it?" I asked.

Ethan looked at his watch. "It's oh-nine-thirty hours."

I blinked at him in surprise. "Wait, it's nine thirty in the morning?" At his nod I asked incredulously, "How long was I asleep?"

"Approximately sixteen hours."

No wonder I feel good. Blowing out a quick breath, I looked inside the refrigerator. "Where's Jeremiah?"

"He's chasing down some possible leads. Left the compound about two hours ago."

I slanted him a glance, setting a carton of milk on the counter. "He left you in charge of me then?" At Ethan's nod, I swallowed down my disappointment and headed to the pantry. *Don't be silly, he probably didn't want to wake you when he left.* Coupled with the standoffishness from the previous day, however, I was confused about things. I wanted desperately for someone to hold me and tell me everything was all right.

Except that everything was not all right, a fact I was having trouble coming to terms with. *One problem at a time, Lucy,* I told myself, pulling open a pantry door.

A few minutes later I was munching on some cereal I'd found, staring at my new bodyguard who was reading a gun magazine. He appeared to be ignoring me, but every so often I'd see him touch the microphone in his ear and knew he was connected with the men outside. I watched him for a few minutes, then pointed my spoon in his direction. "Your wife told me you and Jeremiah used to be Army Rangers together."

Ethan grunted, not looking up from the magazine. *Another man of few words,* I thought, remembering the first limo ride in

France and how silent he'd been then, too. Remembering I'd seen the large man limping when we'd first met, I tried another tack and I gestured toward his lower body. "How'd you hurt your leg?"

"Mission went sour."

"Were you with Jeremiah?"

"No, it happened after he left."

"Why did he leave?"

"Father died."

Getting answers from the bald man was like pulling teeth, but he was talking so I persisted. "What did Jeremiah do with the Rangers?"

"Sniper."

My eyebrows shot up. Really? I digested that bit of information for a minute, munching on cereal, then asked, "What happened when he left?"

The big man was quiet for a moment; I matched his silence for a moment, hoping to ride him out, and finally he answered. "Pissed off a lot of people."

My jaw stopped working, and I swallowed my food. "Why?"

"He left. Found a loophole or put pressure on the right people to get a full discharge. Most people thought he was selling out, abandoning his post. It's tough, becoming a Ranger, and he just gave it up."

"What did you think?"

Ethan glanced up at me. "I made my opinion known to him well enough."

"So you didn't like the idea, either?" I asked, guessing that's what he meant.

He hitched a shoulder, eyes back on the magazine. "He gave up a life many dreamed of having, abandoning his squad. Yes, I had some thoughts on the matter."

"So how did you become head of security for him?"

Ethan sighed and set the magazine on the counter, then turned to face me. Despite his scowl he was answering my questions so I tried not to feel guilty about my persistence. "After I had my accident, Jeremiah shows up at the hospital. Offers me a job if the army doesn't want me anymore. I tell him to get the fuck out and he leaves. Lo and behold, a few months later I get my discharge papers and Jeremiah shows up again, offering me a chance at the business we used to talk about starting when we retired."

"Your security business?"

Ethan nodded. "Jeremiah funded the initial costs but I hope to buy out his portion soon enough."

"Why leave the partnership? Don't the two of you get along?"

Ethan shrugged. "He has bigger fish to fry and I'd rather be in business for myself."

That seemed to conclude any more on the subject but I was still curious. "What was Jeremiah like back then?"

"Younger." At my droll look, a hint of a smile twitched one corner of the man's mouth. "He felt the need to prove himself constantly," Ethan continued, thinking. "He always wanted to be at the forefront of anything, so it came as a surprise when he settled on being a sniper. It helped him, I think, to hone his patience." Ethan cocked his head to the side. "He was never the life of the party but he did know how to relax. Since his father's death, though, I don't think he's been given much time to do that."

In for a penny, in for a pound. I was getting my questions answered so I might as well ask what else was on my mind. "What about Anya? How did they come together?"

His eyes narrowed and he peered hard at me. I chewed another mouthful of cereal, trying my best to appear innocent. "I probably shouldn't be telling you this," he muttered.

I just munched on my food, giving him an expectant look. It took a minute but he finally rolled his eyes and answered. "Jeremiah had some big Russian deal going down and he needed someone to translate, both for written and verbal communications. Anya fit the bill and became his new personal assistant, moving the previous one to a management position."

"So were they . . ." An item? I couldn't bring myself to say it outright and wasn't sure how much the big bodyguard knew about my relationship with my boss. I colored at his probing look, reaching and pouring more cereal even though I was already full.

"Their personal relationship wasn't any of my business. I could tell she carried a torch but he was impossible to read. Either way, when he found out she was sneaking secrets to his brother, Jeremiah fired her and threw her out. That was probably close to three years ago now."

"What was she like?" I couldn't help but asking.

"Young. Inexperienced. 'Fresh off the farm' like my grandma would say. Smart though, and fluent in two languages. Jeremiah actually found her in Russia and brought her over here, but once he kicked her out she was on her own."

Poor Anya. Despite the blond woman's arrogance now, I felt bad for the poor displaced young girl. Maybe she got what she deserved, but it was harsh nevertheless. "What about Lucas? Why did Jeremiah call him Loki?"

Ethan shifted, his frown deepening into a scowl. "Loki is the rotten vine on the family tree, and that's saying something. Fucking waste of space, if you ask me."

The sudden vehemence in the bald bodyguard's voice surprised me. Wow, tell me how you really feel. "Is Loki a childhood nickname, or something else?" I persisted, wondering if I had pushed my luck bringing up the obviously volatile subject. "What happened between him and Jeremiah?"

"Besides Loki becoming everything Jeremiah and I once stood against?" Ethan growled. "His problems with Jeremiah happened before I left the military, but the little shit stole thirty million dollars from the company right as Jeremiah took over, then fled to parts unknown."

I blew out a breath. That's a lot of money. "What did he do with the money?"

"Hell if I know—probably started buying weapons." At my confused look, Ethan shrugged. "Loki is the name he goes by now, chose it himself as far as I can tell. I guess his old name sounded too posh to use. He's an arms dealer, makes his money selling weapons to countries that want to blow others up."

My spoon clattered in my bowl as I stared, dumbfounded, at the large man. Ethan's thunderous expression was intimidating and he looked like he wanted to say more, but when he saw my shock his jaw tightened. "I shouldn't have said anything," he muttered, grabbing the magazine again. "Those weren't my secrets to tell."

My brain meanwhile had a hard time wrapping itself around the facts. I danced with . . . an arms dealer? The sarcastic blue-green eyes popped again into my mind's eye, the familiar and beautiful face marred by a scar across one cheek. What have I gotten myself into?

There was a click as the front door opened and Ethan shot to his feet, startling me. He relaxed almost immediately, and a second later Jeremiah walked through the entryway and into the kitchen. I smiled, relieved to see him, but my happiness dimmed when he barely spared me a glance.

"Any luck?" Ethan asked.

Jeremiah shook his head, lips thinning. "I've made inquiries," he said. "I should know in the next day or so."

Ethan frowned but nodded. "I'll be outside then if you need me."

I watched Jeremiah as Ethan strode out of the room. "You look tired," I said, tilting my head to the side.

"I'll be fine." Jeremiah blew out a breath, then looked at me. "How are you?"

"Better." I gestured at the empty bowl in front of me. "Got my appetite back."

He nodded, then his gaze zeroed in on my rumpled

clothes. "I left you some bath supplies and clothes at the foot of your bed."

"I saw that, thank you. I was going to shower after I had breakfast." I shivered, suddenly nervous—I had little experience with outright seduction—then looked up at him through my lashes. "Want to join me?"

He went rigid, hands curling along the edge of the countertop. I saw the fire in his eyes, then to my surprise he shook his head. "I have things I need to take care of before the morning's over."

I hadn't expected his denial, and even though I knew he had every right to say no, the rejection stung. He's busy, someone's trying to kill us plus he has a big business to run.

"Let me help you upstairs."

His hand wrapped around my upper arm but I dug in my heels. "What have you found out so far?" I asked, looking up at him. Jeremiah pursed his lips, looking annoyed—whether at my defiance or the situation at large, I couldn't tell. *Damned if I'll let him see me cry,* I thought furiously, staring defiantly into his eyes.

"Nothing yet," he said, tugging on my arm. "Let's get you upstairs."

I pulled my arm from his grip. "Thank you, I can manage fine on my own," I said with as much dignity as I could muster. His subtle rejection, combined with the previous night's dismissal, left me annoyed and determined to do without his help. I'd barely taken a step up the stairs, however, when Jeremiah grabbed me and swept me into his arms. I squeaked, latching on around his neck, then frowned as he carried me up the steps. "I could have done this, you know," I said, trying not to sound pouty.

"You're my responsibility," he said, taking the stairs two at a time.

Yay, I'm a "responsibility" now. I snorted. "You sure know how to make a girl feel good."

"It doesn't matter as long as you're safe."

I rolled my eyes but tightened my grip around his neck. While he wasn't always the most romantic sort, I did feel safer with him. "Maybe later you can give me a tour of the grounds?" I said as we reached the top of the steps. "I'd love to go down by the water."

Jeremiah shook his head. "Until we figure out what's going on, you're to stay inside the house."

My jaw dropped. "I'm under house arrest?"

"There are too many places outside that are accessible from long-range. Until I can figure out a way to mitigate those risks, you're staying inside these walls."

His tone brooked no argument, which automatically made me want to rebel. I tried however to see from his point of view. He used to be a sniper so he'd know all about long-distance dangers, and while the thought of someone watching my actions through a scope was disconcerting and more than a little frightening, the prospect of being a shut-in rankled. "What if I wore a bulletproof vest?" I asked. "Maybe a Kevlar helmet? Do they even make those?"

My request made him snort what might have been a small laugh. He set me down outside my room door, and gently directed me inside. "Go shower. The house is yours, but no going outside." He brushed an errant strand of blond hair behind my ear, fingers running along my jaw. "I need you safe, that's all that matters at this point."

I tried to lean my face into his hand, aching for his caress, but he pulled away his hand and stepped back. Giving me a curt nod, he turned and left me standing in the doorway, silently fuming. *This makes no sense,* I wanted to rail at him, *you're the one the assassin is after yet YOU get to traipse all over the grounds!*

The shower was quick and did little to calm me down. I slung the robe around me, wrapping my head in a towel, and headed downstairs again, only to be brought up by another large guard at the base of the steps. I hadn't expected strangers inside the house and wrapped the robe tightly against me as his gaze turned upward. "Where's Jeremiah?" I asked.

"He had business outside, ma'am. We'll be down here if you need anything."

Swallowing, I nodded jerkily then fled upstairs for clothing.

16

After two days in the gorgeous mansion, I was going stir-crazy.

There was only so much a girl could do inside and, while the house was large, I'd exhausted its mysteries. Well, as much as one could with only their curiosity and the Internet. I watched television, surfed the Internet, and tried to keep myself as busy as a house arrest would allow. I was hyperaware of everything going on around me, always expecting some armed bandit or assassin to barge through the door, and it was exhausting. Worse yet, nobody would tell me what progress if any was being made. Jeremiah more often than not was absent from the house, and the bodyguards weren't talking, so I was on my own. It felt illogical to resent my captivity since it was for my own good, but I found small ways to rebel, even if only in my mind.

There was one bathroom window that wasn't barred or fogged, looking out over the side of the building across a well-manicured landscape. I took my showers there every morning to peek outside, feeling silly for the thrill the small defiance gave me. The window looked out toward the ocean butting up against the rear of the property, with a boathouse sitting near the water's edge attached to a long pier. There was usually a guard in view, and a gardening truck with a small group of workers arrived every other day to make sure the grounds stayed gorgeous. I longed to go down by the water, maybe dip my toes off the pier, but invariably I'd remember Jeremiah's words about long-distance sniping and would close the window in fear. That emotion more than anything kept me imprisoned inside the house and only added to my bitterness.

That didn't mean, however, that everything was boring.

I had free reign to the entire house, with the exception of Jeremiah's office. Eager to learn more about my employer-slash-lover, I made my own tour, noting everything I could find. There were surprisingly few personal effects, with no pictures of family on the wall or mantel. While beautifully decorated, it could have been anyone's palatial mansion. Considering the history I'd been told about the house, I would have expected something unique, yet never found anything that tied it to the Hamilton family.

Until day three, when I found an old painting at the back of the master bedroom closet.

The picture was large, almost as tall as me and framed with a thick, heavy wood. I muscled it out of the large closet and leaned it against a nearby wall facing the light, then took off the covering sheet. At first I thought it was an actual photograph, blown up to nearly life-size, until I noticed upon closer inspection around the face and hair the subtle, telltale sign of brushstrokes. I didn't immediately recognize the face staring at me, although I could see a resemblance to both Jeremiah and his brother, Lucas. The man was young and wore a suit and tie, no different to my untrained eye than any today, and appeared to be about the age of Jeremiah.

The artist, whoever he was, was a master of his craft, capturing the haughty domination in both the eyes and face of the subject. As I stared into the face captured forever on the canvas, I finally realized with a shock the man's identity: Rufus Hamilton, the former patriarch of the Hamilton family and Jeremiah's father.

"What are you doing?" a sharp voice came from behind me. I jumped at the voice and twirled around to see Jeremiah standing framed in the doorway, eyes fixed firmly on the painting. He moved farther into the room but didn't approach, as if the very sight of the portrait repulsed him.

I started to stammer out an apology, then an idea struck me and, nervous at being caught, I blurted, "Did this used to hang in the dining room?"

The question was a diversion, an attempt to dodge any possible wrath coming my way, but I could tell from his reaction I was right. "Why aren't there any family photos in the house?" I asked when he didn't answer. "You grew up in this house, surely there are some mementos from—"

"I had them taken down when I acquired the property." Jeremiah's voice was curt, his demeanor stiff. He finally turned his gaze to me. "I preferred not to have the reminders of my childhood."

"Really?" The answer seemed so foreign to me, but I knew my upbringing had been radically different. I'd met his mother, and from all I'd heard about his father, Rufus, Jeremiah's life hadn't been all sunshine and roses. Still, it was hard for me to grasp. "You don't have *any* happy memories of this house?"

Jeremiah's mouth twisted cynically as he eyed the painting. "My father didn't like fun unless it was only to impress others. Trips to this house were more for business than any kind of pleasure, usually to court new clients." He snorted. "Rufus's was the old-school style of parenting: children were to be seen and not heard. We . . . weren't always accommodating."

I tried to imagine a younger Jeremiah, but found it difficult. If Lucas was anything like now, I'm sure he made himself heard. Jeremiah though . . . "What was your childhood like?"

The question was impertinent and probably too personal; I wouldn't have been surprised if he hadn't answered. So it surprised me when he replied, "Very structured. You knew your place, or faced dire consequences. Rufus was older when he married my mother and had children; I honestly think my mother didn't know what she was getting into. He had his idea of the perfect family that would look good on paper, but controlled everything about it with an iron fist." He lapsed into silence, staring hard at the picture beside me. "My brother, as you might suspect, didn't always play along. Eventually when I was in high school, however, Lucas seemed to straighten out his antics and genuinely learned how to run the business."

There was a fondness in his words that intrigued me. "You idolized him, didn't you?" At Jeremiah's severe look, I quickly amended my statement. "Your brother, Lucas. Did you look up to him?"

Indecision warred on his face as he debated whether to answer my questions. I wondered how much information I could get out of him before he clammed up again. How much exactly did the world know about the Hamilton family dynamics? Am I encroaching on sacred territory? It was on the tip of my tongue to retract the question when he finally answered. "Lucas shielded me from my father in ways I didn't understand until I grew older. He and my father clashed while we grew up, often when he stepped in to distract Rufus from giving me my punishment for some infraction or another. As we grew older and he moved away for college, then life, I lost that barrier but by then I could take care of myself."

"So when you found out about the money . . ." I said slowly, and watched his mouth purse into a thin line.

"I won't deny it hurt like hell." He raked a hand through his hair, tousling the carefully combed waves. "At first I didn't want to believe it, but the financial records led straight to him and I was forced to go to the board with my findings. By then, however, he'd already fled the country, not bothering to defend himself, which damned him in the eyes of all those involved."

I stepped forward to comfort him then paused halfway, not sure what to do. "What sort of clients did your father entertain here?" I asked instead.

"The really lucrative ones, those he wanted to impress. I

remember one man, a retired Air Force general, my father was trying to wine and dine. He spent more time answering questions from me about military life than with my father. The interruption didn't go unpunished; my car was "mysteriously" impounded and certain privileges revoked, but it didn't matter. Less than a year later, I signed up for the army without my father's knowledge, one final fuck-you to the old man." He gave a harsh laugh. "Guess he still managed to one-up me in the end."

I crossed the remaining space until I was standing in front of him. Spontaneously, I threw my arms around his waist, pulling him tight in my embrace. The thin material of his shirt was soft against my cheek. "I'm sorry your childhood was rotten," I murmured against his body, wishing I could somehow hug away the pain and memories. "Maybe you can start to make some happy memories now . . . it's not too late."

Jeremiah stayed silent, and I slanted a look up into his face. He was gazing down at me, head cocked to one side, and a hand came up to caress my face. The slow burn in his eyes, a kindling of desire, made me realize how closely I pressed myself against him. Just as in the airplane, I found myself moved around and pressed up against the wall, Jeremiah's beautiful face looming above me. A telltale bulge pressed against my belly and I sighed, raising my face for a kiss.

Only to have him step back, moving out of my arms. "I can't," he murmured, eyes on the ground beside me.

I blinked, confused. "Why not?"

He looked frustrated by the decision as well. "I don't want . . ." he started before pausing. "Anya . . ."

"Anya," I repeated sharply, aggravated by the connection. What did she have to do with this? I crossed my arms over my chest, trying to stamp down the jealousy tugging at my heart. "Did she and you have a thing?"

The words hurt to say, but the pain in my chest eased when Jeremiah shook his head. "No, we were never an item. But you remind me of her, how she was before everything happened." He stopped again, clearly flustered by the line of conversation. Then the mask slammed down, ironing out his face into the stony expression I always saw. He drew himself up straight and indicated the painting with his chin. "Please make sure that gets put back away."

I watched him walk out of the room, the whole conversation leaving me wondering what other secrets I didn't know about.

On my fourth day of captivity, I was walking by Jeremiah's office when I heard his voice coming from inside. Since our cryptic conversation the day before, I hadn't seen or talked to the man, and nobody would tell me what was happening with the investigation. Determination bubbling through me, I pushed open the door without knocking, barging into the office. It was immediately apparent we had a guest at the house, although I hadn't heard anyone come inside. The red-haired woman sitting in front of the big desk turned to look at me, and my eyebrows shot up as I recognized Celeste, the chief operations officer for Hamilton Industries. She seemed surprised to see me as well, and looked between me and her boss seated behind the desk.

"Can I help you?"

Jeremiah's voice was stiff as he addressed me, his gaze disapproving of my entrance. Both helped stiffen my resolve and I lifted my chin in bravado. "I'd like to know when I can go home." I'd meant to ask about the investigation but Celeste's presence threw me off. She was the first woman I'd seen on the grounds since I'd met Jeremiah's mother. Her confusion, whether to my presence or the situation at hand, was a welcome balm—at least I wasn't the only one uncertain what was going on in this household.

"We can speak later, Ms. Delacourt." The cell phone on his desk vibrated and he snapped it up, standing to his feet. "One moment, ladies," he said, stepping around us and out the door. I was left gaping at the space he'd just been occupying.

"Do you have any idea what's going on?" Celeste asked. She sounded indignant, sharing my frustration about the state of affairs.

I could only shrug and shake my head. "What do you know?" I asked, trying to gauge her knowledge of the situation. Perhaps she knew something I didn't.

"Nothing, except Ethan won't let me out of his sight." The redhead threw her hands up in frustration. "He's set a constant security detail on me but wouldn't tell me why. Jeremiah left me in charge of everything, too, and I've been scrambling to keep up." She turned an irritated look to me. "You've been here the whole time?"

I nodded. "He doesn't even want me to leave the house."

The redhead's eyes narrowed shrewdly. "Do you know anything about what's happening? I swear, I hate it when Ethan and Jeremiah go all alpha male, it makes me nuts."

"No kidding." I snorted. "There's overprotective, then there's just plain rude." Her words confirmed my suspicion that she didn't know about the poisoning but I wasn't sure how much to reveal. The temptation to tell all was strong, even if only to have somebody on my side. Unfortunately, the opportunity was lost as Jeremiah stepped back through the door, followed closely by Ethan.

"Remi, tell me what's going on," Celeste demanded. "I'm fielding all sorts of requests for meetings and appointments with you, and have nothing to tell these people."

"Do you need help doing your job?" Jeremiah's voice stayed cool as he cocked his head to the side, staring at the redhead. "Should I reassign some of your duties to other officers?"

Pride warred on the other woman's face. Clearly the idea of delegation didn't sit well with her. Finally she pointed a finger at the billionaire. "You have the rest of the week, then I need answers," she said, glaring as if daring him to disagree with her terms.

Jeremiah's nod seemed to mollify her and Celeste turned to leave. She shrugged off Ethan's arm on her shoulder but the big man didn't seem to mind, hovering over her as they left the office. The door clicked shut, then I turned to face Jeremiah, only to see him already watching me. He was as difficult to read as ever so, taking a deep breath, I stepped around the desk so I was beside him. "Please tell me what's going on with the investigation."

I hadn't meant to word my request as a plea. Celeste had been more stern in her demand for information and part of me wished I was more like her. However, I saw a faint softening in Jeremiah's eyes, and a large hand reached out to brush a strand of hair from my face. My breath caught as his fingertips skimmed my jawline, cupping my neck just below the chin. Immediately I melted, pressing against his touch.

Only to once again have it taken away. Unbalanced, I put a hand on the desk as Jeremiah stepped back, eyes suddenly hooded. "It's my responsibility to keep you safe," he said, his voice cold as he turned back to his desk.

Anger spread through me. "I could walk right out those gates and you can't stop me." That statement finally got his full attention. Jeremiah rounded on me, face stormy, but I refused to back down. "You've made me little more than a prisoner in this house," I continued, "you won't tell me anything, and I'm sick of it."

"You signed a contract stating you would do as I said," he growled, face ferocious. "You're not leaving this house."

I took a step back and he followed, then I stiffened my spine and glared up at him. "That contract also stated I could terminate my 'employment' at any time. If you won't let me know what's going on, I'll quit and walk right out those gates down there."

Point made, I turned around to leave the office. I hadn't taken more than a step however when the room spun and suddenly I was pushed against a wall. The impact didn't hurt but it did startle me, and I looked up with wide eyes at Jeremiah's face. Gone was the stoic CEO; I'd poked too hard and the beast had reared its head. He towered above me, the grip on my arms like steel, but the outburst seemed to have calmed something inside him. The fire still burned deep in his eyes, however, as he caressed my face again. "I've been trying to resist you," he murmured, eyes following his fingers across my skin. "Being close to me is toxic, and you were caught up in that. The right thing would be to forget you, get you someplace away from me. . . ."

My heart melted. *Don't leave me, please,* I thought, not caring to look too deep into my sudden swell of emotion. As his thumb skimmed along my lips I reached out and took the pad between my teeth, running my tongue along the hard skin. He sucked in a breath, his grip on my arm tightening, and his Adam's apple bobbed as he swallowed. My gaze dropped to his mouth, memories of his lips and tongue on my body making my breath stutter.

"I'm no gentleman," he growled, eyes tracing the lines of my face. His hand lowered toward my breasts, but he clenched his fist instead, stopping short of touching me. "I look at you and all I see is how easily I can break you. You almost died once because of me and . . ."

I shrugged my arms away from his grip, and to my surprise he released me. Jeremiah's eyes clouded and I knew he thought I was rejecting him, but before he could step away I cupped his face with my hands. "Do you want to know what I see?" I said softly, staring into his eyes. My heart twisted at the yearning I read there. "I see an infuriating, beautiful man who's had every dream he ever dared imagine ripped to shreds by life. I want nothing more than to make it all better, but that's beyond my ability." I caressed his cheek with one thumb, then reached down and brought his knuckles to my lips. "I promised to give you anything you want and I meant it," I continued, raising his hand to my lips before letting it rest below my neck. "Believe me, I'm tougher than I look."

Jeremiah swallowed, staring at the large hand that wrapped itself around my throat. He adjusted his grip higher and I tilted my head back, not breaking eye contact. I kept my hands at my sides this time as he studied the contrast between his hand and the soft pale skin of my throat. When he finally raised hungry eyes to mine, an answering fire lit inside my belly. "Take me, sir," I murmured, and literally saw in his eyes the moment my words finally broke down the last of his resistance.

He swept me up in his arms wordlessly and carried me out of the office, padding silently down the hall to the large bedroom nearby. He set me down beside the bed, then shut and locked the door behind us. I watched silently, awaiting his command, as he turned back to me. "Remove your clothing and kneel beside the bed."

Relief rushed through my body, leaving me giddy and excited. My mind flashed to the first time I heard his voice, the command and power that resonated in every word. He could be reading the dictionary and I'd get wet, but when his eyes regarded me as they were now I positively burned. Holding his gaze, I slowly unbuttoned the shirt I was wearing, shrugging it off my shoulders to fall into a loose pile behind me. My pants were next, the loose fabric pooling around my feet as I stepped out of them.

Jeremiah gave me a quick once-over, then shook his head as I moved toward the floor. "All of your clothes."

My heartbeat sped up but I complied, reaching around behind me and unclasping my bra. I pulled the straps from my shoulders, hands trembling as I exposed my breasts to his gaze. Liquid heat unfurled in my belly; I could almost feel his eyes caressing my body, which responded to his obvious desire, quaking with need. The cool air across my already hard nipples made my breath catch as I removed the thin flap of fabric from my breasts and let it fall to the ground beside the discarded shirt.

Swallowing hard, I hooked my thumbs through the top of my panties and slid them down my thighs. Jeremiah made an appreciative noise as my backside rose in the air so I continued the movement, almost touching the floor with my fingers before stepping out of the thin material. When I straightened he was watching me, the approval in his eyes a glorious shock to my system. "So beautiful," he murmured, and I flushed with pleasure.

He moved over by the nightstand and, reaching behind the wooden piece of furniture, pulled out an expensive-looking black paper bag with handles. There was no writing on the side to indicate what was inside, and I watched curiously as he set it on the small table. "Hands and knees, on the bed."

My eyes widened, my breath catching in my throat. The position would expose me completely to him, leaving me at his mercy. Nudity, especially in the presence of another, was still a new concept for me but Jeremiah's look brooked no argument. Limbs stiff, I climbed onto the tall bed but kept myself facing him. The thought of exposing the most intimate bits of myself to his open perusal was still too much—my whole body flushed just thinking about it—but he seemed pleased with what he saw. He rattled the bag. "Care to guess what's inside?"

The contents had a solid sound, but my mind blanked on me. "Lingerie?" I hazarded, even though I knew it was much more than that.

Jeremiah smiled, a small quirk of the lips that made my insides flutter. *He really is beautiful like that,* I thought as he reached into the bag and began pulling out items. "These were purchased with you in mind," he said, setting them one by one on the nightstand.

My brain refused to comprehend what I was seeing at first until he pulled out leather cuffs and set those aside on the bed. I stared at the black leather for a moment, then at the plastic items spaced out over the top of the wooden stand. Oh, my God . . . My sexual experience was limited, but while I couldn't name most of the items laid out in front of me, I had an inkling as to how they'd be used.

Jeremiah picked up a slim dark plastic item and a small container of clear lube, then moved around the bed behind me. "Eyes forward," he ordered when I half turned to keep him in sight.

Trembling with uncertainty, I looked forward again. Not knowing what would happen left me apprehensive but part of me was breathless with anticipation. Since I had met Jeremiah I'd seen and experienced things beyond my wildest dreams, and something told me this would be no different. I still jumped when his hand rested on my backside, however, and heard the low rumble of his laugh. So sexy.

"You're so beautiful," he murmured, his hand stroking down my legs then back up the inside of my thighs. "I enjoy having you at my mercy like this."

Slick fingers pressed against my folds, gliding over my throbbing entrance, and I surged forward in surprise. Another hand grabbed my hip, steadying me as the fingers continued to slide down and around in a way that left me panting. One finger dipped inside, pressing around the tight walls of my opening, and a loud moan escaped my lips.

Jeremiah chuckled again, then his thumb moved up toward my other hole, smoothing over the entrance. He had played there before so I half expected it, but the surge of heat I felt as he pressed against the small strip of skin between the two openings shocked me. The pressure felt good in its own right, not necessarily coupled with any other touching. Jeremiah's thumb circled the small puckered hole before pushing inside and I moaned again, confused by my response but no less turned on.

The slick finger disappeared, then something blunt and hard took its place, pressing firmly inside. I whimpered as it stretched me, moving slowly but inexorably deeper into my body. There was very little pain as Jeremiah made certain to move in tiny increments, but the pressure the object created was foreign. It seemed like an eternity before he finally stopped, the strain uncomfortable but not painful. I chanced a glanced backward and saw him admiring his handiwork. He saw me looking and, one corner of his mouth lifting ever so slightly, he motioned with one finger for me to turn back around.

"You've never done this before, have you?" At the fervent shaking of my head, he chuckled. "I teased you before, but I've been waiting to get you and this sweet ass alone."

My breaths came in pants as he spread the cheeks of my backside. I trembled, uncertainty warring with desire. The sensation of my fluids trailing down the inside of one naked thigh made my body flush in embarrassment, but I heard Jeremiah breathe deeply. "God, the way you smell," he growled, fingers digging into the skin of my hips. That was all the warning I had as his face dipped down to my exposed core, mouth and tongue moving through the sensitive folds.

Releasing a shocked cry, I surged forward, barely catching myself on my elbows at the edge of the mattress. I had nowhere to go: fall forward and off the bed or push backward into that incredible mouth. Jeremiah's hands on my thighs gave me little room to maneuver however, holding me steady as lips and tongue and—oh, God!—teeth sucked and nibbled the sensitive flesh. One hand left a quivering thigh, then fingers pressed inside my weeping entrance, stroking all the right places to leave me a shuddering mess.

The plug in my butt shifted, barely a small bump, and I tensed at the strange sensation. It was foreign enough to be felt above the pleasure, but didn't detract from the experience. The second time it moved I realized the movements were deliberate as Jeremiah rotated the hard plug, but the fingers moving inside me and the tongue nibbling on my inner thigh kept me from noticing much else.

The mattress behind me lifted as Jeremiah stood and moved around to my side of the bed. I laid there, panting, on my knees and elbows and trying to calm my quaking body. His hand stroked my head then down my back, and I noticed the hard bulge in his pants before me. Mind still foggy, I reached out with one hand and massaged the tip through the cloth, feeling the length and girth of his member. Jeremiah shuddered at my touch but didn't move, his hands dancing along my spine, so I grew bolder. I unclasped his pants and drew down the zipper, then reached inside and pulled him free.

His fingernails scraped up my back as I leaned in and drew my tongue lightly across the bulbous tip. Jeremiah groaned and it was all the encouragement I needed; I leaned forward as far as the bed would allow and sucked him into my mouth. The angle didn't allow me much room to maneuver but I did my best, sucking on the head and running my tongue along the rigid length. Jeremiah's hands returned to my head, thick fingers fisting in my hair. I ran fingers between his legs, cupping and massaging the heavy balls, and was pleased to hear another sharp intake of breath from Jeremiah above.

Part of me was horrified by my wanton behavior, but at that moment it was impossible to want anything else. My body still burned for his touch; every movement reminded me of the object still inside me, stretching my body to accept him. My core ached, desperate for contact, and I snaked my free hand between my legs, leveraging myself on my elbow.

Jeremiah stepped back, his member leaving my mouth with a soft pop, then he delivered a sharp smack to my backside. The spank stung and I flinched in surprise, pausing all movement. "Did I give you permission?"

Unsure how to answer, I drew my hand forward again but Jeremiah raised my head so we were eye to eye. "Were you about to touch yourself?"

The total control in his words, his gaze an implacable request for an answer, made my body clench in need. "Yes, sir," I whispered, knowing instinctively that to lie wouldn't go well.

He nodded, acknowledging my answer. "Did I give you permission?"

"No, sir," I whispered. A delicious dread flowed through my body as he nodded again and released my face, then moved around to the back of the bed. His hand trailed along my backside, lightly passing over the plug again as if to remind me of its presence.

"What should I do to someone who disobeys me?"

Fingers skimmed over the warm flesh still smarting from the spank as if to help me with the answer, but I couldn't speak. To tell him to spank me was beyond my power, but the idea was a powerful and surprising turn-on. I wasn't into pain—even the light spank was way outside my comfort zone—but somehow the idea of being punished made me squirm in anticipation. Two of the items on the small table beside the bed were a paddle and a suede many-fingered whip with a braided handle that looked surprisingly soft. The black and red leather contrasted in a way that grabbed my attention—it was almost pretty, a silly opinion perhaps given its intended use as a whip. When Jeremiah's hand hovered over the paddle I tensed, then relaxed as he settled his fingers around the small whip. "You like the flogger?" he murmured, faint amusement lacing his words.

Flushing, I looked away only to have him lift my chin so I was facing him. "I don't want to see you ashamed of being curious." He stroked my cheek with one thumb. "I know you're an innocent and I'll be gentle, but my goal is to please you and for that I'll need your help. So tell me, does the sight of the flogger turn you on?"

I nodded but Jeremiah shook his head. "I need to hear you."

Agreeing verbally was difficult. I swallowed hard, taking a deep breath, before whispering, "Yes, sir."

"Good." He picked up the flogger and snapped it across his arm. The leather strips made a loud crack against his flesh and I tensed. What was I getting myself into?

"Close your eyes."

I did what I was told, heart racing as a blindfold settled across my eyes. Trembling, suddenly apprehensive, I held myself still as Jeremiah moved back around the bed behind me. The urge to tear off the thin strip of cloth from my eyes was strong, but I imagined the punishment for two slights in a row would be much worse than a simple flogging. *Listen to yourself,* I thought, *this is absurd! Why would you allow this man to touch you like this, let alone spank—*

The first crack of the leather against my backside carried little force, but still managed to surprise me. The second lash stung a bit more and landed closer to my sensitive apex. I clenched my muscles, trying to protect my exposed bits from the tool.

"Keep your knees apart."

Oh, come on! The urge to resist rose up but I beat it down, determined to see this through. Relaxing my body proved more difficult but I forced my muscles to loosen, balling my hands into fists to relieve some tension. The object inside me no longer seemed as obtrusive, or perhaps I was starting to get used to having it there. Either way, the whole experience was proving a lot to take in at once.

Two more cracks of the whip, and when the last one landed across the exposed, sensitive flesh, I yelped. There was a stinging pain but I knew no damage, which allowed me to withstand the next three lashings. By the time the last one fell, I was panting, my backside and thighs stinging. Jeremiah didn't seem inclined to hold much back and I knew my fair skin would show marks from the leather.

A hand smoothed along the tender skin, tracing the burning lines with a soft touch. "Seeing my mark on you pleases me." He laid a kiss on the small of my back. "I have another surprise for you."

I waited, unsure what was coming, then felt something thin wrap around my hips. A small but firm piece of what I assumed was plastic nestled against the tender bud between my thighs, held firmly in place by the straps around my hips. When it suddenly began to vibrate, I gasped.

"I thought you might like this," Jeremiah said, trailing one hand down my damp thigh. "This one is only meant for your clit; I have a larger one that stimulates everything at once but it would get in the way of what I plan next." He held my hips secure as I bucked and trembled, sparks of pleasure flying through my body. "God, you're so fucking sexy."

The bed dipped behind me but I barely noticed, too caught in the sensations rolling through my body. When something nudged against my weeping opening, parting the folds as if asking permission, I pushed back with a breathy moan. The blindfold left me little else to focus on but the pleasure, and I needed him inside me. Jeremiah obliged, pressing his hard length inside my tight entrance. With him filling me I again noticed the sensation of the butt plug, the foreign object creating pressure against my inner walls.

"God!" Jeremiah leaned down over me, his naked torso— When had he taken off his clothes?—pressing me into the mattress as he thrust hard and fast. I welcomed the powerful stabs, a very different pressure building inside me and demanding release. Moans escaped my lips and my hands fisted in the covers, holding me steady as Jeremiah pounded into me from behind. He nudged my knees wider, changing the angle, and hit something inside my body that left me a panting mess. "Pl-please," I stuttered, the word more moan than word. The orgasm I so desperately needed was close; it would only take the right push to . . .

Lips pressed between my shoulder blades, tongue dipping to taste the skin. His hand reached around and pressed the small vibrator hard against my core. "I want to feel you come," he murmured, his voice thick with passion, and I rocketed over the edge with a loud cry, my body exploding with sensation. The orgasm wrung out what little energy I had left and I laid my forehead on my hands, panting.

Belatedly, I felt Jeremiah pull out, then heard the crinkle of a condom wrapper. He finally removed the plug, and before I could understand what he meant to do I felt the blunt tip of his erection against the tight ring of my anus, gently seeking entrance. I squirmed, suddenly uncertain even as I quaked with the aftershocks of my orgasm.

Jeremiah's fingers skimmed down my sides, sliding across the soft flesh of my breasts and down over my hips. "I've dreamed of how your ass would feel around my cock," he murmured behind me, laying a kiss on my shoulder. "I promise to make it good, please . . ."

The raw need in his voice touched a curiosity within me, and I relented as he pushed through the tight barrier ring. In the darkness of that blindfold, there was only sensation. Jeremiah's heavy breathing matched my own, and the obvious pleasure he derived from this small taboo touched an answering fire still ablaze inside me. There was no pain, only a strange and new pressure, but when he made a small roll of his hips, the sudden sensation made me press back against him, hands curling around the edge of the bed.

Jeremiah hovered above, solid arms on either side of my body keeping him from crushing me. I reached out blindly and put my hand over his, and he laced our fingers as his thrusts picked up. His pleasure was my goal but I found myself also into our actions, the foreign sensations melding with the earlier pleasure. His hands tightened around mine and he grunted, forehead falling to my back as he shuddered and came silently.

There was an immense satisfaction in giving such a powerful man this kind of release. *I wish I could see your face*, I thought as he sat up, pulling himself gingerly from my body. I stayed where I was for a moment, basking in the afterglow, then collapsed sideways onto the mattress. Parts of me were deliciously sore, especially when I moved, but I stretched contentedly anyway. "That was incredible," I breathed, closing my eyes and laying my head against the pillows.

"Was?" Jeremiah sounded amused by my statement. Still trapped by the blindfold, I heard but couldn't see a curious clinking noise, then I was twisted on the bed and my arms stretched above my head. Before I could protest, thick cuffs surrounded my wrists and with a *snikt* I heard them secured to the headboard. My mouth dropped open in shock, then Jeremiah lifted one eye of my blindfold. My glare only seemed to amuse him. "You threatened to leave before," he said, letting the blindfold snap back into place. "This will keep you here where I can protect you. In the meantime, however, I can think of a few ways we can take advantage of this.

"Care to find out?"

17

The afternoon bled into twilight, then night, and Jeremiah proved exceptionally attentive. When he finally did release me from my cuffs, I didn't try to run, caught up in the sensual storm he created and never let die. The billionaire proved nearly insatiable, and I had little choice but to rise to the challenge. Four times that night he woke me, intent on delicious torment, and four times I collapsed afterward, spent. The fifth time, it was I who awoke first, taking my time beforehand to watch him as he slept. In slumber he relaxed, his face outlined by the light streaming in through the opaque window. I traced a feather touch along one brow, pausing only when he stirred. So beautiful, and all mine.

For now.

How a man like this would ever notice me was beyond my comprehension, yet here he lay, a feast for my wandering eyes. The soft sheets covered only his stomach and I drank in the sight of his beautiful body, marred only by the small white lines of scars barely visible in the low light. Seeing them, knowing what he must have been through to get them, made my heart squeeze painfully. Knowledge about his life in the military was one thing, but these scars were a testament to the fact that he fought and was wounded, a reminder forever of the missions he went on and the danger he must have seen.

I traced the sparse line of hair leading down his abdomen and saw, with some satisfaction, the sheet below his belly rise as he grew hard again. Slithering down the bed, I pulled the sheets carefully over my head, then bowed my head over his body, licking the heavy tip before drawing him into my mouth.

Jeremiah's hips rolled, pressing up toward my mouth. Emboldened, I put my hand along the base and stroked upward, then followed it back down with my mouth. He grew harder and I smiled, bobbing my head over him. Whatever inhibitions I may have once had were thrown out the window, at least for tonight.

A hand threaded through my hair and I heard a low groan above me. I placed my hands on his thighs for leverage as I took him deep, and felt him arch up into my mouth. Then hands pulled me free, taking hold of my shoulders and twisting me sideways until I was lying on my back with Jeremiah above. He stared down at me, any hint of sleep erased from his beautiful face. I could feel the desperate need in his movements as he opened my legs with one knee, stabbing deep with little preamble.

Throwing back my head with a gasp, I clutched at his back, fingernails digging deep, as he moved over and inside me. Muscles still sore from the night's overindulgences protested but I didn't care; I wrapped my legs around his waist and begged for more as he thrust hard inside me. His mouth crashed down on mine, all passion and no finesse, and I rose to meet him, arms twining around his neck. Our coupling this time was short and fast, but the orgasm that rocked us both at long last drew us down into sleep.

When I finally awoke the sun was high in the sky and I was alone in the bed. I stretched, arching my back and noticing the leather cuffs still attached to the headboard. The sight made me smile, a reminder of what happened only hours before. There was definitely some discomfort from the previous night's antics and I hobbled into the bathroom, drawing a warm bath and giving my sore body a chance to soak. I took my time getting ready, allowing myself a bit of pampering and using the extra time to let the water wash away some of the soreness and aches.

My tummy was ultimately the one that dictated it was time to head downstairs, so I dried off and got dressed, putting my hair up quickly in a plastic clip before heading out. I heard voices downstairs and, curious, went to see who the new guest could be. There was nobody in the entryway at the base of the stairs however so, shrugging, I headed toward the kitchen, making a beeline for the refrigerator.

"I took the liberty of looking you up, Ms. Delacourt."

I almost dropped the milk in my hand at the unexpected voice, whirling to face the woman who'd spoken. "Mrs. Hamilton," I said, her cold scrutiny making me feel as though I'd been caught stealing. "I didn't realize you'd be here."

Her lips flattened into a hard line as she looked me up and down. "Women of your economic stature have a tendency to throw themselves at my son. He usually has the presence of mind, however, to see through their wiles." She sniffed in derision. "You're not even that pretty; at least his previous assistant had that going for her in the beginning. Tell me, do you have something on him?"

My jaw worked but I didn't know what to say. "Excuse me?"

The older woman rolled her eyes. "I see no other reason why my son would associate with you. Both parents dead, barely middle class. You may know French but you appear to have none of the credentials to run any form of business. Did he get you pregnant?"

The brazen question shocked me speechless. Anger built up inside me but I could do little under her condescending stare than move my jaw soundlessly. The cold scrutiny in her gaze offended me on every level but I couldn't begin to put my jumbled thoughts into words. My hands curled into fists—I wanted nothing more than to knock the smile off her sanctimonious face—but a lifetime of good manners kept me rooted in place. "I'm not pregnant," I finally managed to retort, but the answer didn't begin to articulate what was burning through my mind.

"Ah, so just a bit on the side." The older woman *tsk*ed, shaking her head in disbelief. "To think he'd bring you here to the family home. Ms. Delacourt, if you have any sense or class, you'd leave this house immediately. Given the type of girl you are, however, I probably shouldn't hold my breath."

"Enough, Mother."

I was an instant away from throwing the milk jug at the self-righteous woman, and while Jeremiah's presence didn't alleviate that desire it did manage to distract Georgia. The older woman's face reset itself into a pleasant expression when her son walked through the entryway but neither Jeremiah nor I were fooled. "You said you were leaving," he said in a cold voice that seemed to wash right over the older woman.

"Oh, I am, darling, but I saw your lovely assistant and stopped to chat."

"Lovely assistant," my ass! My hand had all but crushed the plastic handle of the milk container. I wanted to scream at the odious woman, but all I could do at the moment was stay in place, shaking and trying not to cry in frustration.

"Please leave, Mother." Jeremiah's tone was firm but tired. "Before I have to bar you from entering permanently."

She waved him off. "Oh, pish tosh, you wouldn't do that. I raised you in this house; it's as much mine as yours. And besides, you know I only want what's best for you because I love you."

The statement made me snort in disbelief, but a glance at Jeremiah's weary expression told me this was an old argument. "Do you have any respect at all for your son?" I asked.

Georgia shot me a snide glare. "Stay out of this," she snapped. "You have no idea . . ."

I slammed the milk container down on the marble counter, the plastic making a popping noise as it crumpled. "Your son owns this house and allows you to visit at your pleasure, yet you walk all over him as if he's still a child. I know what good parenting looks like, and you don't deserve his obvious loyalty."

Georgia's face contorted into a snarl. "You little bitch," she muttered, turning toward me and lifting a hand as if to slap me. Then Jeremiah was there, his hand around his mother's wrist, holding her steady. I kept my chin high, indignation burning a pit in my belly, meeting the woman's hateful glare.

"I won't have you insulting my guests in my house," Jeremiah said, voice low and angry, his words again capturing his mother's attention. "Andrews," he called, and a young guard trotted into the room. Only then did Jeremiah release his grip on the woman's arm. "Please escort my mother to her car and make sure she exits the compound safely. Inform the gate she's only to be allowed onto the grounds from now on with my approval."

"Keep your hands off me," Georgia snapped as the young bodyguard tried to take her arm. "Your approval? Jeremiah, be reasonable, this is silly." Her son, however, stayed silent as she was escorted, protesting loudly, out of the kitchen. I heard the front door open and close, then silence reigned through the house.

I blew out a breath. "I'm sorry for telling off your mother," I mumbled, lifting up the milk jug in my hand. The base had a large dent in the plastic but thankfully nothing was broken.

"She can be difficult."

His reply was simple but held a wealth of meaning. "Still, she's your mom," I continued. "Probably wasn't my place to say anything."

The awkwardness wasn't how I'd hoped to spend the

morning, but the matriarch's presence had soured everything. No longer hungry, I put the milk back in the refrigerator, then followed Jeremiah out of the kitchen. "Have you
learned anything yet?"

"Nothing."

The reply was curt and, frowning, I dug deeper. "Ethan
mentioned you had some other sources, did they have any—"

Jeremiah rounded on me. "What did he tell you?"

I blinked, surprised by his sudden change of mood. "Nothing," I replied quickly, then frustration welled up. "The exact
same nothing that you told me. I don't know what's going on
with the investigation except that I almost died and now I'm
stuck here."

Jeremiah's lips pursed. "We're dealing with it."

"Dealing with what? Nobody will talk to me!"

He raked a hand through his hair, taking a deep breath.
"I promise you," he said in a low voice, "we will find out who
tried to poison you. Once the threat is neutralized, you're
free to leave."

I pointed to the entrance nearby. "You leave through that
door every day, but make me stay inside?"

"Someone could be trying to kill you."

His words rang with truth, but didn't match what I had
seen so far. "I'm not the target," I shot back, matching him
glare for glare. "You said so yourself. I'm not asking you to
paint a target on my back and set me loose in the world, I just
want some answers."

"Dammit, Lucy!" For a split second he looked ready to
burst, a savagery in his eyes I'd never seen before. The sight

shocked me, but as quickly as it happened the emotion disappeared; the gates came down over his features and once again he was the stoic CEO I knew. Thought I knew, I amended, startled by what I'd seen.

"I promised to take care of you." His low voice was even and calm like normal. "I only ask that you don't ask any further questions for your own protection. When it's safe, you can leave."

Defeat bloomed through me, making me want to rip out chunks of my hair. Jeremiah turned his back to me and marched outside, closing the front door lightly behind him. Fingers rigid, I ran my hand through my hair, unsettling the clip so that it clattered to the floor, but I couldn't care less at that moment.

The frustration was overwhelming. I tried taking deep breaths but nothing helped the sudden swell of anger at the situation. This house was my prison, and Jeremiah had become my warden. The opaque window glass might as well have been bars; the technology trapped me inside as surely as any iron or other metal shield. I hadn't seen the outside since arriving except through that tiny bathroom window, and the absurd thought that I might be stuck like this forever propelled me across the living room to the back wall of windows and the door leading outside.

The handle to the door leading onto the patio was cool in my grip. Before I could talk myself out of my actions, I turned the knob and opened the door, peeking out over the landscape and ocean less than a hundred yards from the back of the building. . . .

Only to shut it immediately, overwhelmed by fear of who might be lying in wait for me.

A sob wracked my body, and I clapped a hand over my mouth to stifle more from coming. *Stop being such a ninny,* I admonished myself. *If Jeremiah can do it every day, so can you.* For a moment, I hated him for putting the idea in my head that I, too, could be a target. I'm nobody; there's no reason for him to come after me. The stress of my situation, however, finally caught up with me, and I held tightly to the wall as I tried to get a grip on myself. It took several deep, shuddering breaths before the sobs subsided, leaving me spent and all the more desperate to leave. I need to get out of here or I'll go crazy, that's all there is to it.

I'd been so sure that alarms would sound when I opened the door, but when I turned the handle and pressed forward, there wasn't a peep from the house. No Klaxons rang out, signaling my escape, and part of me was disappointed I'd waited so long. *So much for security,* I thought drolly. Somewhat reassured I wouldn't immediately be caught, I cracked the door further and peeked outside. No bodyguards were visible and the doorway was a direct route down to the water and boathouse I'd seen every day through the small upstairs window. The property was lined with tall trees, obscuring the neighbors' view of the compound. The midday winter chill clung to the air, and there were no boats visible in the ocean before me. My death grip on the doorknob wasn't getting me anywhere, however. Now or never.

Steeling myself, I strode out the door and made my way down the back patio steps toward the boathouse, gait jerky and nervous. I looked back and saw I'd forgotten to close the living room door but knew if I turned around I wouldn't find the courage to leave again. It felt incredible to be outside again and, at that moment, I didn't care if any guards saw me.

The boathouse was even more interesting up close. What I'd thought was only a shack was really a two-story building, following the contour of the shoreline with the lower floor exiting out onto a pier that stretched out over the water. The upper floor was at ground level; stairs along the side of the building took you down to where the boats were kept, but I didn't see anything in the swirling water. As I drew closer I noticed the upper floor looked like a small living quarters although, given the condition of the exterior, I hazarded a guess that nobody had lived there for a while. The boathouse's construction was different than that of the house, much older and more worn down, the aged quality giving it a rustic feel the elegant mansion lacked. While it looked sturdy enough, the elements had done a great job stripping away the paint and finish to the wood; green lichen covered parts of the floor and wood siding, poking through the remnants of paint lingering on the surface.

I'd barely reached the planked walkway of the building, the old wood sagging softly beneath my feet, when a bell rang out from somewhere within the compound. My heart skipped a beat at the sound, and I ran the last few steps to the boathouse before me, looking for an entrance. Glancing back, I saw three guards running toward the mansion I'd just left, splitting up and disappearing around the corners.

Were they looking for me, or an intruder? The idea the

killer could be on the grounds paralyzed my mind, and I mentally kicked myself for my reckless rebellion. *Stupid, stupid! What on earth were you thinking?*

A quick scan of the boathouse revealed a nearby entrance and I hurried toward it, seeking somewhere safe to hide. The door was unlocked and I pushed inside, closing it swiftly after me. I laid my head on the wood, watching through the window as more guards appeared around the open door I'd just vacated in the mansion. Disappointment bloomed in my belly. *I'm going to be in so much trouble,* I thought, suddenly guilty.

From the corner of my eye I saw something move, and before I could react a hand clapped over my mouth. I screamed, or tried to anyway, as I was dragged back from the window by strong arms. I kicked over a wicker chair and a lamp in my struggles, but my assailant didn't release me. I kicked backward but my feeble attack was deftly avoided. *Oh God,* I thought miserably, despair washing over me, *I'm about to die, aren't I?*

Jeremiah, I'm sorry . . .

"Fancy meeting you in a place like this," said a jovial voice behind me. "I really was hoping the next time we saw one another would be under better circumstances."

Shocked, my struggles ceased as I recognized the voice. "You really need to learn a few new defensive maneuvers," my assailant continued. "You're easy to predict after a while. Now please don't scream, my dear, I'd rather the wrong folks not discern our location."

The hand around my mouth lifted and I stayed silent, unsure what to think. His grip on my arms, pushed high up my back, didn't stray an inch. "Am I about to die?" I whispered, heart in my throat.

"That all depends on how quickly my little brother arrives." A smooth hand crept up my torso to encircle my neck, pinning me back against his body. "Care to make any wagers?"

18

I trembled in his arms, casting about for a weapon. Once upon a time, the boathouse had been occupied. Furniture, much of it half hidden by sheets, dotted the floor. At some point, however, the living space had been converted to storage, and numerous items dotted the dusty room, including several which were tied to the high ceilings. There was nothing close by for me to use, however. "Are you the one who's trying to kill Jeremiah?" I asked, stalling for time.

Lucas chuckled, the laugh shaking us both. "While I probably have better reason than most to wish for such a thing, I'm afraid I'm not your man."

Confused, I leaned my head back to look at him. Lucas was shorter than his stockier brother, such that my head lay atop his shoulder, but his grip was like iron. The man's gaze was placid, and his lips curled up into a smile at my perusal. "Surprised? I may dislike my little brother, but I'm not interested in his death. Indeed, I've been doing everything in my power to prevent it."

"Then why are you here?"

He laughed again, then dipped his lips close to my ear. "Maybe I missed you."

Butterflies exploded in my stomach. "Liar," I muttered. Knowing he wasn't going to kill me made me suddenly realize the intimacy of our position, and my body's betrayal irritated me.

"Most definitely." His cheeky response made me roll my eyes. "Or perhaps I know who you're looking for."

I twisted around to look at him. "You know who's after Jeremiah?"

"Perhaps," he repeated, his smirk widening.

My lips pursed in annoyance. Infuriating man. "They're going to find us soon," I said, glancing out the window. "You should let me go," I cautioned, "people might get the wrong idea."

"If I know my little brother, they already know exactly where we are." He motioned at the surrounding ceiling. "There's more than likely a camera or three in the rafters above us, watching our every move." Lucas kissed my cheek, and I flinched away in surprise. "Should we give them a show?"

Irritated by his innuendo, I struggled again but was held fast. "If you had information, why not come through the front entrance like a sane man? Why do all of this hiding and sneaking?"

"It's more interesting this way. My brother can be anal about his security; it's fun showing how easy it is to circumvent." He shrugged. "Besides, my brother would be more likely to call the authorities than let me inside and hear what I have to say."

"Like he won't do that now anyway," I muttered, and Lucas gave a small chuckle. The boards beneath our feet began to quake, and the heavy thump of boots pounding against the boards outside the boathouse shook the old structure.

Lucas merely adjusted his grip, shuffling me between himself and the entryway. "Showtime," he replied, seemingly unconcerned, as the door into the boathouse crashed open. Guards poured in and surrounded the two of us, and my heart skipped a beat as guns were trained on us. I didn't see Jeremiah among them, however, and a shard of disappointment lanced my heart. Lucas merely heaved a sigh. "Looks like Jeremiah's no longer fighting his own fights," the gunrunner added.

The distinctive clicking noise of a handgun being cocked was easily recognizable, especially when it came from directly behind us. Lucas quickly let me go at the sound, hands lifting as I sprang away to see a gun being held against the sarcastic man's head.

"Give me one reason why I shouldn't kill you."

There was death in that voice as Jeremiah appeared behind Lucas, his eyes blazing with a savagery that took my breath away. The obvious height difference between the two men had never been more apparent; Jeremiah seemed to tower over his older brother, the muscles in his arm bulging against the business shirt he wore. The black gun was trained on Lucas's temple, Jeremiah's knuckles around the grip white with strain.

I looked between the two men. Surely Jeremiah wouldn't . . . Not his own brother . . .

Lucas froze, hands up on either side of his head. "Familial loyalty?" Lucas answered lightly, his light words belying the strain I saw in his face. From the sound of his voice he might have been talking about the weather, but the eyes locked on me were bleak.

"Not good enough." Jeremiah pressed the gun harder against his brother's temple, and Lucas closed his eyes.

"No!" I blurted out, heart racing. I moved around until I was beside the two men. "He came to help us, Jeremiah. He knows who's after you, don't kill him!"

The billionaire didn't look at me but I saw the gun tremble against Lucas's head. The bodyguards near the door lowered their own weapons but didn't move to help, leaving the brothers alone. My throat froze, suddenly terrified what I was about to witness, then Jeremiah lowered his gun. He grabbed Lucas's arm and twisted it behind the other man's back, and only then did the bodyguards move in. "Take him to the house," Jeremiah said, voice low and tight.

The bodyguards took Lucas from Jeremiah, snapping a set of handcuffs around his wrists. The older brother didn't put up a fight, seemingly content with the way things were going, but the guards still clustered around him as if he was dangerous. I moved to follow them when suddenly a hand grabbed my arm, bringing me up short. "Not so fast," I heard Jeremiah growl.

I thought that I had seen him angry before, but I'd never seen him like this. There was real fury in his eyes, directed at me, and I knew I had messed up royally. "Jeremiah," I said, trying to apologize, only to cut myself short when I saw his free hand ball up into a fist.

"Do you know what I've done to protect you?" Gone was the total control I had always seen, in its place was a ferocity that looked alien on his face. When I tried to move, the hand around my arm tightened and I tensed, stopping all movement.

"The girl didn't know I was here," Lucas said from across the room. His rapt gaze watched our confrontation keenly. I became aware that the guards were also watching us, having paused in the doorway, but again made no move to help.

"I said, take him to the house!" Jeremiah roared, and I watched in disappointment as the guards shuffled out through the door and back toward the house, leaving me alone with Jeremiah.

I tried to stay calm, even though the heat I felt from him was overwhelming. When the door clicked closed he released my arm, but as I moved away he followed my retreat, stalking me across the room. My hip finally bumped up against a table, then I backed into a wall with no other means of escape. He towered over me, fists clenched at his side, and I tried to quell the sudden misgivings in my chest. "Jeremiah, I'm . . ."

"Do you realize how much danger you're in?" Jeremiah's hands were balled into fists but his arms remained at his side. A scowl twisted his face but he didn't move a muscle to touch me. "Why did you leave the house?"

"Because the assassin is after you, not me?" I hadn't meant

for the statement to be a question, and from the look on Jeremiah's face it was the wrong answer anyway. "Look, I'm really sor—"

I was pinned to the wall suddenly, the hands on my shoulders pressing me back against the wood. Squeaking in surprise, I turned wide eyes on Jeremiah and saw him blink, a small frown furrowing his brow. The anger was still in his voice however as he said, "You saw his face at the hotel. Do you have any idea what that means to a man who lives his life in the shadows?"

I'm sorry, I wanted to say, but Jeremiah's dark look quelled my courage to speak. The hands on my shoulders trembled, Jeremiah's beautiful face contorting in his struggle for control. He bowed his head, and to my surprise laid his forehead against mine.

"You could have been killed," he rasped, the words piercing my heart. "I've done everything I can to keep you safe, gone to people I swore I'd never contact again—all for you. Why did you leave the house?"

Heart twisting, I raised my hand to cup his face but he lifted his head, turning a suspicious gaze on me. "Did you know my brother was here?"

I drew back, stung by the accusation. "Of course I didn't." Frustration bubbled up at his disbelieving look. "I don't know anything about what's going on, thanks to you," I snapped, glaring at him. I slapped his chest in frustration, the movement doing little to make him retreat. "How would I even get information like that while under constant surveillance? You lock me away in that house, guards watching my every move. You don't tell me anything you're doing, lecture me about staying safe without telling me anything, and expect me to go meekly along with it—"

"Goddammit," Jeremiah roared, startling me into silence, "I can't have your death on my hands!" Wild desperation played across his face as his hands left my shoulders, framing my face without touching my skin. "I promised I would keep you safe, then you go and pull something like this."

I watched in wonder as a myriad of emotions played across his face. Despite learning to read his normally subtle body language and limited expressions, the sudden passion on his face struck me dumb. His own battle for control was obvious; he reached out to caress my neck, then checked himself, as if afraid to touch me. "My family destroys any outsiders who get too close; I've watched it happen to my mother, Anya, and countless others." He swallowed. "Maybe I don't deserve happiness, but you do, and I'll get you through this." One finger caressed my cheek. "I'm not a good man," he murmured, staring at his hand fisted near my chest. "I should never have brought you into this. I almost got you killed, and now I need to see you safe."

The pain in his eyes, revealing emotions that were always kept bottled inside, made tears spring to my eyes. I tried to touch his face again but he grabbed my wrist, holding it beside my head. "You can't do this again," he ground out. "We don't know who is after us or what means he has available to get close."

My heart shattered into a million little pieces. Trembling, I searched for a way to show my remorse. "I'm sorry for leaving the house."

"Sorry isn't good eno . . ." Jeremiah retorted angrily, then stopped as I lowered myself to my knees. He released my wrist and stepped back, everything about him going still as he stared down at me. "What are you doing?" he finally said.

I'd never felt so helpless in my life, sitting there at his feet. I had no idea how he'd react, but somehow I knew he needed to be in control, the emotions coursing through him too much to process. "Asking for forgiveness." I swallowed, then added, "Sir."

The remaining wildness in his face drained away but he still hesitated. I stared at his feet, no longer having the courage to watch his face. He still wore the expensive business pants but instead of the dress shoes to which I'd grown accustomed, he wore a pair of rugged black boots. I wondered if they were the same ones he'd used while in the Army, but didn't feel that moment was the right time to ask.

The silence stretched, making me nervous. I stayed where I was, praying I hadn't made the wrong move. My biggest fear was his rejection, so relief shot through me when he finally said, "Stand up and raise your hands over your head."

Swallowing again, I did as he ordered, my eyes moving toward the ceiling. A line of rope hung down from a large roll of cloth above me, likely an old sail, and my heart skipped a beat as Jeremiah wrapped the rope around my wrists. "Hold still," he said, then fished around until he found a small piece of cloth nearby. He snapped it once to remove debris, the sound making me jump, then tied it around my head to cover my eyes. The world plunged to black, and when he tightened the rope above so it lifted me to my tiptoes, I gave a small gasp.

"So, you want to be punished."

I whimpered, heart racing, but didn't negate his question. Despite the heavy boots, he was surprisingly silent on his feet; I cast my head around blindly, trying to find him, then started as I felt his breath on my neck. "What should it be?" he murmured, fingers sliding along my raised arm. "Should I spank you for your disobedience? Whip you? What kind of punishment would teach you not to court death?"

My mouth worked silently but I didn't respond. Somehow, given his current state, I doubt he'd be gentle with me in this situation. I remembered the flogger he used on me the previous night and, despite the current situation, felt an answering heat unfurl in my belly. Now is not the time for this!

"Perhaps a different form of punishment is required." His hand left my arm and unsnapped my pants with deft fingers. They dropped to my feet as he grabbed one leg behind the knee, lifting it high and to the side until I was balancing on one foot, holding the rope around my wrists for support. My face flushed, realizing how I had to look exposed like this. All the underwear I had was of the sexy variety, something I secretly appreciated but that make unexpected moments like this awkward.

A finger slid across my panties and I jerked against my bonds in surprise. "You're wet," he said, his tone such that I couldn't tell what he was thinking and longed to see his face. He let go of my leg, then hooked his thumbs around the band of my panties and slid them down to my ankles. My face burned as he undid the buttons of my shirt, pulling it open to reveal my torso. Rough hands skirted the edge of my bra, then slid beneath the thin material as he spoke. "Perhaps nipple clamps, they can be painful. Is that punishment enough for you risking your life?"

Fingers wrapped around my nipples and I tensed, waiting for the pain, but he only fondled them a bit then let go, leaving the bra displaced and my breasts exposed. A perverse disappointment jolted through me and I stifled a sigh. *I don't like pain,* I thought, but the avowal seemed weak even in my mind.

The rope jerked up again, until only the tips of my toes scraped the ground. Muscles stretched in my arms and my wrists burned, but I clamped my lips together and kept silent. I thought I heard the whisper of footsteps behind me as another hand smoothed over my backside. "Should I take you anally? You seemed to enjoy it yesterday but unprepared it can be very painful. Is that punishment enough for playing fast and loose with your life?"

A hand cracked against one cheek and I flinched, the movement swinging me around. I scrambled for purchase, my panties falling to the ground as Jeremiah disappeared again but I couldn't stop the slow twirl of the rope. Another spank across the same cheek made me spin faster, butt burning.

"Should I use my belt on you?" he asked, voice tight again. The sound of a buckle being loosened came from nearby. "Would that keep you from any more foolhardy attempts like this? Answer me!"

"I'm sorry," I replied, earnestly meaning the words and not just because of his threats. I remembered the desperation on his face, the loss of control when I was in danger, and my throat tightened. "I'm so sorry."

"You're sorry, what?"

"I'm sorry, sir."

"What are you sorry for?"

Hurting you. The pain on his face, the rage when he'd confronted his brother, the surge of emotion, was what I regretted most. I knew, however, that wasn't the answer he wanted. "For disobeying you and putting myself at risk." At the last minute I barely remembered to add, "Sir."

Hands grabbed my hips and hauled me forward against a hard body, knee moving in between my knees. Taken by surprise, I instinctively opened my legs and was hauled up until I was straddling hips. I felt a moment of probing against my naked core, then he plunged inside and I gasped.

"I promise you," he growled, punctuating every other word with a thrust of his hips, "you'll feel every one of those punishments if you ever do this again."

I tightened my legs around him as one big hand moved to my back, holding me still as he rammed into me. The sheer power of each deep stab bounced me into the air; there was little pain, but because my body had been preparing for a much harsher punishment, every nerve ending was alive and on fire. His hands dropped to my backside, squeezing and parting the twin globes for deeper access, and I exploded. The orgasm took me by surprise, my body bucking and twisting as he continued his assault.

Our movements had dislodged the cloth over my eyes and, panting, I looked down to see Jeremiah watching me, his face strained by his own desire. The raw hunger in his eyes seemed more than just sexual, and the sight stabbed through my heart. I wanted to kiss him, caress his beautiful face, but the bonds held me aloft, keeping me from giving him any comfort. *Maybe this is my punishment,* I wondered, feeling the loss keenly in my gut. How oddly appropriate. Then he shuddered beneath me and the moment passed, and we both took a moment to come down from that stunning high.

Holding me tight against his body, he reached up and effortlessly untied the knot from around my wrists. My limbs felt boneless as he set me on my feet. I wobbled, bare feet scraping against the wood floor. His grip was gentle, so different from only a moment before when everything had been quick and rough, but as soon as I was steady he let me go and stepped away. "Get your clothes on and I'll take you back to the house."

Jeremiah turned away before I could get a good look at his face; disappointment churned in my belly at the subtle snub but I set it aside, dressing myself quickly and following after him. He had moved toward a far wall, and as I approached he pulled aside a thin rug covering a pair of rings in the door and hauled open a trapdoor in the floor. The hinges didn't make any noise as the hatch swung open. "This will take us to the house."

I stared wide-eyed down into the darkness. Steep concrete steps led down into the underground passage, and a chilly damp wind blew from somewhere at the other end. "Is it safe?"

"This is how I came in here unseen. It's safer than going outside, at least until we figure out who's behind all this."

Still I balked. "Why do you have a trapdoor to the boathouse?"

Jeremiah's lips thinned but he answered, "There were incidents in my childhood that necessitated . . . additional measures. My father was a paranoid man, but in some instances he had good reason to be afraid. The house has a panic room and this exit in case of an emergency, but we've never had to use either since he died." He held out his hand. "Come on, Lucy," he said, his voice gentler than before, "let's get you to the house."

I tentatively took his hand, still unconvinced whether it was a good idea, but nevertheless took that first step down into the dark passageway.

19

I found out very quickly that I didn't like secret passages.

There was little light along the narrow tunnel. We passed lightbulbs spaced several yards apart but only two worked along the entire corridor. The main light came from a flashlight phone app, reflecting dully off the slick wood floor. I kept a firm grip on the back of Jeremiah's shirt to keep from slipping on the rotting planks.

The passageway's proximity to the ocean left everything covered in moisture; I didn't dare touch the walls glistening in the low light. The tunnel was warmer than above ground but humid, a cloying darkness I was desperate to escape. It seemed to go on forever, the walls pressing ever closer. Right as I was readying myself to push Jeremiah aside and flee the rest of the way we came to a stop and the light shone up at a trap door above. Jeremiah twisted a metal ring and pushed, but the door didn't budge. He heaved at it twice and it finally ripped free, making a sound like wood splitting. There wasn't much light streaming in from the new room, either, but definitely more than in the dark tunnel which was a welcomed relief.

"Climb up," he said, and I noticed a metal ladder against the far wall. The chill from the rungs bit into my hands as I scaled the short distance into the new room. There was a marked difference in the temperature and ambient humidity as I realized we were back in the house. I had only a moment to recognize the kitchen pantry, shelves lined with cans and packaged goods, before the door was wrenched open. Blinded by the sudden light, I gave a surprised squeak and raised my hands in surrender as three guns were pointed in my face.

"Stand down," came Jeremiah's order from below. After a moment's hesitation the guns were lowered, and I sat back on the floor, my feet still inside the hole. The guards stepped back as Jeremiah pulled himself from the dank opening. I scooted sideways to make room, not trusting my jelly-legs after that scare, but Jeremiah lifted me effortlessly to my feet and escorted me from the tiny room.

The living room and kitchen were full of people, mainly guards, so Lucas stuck out among the group. He was flanked by two men, and as I came into view he gave me a quick once-over. I thought I saw relief flash across his face briefly before the smirking mask settled back in place.

Jeremiah fixed his brother with a glare, striding toward the smaller man. "If you don't tell me what you—"

"Archangel."

Jeremiah paused. "What's Archangel?"

"Archangel isn't a what, but a who." Lucas shifted uncomfortably, a petulant look on his face. "Can't we lose the cuffs?"

he asked, rattling the thin chain. "My poor shoulders can't take much—"

"Lucas," Jeremiah growled, cutting off his brother and ignoring the request, "who is Archangel?"

"An assassin, and a very good one at that. Pricey as well." He rolled his eyes. "Contrary to what you may think, I wasn't the one to hire his services; I even tried to warn you as soon as I heard about the hit."

"When?" Jeremiah asked sharply.

"The night of the charity gala in France. I tried to call your cell but there was no answer." Lucas snaked a look at me, a twinge of regret in his eyes. "I should have left a message but instead I decided to contact you directly. By the time I reached your room, however, it was too late."

Jeremiah spoke first, his voice suspicious. "The caller was a blocked number."

"A hazard of the profession." Lucas's lips rose into a smirk that didn't quite reach his eyes. I got the impression the grin was an automatic response, an oft-used professional mask, because something flickered in his eyes and the smile disappeared. "I decided to contact you directly but I was only a minute behind the medical team dispatched to your room. I saw you raging about and knew something had happened."

That bit of information got Jeremiah's attention. "You were there?"

Lucas nodded once somberly. "I knew you wouldn't believe me if I approached you then and didn't want to cause a scene—in the state you were in, you would have throttled me—so I stayed back." Lucas snuck a look toward me. "I apologize for not being faster."

"I'm alive." As far as forgiveness went, the words were a paltry expression of gratitude, but I saw another brief flash of relief across his face. My mind was having trouble equating this man with his chosen career; I couldn't see Lucas as an arms dealer. I guess even bad guys can have a heart.

"What about Archangel?"

Jeremiah's question recaptured Lucas's attention. "He's new in the professional circuit but rapidly working his way up. I know of at least twenty confirmed hits but am certain there are dozens more. The man is a master of disguise and uses any tools necessary for the job. He's good enough to leave no evidence, even so far as to hack surveillance cameras." He jerked his chin toward me. "She's the only one who's seen his face and lives to tell the tale."

I went cold. "So he really is after me now, too?" I whispered. The room suddenly spun and I clung to a nearby countertop for support.

A frown flickered across Lucas's face and he took a step toward me, but Jeremiah was already there, an arm hugging around my shoulders and pulling me close for support. I appreciated the much-needed gesture and gave Jeremiah a smile, even as Lucas was held back again, the guards on either side grabbing his arms.

"Who hired him?" Jeremiah asked, his eyes on me and not his brother.

"It doesn't matter, only that the assassin's coming after you."

The nonanswer drew Jeremiah's full attention. "You don't know, or you won't tell me?"

The deadly note in the billionaire's voice shivered through me, but Lucas merely shrugged it off as if he heard similar threats every day. Maybe he did in his line of work, I thought as Lucas replied, "We can worry about that after the fact."

"We can worry about it now. What are you hiding, Loki?"

Consternation flickered across Lucas's face at the use of his other name. "I wish you wouldn't call me that," he said, the jovial mask slipping for a moment.

"Why not?" Jeremiah shot back. "It's your name, isn't it?"

"That name was given to me, I didn't create it myself." Indecision warred on his face, as if he wanted to say more, explain what he meant, and Ethan chose that moment to come into the room. If the bald bodyguard noticed or cared about the increased tension in the room, he gave no indication. "We have a visitor."

Jeremiah's lips thinned at the interruption. "Who is it?" he asked.

Ethan glanced over at Lucas. "Anya Petrovski."

I was watching Lucas when Ethan spoke so saw the spasm of anger across his face. He saw me looking and tried to cover it up, but his eyes still burned with emotion. *Just like his brother,* I thought. *It's all in the eyes.*

"There's no need to involve her," Lucas said, his voice smooth and dismissive. If I hadn't grown so accustomed to reading Jeremiah's stoic expression, I might have been taken in by the words. "She's probably here to plead my case to you, which is entirely unnecessary."

I glanced up at Jeremiah and saw him studying his brother through narrow eyes. "Would she know anything about this?"

Lucas snorted. "Definitely not, other than the fact I came here to warn you."

He sounded flippant and uncaring, but Jeremiah seemed unconvinced. He turned back to Ethan and said, "Leave her car outside the gate. Search both it and her thoroughly, then bring her to the house."

Ethan nodded and whispered instructions to a nearby guard who disappeared from the room. For all of a second, Lucas's lips pursed and his eyes flashed, then the jovial mask slipped back into place. "I do love drama," he said, his lips turning up into a tight smile.

"What is the meaning of this?" came a woman's voice from the entryway, her strident tones bouncing off the wood and stone. Lucas's smile froze, eyes widening as his head snapped around toward the voice.

Jeremiah glanced at Ethan, jaw tightening in annoyance. "Why isn't she gone?" he demanded.

"She hadn't left the gate yet when you ordered the lockdown," Ethan said just as Georgia Hamilton swept into the room. She was flanked by two more guards who faded back toward the front door, escort duty done. The older woman fixed her eyes on Jeremiah and marched straight up to him angrily. "What is the meaning of this?" she snapped, glaring up at her son. "You throw me out of my own home, send your police force to escort me off the property, then force me back in when I'm obviously not wanted?" She drew in a shaky breath, covering her mouth with the knuckles of her hand. "Haven't you any concern for my feelings?"

The overwrought performance was sublime but, given my experience with the woman, I couldn't dredge up any sympathy for her imaginary plight. Nor, apparently, could Jeremiah who replied coldly, "Rest assured, Mother, you'll be gone from this house as quickly as we can manage."

Annoyance wrinkled her nose briefly, then the waterworks started. "How can you dream of keeping me away from my . . ."

"Well, hello, Mother. Did you miss me?"

Lucas's snide words stopped the older woman in midtirade. Clearly shocked, she turned around to stare at her eldest son, who stood glaring at her from the center of the room. "What is he doing here?" she demanded, all traces of her previous grief disappearing in an instant.

"Lovely to see you, too." Gone was the professional nonchalance Lucas had maintained throughout the conversation with Jeremiah. Sarcasm now laced everything, the bitter sneer across his face angled toward the thin woman who'd just entered the room. The scar across his cheek stood out as the skin around it darkened in repressed anger.

Georgia looked as though she'd bitten into a lemon as she rounded on Jeremiah. "Don't listen to anything he says," she spat. "He's nothing but a liar and a cheat."

Lucas threw his head back and barked a laugh, then bowed toward his mother, a mocking smile on his face. "I learned from the best. Inherited from both sides, in fact."

Puzzled by the exchange, I looked up at Jeremiah for

some clarification but he, too, seemed confused. "What's going on?" he demanded.

"Nothing," Georgia spat, then lifted her chin and squared her shoulders. "I'd like to leave now as it appears family means little in this house."

"Oh, Mother, no. Please. Stay." The sarcasm dripped off Lucas's every word, but the woman merely crossed her arms without looking at her eldest son. A cruel smile tightened Lucas's face but the wounded look in his eyes didn't quite jibe with the expression. "Wouldn't you like to know what happened to that thirty million dollars I was accused of stealing?" Lucas asked. "Surely curiosity had been eating away at you about how I spent it."

Georgia flinched ever so slightly, the sign little more than a momentary purse of her lips. "I don't need to hear this, it's not my business," she said, sniffing in disdain and pivoting toward the entryway. "When your little argument is over, I'll be in my car."

"Stop her." Jeremiah's command was immediately followed as the two guards along the doorway closed ranks, blocking the exit. Georgia squawked in outrage but Jeremiah ignored her, his attention on his brother. "I don't like secrets," he said, voice low.

"Yet you've helped perpetuate one for almost eight years now." Lucas never stopped watching his mother, even when she refused to return the favor. His eyes were a cauldron of emotions, flickering and changing so fast it was difficult to decipher anything in particular. "Come now, Mother, should I tell him or would you like to do the honors?"

Giving an irritated groan that sounded childish coming from the older woman, Georgia turned her back on her eldest son. Suddenly realizing that she had an audience scrutinizing her every move, she smoothed her features and waved her hand airily. "I don't know what you're talking about," she said, rolling her eyes. "Now if you'll excuse me . ."

Lucas's eyes narrowed at the display, then he turned to Jeremiah. "Have you ever wondered where Mother gets all her money?"

The question seemed to startle Jeremiah. He gave his brother a long, hard look before turning to glance at his mother. I followed his gaze and wondered if he was thinking the same thing as me. Georgia Hamilton wasn't a good actress; she avoided anyone's eyes, her head swiveling from one exit to another as if pondering which one would get her away quicker. Finally, she met Jeremiah's look and rolled her eyes. "Come on, you don't actually believe him do you?" she snapped.

"Believe what?" Jeremiah looked between his family members, confusion mixing with annoyance. Neither his brother nor his mother seemed inclined to do more than glare at one another, so he raised his voice and asked again, "I'm not to believe what?"

A cell phone rang, the sharp sound piercing the terse atmosphere. Ethan melted out of the room as the answer to Jeremiah's question hit me like a ton of bricks. Oh, my God. "Your mother was the one who stole the money."

I hadn't meant to vocalize my thoughts, it was only a theory, but the words electrified the audience. "That's absurd!"

she snapped. Georgia rounded on me, face contorting in anger. It was an odd sight to behold, as much of her face had been deadened by Botox injections and their near-tranquility didn't match the obvious rage in her eyes. "What would you know anyway? You're just the trollop my son brought home."

"Wasn't that how you, too, started out this life?" Lucas practically cooed as my hands curled into fists. "Didn't Father find you in a Vegas dance hall? Come now, Mother, projecting your issues on her doesn't forgive you your own sins."

A spasm of pain cracked across the older woman's face at the memory, which she tried and failed to conceal. "I don't need to hear this," she repeated bitterly, but much of the fire had gone out of the words.

She turned away, only to have Lucas block her path and snag her arm. Despite the cuffs around his wrists, he held her firm. "Do you know what you've done to me, Mother?" he murmured as she turned and glared. He leaned in close, their gazes locking, but neither seemed willing to budge first. "Do you know what your lie reduced me to?"

I stared at them, still shocked by my own revelation, then looked up at Jeremiah. He was as still as I'd ever seen, and it was difficult to tell what he was thinking. Part of me wanted to know more about Georgia—had she really been a Vegas showgirl?—but now was definitely not the time for questions. There's so much about this family I don't know.

"Don't blame me for what you chose to become," Georgia spat, glaring up at her eldest son.

"How was anything that happened to me by choice?"

Even from several feet away I saw his body trembling as he released his mother's arm, his hands curling into fists. "Everything I was, everything I had, was locked up in this company. Then that was taken away, I was accused of stealing thirty million dollars, and I took the only option available to me that didn't include jail time."

"Selling weapons to the highest bidder?" Jeremiah interjected in a wooden voice. "That was your only recourse?"

Lucas blinked at the interruption then stepped away from Georgia. He looked shaken, his eyes hollow as he looked back at his brother. "It didn't start out that way. I needed to get out of the country and a man I once considered a friend needed a skilled negotiator to broker a deal on some cargo. I didn't know until I was in the air what that 'cargo' consisted of or I swear, I'd have walked into the jail myself."

Georgia snorted. "And you want to lay the blame at my feet?"

"Take some responsibility for what you've caused," I said, unable to contain myself any more. Every face in the room held varying degrees of disgust and astonishment at the older woman's behavior and words but nobody was willing to speak out.

She rolled her eyes and casually inspected her nails. "The reason doesn't matter. He is what he made himself—I'm not the one who should live with the shame."

I sputtered, unable to control my own anger. "He's your son," I exclaimed. "They're both your sons! Don't you care for them at all?"

"Of course I love them," Georgia snapped, giving me a

haughty glare. "Keep your opinion out of matters that don't concern you."

I wanted to throttle the sanctimonious bitch but at her words Lucas's face shut down. "You're right, Mother," he said, chin coming back up. I recognized the moment his familiar mask snapped back into place. He gave the woman a tight-lipped smile even as she ignored him. "We each have to live with our own mistakes, don't we?"

Jeremiah finally stepped forward. I laid my hand on his arm and felt him tremble, the emotional upheaval locked deep inside. His attention was focused on Lucas, who had visibly retreated from the conversation, locking himself behind a familiar wall of congeniality. "Brother . . ."

"Do you know our mother is shopping around a biography about the Hamilton family dynasty to various publishers?" Lucas said, interrupting his brother. The sudden color in her cheeks betrayed Georgia's anger, but he continued. "An insider's look at our family dynamics, from our dear departed father to the current leader of the family business. She, of course, is the beleaguered heroine in this tale of drama, wealth, and corporate espionage. Reportedly the bids for the book were up close to seven figures before every last editor pulled out." At Georgia's shocked look, Lucas waggled his fingers. "You're not the only one with industry contacts willing to help you screw somebody over."

"What are you talking about? This is absurd . . ."

"*And*," Lucas continued, his haunted smile widening, "she's also selling access to her billionaire son. If a businessperson can't gain an audience with the CEO, why, he or she can be an impromptu 'guest' at the family home, conveniently timed to run in to the new head of the family. All for the right price, of course."

"This coming from a man who sells weapons to dictators and scum of the earth for them to use against innocent people?" The color on Georgia's cheeks was high as she glared down her nose at her eldest son. "You dare come in on some high horse, spouting this load of lies, after what you've done?"

"At least I don't hide what I am," Lucas murmured, parroting his mother's arrogant stance.

Georgia rounded on Jeremiah. "Tell me you don't believe this drivel," she demanded, hands on her hips.

Jeremiah's gaze however was intent on his brother, ignoring his mother completely. Lucas didn't flinch from the probing look. "You can prove this?" Jeremiah finally asked.

"I can," Lucas replied as their mother huffed in outraged affront.

"You take his word over mine." Georgia gave Jeremiah a disappointed look whose sincerity, given her previous outbursts, rang hollow.

Does she even realize how she looks to everyone? I wondered. Judging by the way she ignored the guards and other occupants of the room, I highly doubted it. The woman seemed locked inside her own little world; the opinions of others didn't matter. What a horrible way to live your life.

Jeremiah stepped forward until he was standing in front of his mother. He leaned forward, and while I couldn't see his face I did see Georgia flinch away. "I swear, Mother, if what he says is true, I'll . . ."

"You'll what?" she challenged back. "Throw me out? Cut me off? Do you really think you're the first Hamilton male to make those threats to me?" Georgia snorted. "How do you think I stayed married to your father all these years? Good looks and charm? No, I always had something over him—it was the only security I had." She met Jeremiah's glare with one all her own, but the color had drained from her face, leaving only cosmetics to give her any color. "I knew that old bastard wouldn't leave me a red cent when he croaked, but how was I supposed to know he'd go so soon? You two thought I was no different than your father, and maybe now that's the truth, but I knew for certain the only person I could rely on was myself."

"So you threw me under the bus." Lucas's statement wasn't quite a question, but it was obvious he wanted answers.

Georgia blanched, as if the impact of her actions only then occurred to her. Her mouth moved silently for a moment. "It was never supposed to go this far," she finally said, voice low. She fiddled nervously with her purse, grabbing a tube of lipstick and small mirror, but her hands were shaking too much to apply a new layer. "That bastard father of yours didn't leave me a dime; in fact, he managed to tie everything I thought I'd secreted away into Jeremiah's inheritance. I knew there was no way my sons would take care of me. Don't think I haven't noticed how you act around me," she added as an aside to Jeremiah. "Barring me from my own home, acting as if I'm an infant. You're just as bad as your father, assuming I can't take care of myself."

The accusation jolted Jeremiah, but Georgia continued.

"Everything happened so quickly. I managed to find the will and read enough before the lawyers came to know I'd been screwed. Over thirty years I'd been with that bastard, borne his children, overlooked his infidelities, played my part as the dutiful Stepford wife, and he left me nothing. I helped run some nonessential committees, the ones Rufus felt perfect for my distinct lack of any useful talent. Each had been allocated a certain amount of funds and combined equaled just over thirty million dollars." She lifted her chin. "So I took it."

"And left me taking the blame?" Lucas demanded.

"I didn't think that far ahead," she snapped. "I knew I was on borrowed time so spent as much as I could. Turns out it was tougher to get rid of the money than I thought, at least without attracting too much attention. By the time I found out you were the prime suspect—I didn't bother to participate in the investigation for obvious reasons—you'd already fled the country and I still had a sizeable chunk of money left. So I kept it."

Lucas put his hands over his heart. "I feel for you, I really do."

"Can the bullshit, Lucas. I messed up, plain and simple." She turned to Jeremiah. "Now what?"

"Yes, Jeremiah," Lucas added. "What do you want to do about these new developments?"

The CEO didn't seem in any condition to talk, still obviously startled by the turn of events. I had no advice to give, only tightened my hold on his arm in silent support. *What a horrible choice,* I thought, sympathy pouring through me as Jeremiah looked from his mother, tapping her foot impatiently, to Lucas, who stood quietly with raised eyebrows and obviously expected an immediate answer.

Then the front door burst open and a familiar woman's voice shouted, "Lucas!" Every head turned toward the sound, and a moment later a disheveled Anya Petrovski stumbled in through the entryway door, flanked by a large guard. Gone was the dressed-to-the-nines beauty from the ball; very little makeup graced her face, and the elegant clothes were rumpled and disheveled as if she'd just thrown them on haphazardly. Her hair was pulled back in a loose ponytail, and while her natural beauty still showed as plain as day, her features were less severe, making her appear younger and more vulnerable. Her eyes quickly scanned the room and it was obvious the moment she found Lucas that he was all she was interested in.

Lucas, however, eyed the girl coldly. "I told you to stay away from me," he said, voice devoid of emotion.

His reaction toward the woman surprised me but Anya endured his scorn. She was babbling in Russian, back stiff and face stoic, but tears had pooled in her eyes at Lucas's icy rebuff. Russian beauty moved toward him until he held up a hand to ward her off. "I'm sorry," Anya finally moaned in English, her eyes haunted.

"I told you I never wanted to see you again," Lucas growled. His glare was frightful to behold—in that instant he looked and sounded very much like his brother, and Anya quailed back. This wasn't the haughty, annoying woman I'd met before; the desperation and pain in her tones bled through, even if the exact meaning remained a mystery. I exchanged a look with Jeremiah, who looked as baffled as me. What is going on?

Lucas pointed at Jeremiah. "He's the one you should be begging for forgiveness," he said, voice dark, but Anya continued speaking to him in Russian. She kept clutching the Orthodox cross I remembered hanging from her neck at the gala in Paris, pleading with a stone-faced Lucas to no avail.

"Why is she here?" Jeremiah finally asked. At his words Anya grew quiet suddenly and seemed to withdraw in on herself, looking at the floor and wringing her hands.

Lucas gave the blond Russian a look of contempt. "You were wondering before who hired the assassin to kill you?" Lucas jerked his thumb at the cringing beauty, giving his brother a tight smile.

"Surprise."

20

At first, I didn't understand what he meant. The whole room was silent for a moment, then Jeremiah snapped his fingers and pointed toward Anya. Immediately the two men who had escorted her into the building each grabbed an arm, holding her firmly in place. Only then did Lucas's meaning sink in, and I gasped at the revelation.

"Anya hired the assassin." The words, summing up my own confused understanding of the situation, came from Jeremiah. Incredulity crept into his voice, as he repeated it as a question. "Anya hired the assassin?"

"Never cross a Russian," Lucas replied, rolling his eyes and sighing. "It seems as though the truth of that saying extends beyond my current profession."

"I did this for you," the blond woman said toward Lucas, struggling to free herself from the guards' grip. "I thought this what you wanted!"

"What I wanted?" Lucas sneered at Anya. "You did it for yourself—don't try to lay blame at my feet."

Anya eyed the bodyguards around her but kept speaking to Lucas. "You said you hated him, that you wished—"

"I never wanted him dead," Lucas roared, and Anya flinched.

"You always talk about him," she persisted. She slipped into Russian for a second then caught herself. "When you drunk, you always talk about how you wish to go home . . ."

"And killing my brother will get me my place back?" Lucas barked a laugh. "Anya, you're not a stupid woman, all evidence to the contrary in this situation aside. Look at me!" He spread his arms. "Thousands of people are dead at my hands. Maybe my finger wasn't on the trigger but I provided the bullets, the guns. I'm covered in blood—how can I come home after what I've done, what I've allowed to happen?"

Anya's chin trembled as my own heart constricted at the man's obvious pain. She crooned something softly in her native tongue and reached out to Lucas, but he slapped her hand away. "Don't flatter yourself, my dear." His cold fury sliced through the air, designed only to inflict pain. "I never loved you. Why would one have any affection for a clever tool?"

The blood drained from Anya's face as she gaped at Lucas in disbelief. "You said . . ."

He waved a hand through the air, rolling his eyes. "Words mean little, you should know this. Your usefulness, as well as my patience, has run out. I no longer need your drama." Lucas regarded her coldly, then made a shooing motion with his hand. "You can go away now."

Wow. I watched the scene, uncertain anymore what to

think. As much as I'd detested the woman when I'd met her in France, my heart went out to her now . . . which was silly, given the fact that she'd done so much to hurt us. But at that moment, I had trouble believing that the woman would do such a thing.

Anya drew herself upright in a facsimile of her previous pose but the devastation in her eyes was terrible, the back bone of steel and attitude that sustained her was gone, broken by his words. A single tear worked its way down an ivory cheek. "I give you everything," she whispered brokenly in a thick accent. The fingers where she gripped the ornate cross around her neck were pale and trembling. "I become anything you need, do things that shame me and my family, all for your love. Now you tell me it was a lie?"

I remembered Ethan telling me that Anya was a simple country girl when Jeremiah hired her to help with Russian translations. Looking at her now, I didn't see the haughty, condescending beauty at the party, but a young girl thrown into a world against which she had no defenses. The way she clung to the necklace, a symbol of the religion to which she obviously still clung, made my heart ache for her. Is this where I'm headed?

"We Hamilton men corrupt anything we touch." Lucas gave Anya a pitying look. He spared me a glance before continuing. "You were caught in the crosshairs and that was unfortunate."

"This is not how it was supposed to happen," she whispered. "He said this was what you wanted, that . . ."

She trailed off, but in the dead silence her words carried through the room. "Who said?" Lucas and Jeremiah both replied, echoing one another.

At that moment, several things happened simultaneously. The lights all went out in the large room, casting odd shadows from the muted light streaming in through the window. I had time to realize the glass lining the back of the room, which had stayed opaque for the last several days, no longer hid its view of the ocean behind the house, then it struck. There was a small pop and Anya toppled forward onto the ground, a stunned look on her face. Then I was suddenly grabbed and flung sideways into the kitchen, pressed behind the tall marbled-topped island by a heavy body. Something whistled past my head, the air singing with its closeness. I gave a startled shriek as a jar of flour on the counter behind me exploded.

The room erupted into motion as people scrambled for cover. Guards dove toward the kitchen or the entryway foyer, piling through the narrow passage. There was another pop and a young guard tripped, falling motionless to the ground. He was dragged through the doorway by his comrades, disappearing from my view.

"What's going on?" I asked, heart threatening to tear from my chest.

"Sniper."

Oh God. I trembled against Jeremiah, who pulled me tightly against his body. I heard a loud *thock* inside the island and jumped, but no bullet exited on our side. Beside us one guard broke from his position by the door and headed toward us. Another pop sounded and he spun around, landing gracelessly on his back half inside our cover spot. Surprise and fear flashed briefly in his eyes before his face went slack, and the sickening realization I'd just watched somebody die was almost too much to bear.

"Breathe," Jeremiah ordered, and I let out the air I hadn't realized I'd kept trapped. He nudged sideways and checked for a pulse in the guard's neck, then grabbed the small ear microphone. "Ethan, report."

"Somebody sabotaged the electrical system, including the backup generators." Ethan's voice was tinny and faint but I was close enough to Jeremiah to hear. "We're working to sort that now. What's the situation in there?"

"A sniper has us pinned in the kitchen," Jeremiah bit out. "We need that glass back as cover to get out."

There was a pause, then, "Roger that. Randy says ETA on the power is two minutes."

Jeremiah cursed, dropping the comm onto his lap. "Two minutes," he repeated, and I nodded. "Might as well be forever."

"Visiting with you is always such a pleasure, brother."

Lucas's voice was light and Jeremiah's head whipped around to glare, but the scarred man wasn't even looking at us. All his attention was on Anya, still lying prone in the middle of the floor, clutching her bleeding belly and moaning softly. Lucas had somehow managed to overturn the thick coffee table and one chair as cover, but neither afforded him much protection. Anya reached one arm toward him, sobbing softly as her other hand clutched the gunshot wound in her belly.

232 · sara fawkes

"I'm coming, baby." Lucas made a quick in-out movement with his head, peeking very briefly from cover, and an instant later a bullet tore a hole into the wall behind him. He cursed, then cast about and grabbed a pillow nearby. "This would really be easier without the cuffs, brother," he called out.

Jeremiah dug around in his pockets and tossed a small keychain across the room to land behind the coffee table. "What are you doing?" he asked.

"Probably getting myself killed," replied Lucas, quickly unlocking his cuffs. He paused for a deep breath, and looked over at Jeremiah. "Wish me luck," he added, then tossed the pillow sideways into the open area beside him. It exploded, sending bits of stuffing flying everywhere, but Lucas was already moving, grabbing Anya and pulling her toward his hiding spot. Another pop through the window and Lucas hissed, but he was back behind his barrier and managed to pull Anya with him behind the long table. Two bullets in rapid succession struck the wood table Lucas hid behind with loud *thocks*, but neither appeared to make it through.

Careful to stay hidden, Lucas moved to inspect the wound on Anya's stomach. From the bleak look on his face, I could tell it was bad. Anya sobbed softly, one hand fluttering over her belly while her other hand held tight to Lucas's arm. Out in the entryway, Georgia's screaming reached truly operatic levels. "Mother, be quiet!" Jeremiah shouted, and instantly the screaming stopped. I wondered if it was fear for her life or that of her children that had the woman in hysterics, but right then wasn't the time to consider that.

"Stay with me, Anya," Lucas murmured, carefully removing his shirts and pressing it over the wound.

"I'm sorry," Anya whispered, bloody hand fluttering weakly through the air. Tears tracked down the side of her face into her hair, and the bleakness in her eyes was heartbreaking. "I should have known, I never wanted . . ."

"Shh, don't talk. You're going to be fine."

The lie was obvious; even from this distance I could see the amount of blood pouring from the wound and the increasing pallor in the Russian woman's face. "I never should have listened to him, I only wanted you to be happy . . ."

"You're going to be fine," Lucas grit out, but the reality of the situation was increasingly apparent in his desperate gaze. His hands left the blood-soaked shirt against her belly to cup her face. "Who told you to do this? I need a name, Anya, stay with me here."

She didn't answer him as her breathing grew labored. Her body grew slack, her free hand falling to her chest. "I gave you everything," she whispered, exhalations coming in uneven gasps. "Don't forget me."

"Anya," Lucas said, smoothing back her hair, "stay with me. Hey, you never took me to that little town you were from. What was its name again?" Anya, however, didn't seem to hear his question, her pallid face growing slack. "Everything," she repeated, eyes staring off into nothing. Her hand slipped off the Orthodox cross below her neck, and she drew in a rattling breath. "I sold my soul . . ."

Lucas's face contorted. "Anya, stay with me. Anya . . ."

But she was gone.

Lucas's breath came out in a ragged hiccup, then he smacked the tile floor with a bloody fist and let out a string of curses. A bullet smacked into the wood behind him but he didn't flinch. He sounded angry, but the masks were gone and I saw the profound defeat in his scarred features.

In death, Anya's pallid body looked so small and young. I'd never wanted to see the woman dead, even when I had seen her at her worst. Learning about the young girl she'd once been, then seeing her crying on the ground, had erased my residual bad feelings toward the woman. Her final words had been a sucker punch to the gut, and I could only imagine it was worse for Lucas. Maybe he deserved it. The thought was unkind but I couldn't help but wonder what he'd asked the Russian girl to do on his behalf, manipulating her obvious feelings for him no matter whether they were reciprocated. Does love mean so little to this family?

The lights in the kitchen flickered on as the electricity powered back up, but the glass lining the back of the house remained clear. "Get that safety glass on," Jeremiah barked, holding me tightly against him. A second later someone flipped the switch and the glass fogged over again, the ocean disappearing from sight. The sniper, however, wasn't finished; bullets continued to pop through the fogged glass, mostly centered around Lucas's and Anya's location.

Apparently the gunman didn't like being made a fool.

"Go," Jeremiah said softly, pushing to my feet and propelling me toward the entryway less than ten feet away. He shielded me with his body as we ran the short distance to the relative safety of the main lobby of the house. Lucas came through not long behind us, bloody hands hanging stiffly at his side.

Georgia was at the far end of the lobby, one guard holding her in place. The frantic expression on her face melted as both her sons came through the door, but she paled when she saw the blood on Lucas. Wresting her arm out of the guard's grip, she moved toward her eldest son, jaw moving in helpless shock, only to have him lift a hand to stop her. "It's not mine," he said. There wasn't any emotion in his voice. Anya's death must have burned it out of him, at least for the moment.

Uncertainty marred the older woman's face, clearly debating what to do. I wondered what she would do, perhaps try to mend the relationship with a hug, but her personality won out. Her chin went up as the arrogant mask clamped down hard, and it occurred to me the whole family hid parts of themselves from the world as if showing any true emotion would allow others to use it against them. And perhaps that's what happened in the past.

Ethan came through the front door, flanked by another guard with a cell phone to his ear. "We've got generator power back on but it's going to take a while to fix the mess with the main power lines," he said. "There are three wounded outside, emergency medical is en route."

"We have casualties in here, too, with at least one dead. Get all the wounded upstairs and coordinate to make sure everyone gets attention." Jeremiah put a hand on each of my shoulders, then pushed me toward Ethan. "Take care of her and my brother, there's no time to waste."

"Sir?"

"We need to find that sniper now before he disappears again." He looked at me. "Stay with Ethan; do whatever he tells you."

I had to force myself to release his arm. The urge to try holding him back in the safety of the house was strong, but somehow I knew it wouldn't stop him. He needed this, to be back in the trenches hunting the bad guy. That he was the ultimate target didn't matter to Jeremiah, I could see it in his eyes. So instead of protesting, I swallowed back my fears and said, "Promise me you'll stay safe."

His manner softened at my words, whether in relief or something else. He kissed the top of my head as the wounded guards were brought inside. "I'll be back for you, I promise," he murmured, then headed out the door.

"Take them upstairs," Ethan ordered, and the remaining guards moved up the staircase with the wounded.

"Great," Lucas muttered, staring woodenly at the floor, "I have Captain America babysitting me. Whoop-de-freaking—"

Ethan spun around in front of me, his fist exploding across Lucas's face, sending the man to the ground in a crumpled heap. "I've wanted to do that for years," Ethan said under his breath.

I stared down at the scarred man in dismay. "Did you really have to do that?" I asked, moving forward to see if Lucas was okay. "He wasn't any threat . . ."

A hand wrapped around my head, clapping a cloth over my mouth. Startled, I struggled, opening my mouth to scream but instead breathed in a sickly sweet aroma. Almost immediately the room spun, and I heard Ethan mumble a soft, "I'm sorry for this," as my legs gave out and I was lowered to the floor.

I've heard that phrase too much tonight, was my last thought before losing consciousness.

My dream was weird: I couldn't tell, even within the context of the subconscious fantasy, whether I was flying or falling through the air. Clouds whipped past me, the ground far away like I'd only ever seen from inside an airplane. Something was in my arms, perhaps the reason for my descent, but I wasn't afraid. The ground drew ever closer, yet I felt entirely content with the whole situation, although I had no idea why.

The real-world feel of somebody rummaging through my pockets popped me out of the dream state. Sudden vertigo made my head swim, remnants of the dream perhaps, before I realized we actually were moving and that I was lying on my side. My hands were tied against my lap in front of me, my feet were similarly bound, and I was precariously perched across the backseat of an unknown car. When I tried to sit up, I also discovered that I was tied down by seatbelts, the thick straps pulling me back onto the warm leather.

A man sat in the driver's seat, working with a phone in his thick hand. Figuring he didn't know I was awake yet, I surveyed my surroundings, blinking away the grogginess. Everything was covered in black leather, the textured, expensive type, and it smelled brand-new, but the car itself was unfamiliar to me. The backseat was narrow, with very little leg room—I stayed curled up to keep from bumping the sides—so I guessed it was a sports car of some kind. The whine of an engine used to going fast speeds confirmed that suspicion but didn't give me any other details. I turned myself up to peer up through the window to the overcast skies outside. The leather squeaked beneath me, attracting the driver's attention, and my heart skipped as I recognized the familiar face. "Ethan?"

He turned back around, staring at the road. He tossed the cell phone onto the passenger seat and I realized it was mine, the replacement Jeremiah had given to me after I broke mine in Paris.

"The girl is awake?"

My eyes widened when I heard the other voice. I peeked around at the passenger seat in front of my head but nobody else was in the car. The voice hadn't come from any one direction, and Ethan didn't seem surprised although his jaw did tighten.

"The sedative wore off early," Ethan replied. His voice was gravelly, angry, as if he didn't want to respond.

My cell phone on the seat in front of me burst into sound, visibly startling Ethan. "What is that?" came the disembodied voice, annoyance creeping into its unctuous tone.

"The girl's phone." Ethan picked it back up and looked at the screen. "It's Jeremiah," he added flatly.

My heart raced at the name. Chest tight, I bit my lip to keep from crying out.

"Answer it," the voice directed. "Put it on speaker."

Ethan put the call through, then set the telephone on his lap. Before he could say anything, however, I exclaimed, "Jeremiah!"

"Lucy. Where are you?"

Something cold inside my soul melted at his voice. He sounded strong and sure, and I desperately needed the assurance. "I'm in the backseat of a car," I replied, hating the desperate quality of my voice but eager to get out as much as I could. "Some sports car with all black leather. I can't see anything but overcast skies out the window. I'm with Ethan." I stopped, not sure how to break the news about my kidnapping.

My eyes met Ethan's stony gaze, then the big man sighed. "I'm sorry about this, Jeremiah."

"Ethan?" he growled. Perhaps if I could see Jeremiah's face I could decipher the emotion I heard hanging on that simple word—surprise, rage, betrayal, disappointment—but for now there was only the word and the demand for answers behind it.

"They have Celeste." Profound regret tinged the big man's voice, and I saw his mouth turn down.

Jeremiah cursed. "When?"

"I don't know but I got the call while you were arguing with your family. You know I'd do anything to protect her."

"So you set this up?" Even over the phone, the rage in Jeremiah's voice bubbled over. "You let three men die because—"

"No," Ethan exploded, "that was not me. I didn't know anything until that call and the lights went out before I was off the phone. I swear to you on whatever honor I have left that I had no part in that attack."

"You ask for trust after kidnapping my—" Jeremiah cut himself off, then asked, "Where are you going?"

"To make the trade."

"Goddammit, Ethan!"

"You'd do the same for her, don't bother denying it." Ethan glanced back at me, then gave a harsh laugh. "This whole thing is just like Kosovo."

There was a pause at the other end of the line, then Jeremiah growled again, "Goddammit, Ethan . . ."

"When this is over, don't blame Celeste. This is all my decision." Ethan picked up the cell phone. "I'm hanging up now. Good-bye Jeremiah."

"Ethan, wait—"

Ethan disconnected the call, staring at the phone in his hand.

"Throw the phone out the window."

I started at the smarmy voice beside my head as Ethan did as he was told, lowering the window and tossing out the cell phone. I looked up beside my head and realized the voice was coming from the car speakers. Part of me was relieved there wasn't another person in the car with us but I had the sinking sensation I would very soon meet the voice in person.

"What happened in Kosovo?" the voice asked conversationally.

"An informant betrayed us," Ethan replied, voice neutral. "We didn't realize until after the fact that our target had kidnapped the man's wife and family, so he gave us up to save them."

"Did they all survive?"

"No," came the clipped reply.

"Pity, although perhaps a fitting end for his crimes. Betrayal really is the nastiest of sins, wouldn't you say?"

Ethan's knuckles on the steering wheel were white from the strain of his grip, but he didn't reply to the obvious taunt. "What are you going to do with the girl?" Ethan asked after a short pause.

"Kill her, then kill your friend when he comes to save her."

I moaned and squeezed my eyes shut, tears leaking from the edge of my lashes. When I opened them again, I saw Ethan staring at me in the rearview mirror. "And if I don't bring her to you?"

"I kill your precious wife. Hmm, eventually. She really is a pretty little thing, if you like redheads that is."

Ethan's hands twisted on the steering wheel. "You son of a bitch . . ."

There was a commotion on the other end of the line, then a woman screamed in pain. Celeste. Ethan swerved the car at the sound, bellowing, "Stop it!"

The screaming stopped but the soft sobbing in the background was almost as gut-wrenching. "If you don't want any more marks on your precious wife," the voice stated, no longer amused, "you won't call me any more names. Are we clear?"

"Crystal," Ethan growled, but his profile was a bleak hopelessness.

My heart was pounding, threatening to leap from my chest. My breaths came shaky and fast. "Ethan, please," I whispered, throat constricting at the thought of what was coming. *I don't want to die!*

"Shut her up," the assassin said.

I squirmed, desperate to get free, as Ethan grabbed a white rag from the passenger seat and reached back toward me. His long arms found my face easily but I fought, holding my breath and twisting everywhere I could against the seatbelts to get away. Ethan had the patience of Job, however, and spots danced along my vision as I quickly exhausted my oxygen supply. I sobbed out a breath, the sickly sweet aroma of the drug trickling down into my lungs, and seconds later I fell back into unconsciousness.

This time, there were no dreams.

21

I didn't know how long I was out this time, but the increased rocking and bouncing of the car was what initially pulled me out of my drug-induced slumber. It wasn't until we stopped, however, that I became fully conscious, the sudden lack of movement jarring me awake. There was the sound of a car door and clunk of a seat, then my legs were grabbed. Involuntarily I fought but my struggles were weak and ineffectual as I was pulled from the vehicle and slung over a shoulder. Chill air circulated off the water and I immediately began to shiver, the thin clothing I wore no match for the wet winter gust.

"Can you stand?" Ethan's voice rumbled nearby.

My stomach roiled, nausea threatening to overwhelm me, but I managed a weak, "Yes." The world spun again but Ethan was gentle, setting me on my feet beside the car. I staggered, placing a hand on the glossy sports car for support, and forced myself to look around. Seagulls screeched above, plaintive cries slicing through the air. The ocean surf lapped rhythmically nearby but I wasn't able to see the opposing shoreline with the fog over the water. Factory buildings lined the seaside road, blocking us in. The waterfront road was narrow and hazy, tendrils of fog snaking in over the bumpy asphalt, but I saw another car a few hundred yards away pointed ominously toward us. "Is that . . . ?"

I noticed something from the corner of my eye and glanced back to see a gun in Ethan's hand. My breath quickened but he caught my gaze and shook his head ever so slightly, keeping the weapon pointed to the ground and hidden behind my body. "Where's my wife?" he called out to the assassin who was still obviously listening from the car.

The door to the car nearby opened, confirming my fears. A slim figure with very red hair staggered out of the vehicle as the door was shut behind her. "Ethan?" Celeste called, her voice tinny over the distance.

"I'm here, Celeste," he called back, and I could feel the tension leak out of his body as Celeste's head snapped in our direction. She staggered toward us, and I could see she was both blindfolded and had her hands cuffed behind her.

"Wait for her to reach you," the assassin said, his oily voice through the car's sound system making my hands curl into fists. I bit my lip as a solid *snikt* came from behind me, no doubt Ethan readying his weapon. My chin quivered and I gritted my teeth, determined to be strong. *Oh, but it's so hard.*

"Perhaps now would be a good time to mention that your wife is wearing a bomb?"

I heard a quick intake of breath and Ethan's grip on my upper arm tightened. The pleased note in the assassin's obsequious voice intensified as he continued, "If you're considering any heroics, the first casualty in this conflict will be your beloved wife. So please put away that gun you're hiding behind Ms. Delacourt or my finger might get a bit . . . twitchy."

Ethan immediately raised his hands in the air, brandishing the weapon he held, then tossed it inside the car. "Almost there, baby," he called out to the redhead. My heart ached for the woman, who was stumbling blindly toward her husband, only able to use the sound of his voice to navigate. Twice she almost fell, a dangerous proposition as her hands were tied behind her back, but she managed to catch herself each time.

"How quickly do you think you can take your wife out of range?" Smug superiority fairly oozed from the car speakers. "Let's play a game: Is the bomb on your wife triggered by radio signal or by cell phone? You get one guess. And don't try to use the car when you escape, I might have that similarly wired to blow." A dark laugh came from the sound system. "How far will you have to go to ensure her safety if this all goes sour, or I decide to be a real son of a bitch?"

Ethan growled, his body vibrating with the sound, but his voice was strong and sure as he continued to call to his wife. Her answering cries were full of fear and as she came close, Ethan stepped around me and caught her in his arms. I saw a red mark across one high cheekbone and what looked like a small burn on one shoulder, but otherwise she seemed okay. The redhead's loud sob ripped through the tension as the bald man crushed her against his body, kissing the top of her head for a long moment before pulling the blindfold from her eyes and picking her up into his arms.

I knew the moment Celeste saw me because she gasped. "What's Lucy doing here?" she demanded, voice suddenly strong. Her eyes fell to the handcuffs on my wrists and she gave her husband a piercing look, fear giving way to confusion.

"My finger is getting itchy on this button," the assassin's impatient voice came through the speakers, and a dawning horror flowed across the redhead's face.

"No," Celeste blurted out, "you can't leave her here." When Ethan didn't reply but only turned toward a nearby alley, Celeste's protests rose to shrieking levels and she struggled in his arms. The small woman had no chance, however; her hands were cuffed behind her and there was no way Ethan would let her go. I watched them fade into the distance, the man's huge loping strides taking him far away quickly. A detached numbness came over me as I realized I was well and truly alone, and more than likely about to die. How did my life come to this?

Across the way, the driver's side door opened and a man unfolded himself from the car. He was dressed casually, with only a thin leather jacket to protect him from the frosty air coming in off the water. His slacks flapped lazily in the breeze as he made his way toward me, footfalls from his wingtip shoes growing steadily louder. He wore narrow-framed sunglasses, despite the overcast light, that fit his face well. A detached part of my brain noted he was almost handsome but in a muted way, the "nice guy" who you never really noticed. Given the day's events, I doubted I'd ever forget this man's face if I lived through this.

I stood my ground as he approached, leaning against the car for support. My legs were jelly, threatening to collapse from the fear, but I faced him head-on and tried to emulate Jeremiah's stoic stare. No mean feat, especially when he finally stopped close enough for me to touch. He examined me silently and I met his gaze, my breaths coming quick, but I was unwilling to back down anymore.

"It's rare I actually meet one of my targets face-to-face," he said finally, quirking one eyebrow. "Of course, it's also rare that they see me and live to tell the tale. Truth be told, I prefer it this way, watching a person's face in those final moments." He chuckled, the sound hollow of any real mirth. "Of course, you were never a target until you survived my poison. Tricky girl."

The fake smile on his face didn't reach his eyes and sent a shudder through me. His eyes were dead, dark pools that held nothing else beneath. I struggled to keep myself under control, clamping my lips tightly together so I wouldn't make a sound. As determined as I was not to beg, the prospect of dying left me faint and I clung to the car mirror to keep from collapsing.

"Not that I don't enjoy our time together . . ."—he glanced at his watch—"but we have less than ten minutes until the cavalry arrives. Six, if they have a method in place for physically tracking either one of you that I don't know about. These factories are a maze, tough to get through even with a map." The assassin reached behind him and pulled out a black gun, caressing the barrel with his free hand without taking his eyes off me. He saw me watching and shrugged.

"It was a blow to my professional ego when both of you survived my poisoning attempt. That won't be a trick I use again, but still, I need to correct my mistakes."

I kept my eyes on the other man's, trying desperately to control my breathing. A dozen scenarios flitted through my head on how to get away: hand-to-hand combat, running away, diving off into the water. In every scenario however, I lost. Badly. The quiet confidence in his face told me everything I needed to know, that his skills in pursuit of prey were far greater than my skills at fleeing, especially out here in the open. A detached numbness spread through my body as I watched him prepare his weapon. *Is this really it? Am I merely ending up as bait to lure Jeremiah to his death?*

A narrow tube appeared in one of the man's hands, and he casually connected it to the end of the gun, spinning it in place. He cocked his head to one side and studied me. "You're very brave," he commented. "Most targets would be begging for their lives right about now."

I'd do it if I thought it would mean anything. The wind picked up from the water, waves crashing into the wooden supports beneath us, shaking the ground beneath my feet. My own shivering ceased with the numb realization that I was about to die.

"I prefer it face-to-face like this," he continued, "but most people run away and I have to shoot them in the back. Annoying business, that—almost takes away the dignity and pleasure." He raised his weapon and leveled it with my face. "Don't worry, my dear, you'll see your beloved billionaire again soo—"

Something whistled past my ear and the assassin spun around, collapsing onto the ground. I stared down dumbly as he thrashed at my feet, grunting in obvious pain and holding his shoulder, then common sense flooded back with a vengeance. I spun to flee but hadn't taken a step yet when a hand grabbed my ankle and I toppled to the ground. I managed to catch myself, skinning my knees for the first time since childhood, but was immensely grateful that Ethan had bound my hands in front of me. I squeaked as my hair was grabbed and I was hauled backward and over the assassin until I was all but laying on top of him.

"That son of a bitch," the assassin muttered, and I didn't know who he was talking about until a small device appeared in his hand. It had two small buttons, one blue and one red, and looked much like an electronic car key. I realized, horrified, it was probably the one to detonate the bomb around Celeste.

"No!" I grabbed his hand, wrestling for the controls. Something had obviously gone wrong—Ethan had betrayed him, or the cavalry had arrived early on its own—but it didn't matter; I couldn't allow him to press that button. All I could see was Celeste's panicked expression when she saw me, her cries not to leave me even as Ethan hustled her away, and I couldn't think of letting her die. Not without a fight.

The assassin hadn't expected my resistance, and I almost pried the device from his grip before he fought back. One of his arms was all but useless—blood poured from a large wound in the man's shoulder—so between his wounded arm and my cuffed hands, we were almost evenly matched. I also realized quickly he was using me as a shield against the new sniper and didn't want to compromise that, but he still looped one leg around my waist and jerked me down, trying to wrench the controller from my grip.

A flash of triumph shot through me as I snagged the small plastic device from his hand, but before I could throw it into the water nearby, an elbow exploded across the side of my face. Pain exploded through my skull and, stunned, I hesitated too long and his hand was back over mine, trying to pry the controller from my fingers. Ears ringing, I tried to hold on to it but another elbow, this time to my chest, knocked the wind out of my lungs. Dazed, I struggled to breathe and faltered long enough for him to wrest the small implement free from my grip. Anger and triumph contorted his face, and I watched helplessly as he pressed the red button.

Nothing happened.

He blinked, then looked down at the controls. His finger slid again over the red button, but whatever he was expecting clearly didn't materialize if his expression said anything. "Well, fuck," he said, shoulders slumping in defeat.

I snapped my head back, catching my skull against his nose and mouth. The impact again stunned me, but his grip loosened and I rolled sideways away from him. Our eyes met as his good arm raised up, pointing the gun directly at me.

Then the back of his head exploded, and he collapsed back to the asphalt.

Body quaking, I struggled for breath but couldn't take my eyes off the grisly sight. Hysterics threatened, sobbing breaths forcing themselves from my lips as I pushed myself upright, chest aching from where his elbow had impacted. Tears, however, didn't come; a pervasive numbness overwhelmed me and all I could do was stare at the slack face of the assassin, the hole in his skull, and the . . . the mess behind his head. *I think I'm going to be sick.*

I didn't know how long I sat there, staring at the bloody mess before me, before I heard car tires approaching our location. Too numb to move my head, I nevertheless watched dark sedans and SUVs move in, surrounding us on the narrow waterway road. People exited the vehicles, milling about the scene and wearing the familiar dark uniforms I'd seen for nearly a week now. None of Jeremiah's people approached me, although one man did gently pick up the remote that had skittered out of the assassin's hand when he'd been shot. As much as I wanted to say something, tell them what it was, I couldn't take my gaze off the assassin's face, the man's expression forever frozen in astonishment.

An unfamiliar *whoop*ing sound drew closer, and I finally turned my head to see a helicopter appear through the fog over the water. A tall man stood on one of the skids, and as it approached land's edge he leaped off, landing effortlessly and running straight toward me. The long rifle hooked across his shoulders bounced with his loping gait, and when he came abreast of me he fell to his knees and immediately folded me into his arms.

My body shook, the action uncontrollable and fierce, and a sob burst its way out as I finally gave way to the emotions

I'd kept bottled inside. I clung to Jeremiah as he picked me up gently, keeping me pressed firmly against his body, and loaded us inside one of the waiting SUVs.

The ride home was quiet, for which I was eternally grateful. Jeremiah kept me on his lap, his hands caressing my back and arms in a rhythmic pattern that helped calm me. There was no demand in his touch; perhaps a touch of possessive protection but I desperately needed that form of safety. The earlier numbness had worn off but I was too tired to cry or scream. All I wanted was to curl up in a dark room, safely away from society, and try to forget the past several hours.

My brain, however, kept reliving horrible scenes: the guard dying in front of me at the house, Anya's final moments, Celeste's wails as she was carried away to a safety I'd been denied, the assassin's head exploding in a splash of gore. When I'd found a drop of what I thought was blood on one sleeve while in the SUV with Jeremiah, I'd almost gone crazy trying to strip out of the contaminated clothing. Only Jeremiah's deep voice, his hard hands deftly peeling the offending layers from me, kept me from falling into the hysterics in which I so desperately wanted to indulge.

Any hope of solitude, however, was dashed when I saw the vehicles lining the front of the mansion, unfamiliar shapes and uniforms standing guard at the entrance. I whimpered when Jeremiah's car door opened, not wanting to be in the middle of yet another circus, but only clung to his neck as he carried me out of the vehicle. His lips grazed my ear, breath warm along my skin as he asked, "Can you walk on your own?"

The urge to answer no, to stay safely against him as long as possible, was a strong temptation. I nodded, however, a spark of independence goading me to take control of myself. Jeremiah still didn't release me for several more seconds as we walked through the unfamiliar crowd, then he gently set me to my feet once we were inside the entryway. I teetered for a moment, keeping my grip tight on his arm, but he didn't seem to mind. "Who are these people?" I said finally, clearing my throat. My voice sounded thick to my own ears, likely due to my earlier crying.

"They're government officials, here to take my brother into custody."

Jeremiah's lips were a thin line and I couldn't tell whether or not he approved, but the idea of Lucas going to jail was disheartening. In the lobby, the scarred man was staring at a nearby body bag, a tired look on his face. Lucas's gaze followed the body as two men in Coroner uniforms hefted it up and eased it outside, then he looked up at me. Relief flashed in his eyes. "I'm glad you're safe, my dear," he said, giving me a small nod. "There are already too many casualties in this debacle."

"Thank you for your help," I replied, sighing. "I wish it didn't have to end this way for you."

"It was the risk I took in coming here." Lucas hitched a shoulder, one side of his mouth lifting in a smirk. "I appreciate your concern however. It's . . . sweet."

I frowned, trying to determine whether the statement was

a compliment or an insult, and my dilemma seemed to amuse him. "Good-bye, fair lady," he said as the officials in suits tugged him out of the house. "Hopefully we will meet again soon."

Jeremiah stepped sideways, blocking the path through the door. "Brother," he started, but Lucas shook his head.

"Don't. Whether you're apologizing or condemning me, I don't want to hear it. The truth is out and now we each live with our own consequences."

The brothers stared at one another for a moment, two matching profiles against the fading light outside. Finally, Jeremiah stepped out of the way, and Lucas was led silently out to the waiting vehicle. I watched, disappointed, as the car containing him and the various officials rolled out toward the main gate.

Jeremiah looked around the lobby. "Where's my mother?" he asked a nearby guard.

"The officials took a brief statement, then said she was free to go, sir."

The CEO's lips thinned very briefly, and he sighed. I frowned; I'd hoped for more from the odious woman, but I guessed the habits of a lifetime were difficult to give up. I put a comforting hand on Jeremiah's arm, then tensed as I recognized another familiar figure walking toward us.

Ethan had a wary look on his face but, to my surprise, he wasn't wearing any handcuffs. Celeste was nowhere to be seen, and while I very much wanted to know if she was all right, I kept silent. "I'm glad you're okay," the bald man said to me.

I moved closer to Jeremiah, suspicion and mistrust echoing through my brain. Despite knowing why he kidnapped me, the impossible situation into which he'd been placed, I couldn't bring myself to forgive his actions. Seeing him now only brought back memories of a cloth over my mouth, the sickly aroma of the sedative seeping down my throat, and the terror of him abandoning me to my fate.

"Thank you," Jeremiah said from beside me, his arm pulling me tighter against his body. His body remained stiff as he addressed the bodyguard. "This could have turned out much different without your help."

Ethan nodded. "I managed to find a heavy freezer inside one of the buildings. It kept any signal from getting in long enough for me to disarm the bomb around Celeste." His gaze turned to me. "I hear I have you to thank for the extra delay."

Confused, I turned to look at Jeremiah. He helped? How?

"The Kosovo reference," Jeremiah said, answering my silent question. "Our informant on that mission led us into a trap, giving us faulty intel that got several men killed. However, he dialed the new coordinates on his cell phone so we could complete the mission anyway." His powerful gaze never left the bald bodyguard's. "I'm glad the outcome was better this time around."

Ethan shrugged, but his eyes crinkled in a wince. "Celeste isn't happy with how I handled the situation." He glanced at me. "Leaving you behind with that assassin might be the one thing that costs me my marriage."

Part of me desperately wanted to comfort him—I'd seen

firsthand how much he adored his wife—but I couldn't get any platitudes through my lips. It was all too fresh, too many bad memories and sensory links to work through before I could ever feel comfortable around the man. I think he saw that because regret etched across his face. "I wish I'd seen another way," he said, eyes on me.

Before I could react, Jeremiah stepped forward. His arm was already moving and his fist cracked along Ethan's jaw with a sickening snap. The bald man staggered back, falling to the ground, as Jeremiah towered his prone figure. "You're fired."

A protest lodged in my throat as I stared between the two men. Something silent passed between them, then Ethan nodded. "I expected worse."

Jeremiah stepped forward, extending his hand, and helped Ethan to his feet. "You still have my respect, but I can't afford to trust you again." He stepped away. "Get your things from the bunkhouse and be off the property in half an hour; we'll deal with the business end of things later."

Ethan nodded soberly then turned to me. "For what it's worth, I'm sorry for how I acted."

"Your wife was kidnapped," I replied, surprising myself. "You did what you thought you had to do, and managed to alert the cavalry to rescue me." I struggled to find the words to continue, still conflicted about the day's events. Was I really forgiving the man? "I hope you and Celeste can work things out," I finished lamely, unable and unwilling to absolve him yet. His presence still made me nervous, and I shifted closer to Jeremiah.

Ethan saw the movement and sadness flickered through his eyes. "Take care of him," he told me, the statement a surprise, then turned and walked back out the door.

I peered up at Jeremiah who was watching the entryway his old friend had just exited through. He must have felt my gaze because he turned his head to look at me. My lips parted as I was struck yet again by how beautiful he was, and lifted one hand to caress his face. One large hand slipped up and covered mine, and he placed a soft kiss on my palm that sent sparks through my body. Without thinking, I threw my arms around his torso and buried my head in his chest, tamping down the sobs that threatened to form. *I'm safe.*

And I knew, beyond a shadow of a doubt, that I was irrevocably, madly in love with the man before me. The emotion burst through me, leaving me lightheaded at the realization that I was head-over-heels for the hard yet tender man I'd met only a short time before. Even the logical side of my brain, the part that had railed against such a silly notion before, was in silent agreement.

Jeremiah's arm came around my shoulders and he kissed the top of my head just as another guard came through the door. I peeked sideways to see that the younger man looked nervous. "Um, sir . . ."

"Yes, Andrews?" Jeremiah replied, keeping me tight against his body.

Andrews swallowed, seeming reluctant to speak. "Government officials just arrived at the gate," he finally said, placing his hands behind his back and standing straighter.

The military stance seemed to give him more confidence. "They're here to collect your brother."

I blinked, confused, then looked up at Jeremiah. His face was blank for a moment, then he began to curse.

Ducking my head against Jeremiah's torso, I hid my smile at Lucas's deception and marveled at the day's events.

22

The restraints around my wrists pulled tight, the cool leather holding me fast. The restraints were supple, designed not to cause any irritation, but I'd had them on all night and most of the morning. There was some discomfort, but I was too caught up in other sensations to really notice. Light streamed through small cracks in the heavy drapes, but the room stayed dark and secluded, the perfect getaway for what we were doing.

Jeremiah's lips traveled up my spine, teeth grazing my naked skin as he moved back up my body. Fingers skimmed over my hips, tracing along the sides of my breasts against the mattress. My breath caught as his knee slid between my legs, and I felt his hard length press along my thigh. A hand smoothed my hair to one side as he rained kisses along my neck and up to my ear, teeth tugging gently at the cartilage. My hips rose in silent supplication; he nipped my earlobe but obliged my need, slipping easily inside me.

I sighed, my eyes fluttering closed. Our lovemaking had

been frenzied and passionate before, but now, hours later, the edge had worn off and it was much easier to enjoy ourselves. Jeremiah insisted I stay bound to the headboard, subject to his every desire, and it never occurred to me to deny that demand. His authority and domination helped chase away the bad memories; I was safe, secure in his grasp, and focusing on that allowed me to enjoy the pleasure of the moment.

He rummaged for something, hips continuing to move his hard length in and out of me in long sure strokes, then the small vibrator I wore clicked on again. I let out a gasping breath as his arm slid under my waist, lifting me up to my knees. Fingernails skimmed along my back as he thrust harder, and I grasped the headboard for additional support.

"So beautiful," he murmured, hands caressing my back and over the globes of my backside. "Everything about you is a turn-on."

I bit my lip, his words a balm to my soul, and pressed back for more. He surged inside me, drawing a strangled gasp from my lips. Fingers dug into the skin of one hip, an anchor as he thrust repeatedly inside me, our coupling no longer a leisurely affair. I braced myself against the wooden headboard, shameless moans and cries being pulled from my throat. The tiny vibrator, perfectly positioned so as not to interfere with his access, sent waves through my body with each thrust and spiraled me higher and higher toward yet another orgasm. Other toys lay on the table beside the bed: floggers, feathers, dildos, and several items I wasn't sure what to call, but Jeremiah wasn't interested in any playing—no toys were used except the cuffs and the vibrator, both of which were more than enough in my opinion. I was spent and sore, but just as insatiable as the man inside me.

His thrusts became more erratic, a sure sign he was close to coming. My tired body tightened as well, bracing for another orgasm. I felt his breath along my neck, the rough stubble on his chin scraping along one shoulder. His hand snaked between my legs and pushed the tiny vibrator in closer to my body, straight on the throbbing center of pleasure within my folds, and with a strangled moan I came yet again. Every last bit of tension drained from my body, my forehead collapsing on my arms as my body shook, skin tingling from the overabundance of ecstasy I'd had through the night.

Jeremiah collapsed over me, spent, his welcomed weight pressing me farther into the mattress. I didn't mind at all, grateful for the contact. Eventually, he stirred and reached up to unbuckle the cuffs, freeing my wrists from the restraints. I wiggled around until I was on my back, staring up at his muscled torso. My wrists ached but I didn't care, as I ran my hands along his hard stomach and down his arms.

He drank me in with his eyes, gaze caressing me like silk. Behind his eyes I saw deep yearning, evidence of a hidden need, and love blossomed in my heart. I tugged on his shoulders, pulling him down atop me, and he came willingly, laying across my body so I could wrap my arms around him. His warmth and hard body made my soul sing, and I closed my eyes as I caressed his back. Being free of the restraints, however, made my mind free to wander, and even though I didn't want to dwell on events they still rose to the forefront of my mind.

A lot had happened over the last two days, but the most worrying was the investigation on Jeremiah. The government officials who'd arrived to pick up Lucas hadn't been amused to hear he'd escaped, and they also weren't happy to learn about the additional kidnapping drama that happened the same day. Accusations that he'd allowed his brother to escape paled in comparison to the storm created by the dead bodies. Jeremiah's use of his private helicopter over public areas, ironically enough, was the largest issue keeping his lawyers busy. We had, at least for the moment, been absolved of the deaths both on the property and along the waterway, but the violation of restricted airspace could still be enough to land Jeremiah in jail.

Hamilton Industries had also suffered a blow when Celeste had stepped down as COO following her kidnapping. Jeremiah didn't talk about it and I didn't pry, but I heard enough of his one-sided phone conversations to determine that she didn't appreciate being kept in the dark and put in danger, however indirectly. The status of the redhead's relationship with her husband was still a mystery, but I hoped she would forgive him. Time and space had given me a little perspective: Ethan had been between a rock and a hard place, and chose to save the one thing he loved most. I hated to think what I'd do in a similar situation.

In what I considered a comical twist of fate, I was finally performing many of the duties of a personal assistant for Jeremiah, taking phone calls and messages and helping with day-to-day business activities. It surprised me how much I enjoyed the fast-paced work; Jeremiah forwarded his calls to me and I helped set up his day and keep track of who needed what. To be honest, he threw me into the deep end, sink or swim, but I needed the distraction and I think he knew that. Anytime I slowed down or finished my duties, at those times when I had a free moment to let my brain think of something besides work, I'd invariably flash to an image or memory that disturbed me: the assassin's open wound, Anya's body in that bag, staring down the elongated barrel of the assassin's gun. I'd only managed to embarrass myself once by crying, but with each day the memories became easier to bear. Work, at least, allowed my brain to stay disconnected from the unpleasantness.

A hand slid beneath my head, lifting my head from its position buried in his chest. Jeremiah gazed down at me, eyes searching mine. He traced the outline of my brow, fingers light against my skin as he followed the contour of my face down along my jaw and neck. His caressed lulled me from my thoughts and I closed my eyes, giving myself over to this simple pleasure.

"You're thinking too hard," he murmured, his chest rumbling with the words. "Right now, I only want you to feel."

I gave a soft sigh and opened my eyes, my thoughts pulling me out of the moment. "Are we safe?" I asked, pushing my face into his hand and kissing a knuckle. "Do you know who Anya was talking about, who the person was that convinced her to hire the assassin?"

It was a discussion we'd already had, and I knew Jeremiah was well aware of the continuing threat somewhere out there. Anya's last words before the sniper started firing, mentioning a man she never named, was a dark cloud looming on the horizon. I could feel it casting a shadow over me, but worried more for Jeremiah. He didn't seem to be as intent on finding the mysterious figure as he was keeping me tied to this bed. I remembered my earlier conversation with Ethan at the hospital, where the former bodyguard talked about the CEO consistently shrugging off all kinds of danger. Jeremiah had already rejected his mother as a suspect, despite the new information and the fact that she fled without a word. His nonchalance toward the potential menace bothered me, and I couldn't tell whether it was confidence or if he was doing it for my benefit—I hoped it was the latter.

"We'll get it sorted out," he replied, kissing my forehead. "I'll keep you safe, I promise."

For a familiar argument, a familiar answer. His patience was frustrating, especially since I wanted answers now. *It's only been a few days*, I admonished myself. *You can't expect immediate results on a case with no leads*. Still, I hated being on the sidelines, unable to help in any meaningful way.

I pushed insistently at one shoulder, and Jeremiah rolled sideways onto his back, pulling me along with him so I was lying atop his body, straddling his waist. Tired as I was, I still raised myself from him, staring down at his beautiful face. He watched me, too, the fire in him slaked for now, his face as open as I'd ever seen. His hands smoothed up and over my breasts, then down to rest on my hips as he waited on me.

Everything in me sang at the sight below me. A girl could live forever and not get tired of this. I traced the lines of his muscles, then leaned down so my breasts pressed against his chest. Skimming his lips with mine in a feather-light kiss, I gave him a half smile as I whispered, "I love you."

"No."

My world stopped. For an instant I thought I was falling, but nothing had changed. I sat up straight, confusion racing through me as I stared down at the suddenly stony expression of the man beneath me. My mouth worked, trying to think of something to say, but it was as though my brain had shut down. Jeremiah's hands circled my waist and, as if I weighed nothing, he lifted me off and to the side, then sat up, swinging his feet off the bed. I blinked, the meaning of what had just happened beginning to sink in, and watched as he stood and picked up his clothing.

I looked back down at the bed, trying desperately to keep my breathing steady. Stupid, so very, very stupid. My fists balled up around the pillowcase as I held in my emotion, trying for the stoicism I'd always seen in his face. "Why?" I asked, unable to think of any other question to ask. There was a small break in my voice at the end of the word, but I forced my eyes up, thankful that I hadn't yet shed a tear.

He ignored me for several seconds, quickly buttoning his shirt, then pulling on his pants without looking at me. Finally he turned back to face me, his face as closed off and emotionless as I'd ever seen. The drastic change from only a minute ago was like a death knell in my heart.

He must have seen the distress on my face because he sat down on the bed beside me. "I don't think . . ." he started, then paused a moment in thought. "I'd prefer it if we kept any mention of love out of our relationship for the foreseeable future."

"Why?" I repeated, more forcefully this time. I was slowly breaking apart inside, and keeping myself together was becoming more difficult by the moment, but I needed an answer.

Jeremiah studied me, a clinical examination that was void of any of the tenderness I'd experienced at his hands since our meeting. "Let's think about this logically," he finally said. "You've known me for roughly two weeks now. Is that enough time to build any type of emotional attachment?"

He was being rational, voicing arguments I'd used on myself when the L-word first popped into my head, and part of me still agreed with him. But with every word he uttered, the cracks in my heart grew wider, expanding and multiplying and going deep to the quick. "I'm not asking you to say the same," I finally managed, but the words tore at my soul.

"Maybe not," he replied, "but . . ." He cupped my face, and I flinched. "Why ruin what we have with platitudes like this?"

Pain blossomed, but I kept my face steady. I'd learned from the best, after all. When I reached out to touch him he stood, perhaps a bit too quickly, and retreated back. Grabbing his phone, he added, "Now that you've been cleared in the preliminary investigation, you're free to leave the grounds for anything. With the police presence being what it is, I think we're safe from any more attacks for now. One of the guards can drive and escort you anywhere you want; just stay in contact as to your whereabouts."

A dull ache spread through me as he walked across the room to the door. There he paused, staring at the brass door handle. I thought for a moment he'd turn around and address me again, maybe explain himself further, but he merely turned the knob and left. The latch closed with a finality that was shattering, had numbness not taken over my heart.

Dimly, I felt myself climb out of the bed and go through the motions of dressing myself in clothes still strewn about the room. Cleaning myself up in the bathroom was almost an afterthought, a delaying tactic to keep from showing myself to the world, but when I finally stepped out of the bedroom into the rest of the house, only silence greeted me. From the day I'd arrived at the mansion estate, the house and grounds had been teeming with people, usually the guards or other staff. Now that the danger was past for the time being, they had been moved to their regular assignments, and the sudden famine of souls in the house echoed the painful emptiness within me.

I made my way down the stairs, bypassing the kitchen completely. Food didn't sound good right then; in fact very little sounded good at that moment, so I walked to the front door and peered outside. The air was chill, almost bitterly so. The milder weather we'd had for a while had taken a wintery turn. Snow flurries dotted the ground, but I didn't care that my nose immediately began to sting from the frosty wind. A black limousine sat right in front of the large doors, exhaust a billowing cloud of steam in the icy air. I couldn't imagine it belonged to Jeremiah. Surely he would have already left; it had been several minutes since he walked out. He'd suggested before that I could leave the grounds. Did he call this for me?

I'd stayed away from public places, keeping to the house and not leaving the estate even after the kidnapping attempt. I remained mindful that there was still somebody out there gunning for us, who was willing to use others to do his dirty work. At that moment, however, staring at the limo, I no longer cared—being shot through the heart couldn't hurt any more than this. I left the house and moved to the car, opening the door and sliding inside. The interior was warm, a marked difference from the outside air, and up near the front I saw the dark head of the driver. "Where to, Ms. Delacourt?" he asked.

"Away from here," I mumbled absently. Realizing the distance sound had to travel, I readied to repeat my answer louder but the car lurched forward, heading for the gates. I didn't bother looking out the windows; instead I just stared at my hands, deep in thought.

What if Jeremiah was right? What if my feelings were premature, too soon to be considered genuine? It was reasonable that Jeremiah would hold off on sabotaging a relationship by acting too soon; there were still too many unknown variables in the equation. At least, that was how the rational side of my brain saw it—a man like Jeremiah must have similar issues with moving too fast.

The limo stopped briefly at the gate, and the guards quickly waved us through. I peeked through the back window, watching the great big gates close again, trying to ignore the squeezing in my chest. And really, it was only one part of our relationship with which he took issue. Such a silly word anyway. Love. I'd seen how he looked at me, the way he touched and held me. *Really, Lucy,* I thought, *do you really need platitudes of devotion?* "Love" is just a word.

Right?

A sob welled up from deep inside, surprising me with the sudden depth of emotion. My hand went to cover my mouth, determined to hold the inexplicable grief inside, but I couldn't stop the shuddering breaths or the tears that abruptly appeared and flowed down my cheeks. It's just a word, I thought again, but the pain wouldn't stop. I knew what love was, I'd grown up in a household where it flowed freely. Wouldn't I have a better idea of what the emotion felt like than Jeremiah anyway?

"Is everything all right back there, ma'am?"

"Everything's just dandy," I replied, my voice thick. Then for an instant it all became too much. "Got my heart broken today," I admitted, "but I'm trying to get through it."

"Ah," the driver responded. "Well, my brother always was an idiot."

I was in the middle of rummaging through my purse for a tissue when the meaning of the man's words sank in. My head snapped up, grief and heartbreak momentarily forgotten, as I stared at the back of the driver's head through the small partition. A hat covered his head, and the mirror was angled in a way that made it impossible to see his face. "Lucas?"

"In the flesh." He pulled off his hat, uncovering dark hair. When he turned around to look at me, I saw that he wore makeup of some kind, presumably to get past the guards. His skin was lighter, the nose seemed bigger than I remembered, but the prominent scar on his cheek revealed his identity more than anything else. He gave me a quick perusal. "You look terrible."

His words pricked my remaining feminine pride and I sat up straighter, glaring at him through the tears. Focusing on the matter at hand was a great deal easier than the emotional roller coaster. "What are you doing?" I asked, striving for bravado.

Lucas shrugged one shoulder. "Apparently, I'm kidnapping you. I thought you of all people would recognize that fact."

I stared at him for a moment, flabbergasted, then groaned loudly. Slumping in the seat, I leaned my head back against the cool leather, suddenly too tired to think of fighting. Lucas watched me in the rearview mirror but I didn't care; all I wanted was to not think, not remember my last conversation with Jeremiah.

"Let me guess: you told my brother the dreaded *L* word didn't you?"

I didn't bother responding to his question, instead staring at the ceiling of the limo. Two kidnapping attempts in one week—I'm a very popular girl. The thought held little amusement, however. I just wanted to be alone to lick my wounds in peace.

Lucas didn't seem the least bit deterred by my silence. "My brother is a fool," he continued. "Any minute now he's going to realize what he's done and . . ."

The small telephone on the dash rang suddenly, startling me. Lucas chuckled. "That's probably him now."

I stared at the phone, torn. Thinking about that beautiful, cold face as I had seen it mere moments ago made my already bleeding heart break more. *Why?* I wanted to scream. This was more than a bruised ego—I honestly needed an answer. None of the last twenty minutes made any sense.

Lucas reached out and pressed a button on his dashboard. The ringing broke off on a flat note, and I gave the dark-haired man a startled but dubious glance. "Don't worry, ma chérie," he soothed. "By now my brother has probably discovered the drugged chauffeur and is mobilizing the troops, so to speak."

Speechless, I watched as he pulled us into another parking area alongside a long white limousine. A driver stood beside the front door, a large scary-looking man with sunglasses and tattoos across his knuckles. Lucas stepped out of the car and walked around to the back door, opened it, and poking his head inside. "Coming?"

My mouth worked soundlessly, still trying to grasp what was going on. "Why?" I asked finally. It was the same question I'd asked Jeremiah and held within it all the same doubts and anxieties.

"Maybe I need your help with something," the dark-haired man said, "or possibly this is because I've finally discovered my brother's weakness." Then his gaze softened as I pressed back into the seat. "Or perhaps I want to help you. I knew what would happen the moment I laid eyes on you." Sympathy flowed from his voice. "My brother holds everything inside, while you wear your heart on your sleeve for the world to see. Jeremiah rejected you when you mentioned love. Given that our mother and father are likely the ones to whom he compares the word, is his response so surprising?"

"Is this what happened with Anya?" I asked, looking up into his eyes. "Did he drive her to you in this same way?"

Lucas blanched, the unexpected question hitting him hard. "Not quite," he managed, struggling to compose himself again. "They never had anything more than a business relationship, although I think Anya wanted something deeper. It made my seduction easier . . . but enough of my past. Tell me: Did you ever tell my brother no?"

I flushed, glaring at him, but the sudden truth of his words hit me like a truck. Lucas must have seen my revelation because he continued, "Jeremiah is used to getting his way, and isn't above manipulating others any way he can to achieve his own ends. A valuable skill in business, perhaps less so in a relationship; the thrill of the hunt is what makes the final acquisition that much sweeter. How hard did my brother hunt you?"

As his words sank into my heart, Lucas motioned around the inside of our limo. "This car is being tracked. If we stay here much longer he'll find us. Once he's here, you'll be his again to do as he wants. Where's the challenge in that?"

I swallowed, heart still bleeding as a cold ache suffused me. Lucas reached inside, offering me his hand. The look on his face was mischievous but I saw pity and a familiar longing in his eyes.

"Let's make him chase us, shall we?"

castaway

1

Sweat lined the brow of the small man sitting across from me. The thin comb-over lay plastered to his forehead despite the cool air flowing through a nearby air vent. He hugged a briefcase close in his lap, not looking at any of the men who stood around the table. His eyes kept glancing toward the exit, as if all he wanted to do was bolt and make a run from the tension slowly escalating within the dark room.

I totally understood the sentiment.

"We haven't got all day," muttered a dark-haired Scotsman leaning against the far wall, but he was silenced by the morose glare of the blond man beside him.

Hands clapped down on my shoulders and I flinched. "Right then," came a cheery voice from behind me as my hands curled into fists beneath the table. "Now that we're all here, let's get on with the show. Who wants to start?"

Nobody shared his enthusiasm. Across from me, the thin man flinched at each word, looking like he wanted to melt into the floor and disappear. I swallowed nervously as silence again permeated the room. Finally one large man leaning against a nearby wall pulled himself upright. Everyone else in the room rose slightly in attention, unconsciously deferring to his leadership. "Loki," he rumbled, the thick Russian accent lending weight to his words, "now is not the time for your games."

"If not now, Vasili, then when?"

I noticed several others in the room grit their teeth at the jovial reply. Vasili grunted, then looked across the table from me. "Doctor Marchand," the large Russian murmured, "make your request."

The thin man started, glancing blankly up at the Russian. The hands on my shoulders squeezed enough to get my attention. "Your turn."

My turn? I half-turned toward the man behind me. "To do what?" I tensed as several sets of eyes in the room turned toward me.

"Translation, my dear. Dr. Marchand here is French."

I gave the arms dealer behind me a sharp look. If this had been any other situation, I might also have given Lucas Hamilton a piece of my mind. I'd been born in Canada and spoke fluent French, but I didn't like being forced into things. The dark-haired man behind me smiled placidly, quirking one eyebrow. His momentary glance about the room took in the other men before returning back to me—as if I needed a reminder.

I didn't even know where I was or why I was there; this was the first time anyone had addressed me since we'd entered the room. I'd been given a seat while the others glared

at one another, clearly trying to see who had the biggest . . .
well. I faced the Frenchman, pursing my lips. *"They say to
make your request,"* I translated in a dull voice. The pain of my
fingernails biting into my palm was the only thing keeping
me calm.

Marchand turned wide eyes at me, then licked his lips.
His mouth worked for a moment, as if working up the courage, then he murmured, *"I need help . . . smuggling medicines."*

"They'll want more than that, Doctor," I replied, trying to ignore
the eyes on me. Those slim hands never left my shoulder, but
for now their owner was as much the enemy as everyone else
in the room. *"Where is the medicine going?"*

Defiance sparked in the man's eyes for a brief moment,
then died as he looked around the room. *"To Africa. My hospital needs these supplies."*

I frowned. He sounded like an honest enough man, so
why was he here? *Probably the same reason I'm here,* I thought,
swallowing a bitter pill. *Because I have no choice.* "He wants to
smuggle some medicine to Africa."

"What medicines?"

"AIDS medication," I replied after a brief pause, translating
the reluctant answer from the Frenchman.

"Africa might be difficult," Lucas murmured, and I translated. "Greasing all the right palms there can be an expensive
proposition."

"If you can get them to the Caribbean, he can take care
of the rest." My stomach roiled as I listened to myself speak,
and I forced myself to breathe slowly. The urge to hyperven-
tilate and panic was powerful. I glanced up to see some of

the men eyeing me, and I turned my attention back to the table.

The blond man against the far wall whistled. "That's expensive stuff," he said, his voice a rough Australian accent. "Worth a lot on the black market too."

When I translated this, the Frenchman became incensed. "He insists it's for his village and surrounding areas," I explained as the doctor continued to gesticulate wildly. "He isn't going to sell any of it for profit."

"Too bad." The Australian's laugh was an ugly sound. "He'd get top dollar for it, especially down in Africa."

Doctor Marchand seemed to understand the gist of the conversation because his face turned red in self-righteous anger, but he stayed quiet. He sent an accusing gaze to me, as if I was the one who gave them the idea, and I glared back. I wanted to tell him that I was as much, if not more so, the victim here, but I doubted he'd believe me. *I didn't asked for this job,* I thought silently, trying to shrug off the hands on my shoulders. *Blame the slick-tongued snake behind me for that privilege.*

The big Russian in charge turned to the man behind me. "You can do this, Loki?"

"Indeed." Lucas moved to my side but his one hand stayed on my shoulder. I looked up to see his scarred face study everyone else in the room. "However," he added, quirking an eyebrow, "I don't think that's the whole offer. Am I correct, gentlemen?"

"Right you are, mate." The blond Australian stepped forward. "We'd like to add a bit of our own cargo to the lot, since you'd already be heading that way anyway."

The doctor glanced up at the Australian, then turned to me. *"What are they saying?"* he asked in French. I held up a finger, silently asking him to wait, as the conversation continued around me.

"And what would you be transporting?" Loki asked.

"The usual." Niall grinned. "May as well kill two birds with one stone with this little jaunt."

Lucas eyed the blond man. "You realized this is only to the Caribbean, right?"

"Yup. I just need to get this lot out of the country; distribution should be easier after that."

Loki nodded, as if that explained everything. "I'll need a full inventory."

The Australian man snapped his fingers, and a sheet of paper was passed across the table. Doctor Marchand followed the exchange, dark brows furrowed. Loki read the list and whistled. "Impressive. Valuable too."

"What is it?" the doctor hissed, leaning forward toward me. *"What are they talking about?"*

I stared at the doctor, unsure how to respond. Surely he knew what manner of folk he'd fallen in with. *"How did you meet these men?"*

"When I wasn't able to get enough medicine through approved channels, I approached one of my benefactors for help. He set up the meeting but I have not met the men in this room before today." The thin man slapped one hand on the table, inadvertently drawing attention to himself. *"What is it they say?"*

"Weapons," I replied, sick to my stomach. *"Guns more than likely. They'll be added to your shipment."*

"Non!" Marchand banged both fists on the table and stood suddenly. *"Tell them this is unacceptable,"* he insisted, the briefcase in his hand waving about like a bludgeon. *"This was to be a medical operation; I cannot allow them to . . ."*

Around the room, guns appeared in several hands. The Frenchman stuttered to a halt, his eyes going wide. My heart clenched in shared terror as the men in the room trained their weapons on the doctor. "No, wait," I exclaimed, rising to my feet, only to be pushed back into my seat by the hand gripping my shoulder. "Please, I misinterpreted something." Turning to Marchand, I said, *"Please, think about your patients. If you die now, they'll never have help."*

"If I allow this to happen," the doctor replied, voice high and fearful, his gaze moving between each of the men holding guns on him, *"then I will be to blame for those who come into my clinic because of these weapons."*

His words were like a suckerpunch to the gut. *"Mr. Marchand,"* I begged, *"please sit. This will happen now whether you want it or not, and all we can do is make the best of it."*

The doctor's eyes swung between the men and my face, then with his hands still up on either side of his head he slowly lowered himself back into the seat. The defeat on his face was heartbreaking; he hugged the briefcase to his chest and, from the glare he gave me, I knew I was now firmly lumped in with the "bad guys" category.

I felt like one, too.

"What did he say?" the Australian asked, watching me intently.

"He, um, didn't know about the addition to the shipment."

The other man snorted. "Of course he didn't, love, or he'd never have agreed to throw his money in the pot. As long as he doesn't do that again."

"He won't, I promise." I glanced at the doctor. The thin man's glare nailed me to my seat, and I prayed he would keep quiet.

The Scotsman stepped forward at some silent order, wrenching the briefcase out of the French doctor's arms and setting it on the table. He unlocked and opened it, and my breath stuttered as I beheld more money than I'd ever seen in one place before. "This should cover the up-front costs," the Australian continued. "I am, however, open to certain . . . negotiations."

There was a smug note in the man's voice, and when I looked up I saw him watching me, a lascivious look on his face. His eyes darted down to my chest, his grin widening, then he barked a laugh when I adjusted the shirt higher. "Your little translator amuses me," he said, glancing briefly at Lucas. "Give her to me for twenty-four hours, and you can have ten percent of the profits."

My heart froze, ice shards tearing through my body. I dug my fingers into my thighs until one of the nails broke. The pain jolted me upright, and the hand on my shoulder tightened.

"Ten percent? That's a generous offer."

I twisted my head to see if Lucas meant what he said, but the arms dealer didn't look at me. His gaze was set on the Australian, who was in turn watching me. The blond man leaned close, his hazel eyes searching mine. This close, I could see even in the low light that fighting and age had destroyed the finer edges of his face. His nose was crooked, the white lines of scars stood out on his chin and forehead, and one ear sported a thick layer of cartilage I'd seen on boxers. Even then, he might have been considered ruggedly handsome if not for the decidedly evil twinkle in his eye. I immediately dropped my eyes, and heard him grunt in approval. "She wears fear well."

Behind me, Lucas shifted, clucking his tongue. "And here I thought you were a married man."

"My wife knows her place, and knows better than to question what I want. Whether I take some on the side is no business of hers."

"Ah. Then you wouldn't mind a trade then?"

The blond man blinked, the smirk slipping from his face. Abandoning me, he peered up at Lucas. Jealousy flickered across the Australian's face. "What are you saying?" he growled.

"Your wife for my little translator." When the other man's face mottled in rage, Lucas smiled. "What, are you afraid what your wife might think about a real man?"

"You son of a . . ." The Australian grabbed at the gun on his hip, then the giant Russian was there.

"Enough," he stated, muscles in his arms bulging as he crossed them over a wide chest. Vasili leaned down until he was face to face with the blond man. "Niall," he murmured, addressing the Australian. "Do we have a deal?"

Niall glared at Lucas, then down at me. The hand on my

shoulder clenched ever so slightly, the only sign of Lucas's strain over the argument. Niall subsided. "We have a deal," he said bitterly. Not speaking another word, he signaled to his men. The Scotsman pulled the French doctor upright, dragging the man out of the room with everyone else.

I sagged in my chair, rolling my head backwards in relief. I didn't even realize I was leaning into Lucas's hip until he moved, lifting the hand off my shoulder. Until he pulled away, I hadn't realized how much his presence stabilized me. Swallowing hard, I gripped my knees, grateful when he moved away but ironically missing his strength.

"That wasn't so bad now, was it?"

Vasili ignored him, studying me for a moment. The Russian's stony gaze wasn't as scary as the lascivious look the Australian had given me, but was unnerving nonetheless. "Where is Anya?" he asked finally, thick accent rolling the letters of the other woman's name.

Emotional memories of a beautiful blond woman dying on the ground resurfaced, and I bowed my head. Beside me, Lucas's smile faltered, then finally fell from his lips. "I required a new translator."

Vasili paused, then nodded. "Too bad," the big man murmured, expression never changing, "I liked her." He waved toward the door. "You may leave. I will contact you when ready."

Lucas pulled my chair back and I stood, skittering away when I felt his hand on the small of my back. His response was to pull me tight beside him as deep, thumping music washed over us. We reached the end of the stairs. As one man in a bouncer shirt pulled the rope gate open for us, we exited out into the chaos of music and flesh.

Before today, I'd never been inside a strip club. Two platforms connected both sides of the room, with naked women gyrating on tall poles at each end. Additional poles rose around the room, but most of the action here was done off the stages. Topless ladies entertained the various men seated in plush couches dotting the room. We moved slowly around the back of the club, Lucas keeping me in front of him, and I watched as two women led older businessmen behind curtains to our right. Neither woman was smiling, but that didn't seem to bother the men, whose gazes were not focused on the strippers' faces.

The women were all beautiful, but none of them seemed happy to be there. They ignored my presence completely, and I stayed tense and nervous until we got outside.

Lucas's big driver met us near the door with the car. After so long in a dark place, the bright sunlight momentarily blinded me. I shielded my eyes with one hand as Lucas led me forward toward the car. I climbed inside the limo first and crawled to the far end, while Lucas sat in his normal seat near the door. I studiously ignored the man, staring out the window.

"You did well in there," he said after a moment.

"Not like I had a choice," I replied bitterly, watching as we left this area of the city. I didn't even know where we were; buildings rose up all around me, blocking out any landmarks that could tell me my location. In the short time I'd lived in

New York City and its surrounding areas, I hadn't given my-self time to explore, so the street signs meant little to me.

"There is always a choice," Lucas replied, his voice even. "Sometimes, there just isn't a good one."

I turned to look at my erstwhile captor, but he was staring out a window at the passing city, not at me. Lucas was somber, an expression I hadn't seen on the man's face before. There was always a sneer, a snide remark or some sarcastic comment, but never this kind of quiet introspection. The change threw me for a loop and reminded me of another man who looked so similar.

My heart clenched at the thought of Jeremiah, and I stared down at my hands. *I wonder if he's searching for me.* Not even four hours before, I'd been snuggled in bed with the man I loved, and my life couldn't have been more perfect.

Now I was here.

"Why did you kidnap me?" I asked suddenly, searching for something to drive away the aching loneliness.

A ghost of a smile danced across Lucas's lips. "Would you believe it's because I enjoy your company?" he asked. I snorted. He shrugged one shoulder. "I thought not."

"If you needed an interpreter, you could have asked." *Preferably someone else*, I added silently, crossing my arms.

He looked at me. "What would you have said if I had asked?"

"No."

A true smile graced Lucas's lips. Even from across the car the familiarity of those blue-green eyes on the somber face struck me. *He looks so much like his brother.*

Beyond their appearance however, the two men were as different as could be. The scar bisecting the face of the man before me was only one outward representation. Lucas was lean, lacking the broadness of his ex-Army brother. His hands, I noted absently, were nothing like Jeremiah's. The billionaire's were rough, a workingman's hand, while Lucas's were smooth and well manicured. They were the kind that, to my mind, had never before seen a day of hard labor.

"What do you want, Lucas?" I asked, suddenly tired of everything.

"What do *you* want, Ms. Delacourt?" he mused, watching me intently.

"I want to go home."

"As do I."

A snide remark was on the tip of my tongue but I bit it back as I saw the rueful look on his face. Ignoring him again, I stared out the window. "You could have at least warned me about what was happening in there."

He said nothing to that and we lapsed back into silence. I watched the city pass by without really noticing anything until finally, we turned down an alley and into a gated parking garage. Some trepidation crept over me as we pulled through another inner gate and parked beside an elevator.

"Ah, finally." The light tone was back, and when the door to the limo was opened Lucas scooted sideways and out. "Coming?" he added a moment later, poking his head inside the vehicle.

The urge to stay in my seat came over me again—our last stop had been an unwelcome surprise—but after a moment's contemplation I walked hunched over through the long cab to the door. Ignoring Lucas's hand, I pulled myself out into the cool air, but instead of backing away to give me some space, the wretched man moved in close.

Unable to back away, I turned my head, irritated by his proximity, as he ran a finger down my face. His hand came under my chin, tilting my head back around to face him. "Anger, not fear," he murmured, and then a self-satisfied smile split his face. "I can work with that."

He stepped away, giving me some space, and I breathed a sigh of relief. The driver closed the door and pulled the car away as I reluctantly followed the dark-haired man toward the elevator. Lucas ran a card through a slot and inputted a code of some kind, and then I heard the contraption start its descent.

"Where are we now?" I asked as he held the door open for me. I kept on the opposite end of the small room, and thankfully he didn't try to invade my space again. "Some other meeting where I might get shot?"

"Not quite."

The elevator went up and up, and I wondered how tall the building was. The panel had a single floor button labeled Penthouse, and I realized this elevator was meant only for the top floor. Eventually, the lift slowed, then with a *ding* the doors opened directly into a bright, thoroughly modern living room.

Hmm. Not quite what I was expecting.

"After you," Lucas said.

I stepped out of the elevator, gazing around the spacious

room. The ceilings were tall, with lights hanging down on thin wires to just above head level. Two skylights let sunlight stream inside, but the room was lined with windows that overlooked the New York skyline. The furniture was a pale cream, almost white, and all leather with a few colored accents. It certainly didn't look like much of a bachelor pad.

The doors closed behind me, and a faint *click* came from the panel beside the elevator. A quick glance showed the red light glowing, and I guessed that I was stuck here for the time being. Swallowing back my nervousness, I followed slowly as Lucas moved further into the room, disappearing briefly around a corner. Stepping forward, I looked around and saw that the kitchen was nearly as big as the living room. There was a clink of glass, then he called out, "Wine?"

"Um." He was acting like I was his houseguest, not a captive, and it threw me off. "Water please."

"Coming right up."

While he moved around the kitchen, I shifted further into the living room. The penthouse was modern, with thin steps beside the kitchen, leading up to another floor. I'd spent the last few weeks living inside a huge house in the Hamptons, and while this wasn't quite as luxurious nor as large, it came very close in feel. "Is this place yours?" I asked.

"One of them, yes."

I wasn't sure what I expected from the gunrunner's home, but it certainly wasn't this. As far as I could tell, Lucas Hamilton had a sarcastic, colorful personality. I would have thought his home would be just as ostentatious as the man himself.

This loft, however, looked more like something out of Ikea than Cirque de Soleil.

"Why am I here?" The question poured out of my mouth, all of my frustration behind the simple phrase.

Lucas handed me a bottle of water. "Because we both have something to prove to my brother."

"Can I leave?"

"No."

"Please?"

Lucas sighed. "Would you like a tour of the place?"

"No, I'd like to go home."

"To that little Jersey City apartment, or back to my brother who rejected you?"

I wish I hadn't told him that. My words had been an accident, but the damage was done. The reminder still stung and I swallowed, mouth dry. "He didn't reject me," I murmured, but there was no conviction behind my lie.

Lucas put a hand on my elbow, guiding me around the leather couch. "Sit," he said, and sat down on a matching chair across from me. "Whether he rejected you is beside the point. He needs to learn how to appreciate you, and I need your language skills. If one can help the other, where is the problem?"

I stared at him incredulously. "What world do you live in where you can kidnap people and force them to help you?"

"My world."

I unscrewed the cap off the water, taking an angry swig and wishing it was something stronger. "For someone who says they want to go home," I said bitterly, "you sure seem intent on barreling down the wrong road."

Lucas said nothing to that, and when I finally looked up I found he was studying me intently. I looked away, not wishing him to see how badly I wanted to get away. Not just from him, but from everything.

"It's been a long day," he said after a moment, standing up. "The first bedroom upstairs on the right is made up for you. Let me know if you need anything."

I didn't pause to consider the odd statement but stood up quickly, not wanting to study it too closely. Almost to the stairs, I heard him call my name and turned around. He watched me for a moment before speaking. "You know I never would have given you to Niall."

I swallowed, wanting only to be gone. "I know," I murmured softly. Even when I'd been sitting in that chair surrounded by the strange men, I'd known Lucas had my back. It made no sense trusting him, but I did, at least that tiny bit. Not wanting to talk any longer, I fled up the steps and bolted myself inside the bedroom. The tall bed had been turned down for me, and the shutters to the windows were all closed. Not bothering to take further notice of my surroundings, I climbed into the bed and pulled the covers around me.

The cocoon of blankets wasn't the most perfect shield from the scary world I'd been thrust into, but it would have to do for now.

I must have dozed off because when I finally threw off the sheets, I could see that it was already dark outside. The winter sun set early, and it didn't feel like I'd slept too much, but there were no clocks around to tell me the time. I discovered my room had its own full bathroom, which was a relief, as I didn't want to go outside that door anytime soon.

I thought I heard voices downstairs but ignored them, surveying what was laid out on the granite countertops. Lucas had prepared for my arrival. The bathroom had hair brushes and curling irons, as well as a fully stocked medicine cabinet. I picked up a brush and, looking close, saw a pale blond strand curling around the handle. It wasn't much lighter than mine, and I quickly set the brush down as I realized to whom it had belonged, and whose bedroom I was now occupying.

A quick stroll through the walk-in closet confirmed my suspicions. Gowns, dresses, shirts, pants, all in sizes far too small for my figure, hung in neat rows separated by color and type. I even identified the dress Anya Petrovski had worn when I first met her, the flashy number an eye-catcher despite the low light.

Okay, yeah, this is weird.

There was a knock at the door and I swung around as if caught snooping. *Don't be silly, Lucy,* I chastised myself, still closing the closet behind me. *He put you in here. Obviously he expected you to look around.* There was something not right about looking through a dead woman's things, however. As much as I'd dislike Anya in the brief moments I'd known her, all I could see now when I thought of her was the pale, tear-streaked face lying in a pool of blood.

"Knock-knock?" Lucas called, breaking me out of my reverie.

After a moment's hesitation I unlocked the door and peeked outside. Lucas filled the entryway, leaning casually against the doorframe. In one hand he held a half-empty bottle of wine, in the other two glasses. "May I come in?"

The urge to say "*No*" was on the tip of my tongue. *This is a bad idea,* I thought even as I stepped aside, allowing him inside the room. "You here to let me go?" I asked, crossing my arms.

"Nope, just wanted to talk." He seemed momentarily distracted, looking all around the room as if taking it in. I couldn't see his face so had no idea what he was thinking, but got a clue when he picked up the picture of Anya I'd been staring at. Sympathy curled inside my heart as I remembered that, right behind the Russian girl's tearful face, I'd also seen his desperate one. He'd tried to save her, but there hadn't been any chance, and Anya had died in his arms.

I put my hand out toward his arm as he laid the picture face down, then pulled it back as he turned around. "Thirsty?" he asked, holding out the glasses. When I shook my head, he shrugged. "More for me then."

"You're drunk," I said, giving him a wide berth.

Lucas held up a finger. "Not drunk. Buzzed." He stumbled, leaning against a nearby dresser. "Okay, maybe a tiny bit drunk."

The bottle he carried was nearly empty, and I stared at it disapprovingly. "Is this normal for you?"

Lucas shook his head, paused to think about the question, then shook his head again.

I rolled my eyes, the last vestiges of sympathy burning away. "This isn't winning you any brownie points," I said, but my traitorous mouth tipped up into a small grin despite myself.

"I'm curious what my brother saw in you."

My smile vanished, as did any patience for dealing with the man. "You can leave now." I marched across the room and opened the door. "I'd like . . ."

I turned to see him standing only inches behind me, and my words stuttered into silence. I hadn't even heard him move. I pulled back a step and came up flush against the wall between the bathroom and bedroom doors. Lucas pushed forward, far too close for my comfort, and I put a hand against his chest to keep him back.

It's a curious thing, having someone that attractive standing so close. Even though I didn't particularly like the man, there was no denying he was handsome, or that his proximity made my stomach do flip-flops. The scar across his nose and cheek only served to accentuate his features. The smell of expensive wine was like faint cologne, not at all the cloying odor I would have expected. Beneath my hand, I felt the play of muscles beneath warm skin and silk, and I swallowed.

His fingers pushed a strand of hair out of my face, running along my brow, and I shivered. I pressed back against the wall and he followed, my hand the only thing keeping him at bay. "You're beautiful," he murmured, dipping his face down near my temple. Warm breath flowed against my cheek. "And smart. And fearless. Is that what my brother saw?"

Instead of offending me, his words created a jumble in my head. I stared fixedly at his shoulder, refusing to meet his gaze. His other hand came up to caress my shoulder. The touch burned down my arm, leaving a white-hot trail across my skin, and the hand holding him away weakened its hold, allowing him to press closer.

Perhaps if he'd tried to kiss me or touch me in any way that could be deemed improper, I might have found the will to push him off, but he seemed content to stand this close. Certainly that more than anything left me confused about how to respond. When the back of his hand slid down my neck and across one shoulder, I trembled, my belly clenching.

Remember Anya, part of me whispered. At that moment however, it was difficult to hold my thoughts together enough to remember my own name, let alone the bedroom's previous occupant. I leaned my head back against the wall as another hand glide across my collarbone, the touch feather light. My eyes fluttered shut, giving in to the fragile grace of skin on skin.

Until I met Jeremiah, I hadn't realized how desperately I craved contact. My family was gone; I was alone in the world. For three years, I'd pushed aside all else, striving to preserve their legacy to me, until I'd lost my family home to the creditors. After that, my existence was a struggle to survive, to stay one step ahead of homelessness. Jeremiah Hamilton had plucked me from that reality, his touch making me feel more alive than I had in years. Now he was gone, but that burning desire, the need for human contact, remained strong in me, a live wire I couldn't yet cap.

Lucas leaned his forehead against mine, and as I opened my eyes I saw full lips mere inches from mine. Looking up into blue-green eyes with dark lashes rimming and accentuating the color, I felt my insides melt. "So beautiful," he murmured again, tilting his head to look at me. Then he leaned forward, warm lips pressing against mine.

There was no demand to the kiss, so for a moment I did nothing. He sucked on my lower lip, grazing the soft flesh with his teeth. I didn't kiss him back, my body stiff with indecision, but Lucas didn't seem to mind. When I felt the first dart of his tongue however, my lips parted of their own accord, instinctively allowing him access. My hand on his torso, which had kept him at bay before, gripped tightly at the dark silk, pulling him against my body.

If I thought the soft seduction was all Lucas had, his sudden hunger surprised me. Pressing me hard against the wall, his mouth burned across my lips, and I gave a small sigh. A hand slid around the small of my back, pulling me against his body as the kiss deepened, his tongue teasing me, encouraging me to be a bit bolder. It had the desired effect. I slid my arms around his neck, arching up to him, opening my mouth and allowing him access while at the same time meeting his own ardent advances. Hands curling through his longer hair, I moaned into his mouth, fingers dancing down along his ears and across the rough stubble on his jaw.

"God, you're hot," he murmured against my lips, hands slipping beneath the waistline of my pants to grip my hips. I reveled in his touch, wanting everything suddenly, wanting . . .

Jeremiah.

Guilt stabbed me through the heart, the effect like a bucket of ice water over me. I broke off the kiss with a gasp. Lucas didn't notice the change, his lips falling to nibble tempting patterns on my neck, and an answering fire rose within my belly. My body seemed content to continue what was happening now, while my brain pleaded with me to end this. I rolled my head sideways, and caught the image of the blond Russian woman staring at me from the framed picture. "Is this what you did with Anya?"

The reaction to my question was immediate. Lucas stopped what he was doing, then stumbled back, staring down at me for a moment. The swipe of cold air that swept across me in his absence made me shiver, and suddenly tears threatened to overwhelm me. His eyes followed mine down to the picture beside us, and emotion twisted his face. "Yes," Lucas muttered, staring blankly down at me. "This is exactly what I did."

He stumbled sideways, wrenching the door open beside us, then disappeared around the frame. I slammed the door behind him, bolting it shut, and dove back into the bed. My heart hurt badly, and tears streamed down my face as I tried to drown out the world around me. *Jeremiah,* I thought again, imagining the man's face, his thick arms around me. *I should have given you a chance to explain . . .* Explain what though? I'd whispered my love in a moment of candor, and he'd run from the house as if chased by bees.

Muffled thumps and crashes came from downstairs, but I didn't pay attention, too caught up in my own misery. *How did this happen to me?* I wondered, the events of the day racing through my mind.

What madness have I gotten myself into?

2

A high pitch shrieking tore me from a fitful slumber. Jolted awake, I scrabbled at my sheets, groping for the edge of the bed. The ground was further away than I thought, and I stumbled but managed to stay upright as I ran to the door. Ripping it open, I immediately smelled smoke, and raced toward the stairs, not knowing what to expect.

Lucas peered up at me from the kitchen. Sunglasses covered his eyes, but he gave me a bright smile. "Good morning, sunshine. I'm making breakfast. Care for some?" He had a fork in one hand and an unplugged toaster under his other arm, likely the reason for the fire alarm. Setting the chrome appliance back onto the counter, he moved toward the refrigerator. "How about eggs?"

I watched him, still momentarily stunned by my impromptu alarm clock. He bustled around the large kitchen, whistling a bright tune as he pulled the eggs out of the fridge. Shaking my head, my gaze traveled to the living room and my eyes widened in shock. "What happened?" I exclaimed, moving down the stairs slowly.

"Oh, this? I redecorated."

The room looked as though a tornado had come through sometime during the night. One chair was lying on its side, several paintings had been dislodged from the wall, and the wood coffee table had been flipped onto its top. Nothing looked broken as far as I could tell. It was a mess, but fixable. Eying it dubiously, I kept my mouth shut and avoided the room as I tugged on one of the kitchen stools.

Sitting at the bar and keeping the granite surface between me and my far too chipper captor, I pulled the toaster toward me and peered inside. Frowning, I grabbed the fork and fished out two of the blackest lumps of toast I'd ever seen. "You don't cook much, do you?" I said drolly, pushing the lumps toward him.

"Don't be silly." Lucas set the frying pan atop the stove, turning the gas burner on high, then began cracking eggs. "I've seen all the shows. It isn't that hard."

I watched silently, my eyebrows going up as I realized he had no butter or oil to grease the stainless pan. "Uh huh," I said, resigning myself to more fire alarms.

As the last vestiges of sleep left my system, I sobered up. "So what happens now?" I asked, leaning one elbow on the granite.

"What do you mean?"

"Can I go home?"

I couldn't quite read his expression from my vantage point.

He seemed fixated on the eggs, although he wasn't really stirring them. "It's not that easy," he said after a moment.

"Let me go," I pleaded, giving my pride a break. "I translated for you in that dirty little room, which probably makes me a criminal in some way." The thought made my chin wobble. "Lucas please, let me go. I don't want to become like Anya."

There, I'd said it. Lying in bed last night, it occurred to me that the other woman's death, and possibly her life, was a sore spot for the gunrunner. His reaction now confirmed my suspicion: the knuckles around the spatula in his hand whitened and he sighed. "All right," he finally murmured, but held up a finger before I could start cheering. "But on one condition: you have to attend this last meeting with me."

"What's going to happen?"

"It's cargo transfer, paperwork mostly. They requested everything be expedited, so everything is happening today. I want you there to make sure anything in French is correct, then once that's done you're free to go."

I sagged in relief. "Thank you," I said, smiling in gratitude. Behind Lucas, the first tendrils of smoke wafted from the pan. I motioned toward the oven. "You're burning the eggs."

Lucas let out a curse and pulled the pan off the fire. He quickly switched on the exhaust fan as smoke billowed out from the fry pan, but it was too late. Five seconds later, the fire alarm went off again, and Lucas cursed again.

The whole scene was comical, and I bit my lip to keep from smiling, to no avail. My mood much lighter since I was set to be freed soon, I pushed back the stool and rounded the corner into the kitchen. "Put that in the sink," I said, wrinkling my nose at the sulfur smell of burned eggs. "Don't run water on it," I added quickly, stopping him just in time from ensuring the smell would never leave.

A quick check of the pantry and refrigerator gave me the tools I needed. Two minutes later I was whisking together some batter.

"What are you making?" he asked, peering over my shoulder.

"Pancakes. And you are hereby banished from the kitchen." I pointed the whisk at him, careful to keep it over the bowl. "Shoo!"

"Ooh, I like a bossy woman," he murmured, then fled as I pretended to go after him with the wooden spoon still covered in burned egg.

Four hours later, I wasn't smiling anymore when the limo stopped along the water's edge. Lucas exited the vehicle first and I followed behind, staying as close to him as I could. If it had been Jeremiah there, I would have held his arm for support, but this wasn't the sort of situation the businessman would have willingly put me into. My only comfort was that, after this part, I was done.

I had no clue where we were. We'd left New York City far behind us; my apprehension rose the further we moved from the big city. Any hope of Jeremiah swooping in to rescue me died a slow death during that journey. I tried to comfort myself that I'd see him soon, provided Lucas kept his end of our deal. I wished it didn't come at the cost of having to do this again.

Niall and his men were standing ahead, with a large ship sitting in the water down a short pier behind them. I was no nautical expert, but while this wasn't as big as some of the cargo vessels I'd seen passing along the Hudson River, it was still large enough to carry just about anything. The ship was old. Lines of rust ran down from between the plates and rivets holding the hull together. It looked like at one time it might have been a fishing boat, with the bulk of its storage in the belly. If it was here, I doubted that was its use any longer.

"What's this piece of garbage?" Niall didn't look happy with the ship, jerking his thumb derisively toward the hunk of metal.

"You wanted a transport, here it is." Lucas didn't seem fazed by the other man's irritation. He turned to another older man standing apart from the Australian's group. "Has everything been loaded aboard?"

"Loaded and awaiting your orders."

Lucas nodded, but Niall wasn't finished with his tirade. "Mate, if I wanted a bloody lifeboat, I would have bought one myself!"

"The ship is sound and Captain Matthews will take good care of your cargo. And if you want my help getting your merchandise into the country, you'll use my ship." He grinned broadly at Niall. "Trust me, she grows on you."

The Australian didn't seem at all convinced, but Lucas obviously didn't care. "And where is the good doctor?" he asked.

Niall grunted. "He's taking a different route to our destination. We'll be riding with the cargo."

From the satisfied grin on the other man's face, I got a sick feeling there was more to it than that, but Lucas's smile never wavered. "Ah. Well gentlemen, let's make sure everything is to your satisfaction then we can leave and . . ."

"Oh no, we got other business to discuss." Niall pointed at me. "She's coming with us."

My heart stopped, but Lucas gave a light laugh. "I'm afraid the girl stays with me," he said, taking my arm, but stopped when the men at Niall's back pulled out their guns.

"You didn't tell me this little sheila belongs to your brother. Tell me, how much do you think he'd pay to get her back safely?"

I swallowed, fear causing my stomach to heave and roil. The guns weren't pointing at us, yet, but the threat was obvious. Lucas's smile never left his face, but it took on a flat note as he studied Niall and his thugs. "Quite a bit, I'd imagine." Lucas clapped his hands. The sudden sound caused two of the goons to raise their weapons. "Well then, Captain," he said to the man still standing next to him, "it seems like we'll be having a few guests. Make sure extra accommodations are prepared."

"Yes sir."

"Bloody right." Grinning at having won this argument, Niall stepped forward and reached for my arm. "You're coming with me."

I cringed back, prepared to fight tooth and nail, but Lucas stepped between us. He moved so quickly I didn't even see him pull the gun until it was already under Niall's chin. The big Australian jerked to a stop, rage and sudden fear making his face go florid as he glared at Lucas.

"Ms. Delacourt stays with me." There was nothing jovial about Lucas now. He leaned in close to the other man's face. "My ship, my rules. Do I make myself clear, Mr. Jackson?"

Niall looked like he was sucking on a lemon. Behind him, his men had their guns trained on Lucas and me. I prayed the gunrunner knew what he was doing.

"They'll kill you and the girl," Niall hissed, then grunted as Lucas pushed the gun harder against the tender flesh of his chin.

"Perhaps." Lucas smiled, a hint of amusement in his tone. "But you'll still be dead."

The two men glared at one another, neither willing to back down. When Lucas manually cocked the weapon the fire died in Niall's eyes. "Guns down," he called, and his men lowered their weapons. The blond man stepped back and Lucas lowered the weapon, although it remained trained on the other man. "You'll pay for that."

"I have many things to pay for," Lucas said. "This ranks low on my list." Putting his hand again on my elbow, he steered me away and toward a nearby gangplank. When I struggled against his grip, he didn't waver, forcing me up the narrow pathway to the ship.

"You promised me I could go," I hissed, trying unsuccessfully to wrench my arm free.

"Yes I did." Lucas's lips were pressed in a grim line as he pulled me along behind him down the side of the ship. Much of it looked like a walking tetanus trap, despite obvious attempts at whitewashing and other paint jobs. The boat dipped and swayed, rocking in the turbulent winter waters. As we rounded the main part of the ship, a cabin door loomed into the darkness. "Down here, but watch your step."

Water dripped from somewhere inside, but the stairway led into a cavernous opening within the bowels of the ship. Men were hard at work moving crates around on the bottom floor. Stairs and metal gangways wound around the open area, leading to different levels. Our staircase was long, running all the way to the cargo hold below. Lucas let me down a single flight then turned me onto a landing about halfway down. We passed several doors on the left before Lucas pushed one open, gesturing me inside.

The room was in much better condition than the rest of the ship. While small, it still had a queen-size bed, a couple pieces of furniture and, to my relief, its own bathroom. "Your home sweet home for the next few days," Lucas said as I examined the room. He ran a hand through his hair, the only indication that he was agitated. Like his brother, his face was hard to read, for once lacking its normal cocky grin. "There's tablets in the bathroom cupboards if you get seasick. Keep the doors locked to everybody but myself, and you'll be safe here."

"Oh, you promise?" I snapped sarcastically. "Like how you *promised* I could go home after this?"

He conceded my point with a tip of his head. "Touché."

"Lucas?" I called as he was closing the door. He paused and looked at me. "Is this what happened to Anya?"

"No. She thought the danger was romantic." He shook his head and sighed. "And I, great fool that I was, let her come with me."

I digested that as he shut the door, then hurried to lock it behind him. Collapsing backwards onto the hard mattress, I grabbed a pillow from above my head and covered my face. Oh, what a mess my life had become! Only a month ago, I was an office temp barely managing to get by living in the city. *How on earth did I manage to get aboard a gunrunner's boat?*

I was still lying there several minutes later, staring at the wood ceiling, when I felt the jolt of the ship taking off. Closing my eyes, I turned my head into the pillows, wishing fervently my life wasn't such a disaster.

Now that we were moving and away from the shore, the rocking surf grew more pronounced. My family had never been the kind to take boat tours, so I hadn't developed much in the way of a sea stomach. I was okay so far, but decided it was better safe than sorry and headed to the bathroom to chew a tablet.

Unlike my room in the loft, this one had obviously never seen a woman's touch. Spartan and threadbare, almost everything in the room was either bolted down or braced, which made sense for a seafaring vessel. Even the shelf nearby had a tall lip to keep the books from flying free, and I peeked through the titles. All of them were weathered and beaten, as if they'd seen extensive use. Some I expected, such as Sun Tzu's *Art of War* and Machiavelli's *The Prince*. Others weren't what I imagined to find in Lucas's room, such as Tolkien and C.S. Lewis. *Interesting selection,* I thought, thumbing through the various titles, and then I abandoned that area to look around some more.

A single picture sat on the narrow dresser. When I tried to pick it up, I realized it was glued to the surface ,so I leaned forward to peer closely. It was impossible to tell just how old the picture was, but I hazarded a guess that the two boys were Lucas and Jeremiah Hamilton. The shoreline looked like that of their Hamptons home, to which I'd recently been a reluctant visitor. There were no smiles on their faces, but the way they stood close to one another spoke of a bond that had apparently broken at some point between then and now.

There was a knock at the door, and I bolted upright as if I'd been caught snooping. Rolling my eyes and blowing out a quick breath, I unbolted the door and opened it to see Lucas standing in the doorway.

"Didn't I tell you to ask before opening?" he said, irritated at my lapse as he strode past me into the room.

"Yes, Master," I said sarcastically, getting an exasperated look from him. "What's this?" I pointed to the bundle he set onto the bed.

"Clothing," he replied, for the moment letting the matter of security drop. "I had them picked up before we left. And no, they are not Anya's old clothes. I sent a man to pick up something in your size last night."

I gave him a suspicious look. "How long were you planning on keeping me with you?"

"I have no idea what you're talking about," he said, gracing me with a big smile. "So, how do you like your new room?"

He was talking to me like we were best friends, which made me even more suspicious. *Then again,* I thought, *that's probably how he talks to everyone.* "Not bad," I said in a guarded voice.

"Good. Because I'm going to be staying here with you."

"Oh no you're not." The words poured out of my mouth,

a kneejerk response to his assumption. The idea of sleeping in the same room as the man let alone the same bed . . . "Nope, no way."

"Yes way." He poked the tip of my nose before I could pull away. "And you'll thank me for it. Besides, this is my room. You wouldn't expect me to bunk in a cot with my men, do you?"

"Yes," I blurted out, and Lucas rolled his eyes.

"I need to go make sure we make it away from the mainland all right. Hopefully I greased the right palms this time." He gestured around the cabin. "Make yourself at home."

"This time?" I echoed, but Lucas was already heading out the door. Letting out a frustrated groan, I locked it behind him, determined to keep it closed the next time he knocked. Then I went and grabbed a book, resigning myself to boredom.

An indeterminate amount of time later, there came a knock at the door. I was a quarter of the way through *Art of War*, having given up on Tolkien by the second chapter. I flipped the page, ignoring whoever was at the door. We hadn't made any stops since leaving, and I still wasn't in any mood to entertain visitors.

Another rap at the door, this one louder, had me rolling my eyes and putting the book down on the bed. "Who is it?" I called in a bored voice.

"Much better this time."

I crossed my arms. "You know, sarcasm won't get you through this door."

"What about food?"

My stomach rumbled at the mention, and I quickly unbolted the locks. Lucas stood in the entrance, a tray in his hand. "Mind if I join you for dinner?" he asked.

The polite question startled me, and I shrugged. "Sure." I moved aside as he brushed past. Smells reached my nose, making my mouth water, and I trailed after him as he set the tray on the dresser. "I take it I won't be eating in whatever passes as the cafeteria here?" I peered over his shoulder to see what he brought.

"The correct term is 'galley,' and probably not. I trust my men not to touch you, but Niall brought along a number of his own guards. I'm still not altogether certain of their intentions."

The thought of being the only woman aboard a ship full of men hit me, and I shivered. "Did Anya ever come aboard ship?"

Lucas nodded. "Not often, but on at least two occasions. She liked the attention." He threw me a droll gaze. "I don't think you'd appreciate it as much."

We ate in silence, which I was happy for. The food was decent and fairly healthy, even if the green beans were flavored with bacon fat. "Who's your cook?"

"Alexei. Claims he went to a culinary school, but I don't see it."

"Oh." The ensuing silence was awkward, but tolerable

enough. Lucas seemed lost in thought, which gave me a rare moment to just watch him. Somber like this, he looked so much like his brother. I found it hard to believe Lucas was older than Jeremiah. The man before me was slimmer and shorter than his ex-Army brother, but had the same features and dark coloring. The pale scar along his face stood out against the olive skin, differentiating him from his brother more than anything else.

It amazed me how different the two men were. Jeremiah had the broody, tortured thing going for him, while Lucas . . . I wasn't sure. He held a different type of mask in place, one that I found hard to pierce. There wasn't much brooding here, at least not on the surface; his lips more often than not were locked in a Joker-like smile, as if sarcasm and pleasantries could keep people away.

As much as I enjoyed puzzles, the Hamilton men were a bit out of my league.

"So am I stuck in here until we reach wherever we're going?" The question was matter of fact; I'd resigned myself to another bout of imprisonment by a Hamilton brother. *They certainly had that in common too.*

To my surprise, Lucas shook his head. "You're safest in here, certainly, but you can explore the ship if you'd like. Provided," he added, holding up a hand to keep me from speaking, "one of my men is with you at all times."

I frowned at him, which he appeared to ignore. "From one prison to another," I muttered, poking at the remains of my green beans. I'd been a "guest" at the Hamilton family's house in the Hamptons for nearly two weeks, forced to stay inside the palatial mansion. Despite my captivity, I hadn't fared well; I was shot at, kidnapped, and almost killed before my lover, an ex-Ranger sniper, had taken out my assailant right before my eyes.

The memory killed my appetite, and I pushed the plate of food across the bed. "What now?"

Lucas shrugged. "I don't usually come along for the ride on this kind of trip. I'm more a 'private charter across the sea' kind of guy who'd rather enjoy some tropical scenery and a Mai Tai." He winked at me. "I like the little umbrellas."

"Of course." Conversations with the scarred man were like talking to a child running in circles around your legs: twisted, but oddly amusing. "Five days, right?"

"Right. I'll think of something to get you home between now and then."

I wanted to believe him, but just nodded glumly. Lucas picked up the book off the bed, leafing through the pages. "Good choice," he said. "There's a lot of practical knowledge in here that doesn't have to apply to war only."

"Yeah," I muttered, taking the book away from him and staring at it in my hands.

"All warfare is based on deception." His finger under my chin brought my head up to look at him. "Appear weak when you are strong, and strong when you are weak. The art of war is to subdue the enemy without fighting."

By the third sentence I realized he was quoting the book. "Supreme excellence consists of breaking the enemy's resistance without fighting," Lucas continued, his tone soft. Those blue-green eyes dipped lower, looking at my mouth. "All is fair in love and war."

"To know your enemy, you must become your enemy."

Lucas blinked at my quote, then looked back up into my eyes. A smile, probably the most honest I'd seen on his face, creased his lips. "Very true."

Suddenly shy, I broke off our gaze and rolled sideways off the bed. "Thank you for bringing me dinner." I was careful to keep the bed between the two of us.

"No problem. Get some rest, and I'll see you in the morning." He winked. "Don't wait up for me."

My eyes grew wide in alarm as Lucas, whistling now, moved over toward the door. "Sleep tight," he added, smirking, before letting himself out.

I puffed out a breath, exasperated. *Men.* Pushing the clothes to the ground in a heap beside the bed, I flopped back onto the mattress, staring at the ceiling. I wasn't the least bit tired, but I still pulled the comforter over me, grabbing the book and thumbing back to my place. *This is going to be a long week.*

3

There was no light from within the windowless room
when I awoke, save for the dim glow from a nearby
nightlight. The bed bobbed and swayed beneath me, reminding me via a suddenly queasy stomach that I was aboard
a ship. I flopped an arm sideways and was relieved to find
myself alone in the bed.

Pulling the sheets from my body, I paused when I heard a
faint snort coming from the middle of the room. Crawling
quietly across the bed, I peeked over the edge and saw Lucas
lying on the ground, fast asleep. The dim light still managed
to outline his shape and I bit my lip to keep from smiling.
The man was lying spread-eagle on the floor, taking up as
much space as he could. The blankets he had used for cover
and padding were twisted around his slim body, and from
the amount of skin showing . . . Blushing, I rolled over in the
bed, not wanting to discover whether he really was as naked
as he looked.

I waited a moment before pulling the sheets from around

my body, moving as quietly as I could out of bed and onto my feet. Grabbing the entire pile of clothing on the floor, I tiptoed around the dark man's prone form. The thin carpet was cool, the creaking of my footsteps blending in with the rest of the ship's noises. I breathed a sigh of relief when I locked myself inside the bathroom and quickly changed clothes, washing my face and pulling my frazzled hair back into a quick ponytail. Peeking out of the bathroom, I moved as quietly as I could toward the door, slipping into my shoes and a wool pea coat, then snuck out of the bedroom.

There wasn't a soul in sight, and I let out a relieved breath. From far below I heard someone cough, and there was a low din of voices coming from nearby. I tentatively made my way along the metal ground, moving toward the voices. The last room door was open, and as I poked my head inside all talking ceased. A roomful of large men stared at me.

Cafeteria, my mind registered, but the rest of me froze. I tried to speak but nothing would come out, so I just waved. That seemed to break the silence, and they turned back to their meals as I pulled my head back out of the doorway. *Lucy,* I thought, *you are such a ninny.*

Deciding against going downstairs, I headed toward the upper deck and had to push hard against the door to get it to open. Gray clouds covered the sun, so I had no idea what time I'd awoken. The wind blew across the deck something fierce, the deck beneath my feet bucking and diving. Ocean spray filled the air, covering me with a fine layer of mist within seconds. Pulling my coat tight around me, I held tightly to the thin railing alongside the ship, watching the ocean heave around me. I'd grabbed another seasickness tab earlier in the bathroom and was glad I took the added precaution. My stomach didn't like the rolling seas all that much, but otherwise I thought the whole thing fantastic.

I was the only one foolish enough to be outside this early in the morning. While that meant I had the deck to myself, I could also understand why everyone else preferred to stay inside as the cold penetrated my thick coat. Looking around, I noticed another entrance atop the deck and, staying close to the walls, made my way to the door. Pulling it open, I got a draft of warm air across my frozen nose, and quickly hustled inside. The steps here led upwards, and I climbed them hesitantly, peeking to see who was inside.

Smoky air filled the narrow cabin, the telltale smell of tobacco letting me know I wasn't alone. Voices mumbled overhead, and I poked my head above floor level to see two men sitting in stools bolted to the floor, looking out of windows lining the dash. I recognized the captain from yesterday, but not the man beside him. Both had the same look about them, gruff and weatherworn, but neither exuded the danger of the men I'd seen below.

"Well, lookit what the cat drug in."

I ducked my head, giving a shy wave as both men turned in their seats to look at me. The captain gestured for me to come up. "Well don't just stand there," he continued, old face wrinkling in a smile. "I promise ya, we don't bite."

"I used to," the man beside the captain said, then gave me a gap-toothed grin. "But I've already lost most of the worst offenders."

The captain gave the other man a slap upside the head, eliciting an amused squawk. Biting my lip to keep from smiling, I climbed the remaining stairs and into the captain's area. From my new position, I saw a foldout table sitting between them, with pennies sitting in a wide bowl at the center. The ship listed side to side more up here than down in my room, and I held on to the thick railing beside the stairs.

The captain held out his hand. "Seth Matthews," he said in a gruff voice as I stepped forward, "although nobody calls me by my first name." He jerked a thumb toward the other man. "This rowdy ass is my first mate, Francis Buttercup."

"Bouchard," the other man piped up, elbowing his captain then shaking my hand. "Call me Frank." His hands, like the captain's, were as rough as rawhide. He gestured to the table. "You play Poker, hon?"

Not waiting for an answer, the men fished out a stool from the captain's quarters right behind the wheelhouse, and I was dealt a hand of cards. The pennies were redistributed evenly between the three of us; apparently the two men weren't so cutthroat as not to share their wealth. The captain kept his eye on the ocean ahead, as well as the monitors and gauges on his dash, but was as active a participant in the game as anyone.

"Do you get many people coming up here?" I asked at one point, picking up a Queen of Hearts from the deal.

"Not really, and we try to discourage it when they do." Captain Matthews rubbed his head. "We don't aim to associate with most of the folks who come on this ship, if you know what I mean."

I let out a relieved sigh, glad not to be the only one who thought the same thing. "I've never been on a boat this big before," I said.

"First time at sea then?" When I nodded, the captain waggled his eyebrows. "Want to steer?"

My answer was a big grin and I was soon behind the wheel of the small barge, learning the not-so-subtle tricks of keeping a boat on track. "Oh, you should've seen my fishing ship," Matthews said, grinning at the memory. "She handled like a dream, cutting through the water like nobody's business. Fastest ship in the fleet, and with the best crew to boot. Nothing like this hunk of rust."

"This isn't your ship?"

"No, it is." Matthews didn't sound all that enthusiastic about the fact, but he still patted the dash as if comforting a pet. "We've put some serious blood and sweat into her to make her better and faster, so she's a bit of a sleeper. She may not look like much, but she can outrun most vessels her size. Still, it'll always be like comparing a tank to a high-end sports car."

His wistful tone made me smile and I was about to ask him to tell me more when a chill blast came from the lower entrance. I froze as I heard a Scottish voice say, "I thought I saw her come up this way, boss."

Niall's head poked above the deck, and a wicked grin split his face. "Well well, if it isn't the little sheila herself. We've been looking all over for you, darlin'." He waved dismissively at the men beside me. "You mates stand aside, she's coming with me."

"Yeah," Matthews murmured, "I don't think so." Both men moved in front of me, forming a thick wall. "She's staying right here."

Niall's angry gaze switched to the two men as I saw Matthews reach under the table behind him. "You'll do as I say," the Australian demanded, but his threats didn't seem to faze the seamen in the slightest.

"You gonna let him talk to you like that?" Frank asked calmly, not taking his eyes off the two men.

"No," Matthews replied, "I don't think I much like his tone."

Face mottling with rage at the defiance, Niall pushed his thick coat aside, showing the handgun at his hip. "She's coming," he bit out slowly, "with us."

Frank whistled. "He thinks he's a gunslinger, captain."

Matthews grinned. "That's not a gun." He glanced over at Frank. "I've always wanted to say this to an Australian." He pulled out what he was hiding beneath the table, pointing the shotgun straight at Niall. "Now, there's a gun," he said, lips pulled back in a grim smile.

Immediately both sets of hands across from me went up. "What is it with this bloody ship?" Niall raged. "I didn't pay good money to get treated like this. You work for me!"

"These men are mine, not yours," Lucas's cheery voice called up from the base of the stairs. I breathed a sigh of relief as he ascended, brushing past the two irate men. "Why don't you get downstairs and see what your own boys are up to?"

"Boss," the Scotsman warned, blocking Niall's path when the Australian looked ready to lunge.

Niall shoved his man out of the way and pointed a finger at Lucas. "That girl's ransom is mine, Loki." Niall slapped away the other man's grip but left without another word, banging the door shut behind him.

"Ransom?" Matthews looked at me. "You must be important to someone big to get that man's panties in such a twist."

"My brother." Lucas cocked his head at me. "Who doesn't know she's here with me."

Matthews whistled. "You're on your own there," he said, snorting. "I'm not getting in the middle of that one." The captain pointed a thick thumb toward Lucas. "Did he ever mention how I met this city slicker?"

I grinned, sensing a good story. The tension in the room finally eased as Lucas rolled his eyes and leaned against the console. "You going to tell everyone that story?"

"Only the ones I'm sure will hold it over your head." The captain gave me a wink. "I'm just off the job, at my favorite hole in the ground looking to unwind and get a little drunk. So this man comes up to me in a bar, dressed in a suit and tie, and asks me if I'm looking for work. Mind you, I stink of fish, haven't had a good shower in weeks, just got off my boat. Had to fire a friend's son from my crew because I caught him smoking weed, so I wasn't in the best of moods anyhow.

"He offers me big money, enough to get my attention. I still think he's a pretentious little ass though so I make him a deal: if he works for me on the boat, I'll listen to whatever he has to say. Lad here tries to play up his smirky bullshit but I'm not having it; frankly, I was happy to see his back so I could get back to drinking. Well, imagine my surprise when he shows up the next morning at my boat ready to work. Totally unprepared too, but still there." Matthews snorted. "I immediately regretted my offer, but I'd given him my word."

"You worked me to the bone," Lucas added, crossing his arms. The slight smile on his face took out any bite from his words, however.

"I worked you like I work any of my other greenies. It was the boys that gave you most of the flack." The captain looked over at me. "But wouldn't you know it, the little shit managed to get through it without breaking like a little girl. Even won the respect of my men for giving as good as he got while working hard. Means a lot when you're on the water. So when we get to land and I offered him his share of the take, he tells me to keep it and offers *me* a job."

"Which you took, if I remember correctly."

The captain shrugged. "Made more off that one little run than I'd brought home my previous season of fishing." His face turned introspective. "I miss the men, but they had families to take care of and I didn't want any of this shit to wash over onto them. Frank here," he nudged the first mate with his elbow, "wouldn't leave the boat, so he came along. Hell, we're old with ex-wives and no kids, perfect for this kind of life."

Picturing Lucas in bright waders, handling fish guts, proved impossible for my brain to fathom. He saw me watching him and gave me that trademark smirk. "What," he asked, "don't think I can handle myself with the big boys?"

I was saved from having to answer when a muffled *bang* came from below. Matthews immediately swiveled around in his chair and grabbed the wheel, giving it a few steers, then checked his instruments. "I've lost the engines," he said, amusement gone. "Rudder's still there, but we've got no power."

"Can I help?" I asked as Lucas hustled me down the stairs.

"Sure. Do you know much about diesel mechanics?"

Disappointment stabbed through me. "No," I muttered as we quickly moved to the stairs leading down to our room. The unfairness of my situation was getting to me: not only was I a prisoner, I was a *useless* prisoner.

Some of my frustration must have shown because when we got to the room, Lucas paused. "I need to keep you here for now. All my focus has to be on this, but I'll keep you updated on whatever we find. Will that work?"

Slightly mollified I nodded, and Lucas flashed me a smile that made my insides suddenly melt a little. "Don't forget to lock the door behind me," he said, stepping out of the room.

"Yes sir," I said, saluting smartly. My lips twitched into a smile as I slammed the door in his face. I locked it, true to my word, then went and sat down on the bed.

My eyes ran across the narrow confines of the room. *Wouldn't it be funny if I ended up dying here?* The morbid thought shook me, and I lay on the thin mattress, staring at the back wall.

I wished I could trace back what had caused me to become twisted up in this situation. Lucas was the easiest one to blame. He'd brought me onto this ship. My parents' deaths had kicked me off my college path, but I couldn't bear to blame them. Even now, several years later, their deaths stung too much to linger on. My life had been spiraling downwards for so long, and just as I thought my luck had changed . . .

Why ruin what we have with platitudes?

The memory of Jeremiah's words, spoken to me only a few days before, dashed across my heart like a scalding acid. I closed my eyes tight, fighting against tears that had already spilled too many times. His response to my accidental slip had made me leave the mansion, driving me into my current situation. I hadn't meant to say the words aloud; they just came out. *I love you.*

Like a slap to the face, he'd rejected the words, told me not to say them again, and then left the house.

Was I really so wrong to speak my feeling? The question bugged me more than anything. I hadn't expected to hear him say the words back. I was a rational girl: we'd been together less than a month, and that wasn't long enough for everyone. There had been no stipulations that the word was off limits; if I'd known he preferred those emotions left unsaid, I would have stayed silent.

The whole situation had blindsided me, but to blame him for my current situation? *That would be so nice, to lay all the blame at his feet.* I sighed. Sometimes I wished I were less rational.

There was a knock at the door. I sat up, then got to my feet and slowly padded to it. "Who is it?" I asked.

"Lucas."

The voice was muffled by the door but I grinned. "Figure

out something for me to do?" I asked loudly, unbolting the latch and swinging the door open.

Yellow teeth grinned at me. "Hello, love."

I tried to slam the door shut but suddenly there was a large body blocking my way. Abandoning the door, I raced for the bed, Niall only inches behind me. He grabbed at my hair but I managed to wrest myself free, running across the room only to be trapped by the far corner. Niall paused, seeming to glory in my helplessness, but when he rounded the corner of the bed I leapt atop the thin mattress, sprinting for the door.

I was in the open doorway, almost free, when a large hand grabbed around my midsection and hauled me back. "Lucas!" I screamed, and then I was knocked sideways into the bathroom doorframe, and the door slammed shut.

"Loverboy's on the other end of the ship." He grinned, teeth glinting in the low light. "I'd like to hear you scream my name."

He pressed me backwards and I rolled sideways off the doorframe, my hip slamming hard against the edge of the low dresser. The picture frame, previously stuck to the wood surface, broke free. As Niall leaned in, presumably for a kiss, I grabbed the frame up with one hand and brought it across my assailant's face. My grip on the item was flimsy and the blow glancing at best, but he still pulled back far enough for me to dart into the bathroom.

There was a pause as he surveyed the damage, then a roar of outrage. I tried to close the door but had no leverage, and Niall barged into the narrow room. The Australian's earlier amusement was gone; one hand gripped my throat and he slammed me hard against the back wall of the shower. Off balance and held up by one meaty arm, I scrabbled at his hand and he repeated the move twice more until stars danced across my vision. With his free hand, he wiped the side of his head, then snarled and showed me the blood on his fingers. "You little bitch."

He dragged me out of the bathroom and pushed me back toward the bed. Groggy, struggling to breathe, I fell backward across it and tried to pull myself away from him. He grabbed my legs, holding me to the edge of the mattress, then backhanded me across the face when I tried to sit up. I lay there, pain radiating through my body, as I heard the jingle of a belt being loosened. *No, please . . .*

What happened next was a blur. There was a crash and a bang, then Niall collapsed sideways, squealing like a pig. He crashed to the ground at the end of the bed, and I looked over to see Lucas advancing on him, gun drawn.

"You shot me!"

"Yes I did, and now you have three seconds to give me a reason not to do it again."

Reeling, I struggled upright to watch the entire scene. Behind Lucas, the Scotsman backed into the room with his hands up. Frank followed, holding the shotgun on the bodyguard. Captain Matthews stood beside them, his eyes focused on Lucas.

Niall moaned, rocking on the floor. "You son of a bitch!"

Lucas fired again, and I flinched as the Australian howled.

The bed hid the damage from me, but I heard the pain in Niall's voice.

"You're right about my mother," Lucas said, his voice dangerously light, "but give me something better."

"What do you want to hear?" the blond man said through gritted teeth.

"Why did you sabotage my ship?"

Niall looked perplexed. "Sabo . . . why the hell would I do that? No, no," he hastily added, waving his arms as Lucas stepped closer. "I swear, I didn't sabotage anything! Why would I jeopardize my own cargo?"

"Then I'm to believe your visit here was totally by chance?"

Lucas sounded like he was talking about the weather but, like I'd often seen with his brother, I sensed something dangerous behind the words. Niall on the other hand, didn't seem quite as tuned in. "I saw a chance, and I took it?"

The gun rose, this time aiming straight at Niall's head. Gone was Lucas's happy-go-lucky persona. The change was like flipping a switch; fury suffused the scarred face. Lucas stepped forward, laying the barrel against Niall's forehead as the Australian babbled, falling back to the floor and out of my sight completely.

"Son." At Matthews' gruff call, Lucas froze. The grizzled sea captain was watching the younger man closely. "Don't do it. Not in anger, and not here where the girl can see it."

For a handful of seconds it looked as though Lucas wasn't going to listen. I stared at the scene in shock; Niall had disappeared from view, cowering on the floor at Lucas's feet and begging for his life. The gun shook for a split instant and I saw the trigger finger compress, then the smiling mask came back over Lucas's face. "You're lucky that I'm a nice person," he said, raising the gun so it pointed at the ceiling. He signaled behind him. "Let his man take him downstairs, then lock them both in the hold with a first aid kit."

"You're going to pay for this," Niall muttered as the Scotsman helped him to his feet. It looked as though Lucas had only shot him in one leg both times. "I know people on the outside that won't take kindly when I tell them . . ."

Lucas lowered his gun again, casually firing at the good leg, and Niall howled, collapsing into his bodyguard. "Okay, so I'm not that nice." Lucas shook his head. "Lord save me from amateurs," he muttered as a sobbing Niall was led out of the room. Frank followed closely behind, shotgun trained at their backs. Lucas watched them leave, and then finally looked at me. "How did he get in?" When I didn't answer, he continued in an irritated voice, "I told you to ask whenever someone knocks."

"He said your name." I hunched in, hugging my knees. "I did like you said, asked who was there. I thought he was you, then . . ."

There was a *clunk* as the gun was set down, then arms encircled me. I flinched but they didn't let go, and as the adrenaline left me a shivering mess I clung to that anchor. "I'm sorry," he murmured against my hair as I leaned my head against his shoulder.

Matthews' voice wafted toward us. "I'll head down and keep an eye on repairs." I didn't bother to look, but Lucas nodded his head. "That boy took off like a bat outta hell when he heard you," the sea captain continued, obviously for my benefit, before he closed the door with a soft click.

I clung to Lucas, hiding my face when the sobs hit. Attempts at trying to stop the crying only made it louder, so I gave in to the anger and relief and rage, letting it wash over and through me. Lucas rocked me as I wept, the sobs threatening to tear me apart.

Eventually the emotions subsided enough that I could get a grip on myself again, but I didn't release my hold on the other man. When he made to pull away I clung tighter. "Don't go," I whispered. "Not yet."

He subsided, his hand stroking over my hair. Fingers skimmed down my back and I shivered, but he played the gentleman, keeping his hand from dipping lower. "I shouldn't have brought you aboard," he muttered, and I could hear the self-recrimination in his voice. "Hell, I shouldn't have even brought you into this. There were other arrangements I could have made, ones that would have kept you with . . ."

Lucas broke off and I raised my head off his chest to look at him. He was staring off into nothing, mouth pursed in a grim line, but met my gaze after a moment. I saw something spark in his eyes, and felt my own belly clench as I realized how intimately we were touching. My fists curled around the thin material of his shirt, holding him close. "Thank you," I murmured, pushing into the warmth and safety of his body. His scent and proximity overwhelmed me, but anything was preferable to remembering the day—no, *week*—I'd dealt with thus far.

"No problem." Lucas's voice was strained. I looked up into his face and instinctively understood the hunger I saw in his eyes. Memories of our kiss in the penthouse apartment intruded: the feel of his lips against mine, the scent that was his alone filling my nostrils.

"Lucy," he began, but I never knew what he was going to say because I tilted my head up and laid my lips against his.

He did nothing for a moment, and desperation took hold of me. *Help me forget.* Twisting in his arms, I wound my arms around his body, pulling him close . . . then he took over, his lips parting against my mouth. A sigh escaped me as he bore me back on the bed, pressing me against the mattress. He grabbed my wrists, bringing them above my head, and I moaned. He teased me with his tongue, a smile spreading across his mouth. "You like that, don't you?"

Yes. My hands clenched into fists, wanting desperately to touch him but relishing in the possession. Lucas's knee slid between my legs, pressing against my core, and I jerked, arching into him frantically. For an instant, the face of Niall loomed in my mind and I broke off the kiss with a gasp. Lucas laid his forehead against mine. "We can stop if you . . ." he started, but I shut him up with my mouth, and he didn't protest.

Securing my wrists with one hand, he pushed the other up my shirt, his lips moving to my throat as he thumbed a nipple. I moaned again, craving more, and wrapped my legs around his narrow waist.

"God you're hot," he murmured, shoving my shirt up and over my head. I helped as much as I could, not wanting to

break contact, but when I felt his warmth against my bare
skin I suddenly needed so much more. I struggled free of his
hold and pulled at his shirt, tugging at the pants and belt.
His chuckle at my clumsiness annoyed me so I pushed on
one shoulder, guiding him onto his back. Within seconds
I had his pants free, and somehow wasn't at all surprised he
went commando. I palmed him in my hand, running my
thumb over the thick head, and heard him gasp above me.
Refusing to think about it, I shimmied down the bed, fingernails leaving tracks down his torso, and took him in my
mouth.

He cursed loudly, hips jackknifing off the bed as I pulled
him deep. Fingers tangled in my hair as I kissed and sucked,
digging my nails into his hips for purchase. I flicked the bulbous tip several times with my tongue before pulling him deep
again, rolling my tongue around the thick shaft.

"Christ!" he exclaimed as I ran my nails down his inner
thighs, scraping my teeth along the top of his member ever
so lightly. The hand in my hair tightened, pulling me away
and up. I climbed back over his body, seeking out those lips
again. Lucas met me with a renewed vigor, rolling me over
backwards on the bed. "My turn," he murmured into my
mouth, fumbling with my pants then shoving them down.
I obliged, lifting my hips off the bed as Lucas tore the garments from my ankles, then squeaked as he flipped me over
onto my knees. Hands grabbed my bottom and I pressed back,
mewling with desire, but I wasn't prepared when he spread
my folds and pressed his face between my legs.

I cried out, surging forward, but his hands on my hips

kept me in place. Burying my face in a nearby pillow, I thrashed atop the bed as he licked and sucked. One hand moved from my hip, then long fingers reached deep into my core. Quaking, my whole body tensed like a coil, I was as much a slave to the sensations as if he had chained me in place. Nothing could take me away from the delicious torture, he played me like a master, and my body sang.

The crinkle of a condom wrapper was the only signal things were about to change, but I was too far gone to care. When his mouth left me, I groaned, wordlessly begging him for more. The lack of touch was unbearable, but I heard the bed creak as he repositioned himself behind me. Fingernails scraped down my back, his hands shaping my curves, and my grip on the pillow tightened.

When I felt his blunt tip probe my entrance I gave an excited mewl, and gasped as he entered me with one sure stroke. I was wet and primed, and the sudden stretching brought my orgasm racing to the surface. My cries were coming with each breath now, muffled by the pillow but still audible within the room. Everything inside me tightened, and I knew from the erratic jackhammering behind me that Lucas was close as well.

Then he shifted positions, the new thrusts touching just the right place inside me, and my orgasm rocketed through me. I gave a small scream into the pillow, waves radiating through me as Lucas continued thrusting inside me. Each stab suffused me in pleasure, adding to the sensual storm that had taken me over. However even he could not last forever, and with a strangled sigh he came, fingers gripping my hips tight. His head rested against the top of my back, panting breaths hot against my skin.

We lay like that for a moment, struggling to catch our breath. Finally he pulled himself out with a groan, leaving me while he cleaned himself up. I lay panting on the bed, eyes closed, waiting for the aftershocks to cease. After a moment he returned, wrapping his arms around my torso and pulling me sideways onto the bed. There was safety inside his arms, and I snuggled back against his warm body. "It might surprise you to know," he murmured against my ear, "that I'm a bit of an ass-man. Yours is definitely one of my new favorites."

A giggle escaped me at the unexpected compliment, and I burrowed against him, glorying in the way he held me tight against his body. I traced the outline of lean muscles on his torso and watched as they tightened and relaxed with my touch. For that moment at least, I allowed myself the comfort of his presence, the welcome relief of safety. The gun still lay on the small table beside the bed and I stared at it, absently running my finger around one small nipple on his chest.

We stayed like that for several minutes, the peace a blissful respite. I could have fallen asleep like this, but all too soon for my tastes he pulled away, disentangling his arms from around my body. Bereft of his warmth and suddenly realizing the door to the bedroom probably wasn't locked, I rolled myself in the comforter and watched Lucas get dressed. Seeing the play of muscles on his lean frame was a treat all its own; there hadn't been many beautiful men in my life before . . .

Jeremiah.

The name sobered me, ruining some of the enjoyment and afterglow of the moment. I look down at the covers around me, my skin prickling in confusion.

"I have something for you."

I glanced up to see Lucas holding something long and thin out toward me. Taking it gingerly, I turned it over in my hands. The gray metal object was light and cool, and to my surprise was hinged to open up into a knife.

"It's a butterfly knife. Easy to open and close once you get the hang of it." He took it back briefly, and with a couple shakes of the wrist had it swinging around, exposing the sharp edges. A few more flicks and the blade disappeared, and he handed it back to me. "Keep it on you and practice. It may not be useful in a gunfight, but it might give you enough time to escape in hand-to-hand."

I swallowed and nodded, my gut churning. Lucas tilted my head up to look at him, concern in his beautiful eyes. "I'll be back soon," he promised. "I need to go take care of things, namely getting our ship going again." He looked reluctant to leave, then leaned down and kissed me again. For that brief moment, my fears and doubts fled, washed away by the desire and security I felt from this man. It ended as soon as he lifted his head, and without another word he turned and left the room.

Staring at the knife, I leaned back against the pillows and contemplated my life. Three days before, I had told another man that I loved him. I'd never said that to anyone other than family, all of whom were now gone, never believing he would shove the words in my face. Now, I was kidnapped and aboard a smuggler's ship, stolen away by the brother of the man who spurned me. The brother whose scent was still on my skin.

You wanted no love, Jeremiah, I thought, turning the knife over in my hands. I gave it a casual flick and was gratified to see it open up for me, the two grips coming together in my palm. The sharp blade reflected the low light from above me, and then with another flick of the wrist it disappeared back between the two pieces of perforated metal.

I had never fallen in love until I'd met Jeremiah. His seduction overwhelmed me, taking me to places my heart had never been before. Amidst the danger and decadence of my new life, I had fallen for the billionaire, foolishly believing he had similar feelings. When, at a moment of weakness, I'd spoken the words in my heart, he had rejected the whole notion. Now here I was, not even a handful of days later, in another man's bed.

If sex for me equated to love, then what exactly had just happened?

4

Waiting around had never been my specialty, but it seemed that's what the Hamilton men expected. That didn't mean I had to like it.

I got dressed, played with the knife a bit, browsed books, stared at the ceiling, and twiddled my thumbs. As minutes turned to hours, the rumbling in my belly grew impossible to ignore. I hadn't eaten all day, and as the time went by I began to wonder if Lucas was going to come back before I starved. Even when the engines far beneath me finally roared to life, nobody arrived at my door.

Increasingly, it looked like I was on my own.

I stood at the door, staring at the handle. *Everyone who wants to hurt you is locked up. Hopefully.* The prospect of danger was becoming less important the hungrier I grew. Finally, when my stomach twisted painfully at an imagined smell, I gained the courage to open the door and poke my head outside.

A burly man lumbered past the doorway, but I was ignored as he moved quickly up the stairs toward the deck.

The lower levels seemed to be bustling with activity, rousing my curiosity, but I figured I would learn about it later after I'd grabbed a bite to eat. Tiptoeing was silly on the exposed metal gangway, but I moved as quickly and surreptitiously as I could, slipping inside the galley two doors down.

I breathed a sigh of relief when I saw it was empty, and made a beeline for the big refrigerator. I cringed when I saw what was inside. Raw meat sat open and exposed on plates. Containers with no labels held food I didn't want to check. Disappointed, I closed the big door and rummaged through the pantry nearby. Everything was in boxes except the sandwich bread, which I pulled out and checked. No mold that I could see marred the white surface, and as hungry as I was that was enough.

While not the most nutritious meal in the world, I scarfed down three plain slices before I searched around for sandwich material. I quickly ruled out anything in the refrigerator and began scanning shelves looking for something to put on a sandwich. I found no peanut butter, which I'd been hoping for, but did find a squeeze tube of something called Marmite. One whiff of the unknown topping had me quickly changing my mind, but as I turned to put it back, I noticed someone across the counter watching me.

Startled, I gave a little squeak, dropping the plastic container in my hands. "Um, hi," I said uncertainly, bending quickly to retrieve the weird spread.

The boy looked nervous to see me, which calmed me down a bit. He was much younger than most of the others I'd seen on the boat, closer to my age, so I attempted a smile. "I was looking for something to eat." At his blank stare, I realized there was a possibility he couldn't understand me. "Um . . ."

There was an unintelligible shout outside the door to the cafeteria, drawing my attention. The boy's head snapped around toward the rising voices, then back toward me. I recognized the desperation in his eyes.

Uh oh.

I bolted toward the door but wasn't fast enough. The boy grabbed my arm, spinning me around and sending me hard against a nearby table. People began filing into the room and he hauled me back against him. The glint of something reflective caught my eye, then I froze as a butcher knife was held against my neck.

Lucas pushed his way to the front, then stopped when he saw me. I glared at him, and the man had the gall to smile. "You must have the worst karma."

"I know, right?" I answered, exasperated, then the knife was pulled harder into my flesh. Every emotion evaporated except fear; when I swallowed, I felt the knife bite into the tender skin of my throat.

"Alexei," Lucas said in a low voice, smile fading quickly, "put the girl down."

The boy spat at Lucas, then let go a string of words in a language I didn't know. From the way he spoke, I knew they were curses, and all directed at Lucas.

"Kolya," Lucas said in a sharp voice, and the man I recognized as Lucas's driver stepped forward. "Please translate."

"Fuck you."

Lucas glanced at the tattooed Russian, then snorted. "I figured as much. Tell him to please let Ms. Delacourt go."

The big driver translated, but Alexei shook his head and let loose another round of angry words. "He said no," Kolya translated, obviously paraphrasing.

"Ask him why he sabotaged this ship."

"Sink everything." The words this time came from Alexei, who again spat at Lucas. "Especially you."

"Ah, the boy speaks." Lucas gave a grim smile. "And what, may I ask, have I ever done to you?"

"You kill my family," the boy snarled. "Your guns, slaughter them."

Lucas's smile slipped. "Who told you that?"

I realized he wasn't even bothering to deny the claims.

"I set bomb, but it not go right." Alexei ignored Lucas's question. "You at the bottom of the sea, then I see my family again." He indicated the room with the knife, shouting something else I didn't understand.

"That was for us," Kolya said when Lucas glanced at him. The driver's eyes were on Alexei. "For working with you."

"Ten years." Alexei's body tense with rage and pain, "I wait for revenge ten years. And now, I fail."

Lucas's head shot up. "Ten years was before my time," he said, face deadly serious. "I didn't sell those weapons that killed your family."

Against my back, Alexei's body began to shake. "You lie," he murmured, and I felt the tension in the room escalate.

Something in my pocket bumped against my thigh, and

a bulb went off in my head. *The knife!* I pulled it out slowly, lungs quaking with the fear of being caught, and unfolded it close to my body where I prayed Alexei wouldn't see.

When it was open I gripped it tight in my hand, but paused when I saw Lucas's hand make a patting motion in the air. *Don't make me wait.* I held off, hoping the gunrunner knew what he was doing. I tried not to swallow for fear the blade would cut deeper into my skin.

Lucas shook his head at Alexei. "Whoever told you I was the broker ten years ago is the liar, not me. Tell me, boy, who gave you that information?"

Alexei seemed to struggle with an answer, and my hand trembled around the knife. A tickle flowed down my neck right where the blade sat, and I knew I was bleeding. An inch deeper, and there would be a whole lot more blood.

"But you sell more weapons." The boy seemed to rally with this revelation. "You kill more families." The hands holding me tightened. "Why should I not kill yours?"

I wasn't waiting on Lucas anymore; I heard my death in those words. *You had your chance, buddy.* Shifting sideways, I plunged my knife backwards until I felt the sickening jolt of it hitting flesh, then bone. Alexei's cry rang out in my ear and we tumbled to the ground. The arm holding the butcher knife to my neck relaxed enough to let me push it away, but I still felt the tip graze my neck as we hit the ground.

In the tangle of bodies, I lost my grip on the butterfly knife, and panic scorched through me. Scrabbling along the floor, I glanced back to see Alexei still gripping the kitchen knife. He grabbed my ankle, pulling me back toward him. I slipped on the dirty surface as he raised the blade again, looming over me. Then gunshots filled the air and Alexei fell backwards, crashing back against the refrigerator.

Whimpering, I skittered across the floor away from the body, then beat at the hands that tried to help me up. "What the hell," I screeched, jumping to my feet. Adrenaline coursed through my body and all I could do was pace, heart racing and body jittery. "Why does this always happen to me," I demanded, unable to stand still.

Kolya reached down to the boy, checking for a pulse, but I already knew the big man wouldn't find anything. I dug my hands into my hair, pulling at it in frustration. At that moment, I needed to get away, be anywhere but on that ship.

Then Lucas was in front of me, blocking any escape. "Hold still."

I fought to get around him, and he grabbed my shoulders. "You're bleeding, let me take a look." His eyes narrowed when I still pushed him away. "Would you feel better if I slapped you?"

"Don't you dare," I said, glaring at him. The threat did manage to calm me enough for him to press a dishrag against the wound. I winced at the sting, and prayed the cloth was clean.

"I have a first aid kit in my bathroom. Kolya, take care of the body and figure out how Alexei got a bomb onto this ship."

I slapped away Lucas's hands again, determined to walk by myself. Then the world tilted and I screeched again as he lifted me up in his arms. All I wanted was to be left alone, but he carried me kicking and screaming back to the room, dumping me on the bed before shutting the door. He rummaged through the bathroom, and then came out holding a big red box. "Hold still. I need to look at that."

Still grumpy, I complied, flinching away with a hiss when the alcohol hit the wound. "My life was so boring before I met you and your brother," I muttered, holding pressure to the cut as Lucas rummaged through the first aid kit. "Is this some cosmic payback for being the dullest girl on the planet?"

"Perhaps," Lucas quipped, and at my dark look he laughed. "Go take a shower. I wouldn't touch anything that's been on those cafeteria floors, even you, without a thorough decontamination first."

I agreed: the kitchen had been disgusting, and I doubted the floors were any better. Closing myself into the bathroom, I stripped out of my clothes, started the shower, and then examined my neck in the mirror. Lucas used enough tape so water wouldn't get inside, but the area was tender. A faint red line trailed over one breast, leftovers from the knife wound. I shivered, partly from how close to death I'd come and the adrenaline leaving my body. Jumping into the shower, I let the warm water just flow over me for several minutes

The bathroom door squeaked open, and I heard Lucas enter. "Go away," I snapped, but he only chuckled. I heard him take his clothes off too, then he pushed the curtain aside and stepped in the shower. To hide my nervousness, I turned away and started soaping my body.

"Finish with that, then hand me the soap."

The commanding tone made my belly quiver, but I didn't reply. Handing the thin bar back to him, I rinsed off quickly, trying to ignore the man behind me. Lucas kept his hands to himself, which was a relief, but I couldn't face away from him forever. Finally I turned, closing my eyes to block out the view as I rinsed my back and hair. I heard Lucas make an appreciative noise and, despite the warmth of the water, my nipples pricked up in response.

"My turn," he said, and when I opened my eyes he handed me a soapy rag.

I frowned at him. "I'm not your slave." I gingerly took the washcloth despite my protest.

Lucas waggled his eyebrows at me. "Do you want to be?"

I rolled my eyes, trying for nonchalance, but it was difficult. Refusing to look down, I started scrubbing away around his neck and upper chest and was surprised by how much grime came away. "You're filthy."

"That's what happens when you're working on a boat engine all day long."

Indeed, the little rag I held was woefully inadequate for the job at hand. I rinsed it off twice, adding soap each time, before finishing with the front of his torso. Having the job helped me not focus on the feel of his muscles beneath my hands, or how I was naked with a strange, beautiful man in a shower. There was something intimate about showering together, and I wasn't sure my brain could handle more complications. I stopped scrubbing before his groin, but didn't miss the stiff shaft poking out toward me. "Turn around."

"Heh, bossy little slave."

He obliged and I scrubbed at his neck and shoulders, working my way down. This side wasn't nearly as bad, and as I reached his lower back I bit my lip in appreciation. He had a gorgeous backside, and my fingers itched to touch him, but I stepped back. "Okay, rinse off."

We squeezed past one another in the narrow stall, my heart skittering as our flesh met and slid. He washed the soap off, giving me a full and unabashed view, and this time I couldn't look away. Lucas was not as tall or muscular as his brother Jeremiah, but he was just as beautiful to watch in his own way. I came close to touching him a couple times, always snatching my hand back at the last minute. My heart was hammered and a dull ache throbbed between my thighs.

His eyes opened as he pulled his head out from under the stream of water and smirked when he saw me staring at him. "You going to wash your hair?"

"I, um." At a loss for words, I looked for a shampoo bottle then froze as Lucas took a step toward me. He cupped my breasts, thumbing the nipples, and I shivered. I didn't know what to expect with this man. He was alternately a gentleman and a rogue, but my body came alive at his touch.

He peered down at me, a lopsided smile on his face. "Once with you isn't nearly enough," he murmured, stroking my cheek. I couldn't stop the needy sigh that came out of my mouth, and saw an answering spark in his eyes. My hands sought out his body, tracing the lines of muscles along his torso.

Lucas thrust the shower curtain aside. "Out," he ordered, and followed me as we stepped onto the small rug beside the tub. He didn't bother with towels. I was swept off my feet and taken to the bed, his long strides covering the distance quickly. We fell onto the bed, each of us seeking out the other's mouth, hands moving across wet skin.

Our kissing wasn't the frenzy of earlier, but that didn't make it any less intense. I gasped again as his mouth slid to my neck, teeth nibbling and biting. A hand moved down the side of my body, opening my legs so that he lay between them. His lips came back up to mine, teasing and promising, and I moaned inside his mouth.

Once again he brought my wrists above my head, but this time I felt something loop around them. I broke off the kiss to look upwards at my bound wrists, then back at his cheeky grin. "I have a feeling you like this sort of thing," he said, grinning as I pulled unsuccessfully at my new restraints. I didn't even know where he'd gotten the cord, and certainly hadn't noticed it on my way to the bed. The rope he used was thick, half as wide as my wrists but with enough slack for my bound hands to have some freedom of movement.

Lucas seemed satisfied with his handiwork. "Now I can do what I please." He winked at me and lowered his mouth to suck one nipple. A rush of air escaped my lungs and I arched my back, craving more. He moved to lick the other nipple, teeth grazing the tip, then trailed his lips down my quivering belly. Slinging my knees over his shoulder, he gazed at me as I tried mightily to maintain some dignity, to no avail.

"I love the way you taste," he murmured, igniting a flame in my heart. Spreading my knees apart, he lowered his head, and at the touch of his tongue my hips surged off the bed. I strained against my bonds, thrashing and trembling as his tongue probed at my entrance. Fingers pressed against the sensitive tissue, opening me farther as he pressed his face against me, and I let out a loud moan.

"Ooh, a screamer? Let's make the boys below jealous."

I clamped my lips tight, clenching my jaw, as Lucas dipped his head again. My body jerked and spasmed at his ministrations, small grunts and cries still working their way free, but nothing loud enough to make their way past the door. Lucas did his very best to work my body, pressing all the right buttons and secret places until I was a tense, shaky mess.

He pulled his mouth away then raised himself up suddenly, lifting my hips off the bed. Twisting me sideways on the bed, he lifted one leg to rest on his shoulder as he pushed my body into position and thrust up inside me. I pulled against my restraints, a loud cry coming from my lips before I clamped them shut again. He didn't seem to be in any hurry, thrusting slowly and deliberately, hitting a point inside that sent shivers up my spine. The new position hit all the right places, and my orgasm rose quickly toward the surface, but Lucas wasn't ready to be done so soon.

He pulled free and spun me over again so I was laying face down on the bed. Grabbing the lobes of my backside, he gave them a little shake, then a teasing smack at my annoyed look. "I like playing with your ass," he said, giving me a cheeky grin. "Almost as much as I like plowing it."

His thumbs traced the crease, spreading me open as I pulled my knees up under me. I pressed my face into the pillow, tensing as one finger slid over my rear opening, but he bypassed that and moved to the sensitive flesh below. He positioned himself behind me, the thick tip pushing slowly inside. My belly clenched in anticipation and I heard Lucas hiss, his hands pulling my hips back until he was sheathed fully inside me. His forehead pressed against my shoulder blades, hands moving up to my waist as he pulled out then back inside, repeating the movement more forcefully a second time.

I grabbed the extra length of rope, holding tight as the thrusts grew quicker and more forceful. Moaning loudly into the pillow, I tilted my backside higher, nerve endings screaming at the pleasurable friction. Teeth grazed the skin behind my neck, and when the first bite came the sharp pain only added to the pleasure.

"God, you're sexy," he breathed into my hair. The compliment made my heart sing and I clenched around him, pushing back against his hips. He cursed and I grinned, doing it again. He plunged forcefully inside and I groaned into the pillow. So much pleasure, with my release just out of reach.

He pulled free and flipped me over onto my back. There was no pausing this time; he was back inside me within seconds, face only inches from my own. I couldn't hold in my cries but he covered my mouth with his, swallowing my moans and sounds. My legs wrapped around his narrow waist, locking behind his back. I sobbed as I felt the orgasm rise slowly toward the surface, threatening to overwhelm my senses. Pulling at my bonds, I ached to touch him, hold him against me.

"Let me see you come." Lucas's voice was breathless, his face inches from mine. Those gorgeous eyes were a deep blue, darkened with lust and need. The pale scar stood out, an angry slash on his beautiful face. Then my world was consumed by the whirlwind ripping through my body, every muscle tensing as I exploded. Even Lucas's lips couldn't hold my cry this time as I moaned and thrashed.

The scarred man continued to hammer into me, his breathing ragged, and every stab only made the waves continue longer. I closed my eyes, body beyond spent, as Lucas finally came deep inside, collapsing atop me. My heart thundered in my chest as we both struggled to catch our breath. "I didn't think it could get much better than earlier today," Lucas murmured, not even bothering to lift his head.

I didn't answer, my mind too blown to formulate a proper response. After a moment, Lucas pulled out but kept me close, his warm body a comforting weight bearing me down on the mattress. He released the rope from around my wrists, and my arms dropped limp to the pillow above my head. We lay there for a moment, struggling to breathe normally again.

"Why is it," I asked after a moment of silence, "that most of your men are Russian?"

The non sequitur comment drew a startled chuckle from Lucas. He folded his arms across my breasts and rested his chin atop one wrist, looking at me in amusement. "Many of my early associates were from Eastern bloc countries. Also, while Anya was with me, I had an easy translator for certain segments of that population."

His eyes clouded at the mention of the Russian girl, killed by an assassin not even a week before. "Did you love her?" I asked bluntly, aware of the awkward direction our conversation was taking.

He started to speak, then paused. "Maybe once," he murmured, apparently not thinking this was an odd discussion topic given our current position. "When I first met her, she was young and naïve. I was angry and selfish; stealing her away from my brother was a way to get back at him for taking over my life." He sighed, staring blankly beside me. "Times change. People change. I didn't do enough to keep Anya sheltered from this lifestyle, and now she's dead." He met my eyes again. "What about Jeremiah? Do you love him?"

"I . . ." My heart clenched painfully. "I thought I did." Right now, my opinions about Jeremiah were all jumbled, due in no small part to the man lying naked atop me. "He saved my life."

"I saved your life too. Twice."

I winced at the reminder, hand going to the bandage at my throat. "Yeah," I mumbled, dropping my gaze. A lump formed in my throat and I screwed my face up against tears. "When I told him I loved him, it was the first time I'd said that to anyone since my parents died." The memory was powerful enough to pierce my heart again. "He just called the words 'platitudes.'"

"My brother is an idiot." Lucas said it in a matter of fact way, as if the phrase was as common to his lips as breathing.

Then he sighed. "Love is a fickle and cruel mistress. Confusing as hell too."

"Yeah."

We stayed in amicable silence for another moment, then I put my hand up to my hair. "I should probably finish my shower," I muttered, grimacing as I felt the damp, tangled locks spread out over the pillow.

"I think you look fantastic," Lucas said with a straight face, and I swatted him on the shoulder. He grinned down at me. "In fact . . ."

He nudged my thigh and I realized, with some shock, that he was hard again. His amusement grew at my surprise. "I want to taste you again." His throaty voice set fire to my insides.

I ran my fingers in his hair as he gave me a soft kiss, and then closed my eyes as his lips trailed down my body once again.

We made love twice more before falling asleep curled up around one another. Time meant little in that dark room. No sunlight pierced the gloom, and nobody disturbed us.

Made love. When Lucas touched me, fingertips burning brands into my skin, I tried hard not to think about what those words meant to me anymore.

A loud hammering on the door jolted me awake. "Lucas, we need you outside," Frank's voice shouted through the door. "Captain swears he saw a boat coming up on us. Might be pirates."

I paused in confusion, but Lucas leaped out of bed, turning on a lamp and throwing on clothes. "Pirates?" I asked, failing to reconcile the peg-leg image in my head with the modern era.

"We're getting close to the Caribbean," Lucas said, stepping into his pants, "and a few roving bands of outlaws still prey on ships down there. I didn't think we'd come across any this far north though." He looked over at me. "You'd better get dressed."

He slipped out the door as I rolled out of bed, and I hurried to lock it behind him. Grabbing up clothes from the bathroom, I quickly dressed, keeping an ear open for anything strange. The tamping of feet outside my room shook the floor, but I didn't hear anything else suspicious. For a second I looked for the knife and then remembered that I'd left it stuck inside Alexei's leg. The most dangerous thing in the room was the picture frame. I clutched it, wishing I'd been left *something* with which to defend myself.

From somewhere on the ship, there came a series of pops. I froze, clutching the frame in both hands, the edges cutting lines into my palms. More footsteps sounded outside the door, quiet this time but I could still feel each footfall. *Don't come in here, please don't come in here . . .*

The handle shook, then a crunch as someone attempted to pound it open. I gave a terrified squeak, racing for the bathroom right as the door gave, slamming open. A black figure filled the doorway, and I stopped immediately when I saw the big assault rifle in his hands turn toward me.

The gun lowered almost immediately, and I screamed as the figure reached for me. Batting away the hand with the frame, I turned to run toward the bed, but an arm wrapped around my waist, hauling me off the ground. Thumping at the bare arm with the picture frame, my second scream was cut off when a dark hand wrapped around my mouth.

"Lucy," a familiar voice muttered in my ear, and I stopped struggling in shock. "I'm getting you off this boat."

The frame fell from my numb fingers, cracking against the thin carpet. The hand lifted off my mouth. "Jeremiah?" I whispered, struggling to turn around.

He put me back on my feet, and I stared up at the man. Black grime streaked his face and arms, but those oh-so-familiar green eyes blazed like torches. I put my hand out to touch his face, then covered my mouth, unable to believe what I was seeing.

Then from the doorway came the click of a cocking gun, and Jeremiah froze, head snapping upright.

"Hello, little brother." Jeremiah shoved me behind him as he turned to face Lucas.

The gunrunner quirked an eyebrow, then glanced at me. "Well, isn't this awkward."

5

I just had the most amusing thought. Do you want to hear it?"

Jeremiah glared at the smiling Lucas, but the gunrunner didn't seem fazed in the slightest. The grin on his face was stretched almost garishly wide, teeth shining white in the dim light, as he stared at his larger brother. "The last time we were in this exact same predicament, our positions were reversed. Didn't you have the gun pointed at *me*, little brother?"

"Loki . . ."

"Oh yes, I remember! You said I had to give you a good reason why not to kill me." Lucas cleared his throat dramatically, the gun not wavering a bit. "So, dear brother, it's your turn. Why shouldn't I kill you?"

"For me," I blurted out, trying to move around to the front. Jeremiah however shifted to keep himself between me and the gun, effectively blocking my path. His response annoyed me, but I persisted. "Lucas, please."

miah glanced back at me, and missed the brief dis-
intment that flashed across his scarred brother's face.
disappeared almost immediately, hidden by that manic
mile as if it never existed. "She said 'please,'" he murmured
conspiratorially, and for a moment I thought for sure he
would tell Jeremiah about what had happened in that room
only hours before.

"However, unlike my brother," Lucas continued, lifting the
gun to his shoulder, "I won't actually shoot family."

Jeremiah stepped forward the moment the gun moved toward the ceiling. I couldn't even call what he did grappling;
like magic, he tore the gun from Lucas's hand, slammed the
man against the opposite wall and turned the gun on him.

"My men however," Lucas continued quickly, grunting
at the effort of speaking with a compressed rib cage, "have a
rocket propelled grenade aimed at your ship and if I don't
call them off in ten seconds they shoot." He held up a radio
in one hand. "Nine."

"Call them off."

"Ah." Lucas glanced at the gun shoved in his face. "No.
Threats like this tend to turn me into a rebel. Sorry."

"Lucas . . ."

"Why yes, that's my name, and you know I don't bluff.
Six."

I stepped forward and grabbed Jeremiah's elbow. "I'm
fine, Jeremiah," I said, a little desperate. "Let him go."

The big man looked at me, eyes blazing, then back at his
brother who held up a hand showing four fingers. Cursing,

he released Lucas, lowering the gun, and immediately the gunrunner lifted the radio to his lips. "Give me another thirty seconds, and stay on them if they move."

"Yes sir."

Lucas lowered the radio. "Call your men off my ship, Jeremiah."

The two were standing nose to nose in a battle of wills. Jeremiah's hands worked at his side, clenching and unclenching like he fantasized wringing his brother's neck. Lucas seemed unfazed by the posturing, but a thick muscle in his cheek gave away his own tension. Seconds past, and I was ready to start wringing some necks myself when Jeremiah lifted a hand to his ear. "Pull out." He paused. "I'm staying here. Pull back to the boat."

I sighed loudly in relief, but neither man broke their stares. Figures appeared through the doorway, and I recognize Kolya and several others. They leveled their guns at Jeremiah as Lucas spoke into the radio again. "Let the ship go."

There was a significant pause, then another, *"Yes sir."*

"Strip him of his weapons and gear," Lucas said, "then take him downstairs. Don't take any shots at him, he holds grudges and doesn't play fair when he gets payback."

One of the men tried to grab Jeremiah's arm but the black-clad commando slipped easily from his grasp. He didn't protest however as they removed the assault rifle and side-arm, then looked at me. "Are you really okay?"

A lump formed in my throat at his simple question and the myriad complexities that came with it. "Yes," I whispered, a queasy churning starting in my gut. Then, without any warning, Jeremiah swept me into his arms and pulled my lips to his.

The kiss was as strong and solid as I remembered. For a moment, I lost myself in his strength, forgetting my surroundings and the stress of the last few days. The second the kiss ended however, it all came crashing back, a jumbled disaster that made my heart sick.

Jeremiah pressed his forehead to mine. "I'll get you home," he murmured, big hands cupping my face. Stepping away, he moved out toward the gangplank without another word, the two men with guns following closely behind.

"Make sure everyone is accounted for," Lucas told Kolya, who nodded and disappeared through the door.

I sat down on the bed, covering my mouth with one hand. I felt like I was going to be sick. Horror dawned as I was brought face to face with the potential consequences of my decisions, and I drew in several shaky breaths before I could look at Lucas. He said nothing, merely staring down at me in uncharacteristic silence. His mouth was set in a flat line, then without a word he left the room. The door clicked shut behind him, leaving me alone with my misery.

What have I done? Not even three days before, I'd said words that came from the heart. Now, I was left to wonder what exactly those same words meant to me anymore.

Falling back onto the bed, I pressed fingers into my temples to ward off the headache forming behind my eyes. *What did I feel?* Right at that moment, I wanted to feel nothing, but my heart wouldn't allow that. Every emotion under the sun swirled inside me like a churning cauldron. There was no making sense of anything, let alone make decisions.

I wasn't sure how long I sat there, wretchedly contemplating my future, before Lucas returned. A duffle was slung over one shoulder, and I watched as he stuffed clothing from the drawers inside without once looking at me. The lump in my throat grew bigger, and I had to swallow several times before I could speak. "Where are you going?"

"I'll be bunking up top with Matthews and Frank. You can have this room to yourself."

"Why?"

He said nothing for a moment, pushing clothes into the small sack. "My selfishness ruined the life of one innocent girl already." His normally expressive face was carefully blank. "I won't repeat that mistake again."

I watched him move around the room, picking up things he would need. One guilty subject weighed heavily on my mind, and finally as he threw the bag over his shoulder, I couldn't hold myself back anymore. "Does Jeremiah know about . . ." I started, but Lucas interrupted as though he'd been expecting my question.

"He thinks you are my prisoner, and you are. Anything else that's happened is up to you to tell." Lucas's voice was bereft of any emotion but at least when he finally turned around there was no condemnation. His mouth twisted ruefully. "You're free to leave the room, my men have strict orders not to touch you."

I flinched at his choice of words. *You're free to leave.* Jeremiah had said the same thing to me when I'd said I loved him. The memory stirred up more confusion in my heart as Lucas opened the door. "Don't go."

The words were barely above a whisper but Lucas paused, then turned back toward me. I couldn't meet his eyes, my vision blurring with sudden tears, but he set down the bag and knelt at my feet. A hand tucked a lone strand behind my ear, and I leaned into the touch. "Lucy," he said, waiting until I raised my eyes to his. "Tell me why I shouldn't leave."

"Because . . ." I stopped, unable to form a response. My mouth worked as I desperately tried to come up with a reason that made sense. Considering how unreasonable the last few days had been however, nothing convincing came to mind.

After a moment of silence, he nodded slowly. "I thought so." Standing back to his feet, I watched as he picked up the duffel and slipped quietly out the door, the latch clicking shut behind him.

I felt as though my heart was breaking, and couldn't understand why. Jumping to my feet, I paced along the room, nervous energy making me go stir crazy. I'd been locked up inside for too long; time had no meaning anymore. I had a vague feeling that, outside the metal walls, night had fallen, but right now I was wide awake and needed answers.

Something cracked under my foot and, looking down, I saw the framed picture beneath my foot. Picking it up, I saw with some dismay that I'd broken off an edge of the frame itself, but the glass had miraculously held up to the recent beatings. The two boys stared at me, so young and full of life and love. Their eyes lacked the anger and mistrust of the men I'd seen earlier, and I wondered if those days were forever gone from their lives.

Setting the frame carefully atop the dresser, I slipped on my shoes and opened the door. Jeremiah and Lucas would have to work out their differences on their own time. I had too many questions that I needed answered, and knew only one person who could do that for me.

Jeremiah's prison wasn't really a cell so much as a dank room at the bottom of the ship. The rumble of the engines was much louder here, the walls and floor vibrating from the proximity. Two of Lucas's men stood outside, but when they saw me, one of them casually unlocked the door. "Might want to knock first," one of them rumbled, and I noticed even in the low light that he had a dark bruise forming around one eye.

Taking a deep breath, I knocked softly against the wood door, then opened the door carefully. Poking my head around the frame, I found Jeremiah's hulking form sitting on a bunk. The large man stood to his feet as I came into the room, and I shut the door behind me to give us some privacy.

"Hi," I murmured, taking another moment to gather my thoughts by looking around the room. The room was small, with two sets of recessed bunk beds at one end and an open toilet at the other. A solitary light on the ceiling illuminated the room, showing me that Jeremiah had removed most of his gear and only wore the black shirt and pants now. Leftover war paint showed as streaks to his arms and face, but I could feel his gaze on my skin. It still took me a minute to get up the courage to look him in the eye.

"What happened?" he asked.

I knew immediately what he was asking, and it was as good a place to start as any. "After you left, I got into a limo outside the house that I thought you'd left for me. I had no idea it was Lucas behind the wheel. He drove me to another car, then offered to let me come with him."

"What did you say?"

"I asked him to take me back." My mouth twisted down at the memory. "So he kidnapped me for real, sending his driver in to drag me out kicking and screaming."

Jeremiah grunted, and when he shifted I became aware of his proximity. As much as I wanted desperately to touch him, there might as well have been a wall between us. He was less than four feet away from me, but neither one of us would take that first step. Finally, Jeremiah spoke. "When I heard they'd found one of my drivers tied up in the bunkhouse, I knew something had happened. Then I was told you weren't in the house, and Jared was found unconscious. I couldn't . . ."

Jeremiah cut himself off, and I saw a myriad of emotions race across his face. The stoic mask was gone, and he seemed to struggle with his next words. "By the time we started tracking the car, it had already stopped moving, and when we got there everyone inside was gone. You were gone."

My chest tightened at the unexpected emotion I heard in his voice. "So what did you do?" I whispered, scarcely able to breathe.

He stared down at me, green eyes bright in the dim light. "Moved heaven and earth."

I gasped, throat tight, and covered my mouth to hold in the choked sob. The wretched space between us disappeared; Jeremiah took the step we'd both been avoiding and pulled me into his arms, and I broke down. He trembled against me, thick fingers digging into my skin. Everything that had been weighing on my mind exploded out, and I cried against his chest.

He held me, stroking my back as my emotions leaked out. "I'm sorry I couldn't protect you," he murmured, squeezing me tight. We stayed that way for a long time, content to be touching one another. Eventually my sobs lessened and, drained of emotion, I clung to his solid mass.

He laid a kiss to the top of my head, both hands running down my back possessively. "That son of a bitch Lucas. You're *mine.*"

The words were out before I could stop them. "Your what?"

I don't know what I expected to hear from my spontaneous query. So much of my uncertainty and doubt funneled into that single statement, but Jeremiah paused. Disentangling myself from around the big man, I looked up into his face. "I'm your what?" I asked again, detachment growing in my heart.

The question seemed to confuse the other man, who frowned down at me. His reaction touched a nerve, and resentment built quickly. "When we last spoke," I said, keeping my voice low and embracing the anger, "I said some words to you which you rejected. So please tell me what I am to you."

"Lucy . . ."

"Don't." I stepped away, allowing the anger to flow. Rage was so much easier to deal with than pain; it allowed me to say the things I needed to get out. "You say I'm yours, but I'm not allowed to love you. So what am I? A responsibility? A liability?"

His chin came up. "I swore to protect you."

I gaped at him. Surely he understood what I was asking. "I don't care about my safety," I snapped, "that's not important right now . . ."

"It is to me."

"Why?" My last word was a shout, and Jeremiah straightened up. I waved my hands around my head, unable to contain my energy. Giving an exasperated groan, I turned away, rubbing a hand over my face. When I looked back, that stoic mask was back over his face, and I suddenly wanted to cry again. "Why do you think you can claim me, yet reject my love?" I murmured brokenly. "What gives you that right?"

He didn't answer for a long moment, and I almost turned to leave when he finally spoke. "Love isn't a happy ideal in my family." The mask threatened to crumble for a moment before clamping back in place. "I don't wish for the . . . complications love might bring."

My shock at his attempt to justify his actions faded quickly. "That may be so," I conceded, "but my parents were happily married for twenty-four years before they died. My grandparents, fifty-two. The words meant something to *me*." I sighed. "I never asked for you to reciprocate, I only wanted to tell you how I feel."

But Jeremiah just shook his head. "That word is a mere platitude. If the affection is there, why does it need to be named?"

Platitude. That word again. Oh, how I hated that word. My hands balled into fists, insides quaking at the sudden rage it induced. "You won't even try to see my side, will you?" If it didn't fit in with the way he believed, it was wrong. Was this the real Jeremiah? Had I been so blind this entire time?

"Fine," I snapped, not bothering to wait for his answer. "No love then. Let's see what that feels like." Without bothering to think about what I was doing, I grabbed his head and hauled his face down to me.

The kiss was a disaster from the start, but I didn't care. I'd surprised him, that was obvious, but Jeremiah recovered quickly. He pulled back and I followed, determined to teach him a lesson, if I only knew what lesson that was.

"Lucy," he growled, hands clamping around the tops of my arms. I abandoned kissing his mouth and moved down to his neck and he froze, not pushing me away. The acrid taste of sweat and salt water filled my senses, and for a moment I forgot myself. I skimmed my teeth along his skin and felt him shudder against me. My hands moved under the shirt, tracing the familiar pattern of muscles there. I heard the sharp intake of breath when I pressed myself close, nipping lightly at one nipple through the thin material of the shirt.

No love.

Pulling my hands off his body, I wrenched free of his grip and sank to my knees. I could see instantly that he was turned on by the play; his pants bulged beneath my fingers as I worked the clasps. He tried to grab my arms to pull me upright as I worked the clasps to his pants and I pushed at his hips. While he grabbed the bunk for support I unhooked his pants and reached inside.

"Lucy, stop."

"No love, you say," I muttered, ignoring him. "All we had was sex and a little danger. Why stop now?"

"That's *enough.*"

Hands gripped my arms and hauled me up to my feet. Jeremiah's face filled my vision. "It wasn't just sex," he exclaimed, shaking me. "I was . . ."

Crack!

My hand smacked across his face, stopping whatever he was about to say. The blow startled him; Jeremiah blinked down at me a few times before releasing my arms. "Do you feel better now?" he said, lips compressing into a thin line.

My slap had been from a bad angle, with barely any force behind it. The callous disregard in his tone fired me up again. "No," I answered, and balling up my fist I threw my arm into a hook, landing right in his jaw.

Pain bloomed almost immediately and I gasped. I saw Jeremiah stagger sideways at the blow but whatever triumph I might have felt was eclipsed by the agony in my hand. Moaning, I looked it over, tenderly probing the swollen flesh.

"Let me see it," Jeremiah said, but I skittered away from

him. At the same time, the door opened and both guards filled the entrance, presumably to see what was going on inside the room. Their presence made Jeremiah pause, and he seemed genuinely regretful as I straightened up. "Lucy . . ."

"Shut up." Cradling my hand to my belly, tears of pain leaking from my eyes, I glared at him. "I don't want to love you anymore, Jeremiah Hamilton," I said, my voice cracking on his name. "It hurts too much."

Not wanting him to see any more of my tears, I turned toward the door. The two guards parted to give me enough room to pass. I made my escape, fleeing upstairs to my empty cabin and praying nobody would see me.

6

I would have given into the temptation of staying inside for the rest of the trip had Captain Matthews not knocked on my door the next morning. "We just entered the Caribbean," he called through the door. "Thought you might want to have breakfast with one hell of a view."

The urge to say nothing, sit inside my little box and avoid any and all people to sulk, was strong. However, I'd never seen the Caribbean before; the furthest south my family had ever gone was the Carolinas for vacation. I got dressed silently, realizing it was rude not to acknowledge his offer, but when I opened the door the grizzled sea captain was still outside.

He whistled when he saw my wrapped hand. "I'll take a look at that when we get up top. Rumor is you tried to take down that bigger brother; looks like you gave it a hell of a shot."

I said nothing, but felt a traitorous smile tip one side of my lips. "He had it coming."

"I'll bet. Come on, Frank's broken out the pineapple. Our little tradition whenever we're down this way."

Following the older man up onto the deck, something inside me eased as the warm sun caressed my skin. Being cooped up in that windowless room, I realized, had kept me grumpy; my mood immediately lightened as I took in the sunny skies. The boat still rocked in the waves, but not nearly as badly as it had when we were farther north. Refreshed, I climbed the steps up into the captain's deck to find Frank and Lucas had already started eating.

"Hang on lass, let me get some ice for you."

Matthews busied himself putting ice into a plastic bag, but when Lucas saw my swollen hand his jaw immediately clenched. He was beside me in an instant, picking up my arm delicately; I moved away, not all that happy with the Hamilton men at the moment, but he persisted. Thankfully he didn't touch the still-painful digit, just giving it a close look. My knuckles had swollen overnight but I'd refused to put up a fuss. Pain medication and wrapping the hand in a towel before going to bed let me sleep.

I'm not sure what I expected, but the smile that tipped his lips wasn't it. "'Atta girl."

A surprised laugh pushed free as I pulled my hand away and sat down in one of the chairs. Frank steered the boat this morning but still managed to hog most of the pineapple. While he and Captain Matthews argued over how much of the tropical fruit to divvy up to the guests, I let my gaze wander outside. The windows on either side of the cabin were open, the warm sea breeze circulating the small compartment.

Outside, the ocean stretched out around us but the waters were tinged a pale green, different from any ocean I'd seen before.

Lucas leaned in close to me. "If you think this is nice," he murmured, nodding his head toward the sea, "wait until you get closer to land."

I pushed him away with my good hand and he sat back, grinning. As much as I wanted to be mad at him for bringing me on this journey, the mood within the cabin was too happy to ruin. A smile tipped my own lips as Matthews handed me a bag of ice, which I carefully laid atop my bruised knuckles.

Frank waved two decks of cards above his head. "Okay, who's up for a game of Pinochle?"

We made landfall late that afternoon, although we were in sight of the shoreline long before that. "Which island is it?" I asked the captain.

"Jamaica. Winter is the best time of the year too; can't get more perfect weather."

My first view of land however was somewhat lackluster. Palm and thick-leafed tropical trees lined the shoreline, but the ramshackle port we pulled into would not have been on any tourist map. Lucas went below, leaving me up top while he dealt with his business on the docks. The sudden reminder of what kind of ship I stood upon was a hard pill to swallow.

"How do you cope with knowing what you're carrying?"

I asked the two seamen, watching as Lucas's men started moving the crates off the ship.

"We don't look." Captain Matthews was somberly watching the proceedings below. "This ain't a dream job, but the money is good and neither me nor Frank put anything away for retirement." He sighed. "I hate lying to the boys that give me a call, wondering what their old captain's up to nowadays. That part stings the most, I think, but I want the lot of 'em to stay as far from this life as possible."

I couldn't imagine doing work like this for a living, and meeting good people like the captain and first mate confused me. Perhaps I could have vilified all of Lucas's men if I hadn't met these two; now, through the lens of their experience, I had some sympathy for the rest. And then there was my part, merely as a translator but my words and actions may have killed that French doctor. Pushing those thoughts out of my mind, I contented myself with staying as far away as possible, not leaving my current location until everything was done.

Until I saw Jeremiah being led down the gangplank to the docks.

The tension in my heart escalated as I watched Lucas's men escort a handcuffed Jeremiah to the pier, and suddenly I couldn't stay in my safe little box. "Excuse me, gentlemen," I said, making my decision. "I think it's time for me to go."

"It was good to meet you, missy," Matthews said, shaking my hand. "I hope to see you again someday, albeit under better circumstances."

I felt bad for leaving them and wondered if I was making

the right decision, but still hurried down the steps and around the side of the ship. The water here was more stable than when we'd left New York but I still took the gangplank to the shore carefully. Watching the bustling proceedings was very different than when I was up in the captain's area, and I didn't breathe easy until I was beside Jeremiah. I could feel the big man's gaze on me, a heavy weight that I tried to ignore. "I thought you never wanted to see me again," he murmured.

"I thought so too." I fought the urge to look at him, desperate to see his expression. I cringed toward him as a forklift veered dangerously close. The two guards still flanked the big man but despite the flurry of activity, I felt safest beside the ex-Ranger.

Loud cursing preceded Niall's arrival onto the docks. The Australian was supported by two of his men and didn't look at all thankful for their help. "Where's that son of a bitch?" he shouted, scanning the docks. "He's going to pay for what he did."

"Somebody called for me?" Lucas stepped out from between two crates, smiling at the furious blond man.

Niall pointed a finger at the gunrunner. "When Mr. Smith hears about what you did to me, he'll . . ."

"Mr. Smith can hear quite well, thank you."

Niall's eyes bugged out as another man stepped out of the shadows beside Lucas. "G . . . Good afternoon, sir," he stuttered. "Didn't expect to see you here."

"I didn't expect I'd need to make the trip." Smith was an older man, maybe in his mid-fifties, but he wore his age well. Silver hair streaked his temples, and the wrinkles on his face only served as character. Much like Jeremiah, he had a commanding presence you couldn't help but notice, and right now he didn't seem to approve of his Australian lackey. "Tell me, Mr. Jackson," Smith said conversationally, "where is Doctor Marchand?"

Niall licked his lips nervously. "My men couldn't find him before we left," he said, then quickly added, "sir."

"I see. So you didn't intend to take his shipment of supplies and try to sell them without my knowledge."

The blond man's mouth worked for a moment, his face white, then he shook his head. "No, sir," he whispered.

"Because word about special sorts of deals get around, and people frown on betrayal like that. Those feelings affect business, which isn't something I appreciate. Fortunately, I'm in a good mood today." Smith looked at the two men carrying the terrified Australian. "Take care of him."

The two goons who had been propping the man up suddenly became his captors, dragging the man quickly out of earshot. I clenched my fists, pressing my forehead against Jeremiah as Lucas asked, "What are you going to do with him?"

"Unfortunately, this one is my wife's nephew so my hands are tied. However, I don't think he'll make this same mistake twice. Thanks for the call, I'm certain the authorities will find the poor doctor eventually."

"A shame," Lucas replied. "There are so few chances to do any kind of good in this job, but the medicines will reach the doctor's hospital."

"Agreed." The two men shook hands. "Pleasure doing business with you as always."

As Smith walked away, Lucas moved toward Jeremiah and me. His gaze flickered to me as he pulled around behind us. Whatever he thought about my proximity to Jeremiah, Lucas kept it to himself as he unlocked Jeremiah's shackled wrists. "Sorry about the cuffs, I had to be sure you wouldn't do anything stupid."

Jeremiah rubbed his wrists. "I still don't understand how you can do this kind of thing."

"Practice makes perfect."

There was no smile on the gunrunner's face. As far as I could tell, he was being truthful to his brother, but not giving away much else. I was just stunned they were speaking to one another at all. "Didn't you two hate each other a few hours ago?" I asked hesitantly.

The chorus of "Yes" left me even more confused. The two men exchanged a glance. "We spoke last night," Jeremiah said in a careful voice. "Came to a few understandings."

I peered between the two men, expecting more of an explanation but not getting it. Standing in front of both men side by side, the family resemblance was pretty stunning. Despite the different physiques, both men had the same coloring and facial features, minus the scar across Lucas's nose and cheek. I'd seen scars as bad or worse on Jeremiah's body, a testament to the life he led in the Army Rangers.

Finally, Lucas spoke. "Come on, let's get to the hotel. Business always makes me hungry."

"Hotel?" I asked, trailing along beside Jeremiah. "We're not going home?"

"Not yet," Jeremiah murmured as Lucas led us to a large

SUV. "I'll explain later but . . ." He blew out a breath. "For now, we're safer here with my brother than in New York."

He didn't sound any more pleased by the situation than I was. Unfortunately, there was little comfort to be had from that realization.

The short ride to the hotel was quiet, tension between the siblings thick in the air. The two men sat on opposite ends of the vehicle with me alone in the center. The awkwardness made me somewhat happy that I had grown up an only child, and I was relieved when we pulled up to the hotel with little fuss.

I wasn't sure what I was expecting, but there was a distinctive island feel to our home for the night. Tiki torches lined the driveway and entrance, the small flames flickering bright in the dying light. A five-star resort this was not; it seemed more like a local hangout than a tourist dive. Our rooms were already reserved, with the clerk merely handing Lucas the keys as he came to the desk. I was relieved to find I had my own room, not realizing until the tension eased that this situation was something I'd been unconsciously dreading.

Of course, my room was sandwiched in the middle of the three. I sighed. *Hamilton men.*

"So can someone fill me in on what's going on?"

Ours was a late dinner, but the hotel restaurant showed no signs of slowing down. Music flowed from the bar area inside, and some of the guests there occasionally spilled outside where we sat, but for the moment we were still alone.

Dark trees blocked any view outside the grounds but there was a distinct lack of traffic. In quieter moments, I could still hear the ocean nearby.

"Somebody is doing their damndest to ruin or kill us." Lucas didn't sound too threatened by the fact, but then again even a gun to the head didn't faze him. "First it was the hit-man sent after Jeremiah, then a saboteur with a bomb I'm certain he didn't understand shows up on my ship."

"I thought Anya hired the assassin," I said, but both Jeremiah and Lucas shook their heads.

"Whatever she may have been," Lucas replied, "she wasn't evil enough to come up with this on her own. Someone coached her into that decision."

"I've got my men looking into it." Jeremiah didn't look hungry, as most of the food on his plate remained untouched. He seemed to be deep in thought, and occasionally sent glances my way, which I ignored. "I could tell you as soon as they discovered anything if you'd give me back my communication equipment."

"Like I told you last night, no matter the network you're working with, it's closer to the bottom of the information ladder." Lucas leaned back in the booth, steepling his fingers. "I can get you straight to the top."

"I don't like your methods."

Jeremiah's low answer only made Lucas's smirk widen. "But they work far better than anything you've access to."

Both of Jeremiah's hands clenched into fists atop the table. "I spent years fighting against people like you in the Army . . ."

"Then you *quit* that life to take over mine." Lucas's lips kept their upward tilt but lost what humor was left. "I was pushed out of the only existence I knew by my own brother. He took over the gilded throne and let me fall to the wolves."

"You didn't fall," Jeremiah said, voice as cold as ice, "you jumped. You *kept* jumping, and now you're trying to drag me down with you. Our father . . ."

"*Your* father gave you everything and left me nothing," Lucas hissed.

"I didn't want this!"

"But you took it anyway, didn't you?"

"Hey," I snapped, aware that the two men looked poised at any point to leap over the tables at the other's throat. Peering around the room, we didn't seem to be attracting any attention in the empty outside area, but if the conversation continued, that would change. "Can we stay on subject here?" I asked in a low voice.

Both men turned angry gazes on me, and for a moment I thought they were going to band together against me. As if on cue, a conga line appeared from the bar, breaking up the tension at the table. They sat back down, still glaring at one another, and I breathed a little sigh of relief. "Now what?"

Lucas glanced at me, then back to Jeremiah. "Do you have your passports with you?"

I shook my head, and after a moment's hesitation so did Jeremiah. Lucas nodded. "It should be easy enough to get replacements, provided you," and he pointed at Jeremiah, "aren't already an outlaw." At my confused look, Lucas grinned. "The media is trumpeting the news that our golden boy here has skipped the country, although nobody seems to know why yet. Authorities don't sound pleased but so far there hasn't been any arrest warrants posted. Uncle Sam must love you right now."

"Arrest warrants?" I echoed, my brow furrowing. "What's he talking about?"

"My baby brother wasn't supposed to leave the country, what with him shooting someone and all." Lucas waved his hand through the air. "But no, he takes his armed troops and rides off into the unknown. Without him there to keep an iron grip on the media, the truth, or variations of it." He glanced at Jeremiah. "I have it about right, don't I?"

Jeremiah looked away, clearly uncomfortable by the conversation, but I wanted to know more. Despite my best efforts, my heart ached for the large man. Jeremiah Hamilton thrived on control, and if his brother really had taken away all communication equipment, then he'd lost the upper hand.

For the moment, however, his public image paled in comparison to my own questions. The memory of our argument on the ship still smarted; the answers he'd given me weren't enough. Had he followed me here out of some misguided sense of duty, or was there more to our relationship than even he wanted to admit?

Or had his flight out here simply been to settle the vendetta with his brother? Not knowing the truth had me tied in knots, but there was no denying he'd risked everything by coming here. Thinking about it made both my head and my heart hurt.

"Tonight we rest." Lucas spread his arms wide. "Tomorrow, we leave for Dubai."

Maybe I should have been used to the weird turn my life had taken by that point, but I still blinked at the sudden news. "Dubai? As in the Arab nation?"

"One of the richest."

I frowned. "Why are we going there?"

"There's an information broker there who owes me a favor, and I'm hoping he can shed some light on who's after us. Plus, I'd much rather keep moving than stay in one place and be caught." Lucas winked at me. "Relax, I think you'll enjoy it."

"But why can't I go home?" Perhaps I was whining, but I figured I was entitled to lodge some form of complaint. "I'm not related to either of you, this isn't my battle. If it's really as personal to the Hamilton family as you say, then I wouldn't be a target."

"And what would you do," Jeremiah asked, "when you got home?"

I glared at him. "Contrary to what you obviously think," I snapped, "I can stand on my own two feet."

"I didn't mean . . ."

"Yes you did." I crossed my arms, irritation bubbling up. "Since I've met you two, I've been shot at, poisoned, kidnapped—twice I might add—and attacked by strange men. I don't care how rich you are or how many foreign countries you drag me into, this whole thing is ridiculous."

"See?" Lucas spread his arms and gave me a bit smile. "Bet your life has never been this interesting."

There was nothing I could say to that. I sat back, wordless, watching in a daze as the conga line disappeared back inside the bar. Two beautiful faces, so very similar to one another, stared at me: Jeremiah's gaze was as stony as ever, and Lucas grinned at me like a buffoon. As much as I wanted to scream and rail at them, I couldn't seem to form the words.

"There are many ways to hurt a man." Jeremiah leaned forward. "Sometimes, the easiest is to go after those in our care."

"What, like the girl you're sleeping with?" My voice had a nasty, self-recriminating note and I bit my tongue. "You've made it clear what I am to you."

"Others might see it differently," Lucas murmured, but I just stared at the table, trying to hang onto my anger.

"This is stupid," I muttered after a moment of silence, as the conga line appeared again from inside the bar. "What about your mother then? Why isn't she the one you're whisking off to foreign lands?"

Lucas snorted. "They probably know better than to try hurting us from that angle," he said.

"My men are keeping an eye on her," Jeremiah said, and I looked over to see him watching me. His eyes flickered to his brother. "I agree however that she's not likely in any danger."

"Imagine, my little brother agreeing with me." Lucas smirked. "Boy, it must have hurt to admit that." Not waiting for a response, he suddenly stood. "We're in the Caribbean, let's have a little fun." He held out a hand. "Dance with me."

I rolled my eyes and looked up to see the scarred man waggle his eyebrows. "It'll make my brother jealous."

"Maybe I don't want to make your brother jealous," I muttered, not looking at the man in question, but when Lucas grabbed my hand and pulled me up I didn't protest. The conga line was passing near our table and it didn't take much for Lucas to steer me to the end of the line.

"I'll be good," he said, laying his hands on my waist. When we entered the bar however, he still pinched my rear. "Okay, mostly good," he murmured in my ear as I elbowed his rib cage.

I hadn't really noticed what was happening inside, and found that a wedding party had taken over the bar area. The twang of the steel pan drums and the overall festive atmosphere in the room brought a reluctant smile to my face. It was impossible to keep a sour mood amidst the crowd of people; between the loud music and dancing figures, I felt my temper ease a bit. Lucas kept his hands to himself, which likely contributed to my improved disposition, and for a brief moment I let myself get caught up in the party environment.

When the conga line made its third trip through the outside dining area, however, I noticed that Jeremiah's seat was empty. Scanning the murky area outside the dining area, I saw a familiar shape, outlined by the Tiki torches, walking alone into the darkness. Abandoning the conga line, I pulled free from Lucas's grip and followed after Jeremiah's retreating figure.

He stopped beside a maintenance hut when I called his name, but as I came to his side I didn't know what to say. My eyes were still growing accustomed to the darkness so it was hard to see his face. His shoulders were hunched forward and he kept his face turned from me, and although my heart ached I tried not to read too much into it. Reaching out, I laid a hand on his arm, and was gratified when he didn't pull away from me.

"I don't like feeling useless."

I blinked at his words. Jeremiah didn't move, just continued to stare out into the darkness. "Well, join the club," I murmured, and felt the muscles under my palm tense.

"Maintaining control keeps me sane. My father . . ." He stopped talking for a moment, and I squeezed his arm. "When my father died, I lost control of my life. My brother's right: I took his as surely as Rufus Hamilton took mine."

Moving closer, I curled my hand around his arm, pulling him close. "You did what you had to do back then," I murmured. "If you hadn't taken over the business, thousands of employees would have lost everything. Yes, it's terrible that it led to Lucas going down such a dark path, but don't you see? It's not your fault."

Jeremiah ran a hand through his hair. "And yet I'm still stuck under the thumb of a brother who hates me, forced to take part in activities that I once fought against, and facing an unknown enemy." He sighed. "Meanwhile at home, my family name is being dragged through the mud, the business I sacrificed everything for is slowly crumbling, and I can't do anything to protect those in my care."

I didn't really think about what I did next: sliding my arms around his body, I hugged Jeremiah, laying my cheek against his chest. He stiffened against me for a brief instant, then his arms fell against my back and shoulders and he pulled me close. I closed my eyes and breathed in the familiar scent of his body, tightening my hug.

Why do you have to be such an utter fool? I thought, miserable about how bad affairs had grown between us. Days ago, I would have done anything for the man in my arms. Now, I wasn't sure why I was even touching him. I sighed inwardly, knowing the answer. *Because he needed comforting and, despite everything, I still loved the bastard.*

It would be so much better if I could switch off that part of my brain. There was so much clarity when I was alone and angry, but the moment I stepped back into Jeremiah's presence, everything grew muddled. Even at the worst of times though, I didn't hate him. His privileged life had been rough, and I understood at least partly why he was who he was. However, that didn't make dealing with him any easier.

When his hands moved up my back, a flame flickered to life in my belly. I didn't protest as he maneuvered us around until my back was against the maintenance shed beside us. He lifted my arms up and around his neck, pressing me back against the rough wall, and I trembled at the contact. My body betrayed me, melting at his touch, and when he lifted my chin and leaned down to kiss me, I didn't protest.

Always before, Jeremiah had been in control, but somehow this was different. He didn't try to restrain me in any way; his kiss wasn't an assault or struggle. His lips caressed mine like a lover, making no demands other than for permission to continue. When I opened to him, still he held back, tongue dancing and teasing. I tightened my grip around his neck, pulling him close and wanting more, but he took his time, lips and tongue a gentle torment that was nothing like I'd experienced in his hands.

He broke off the kiss, leaning his forehead against mine. Firelight danced in his eyes and, my breath catching, I traced his beloved face with my fingertips. His eyes searched mine, holding back none of what he was feeling. I read him like an open book, and the knowledge was intoxicating.

"Lucy," he murmured, my name a benediction on his lips. Desperate longing shone through his eyes as he kissed me again before asking softly, "Stay with me tonight."

I shut my eyes, licking my lips, then looked back up at him. Desire ached in me, alongside a bleak loneliness, and every fiber of my being screamed for his touch. He shifted, running a hand down the side of my neck and arm. A cool island breeze brushed against my hot skin, and I shivered as he whispered my name again, lips moving across my forehead.

"I'm sorry, Jeremiah."

For a moment, I thought he hadn't heard my low answer, then without a word he pushed free of me. Cool air swirled around me at his sudden absence and I gripped the wall for support, but Jeremiah didn't speak. I swallowed my agony as he walked away, disappearing into the dark night. Covering my eyes, I bit my lip and tried not to cry even as my heart broke for him.

"My brother isn't good with rejection."

I dropped my hand and looked over at Lucas standing against a palm tree nearby, but the gunrunner's eyes were off into the darkness where Jeremiah had disappeared. I didn't trust myself to speak without breaking down however, and Lucas seemed to understand. "I'll walk you to your room."

We stayed silent all the way up the elevator, Lucas trailing a step behind me. The hotel rooms ran along the outside of the building, and in the light of a rising moon I could see the reflection of the water just beyond the tree line. I pulled my card out and opened the door just as a voice behind me asked, "Do you want some company tonight?"

I looked back to see Lucas studying me. Any hint at a smirk was gone; he waited patiently for my answer, but the words wouldn't come to my lips. I looked at him and realized, with no small amount of regret, that I wanted to say yes. I wanted to be held tonight, told everything was going to be all right. But, more importantly, I wanted it to be with Jeremiah, and my pride wouldn't allow that.

He seemed to read my decision because he nodded and took my hand. "Good night," he murmured, laying a kiss on my knuckle before turning away. I watched his retreat until he disappeared around the corner of the walkway, and then closed myself in my room. Skipping a shower for morning, I left the lights off and curled into the bed, wrapping my arms around myself and trying to hold on to the remnants of Jeremiah's scent still on my skin.

7

Nothing I'd ever seen in my life could have prepared me for the Arabian city we flew over.

Dubai itself was not a mystery to me. I'd read about it online and in the news, and had at least a basic understanding about the many sights and attractions. Nothing however could have prepared me for the real deal. Not even a seventeen-hour plane trip dimmed my excitement at seeing the coastal emirate from the sky. The shaped islands, the Babel-like spire reaching into the heavens—everything was larger than life, so over the top and stunning.

When we'd left Jamaica, I'd been depressed that our time there was so short. I had never been to the Caribbean islands before, and would have enjoyed a tour or some fun, but the Hamilton men were all business. At breakfast, Lucas gave us both passports that were identical to the ones we'd left behind. Oddly enough, he'd chosen to replicate my Canadian one, saying it offered greater potential mobility within the

Muslim nations. While I knew he was right, now I worried about what he planned to do with that dubious "bonus."

There was no private jet this trip, at least not for the first leg of our journey. We still flew first class, landing in London's airport before continuing to Dubai. Once we crossed Customs and Immigration in the Arabian city however, a helicopter had been waiting to take us to our hotel.

"Is this one of yours?" I asked both Lucas and Jeremiah through the headsets we'd been given.

Lucas shook his head. "Belongs to our host," he said. "A welcome gift of sorts."

Jeremiah didn't say a word, just stared out the window at the view below. I found it difficult to look at him; he hadn't spoken to me since the previous night when I'd rejected his advances. There was no way for me to tell whether he was angry with me, or angry at the situation, and I feared the answer enough to not ask the question. Still, his silence upset me, and the knowledge that I might have hurt him made my heart ache.

I need him to understand what he's done. Principles, however, were useless when all I wanted was his arms around me, to bury my face in his neck and breathe his scent. Jeremiah was close enough to touch, but he ignored me, and I in turn was forced to pretend to ignore him.

Lucas, on the other hand, seemed quite chipper for a man who'd stayed awake for most of the trip. I might have been annoyed at his constant jabbering except the impromptu tour he gave of the city was fascinating. He seemed to know a lot about the city and country, which made me wonder how often he'd been to the opulent area.

We were high enough to see the full outline of the man-made land extensions. I remembered hearing about the palms, but my breath caught as I saw a series of smaller islands only a few miles down the shoreline. They were arranged in a flower pattern, with a "stem" leading to the mainland. While smaller than the palm islands, the flower seemed almost delicate, and as we drew closer I saw each individual island was actually very large. I counted at least twelve small "petals" surrounding a larger central island, and as we veered toward it I noticed a large structure. "Is that our destination?"

Lucas nodded. "The Almasi Hotel," he said as we moved in closer. "The latest addition to an already flamboyant city."

The hotel wasn't as tall as some I'd seen, maybe twenty or so stories. The structure had a thoroughly modern appeal, yet hearkened back to an older Arabian style. A huge glass dome dominated the structure, the windows gleaming like diamonds in the Arabian sun. A flat pad spread out across the top of the main tower, a helipad for our transportation. Our helicopter made its landing atop the building, powering down the engines and rotors.

Lucas disembarked first, followed swiftly by Jeremiah. I unbuckled the belt and found, to my chagrin, two separate hands held out to help me down. Jeremiah and Lucas both looked at me expectantly, and I hesitated. *You have got to be kidding me.* I looked between the two men, then grabbed the handrail beside the door and lowered myself to the helipad.

I smoothed out my clothes, deliberately not looking at either man.

On the stairs across from us, a small retinue of people appeared as the large blades overhead finally stopped. Lucas turned toward the man and I followed slowly, Jeremiah bringing up the rear. The stranger leading the small group spread his arms as he saw Lucas. "Ah, Loki my friend, it has been a long time."

"Rashid," Lucas said, his lips folding back into another smile. Neither man put out their hand in greeting, which I found odd. Lucas turned and gestured grandly toward us. "May I introduce my brother Jeremiah, and Miss Lucy Delacourt."

"Ah, so this is the brother I've heard so much about." Rashid stepped forward and held out to Jeremiah in greeting. "I have wished to meet you for some time. Business does not bring you to our shores often enough."

Jeremiah inclined his head, his face a blank mask, but didn't reply. Rashid turned to me, smiling big. "Ah, Ms. Delacourt," he said grandly, inclining his head. "A woman like you would have garnered many camels from my ancestors."

The words sounded like something he told every woman, flattery without anything behind it. Or perhaps that was my own bias from being dismissed so quickly. I sensed a faint bit of hostility toward me; his gaze was quick to dismiss me, nor did he offer me his hand, and I struggled not to be offended. "Welcome to the Almasi Hotel, the jewel of Arabia. Gentlemen, let's retire inside and talk. My sister Amyrah will help your woman to the rooms."

I bristled at the phrase, then again when neither Lucas nor Jeremiah spoke up in my defense. A woman dressed all in black, a white scarf carefully covering her hair, stepped shyly forward. She had an earnest expression on her face and was studying me like I was a rare and beautiful gem, which was a bit disconcerting. "Hi," I ventured weakly.

The girl's face lit up, and she seemed to remember herself. "I am Amyrah," she said softly, holding her hand out. Her handshake was limp but she seemed pleased with the contact, and I made a mental note to read up more on Arabian customs. "May I show you to your rooms?"

She sounded very formal, but something told me she was near bursting to ask questions. She spoke English very well but her garb was so foreign to me; the scarf covered all of her hair and her clothing was more like billowing robes, robbing her of any feminine shape. We walked silently down toward the elevator, the men having already disappeared, and I struggled with what to say. Finally, I gave in to my curiosity. "What do you call the scarf on your head?"

Amyrah looked confused for a moment, putting a hand atop her head, then she smiled. "You are American," she said, nodding, as if that explained my obvious lack of knowledge. "This is my *hijab*."

"And the rest of your clothes?" I asked, vaguely gesturing to the dark robes shrouding her figure.

Her smile widened. "They are my clothes."

There was no guile in her response, nor did she seem to be making fun of me. I laughed at my own ignorance, but the questions seemed to break the ice. "I must ask," Amyrah

said as we boarded the elevator. "Have you been to Holly-
wood?"

Amyrah was fascinated by American culture, and I quickly
realized the Muslim girl hadn't seen much of the world in
her short life. She seemed excited when I told her I'd lived
and worked in New York City, asking me questions ranging
from the Statue of Liberty to the New York subway system.
I found it impossible to tell how old she was. Sometimes,
she seemed like any other well-educated young college-aged
woman I'd met, and other times her questions were as naïve
as a child. One thing was clear however, she'd led a very
sheltered existence but sincerely wanted to see more of the
world.

"Does your brother own this hotel?"

Amyrah shook her head. "He is one of the major inves-
tors and helped build it, but is not the primary owner." She
opened a door, and then motioned for me to go inside. "These
are your rooms."

Rooms? I slipped through the door then stopped and stared
around me. "Wow," I said, a quick exhalation that didn't at
all cover what I was seeing. I turned back to Amyrah. "This
is all mine?" At her nod, I turned back and stared around
me in wonder.

Less than a month ago, I had been lucky enough to stay in
the Ritz Carlton Paris, one of the richest hotels in the world.
There, every decoration, every inch of floor space, had been
old-world decadence. Ceiling to floor, the rooms and various
hotel sections had been as ostentatious, as opulent as a person could imagine. No penny had been spared, no section

left ungilded; the hotel had screamed its wealth and prestige, and I had loved every inch.

This room had a similar feel, but with a much more modern twist. The ceilings were tall, lending more vastness to an already-spacious room. None of the furniture was ostentatious, at least not at first glance; indeed, the entire suite had an almost spartan feel, at least in comparison to the Ritz. Yet the tiles and wood floors, the vibrant accent walls and dark wood furniture, lent it a modern appeal that was as rich as anything I'd seen in Paris. The farther I ventured into the suite, in fact, the bigger I realized it was. "This is *my* room?" I asked incredulously.

Amyrah nodded. "Your two men will be in the suites beside this," she said, blushing. "My brother finds it unseemly for an unmarried woman to share a room with a man."

My two men? "Oh, no," I said quickly, shaking my head emphatically. "They're not both mine, seriously."

"I am not judging you," Amyrah continued quickly, mistaking my answer. "Many westerners come here with their own beliefs and practices. But my brother is very strict on the separation of sexes, at least while you are his guests."

My jaw worked soundlessly and I groaned inwardly. This wasn't a reaction I'd expected, and hearing the girl beside me speak so candidly made me blush. "I belong to neither of the men I'm with," I said firmly, telling myself that it was not technically a lie. "What's downstairs?" I asked, desperate to change the subject.

"The main floor has a variety of shops, catering to the

hotel's diverse clientele." This part seemed almost a rote delivery, as if she'd rehearsed or practiced this part several times. "The concierge can help you with any tour options, and access to a private car comes as an option with these rooms." Amyrah beamed at me. "You can also ask me any questions and I will do my best to help you."

I studied the girl before me. "You live here in the hotel, don't you?" Something about the delivery of that speech made me think she was often called to help out the guests.

Amyrah flushed and looked down shyly. "We do have a family home," she conceded, "but when my parents died, my brother moved me here permanently."

The simple way she spoke about her parents' death made my heart break. "I lost my parents a few years back too," I murmured, looking around the room to control my sudden tears.

"Oh!" Amyrah touched my arm. "I am so sorry for your loss."

I almost broke down in tears at her selfless expression. Time, it seemed however, had given me enough strength not to do so; the memory hurt, but it was not the horrible ache I'd once been faced with. A thought occurred to me and I latched on like a bulldog. "That's it, we're going shopping."

The sudden change in conversation left Amyrah blinking. "What?"

I smiled at her surprise, tugging at her arm. "Come shopping with me. We don't have to buy anything, but we can still have fun. Anyway, the guys are probably doing their manly stuff, so let's be girls for once."

A bemused smile crossed the girl's face, and I winked. "It'll be fun, I promise."

As it turned out, Amyrah was a lot of fun when it came to "girl stuff." The rarity of this kind of trip for her was immediately apparent. From the way she ogled many of the window treatments for the stores, I could tell she didn't do this often. She knew where each and every store in the hotel was located, but her wide eyes told me she rarely, if ever, went inside.

So I dragged her into several high-end boutiques, pulling out dresses and holding them up against her. The idea of showing her legs or arms in public seemed scandalous to the Arab girl, so I changed my criteria a bit and began looking at floor-length, long sleeves gowns. Not too surprising, there were quite a few of those to be had, as well as many different headscarves in a variety of styles. For me, it was a slight culture shock; from the outside, the stores all looked like what you'd find in expensive American shopping areas. Once you started taking a closer look however, their selection obviously catered to a different, more local crowd.

Amyrah tried on several of the more colorful scarves and I was able to see her hair down. She really was a pretty girl, with long hair as dark as her brother's. I finally managed to get her to try on some of the dresses, promising her that nobody else would see her. It took a few dresses before she let me see her in a floor-length, long-sleeved red gown that went up to her neck but otherwise showed her curves. She fidgeted in front of me, tugging at the fabric. "It's very tight."

As far as I could see it was probably a size too big, but I beamed at her. "You look fantastic!"

A shy smile tugged at her lips. "I do, don't I?" she murmured, looking at herself in the mirror. Then her face fell. "But my brother would never approve."

"He doesn't have to know about . . ."

"My brother knows everything." She pinched her lips. "I should not have done even this."

I tried not to let her see my own disappointment when she walked out of the dressing room in her old clothes. "Not even any of the scarves?" I asked, and saw the reluctance in her face as she shook her head.

"Thank you for coming with me," she said, lips tugging up in a smile that didn't quite reach her eyes.

Well, this didn't turn out like I'd planned. Not that I'd had much of a plan, but I hadn't thought things would end on a sour note. There was a lot about Arab culture I didn't get, but I could see that Amyrah was unhappy, and I felt like much of the blame was mine. We exited the shop quietly, heading back toward the lobby, and I snuck a look at the other girl. I'd been cooped up with too much testosterone lately; first, locked in a house under constant guard, then stuck aboard a ship full of men. ·

What I really wanted to do was be girly, even if only for a little while, but apparently I'd screwed that up too.

"Listen," I said, trying to salvage the day, "I had fun. I'm sorry if I pushed you down a road you didn't like, but I'll try to be better." I poked at my clothing. "What I need right now is to change out of these clothes and wash up, but maybe we can meet down here afterwards?"

I didn't realize I'd been bracing myself for a refusal until I saw her answering smile and felt the tension drain out of my body. "I would love to," she said, her air regal but the smile showing her true feelings, and I grinned back in response.

We quickly arrived back at the lobby, and as I glanced toward the entryway I saw a dark man watching us. My smile wavered and I looked away, and then back behind us. My time with the Hamilton men, it seemed, had made me paranoid, and I nudged Amyrah when I saw another man staring in our direction. "Do you have anyone watching over you?" I murmured.

Amyrah gave me a puzzled look. "When I leave the hotel, yes, we do have security," she replied.

Maybe that was it. An overprotective brother would probably explain the dark figures I was sure were following us. I snorted. "Men."

I wasn't expecting an answer, but beside me Amyrah laughed. "Yes," she said simply, and we shared a smile before parting ways, promising to meet down here in an hour. That gave me enough time to shower and change clothes, and I was looking forward to it.

Unfortunately, the moment I came to my room, I realized that my plans were going to be difficult. Arguing male voices came from inside, and I groaned aloud as I pushed the door open. Lucas was sprawled in a chair just inside the doorway, a glass of some concoction in one hand. Nearby, Jeremiah was pacing, clearly agitated about something.

"What are you two doing in my room?" I demanded as I moved into the large living room.

Lucas raised a glass to me. "You have the biggest room," he said lightly, gracing me with a trademark grin.

I rolled my eyes, not in the mood to deal with either man. "You two can head to your own rooms," I snapped, folding my arms. "I need to take a shower and change clothes."

"Fantastic!" Lucas set his drink down on the end table. "I'll join you."

I couldn't do anything more than stare in shock, but Jeremiah stopped pacing at his brother's glib statement. "Loki," he growled, clenching his fists.

"You know, I can always tell when you're angry," Lucas said, pointing at his brother. "It becomes 'Loki this' or 'Loki that,' which I think translates to 'I want to wring your neck.' No, seriously, tell me I'm wrong."

The two men seemed to have forgotten about me, and for that I was glad. My heart was beating too fast, and I struggled to collect my thoughts. The reminder of my actions aboard the ship was painful, harder still because Jeremiah was standing right there. If I looked at it too close, the guilt threatened to eat me alive.

"Anyway," Lucas continued, "you'll have to excuse my brother. He found out today that he is *persona non grata* back in America."

The news jarred me back to the present. "What do you mean," I asked, "he's not allowed back in the country?"

"Oh, nothing so interesting as that. Little brother here kept a stranglehold on the media, and with him out of the picture they're suddenly publishing all sorts of fun facts."

Jeremiah grunted. "I'm telling you, the timing is too much of a coincidence."

"And I think you're just bitter not being in total control anymore."

"The best way to deal with this is to be there in person." Jeremiah paced the floor, alive with nervous energy I didn't remember seeing before today. "Instead, I'm stuck half the world away while my name is dragged through the mud."

"Oh, boo hoo, poor little brother is worried about his *reputation*." Lucas rolled his eyes. "Excuse me if I don't shed a tear about the horrible loss."

Bitterness rang loud and clear from the scarred man's voice, and his words only served to make Jeremiah angrier. I knew I'd stepped into an argument that had been brewing for quite some time. The humorless mirth with which Lucas egged on his brother and the tense set to Jeremiah's shoulders told me this would be a fine time to make an exit.

"Fine," Lucas said to his brother as I turned to go, "you leave. Go home to your ivory tower. But Miss Delacourt is staying here with me." He snorted. "You've proven incapable of keeping her safe. How many times has she been taken out from under your nose?"

I whirled around at my name, staring at the arms dealer incredulously. Indignation robbed me of speech, but I saw

Jeremiah turn at the insult. Lucas didn't seem to care about the danger he was in. He stared out the window over the desert skyline, sipping from his glass, as Jeremiah advanced.

There were small bottles in the bar before me, but I didn't want to throw anything hard at them. I could tell that, in a minute, there would be enough fighting where I couldn't do a thing. A spray nozzle lay beside the sink and I grabbed it up, aimed at the two men nearby, and pulled the trigger.

Seltzer water gushed out, dousing them and momentarily distracting them from mutually assured destruction. Lucas cursed, bolting up from the chair. Jeremiah also reversed course, backpedalling from the stream of liquid. I followed their retreats, keeping the spray trained on each man as they tried to get away. The extension for the nozzle only went so far, eventually tugging me to a stop a few feet from the bar.

"If you want to fight," I said, giving in to anger, "do it in your own rooms. Now get out of mine!"

The ground beneath me was slippery but I kept my focus on the two men who had matching faces of incredulity. Dropping the seltzer sprayer, I lifted my chin and glared at them. "I'm going to take a shower," I said with as much dignity as I could muster. "When I get out, I want both of you to be long gone."

Not bothering to wait for a response, I swept past them and stomped down the hallway, slamming the bathroom door in an undignified fashion. The bathroom was just as gorgeous as the rest of the suite, but I was too worked up to care. Making sure the door was locked, I started the shower and grabbed a towel, stripping and stepping into the warm spray.

With the water going, I couldn't hear anything going on outside and prayed they had left. I took my time in the shower, but eventually switched the water off and stepped out. Once I'd dried myself off, I poked my head out into the hallway. Silence greeted me. "Hello?"

No replies.

I padded down the hallway, peeking into the living room. Someone had wiped up the mess made by the seltzer water, leaving the damp rags in the bar sink, but otherwise I was alone. Huffing again, I went back to the bedroom to ready myself to meet Amyrah.

The downstairs lobby was full when the elevator doors opened, many of the people congregating at the nearby bar. Most of the people milling about were obviously westerners; I heard English being spoken with a variety of accents. I guessed it was some kind of conference just letting out from somewhere in the hotel, and hurried through the crowd toward the res-taurant. I'd promised Amyrah to meet her within an hour, but had taken a few minutes too many with getting ready.

The restaurant also looked full, and I craned my neck to look for Amyrah. Sometimes I wished I was taller, as the flats I'd worn didn't lend me much height. Squeezing through the crowd, I leaned in toward the curved bar to get what I hoped was a better view and saw a woman in a white head-scarf. I wasn't sure it was Amyrah until she waved to me, then disappeared into the crowd of people.

There weren't as many people away from the bar itself,

which made moving through the crowd easier. When I saw the woman again, I relaxed as I saw the big smile on her face. The bustle of a nearby kitchen grew louder, and as I neared Amyrah she jerked sideways suddenly, disappearing from my view.

I stopped, surprised. Craning my neck around a man who'd moved in front of me, I found I couldn't see Amyrah anymore. My skin prickled and, shoving the man aside, I ignored his angry yell as I moved quickly to the last spot where I'd seen the Muslim girl. When I'd gotten to the spot near the kitchen door where I'd last seen her, I looked all around but saw no other white headscarves, only the flowing hair of the Western female guests.

There was a crash in the kitchen, and my head jerked sideways. I gave a moment's pause, biting my lip as I realized I could get into real trouble if I was wrong, then barged into the kitchen. The sound of cutlery and fire rose up around me, but I could have sworn I heard a woman's cry from my left. The kitchen staff were agitated, several of the men waving their arms in the air and shouting in Arabic, but I ignored them and took off after the cry. Several were incensed that I'd entered but I danced away from them, following what I hoped was the right lead.

I heard another angry woman's cry and, rounding the corner, saw a man carrying a robed figure in his arms. The figure was putting up a fight, and I recognized the now-dislodged white scarf still half-covering dark hair. I passed a tray holding an empty champagne bottle and grabbed it up as a weapon. Amyrah struggled in the man's arms, and I knew the moment she saw me because her dark eyes widened. The last of my indecision melted away and I took the last few steps necessary and brought the bottle hard against the man's head.

He staggered, dropping Amyrah to the floor. When he turned back toward me I was already swinging the bottle a second time. This time it clipped him on the temple and he went down, sprawling across the ground as if dead. Dropping the bottle through limp fingers, I stared at the figure at my feet in horror. He was wearing hotel employee colors, and blood trickled down a gash to the right of his forehead.

Ahead of me, Amyrah struggled to stand, and I stepped over the prone man to help the girl to her feet. She was staring down at her assailant, babbling in Arabic and clearly scared out of her wits. I said her name, then repeated it before she finally raised her eyes to me. "We need to go."

My words took a moment to register but she nodded. I grabbed her hand and pulled her after me, already lost in the maze of corridors. This looked more like the servants' entrances than anything a hotel guest was meant to see. The walls were a pale utilitarian cream, nowhere near as decadent as the rest of the building. I pulled us through several twists and turns, then stopped and faced Amyrah. "We should get to a public area. Do you know your way out of here?"

Having something to do snapped the girl out of her shock. "The shopping area is this way," she said, turning down yet another of the hallways. I followed close behind, wishing now that I'd kept ahold of that glass bottle. The halls in this section were mostly empty, but I knew when we grew closer to the shopping district because I could hear the hum of voices grow louder.

The door Amyrah pushed through led us out into another hallway that was different from the ones behind us. This one had mosaics on the wall and tiled floors, and I realized we were somewhere that guests would normally see. Sure enough, we spilled out directly into the main shopping area. I breathed a sigh of relief the moment I knew we were in public. Most of the people walking past ignored us, but at least I knew they were there to see if we needed help.

I nudged Amyrah. "Which way to the lobby?" All I could think about was finding Jeremiah or Lucas. They'd know what to do with this situation.

"Yes, this way."

We walked quickly, trying not to appear like we were running from something or someone. I looked around, trying to spot anyone else out of the ordinary. For the most part we were ignored; the mall was filled with a myriad of different cultures and nationalities, none of whom seemed interested in us. We were almost to the lobby and, I hoped, safe when I saw a man on the far wall zero in on our location. *Uh oh.* "Amyrah," I murmured as the dark figure started toward us, "we may need to run."

The shorter girl needed no encouragement; she took off immediately, and I followed right behind her. Sure enough, the man I'd been watching started after us, bringing his hand to his mouth. *Oh God,* I thought, *there's more of them?*

Ahead of us, at the mouth of the lobby, two more dark figures appeared. We skidded to a halt, looking for somewhere else to duck and hide. The ramp however was only wood paneled walls and mosaic tile floors; no doors or exits of any kind marred its surface. Amyrah huddled close to me as the three men rapidly advanced on us.

Up toward the lobby, a familiar silhouette stood outlined by the glass entrance. "Help," I all but screamed, and nearly collapsed in relief when the figure turned toward me. My cry made the three men pause and look toward where I'd called.

That was all the time it took for Jeremiah to reach our position.

The single man who had followed us up the ramp took off back toward the mall, but the other two waiting in the lobby weren't as lucky. Jeremiah grabbed both, throwing one to the wall while he dealt with the other. I covered my mouth when I saw a knife appear in the other man's hand, but the commando quickly disarmed him, then lashed out at our assailant's knee. The man went down with a howl, and Jeremiah turned to face the other man who seemed intent on following the third man back into the crowded mall. Jeremiah swung the man around into one of the tables as I realized a crowd was forming around us.

From the lobby, large men in suits barreled toward our location. The man on the ground struggled to his feet and Jeremiah turned, swiping the man's legs out from under him. The injured attacker went down but the distraction was all the second needed; he pushed away from the door, slipping past Jeremiah and taking off toward the mall. By then, security had arrived at our location, and Jeremiah raised his hands to show he wasn't a threat. The man at our feet tried to crawl away and Jeremiah put a foot down heavily between the man's shoulder blades, holding him on the floor.

Rashid appeared through the crowd of people and shouted orders in Arabic to the men who had been about to grab Jeremiah. They subsided and instead hauled up the man on the floor; Jeremiah stepped back to allow them access. I breathed a sigh of relief when he was hauled away, but still cast a quick glance back toward the shopping area. Two more had gotten away, and I wasn't happy about that.

Amyrah launched herself at her brother, who enveloped her into his wide embrace. The girl sobbed against him, hiding her face in his shoulder, and Rashid himself struggled not to be overcome himself. He faced Jeremiah, who stared back stoically. "I thank you," he murmured, laying a hand on his sister's head.

Jeremiah shook his head. "I wasn't the one who saved her," he murmured, moving in behind me.

The Arab man finally looked at me, *really* saw me, and gave a jerky nod. "Anything," he told me, then paused as Amyrah tightened her hold. The depth of his love for the sister in his arms shone through his eyes. "Anything you need that I may provide, it is yours."

I nodded back, unable to speak. Jeremiah's hands crept to my shoulders and without thinking about the possible consequences I leaned back against him. The adrenaline was still coursing through my veins, making my heart race. My heart sped up yet again however when the billionaire wrapped his arms around me, holding me close to his body. The inexplicable urge to cry came over me; oh, how I'd missed this!

As the throng of security thinned, I watched as Lucas pushed his way toward us. He took one look at me, his gaze flickering to Jeremiah, and a rueful smile tilted his lips. "Looks like I missed out on all the fun."

I wasn't allowed to leave immediately. In fact, I had nearly another two hours of questioning before I was finally free to go back up to my room for the night. Amyrah had disappeared, likely under her brother's lock and key after the kidnapping attempt. Security and what I assumed was Rashid's own team questioned me relentlessly about what had happened. I repeated my answers over and over again, growing more agitated with each passing minute, until finally Jeremiah ended the interrogation for me. He appeared halfway through my questioning and stayed, but finally he had swept me into his arms and stormed from the room. They let him go, either done with me or not wanting to get in front of the raging bull.

I managed to learn that, right about the time I was heading downstairs to meet Amyrah, her brother had received word of the imminent kidnapping. He'd immediately set out to find her, but the kidnappers had done so first. A van outside one of the catering entrances was spotted on surveillance video leaving with the other two alleged kidnappers. If I hadn't freed her from the man who'd snatched her, Amyrah would have been inside that van and headed only

God knew where before her brother could lock down the building.

The timing seemed too coincidental, and that probably accounted for the length of my questioning. Nobody ran after us or tried to arrest me however, and I laid my head on Jeremiah's shoulder, exhausted by the whole ordeal. He didn't release me until we got to the door of my suite, and only then so I could pull out my key card.

All I wanted was to collapse into the bed and not have to think any more about the day so far, but Jeremiah had other ideas. "What kind of self-defense do you know?"

I sagged, groaning, but shook my head in response. He took my hand, flattened my fingers, then pulled it toward his neck. "If you ever get in close quarters, there are several weak areas. The side of the neck is one." He pulled my hand around so the heel was just touching the tip of his nose. "Hitting the nose like this can incapacitate an attacker long enough for you to get away."

"Jeremiah . . ."

Ignoring my plea, he twisted around me, angling one booted foot over my knee. "If you can strike anywhere at the knees, take the shot. Anything to hinder them from running after you."

"Why are you telling me this now?" I moaned, looking back toward my bedroom.

"I don't like seeing you helpless."

That statement got my attention. Jeremiah was staring down at me as passive as ever, but within that stillness I saw the predator struggling to get free. I also became aware of our nearness, how close we were to one another. I stared up into those green eyes and my heart stopped at the depth of emotion I saw there.

He stepped in close so that we were almost touching. I didn't move, breathing in his exquisite and unique scent. A hand smoothed my hair behind my ear, fingertips running down the side of my neck. I couldn't drop my gaze; his eyes held me in their power. Reaching up, I traced the lines of his face and my heart skipped as he leaned into my palm.

"Let me stay tonight." His voice was rough with need, but his touch remained gentle, almost featherlike.

I took a deep breath and let my eyelids fall closed. Blindness didn't remove him from my senses; I could feel him standing close, his scent and *presence* enough to make my heart want to beat out of my chest. But it gave me the strength to say three of the most difficult words of my life.

"Good night, Jeremiah."

The hand caressing my face stopped, then fell away. Everything inside me strained to follow, to reach out again for his touch. I opened my eyes and looked up to see him still watching me, a thoughtful look on his face. Then, to my astonishment, a *smile* creased his lips. My mouth dropped, the expression so foreign to me coming from his face as to make me speechless.

"I didn't know what I had until it was too late," he murmured before stepping away. "Good night, Lucy Delacourt. Our conversation is not over."

My breathing came in little gasps as he let himself out. I

stood still for several minutes, afraid that if I moved, it would be to run after him.

Would that be so bad?

I didn't know anymore.

Part of me wasn't sure whether my defiance was a result of self-preservation, or a way to punish him. Except, now I didn't know whom I was punishing more, Jeremiah . . . or myself. I craved his touch, needed him with every breath in my body. Being around him brought out the best and worst in me; as much as I wanted him, I feared what would happen if I gave in. All I knew was that, this time, I wouldn't survive it if he rejected me.

The last time I'd bared my feelings, he'd walked away, leaving a crack on my heart that I still had no idea how to fix. How could I even consider trusting him with that power again?

And would he even want me when he learned my secret?

I staggered zombie-like to my bedroom, pulling the covers up and sliding beneath them without even taking off my clothes. Curling into a small ball, I stared out into the darkness, my mind a black wall of pure emotion, until finally at some point I fell into a fitful slumber.

8

I wasn't sure how I'd come to be riding a four-wheeler through the Arabian Desert sands, but I was having too much fun to care.

We'd left the city far behind us, invisible to the naked eye from the roll of dunes. Even from my current vantage point I saw no sign of the tall buildings anywhere along the horizon. Below the dune, others moved along like ants toward our destination, a Bedouin encampment in the middle of the desert. I'd grown tired of playing follow the leader and, in a spontaneous moment, had scaled a nearby sand dune. It had been steeper than I first thought, but not so bad that I was afraid.

The desert sun shone directly into my eyes as I crested the dune, and I stopped atop the sandy ridge. The ATV rumbled beneath me as I surveyed the landscape stretching out to the horizon. Never before had I seen anything like it; the hills of sand, contrasted by the blue skies above, took my breath away.

My wakeup call that morning had been quite the surprise. Given what had occurred the previous day, I would have thought we'd be under lock and key, or at least confined to the hotel. So it had been surprising when Lucas showed up at my door, inviting me with a big grin on his face to have a desert safari.

There was no way I was saying no to a once-in-a-lifetime experience!

We'd gotten a late start, thanks in part to the security detail that was coming with us. Rashid seemed excited to give us this gift, but I could tell the men guarding him had their doubts. Amyrah was nowhere to be found; I hadn't heard from the girl since the previous night. My guess was that her overprotective brother had her under constant guard, locked away in his ivory tower.

It would have been nice to have her here with me. *I wonder if you ever get used to these kinds of views?*

Twin rumbles came from the hill behind me, and I turned just as Jeremiah and Lucas rode up and stopped on either side of me. I rolled my eyes, remembering I had my own overprotective goon squad.

"You shouldn't leave the group," Jeremiah said. "We may not be safe out here."

"Oh, lighten up little brother." Lucas grinned out from beneath a ratty ball cap at Jeremiah's answering scowl. "Admit it; you just don't like having fun."

Being between the two men was like wrangling a pair of kids. Lucas seemed determined to goad his brother, and wasn't above using me as bait. At the hotel, I'd been hustled to the car by Lucas before Jeremiah even appeared, and had watched through the window as the two men bickered. I wasn't sure who the victor was but both men entered the car, sitting on either side of me. Any attempts on my part to lighten the mood through conversation didn't work, so I stayed silent as we drove out of the city.

Nobody had told me what to expect, so when we pulled off the road onto a side road, I was confused. Our cars bumped along a road that was little more than a trail between dunes, usually with large sand drifts that lifted one side of the car higher as we rolled over them. I was jostled between the two men, which didn't help my mood any, and was relieved when we finally stopped near the small fleet of ATVs and camels.

I'd then been given the task of choosing which mode of transportation we'd take to our next destination. The camels didn't look all that appealing up close, so I'd opted for the machines instead.

"You've done this before, haven't you?"

I grinned at Lucas, feeling a little self-satisfied. "What, afraid a girl's going to beat you at manly sports?"

The scarred man laughed. "I'll race you then," he taunted, "first person back to the group." Without waiting for my reply, Lucas gunned the engine and turned his ATV around in record time. He took off down the hill, the paddle tires spraying us with sand.

I revved my engine, then paused when I saw Jeremiah's face. He was scowling at the horizon, and after a moment looked over at me. His gaze softened, but his mouth and jaw remained tight.

"You didn't want to come, did you?"

My statement was pure conjecture, but he nodded. "We aren't safe out here," he said over the rumble of the motors. "I don't know why Rashid or Lucas would agree on an outing like this."

The exact same thought had been bouncing around my head all day. We were isolated out here, caught in the middle of nowhere. "Lucas said the trip had been given as a gift, and we'd be rude to say no."

"That's what he told me, too." Jeremiah scowled at the sandy view. He looked uncomfortable, which was something I didn't equate with the big man. I knew it wasn't our impromptu mode of transportation; he rode the quad easily, even through the more technical areas I'd gone around. He was always in control, keeping an iron fist on his life, but the last few days had stripped him of that.

"So why did you come?" I asked, genuinely curious.

For a moment I wasn't sure he was going to answer me. His gaze didn't waver from the horizon where the sun was closing in on twilight. Finally he spoke. "Right now, Rashid controls everything. Because Lucas took all of my equipment, I don't have any access to my own network so can't do my own research on our host, my brother's "friend." I don't know how to feel about accepting his help when I don't know anything about the man."

"Lucas seems to trust him."

"Yes, another fact stacked against the man."

I blew out a breath, silently commiserating. For someone so used to controlling every aspect of his life, this had to be a major blow.

Finally Jeremiah turned to me. "What happened when he took you?"

My heart froze. I swallowed hard, staring at the horizon. "I translated for one of Lucas's deals. Got Shanghaied, almost killed by a deranged saboteur." I shrugged, although my heart wasn't in it. "You know, the usual."

"That son of a bitch." I felt Jeremiah's eyes on me. "I should never have left you alone in that house like I did."

My chest hurt, the desire to tell him everything strong enough to bring tears to my eyes. *Oh God, what have I done?*

"You guys coming or what?"

Lucas's voice drifted up the dune, snapping us both from our thoughts. Jeremiah glared down the hill as I looked away, blinking back tears. Without looking at the man beside me, I turned the quad around atop the dune and headed slowly down the sandy surface.

"What took you so long?" Lucas asked as I reached the bottom. When I didn't answer, his grin turned brittle along the edges. "Did my brother say something to you?"

I shook my head and, thankfully, the gunrunner backed off that line of questioning. "Where did you learn how to ride these things so well?"

"My great-aunt had some land up in Quebec when I was growing up," I replied, glad for the subject change. Jeremiah pulled beside me as I continued. "We used to race snowmobiles around her property in the winter." I didn't tell them that it had been over a decade, and I'd never driven one by myself. I was having fun with the quad anyway and doing well enough on my own.

Lucas laughed. "Sounds like fun."

"I thought you didn't have any family left."

I shrugged at Jeremiah's question. "When my parents moved to New York, we fell out of touch. I don't know them except for a few childhood memories. So when my parents died, asking them for help seemed like asking for charity."

"Pride cometh before the fall," Lucas quipped, and I flinched. The smile slipped from his face. "I'm sorry, that was insensitive."

I maneuvered the quad back and around both of the other vehicles. Right at that moment I didn't want to talk to either man about my family or the choices I'd made in life. My secret gnawed at my soul; being with both men only made my guilt that much sharper. Flying down the tall dune, I followed after the main group that was waiting for us. We were the only ones riding on the quads, Rashid and his men preferring the relative safety of the SUV.

The shadows cast by the sandy hills were growing larger by the minute as the sun set along the distant horizon. The wind on my face helped clear the twin tears sliding down my cheeks. By the time the two Hamilton men had caught up with me, the dry desert air had already soaked up the moisture on my face.

When we reached the encampment, the sun had already disappeared below the horizon, leaving the last tendrils of twilight to guide our way. The camp however was difficult to miss; it glowed like a fiery brand against the fading light, an oasis of light in the growing night.

The entire encampment had a wall surrounding it made up of reeds or some kind of vegetation. As we came inside, I saw that the area was lit with a combination of fire and electricity. I neither saw nor heard any generators running, and although I saw no panels, I wagered a silent guess that the Bedouin camp used solar energy. Perfect for a desert people, if not quite as rustic as one might imagine.

We parked the vehicles near the entrance, and I winced as I swung my leg from the ATV. Much of the afternoon had been spent on the four wheelers, and I walked bow-legged for a moment before my muscles stopped cramping. Away from where the vehicles were parked, large rugs lay on the sand around the areas where people could walk. The wind had picked up, swirling little eddies of sand around the SUV.

"Lucy!"

At the familiar voice, I turned to see Amyrah walking toward me. A big grin split my face as we embraced. "I thought your brother wouldn't let you out of the hotel," I said incredulously.

"Oh, he almost wouldn't. I had to plead and beg to come see you again." She tugged at my arm. "Come, we have food and entertainment waiting."

"Entertainment?"

I had no idea what kind of extravaganza we'd be in for at the desert camp.

While we ate, Amyrah introduced me to several of the

women in the group. Several of them were dancers, the thin veils they covered themselves with barely hiding the curves of skin and gilded outfits. They were all beautiful, and Amyrah seemed to be friends with many of them. I got the impression the young girl desperately wanted to be amongst their ranks, be allowed to wear the sparkling, skimpy outfits and dance on stage.

The furtive looks over her shoulder toward her brother, and the constant guard detail she had flanking her, told me Amyrah's struggle in that respect would be long.

The entertainment began before everyone had finished eating. The belly dancers started the show, and I was mesmerized by how their bodies moved to the beat of the nearby drums. The wind blew their veils all around but the dancers moved with it, allowing the currents to only add to the dance. I watched, fascinated, by the movements of the women; they were so much more sexual than I would have thought from the Arabic country.

When my wood plate skidded across the table with the wind and people began milling about in the background, I realized something was amiss. The dancer on stage finished her routine, the veils whipping around her, then as she exited the platform Rashid stepped toward us. "We will be staying here tonight," he said, directing his words at Jeremiah and Lucas who flanked me. He beckoned Amyrah to him, then gestured to one of the male dancers. "Hassan will show you where you will spend the night."

The wind was howling now, sand pelting my exposed skin. Jeremiah tucked me in to his side, shielding me with his jacket as we followed the dancer toward a row of tents at the far end of the complex. Around us, lights were going out one by one, plunging our path into near darkness. Fortunately, Hassan had a flashlight which, if we stayed close to him, was still visible through the sandy air.

We ducked into a small hallway lined with rugs and woven blankets, a brief respite to the sandy conditions. Hassan, it appeared, couldn't speak English but he did just fine by pointing: I was to go there, Jeremiah there, and Lucas over there. Without a word we parted ways, although I was loathe to release the large man holding me. Being back in his arms was pure heaven; the guilt weighing my soul was still there, but I wanted to cling to this moment for as long as possible.

The interior of my tent was much like the outside. Thick cloth protected us from the elements, the material rippling with the wind. The floor was covered by rugs, with a single solar lamp on the floor lighting the room. To one side, there was a low bed, only raised a foot or so off the ground. Pillows lined the room, and an ornate hookah sat on a low table at one end.

Despite myself, I paused to marvel at my surroundings. I was in a *Bedouin* camp, inside one of their tents, on the Arabian desert. This was not at all where I thought I would ever find myself, and despite everything I was happy to be part of this.

I heard the howling winds grow louder behind me and turned to see Jeremiah close the flap over the door. My breath caught as we stared at one another from across the small room. His face was as open as I'd ever seen; deep emotion warred across his features, but he didn't step forward. I was rooted in place, unable to make a move.

Finally, he spoke. "I admit that I've put you through a lot in our time together." His voice was rough, but his gaze on me didn't waver. "Say the word and I'm gone."

My gut clenched at his words, but he wasn't finished. "I need you." His words were like the gasp of a drowning man. "I should never have run like that, back at the house, but l-love . . ." He paused over the stammered word, face twisting in frustration. "All my life, that word, that *feeling*, has been a crutch I was forced to overcome. You've seen my mother, and I thank God you never had to meet my father because he, he was ten times worse."

"Jeremiah," I whispered, breath shaky.

"But I *need* you," he rasped, taking a jerky step forward. "Every cell in my body is telling me to run away, leave you alone, and I *can't*."

I took the necessary two steps forward, and stared up at him. His fists stayed by his sides, but from here the desperation in his eyes overwhelmed me. Choking back a sob of my own, I reached up and cupped his face, stroking his cheek with my thumb. His body tensed as if holding him back, and I felt a tear streak down my face.

My future was laid out before me in sudden and stark detail. No matter what I chose to do, it led to the same outcome: heartbreak on a scale from which neither of us would recover. I had betrayed the man I loved because I thought he had rejected me, and yet here stood as firm a testament to his affections as I'd likely ever see. That he couldn't say the words didn't matter; I saw everything I'd ever hoped for in my life shining from his eyes.

And I couldn't bear to let him go. Not yet. Pure selfishness on my part, but I knew that to give him up would break me, knew *now* what the revelation would do to Jeremiah. Our fate was sealed but for this one moment.

"Please," he ground out, body quaking beneath my palm, and the last of my resistance fell away. Rising up on my tiptoes, I pulled his head down and brought his mouth to mine.

That small kiss, barely a brush of lips, shook him free of his paralysis. He cupped my face tenderly in his hands, the touch feather-light, which only emphasized the shaky control he exerted. Deepening the kiss was therefore left to me, and I crushed myself to him, desperate for as much contact as two bodies could allow.

Outside our little tent, the wind roared and howled, drowning out the sounds we made. Jeremiah swept me off my feet, moving us across to the small mattress. He laid me carefully on the bed, kneeling above and wiping another tear from my eye before settling between my legs and taking my mouth in another kiss.

In the darkness of our little world, there was only Jeremiah and myself. We were insatiable, neither of us able to take our hands off the other. What sleep we managed was only in between bouts of activity. Long after I'd grown sore and weary from our lovemaking, I still climbed on his hips when I felt he was hard again, riding him to another mutual orgasm.

My desperation for him was matched by his for me, and in those hours when we were together, I could pretend that this could be forever. That I would never have to give him up.

That I hadn't made a mistake that would shatter us both.

The darkness hid us from view, but that didn't stop my hands from tracing every outline of muscle, every curve of his beloved body. I memorized every inch of him, stowed the knowledge away in the back of my mind for the future. If tears wet my cheeks, he never saw them; I buried my own pain to give him everything he wanted, for this one night at least.

The sandstorm had died down by the last time I awoke to find him already inside me, staring down from above. Sated and deliciously sore, I still twined my arms around his neck and tilted my hips to meet his thrusts. Remnants of a dream where I had been one of the belly dancers still flitted through my head, and I rotated my hips, grinding against him to the beat of our hearts.

He exhaled raggedly before rolling us sideways so that he lay beneath me. I peered down at him through my hair, then coiled my naked body above him. Closing my eyes, I flipped my hair back and danced above him, a slow and sensual rhythm flowing through me. His fingers dug into my hips as I swayed above him. Gone was the fierce need for completion; I danced for him, twisting myself to the music in my head. His hands smoothed up my sides to cup my breasts, thumbs flicking the nipples.

I splayed my hands across his wide chest, leaning forward as I rolled my hips, bringing him in and out of my body.

Only then did I finally open my eyes to see him staring up at me, an awed fascination in his gaze. "So beautiful," he breathed, before capturing my face and bringing me back down for another kiss.

We stayed like that for a while, no goal except to pleasure and find pleasure in each other. Finally, at long last, I slept, unable to keep myself awake any longer.

When I awoke, I was alone. Sunlight poked through the cracks in the tent, enough light for me to see my clothing strewn across the room. There was no sign of Jeremiah, but I could still smell him on me, feel his lingering presence on my skin. The ache between my legs was no lie, but I ignored it as best I could, dressing quickly before pulling back the flap on the door.

Light streamed in, and I squinted down the makeshift hallway into the bright area that was the camp's center. My eyes hadn't yet adjusted but I could make out figures milling about. It was still too bright for me to watch for more than a couple seconds.

"Don't worry, nobody saw him leave your tent."

I jumped, startled, and looked the other direction to see Lucas sitting on the ground next to my room. He was staring at his hands, idly wiping sand from between his fingers. All I could do was stare, frozen in place, wondering how long he'd been sitting there. The silence stretched too long, and finally I had to say something. "Obviously, you saw him."

"Yes, but apparently I'm nobody." He stood to his feet, continuing to stare at the other wall before turning to look at me. The smiling mask was gone; he wore a stoic expression that would have done Jeremiah proud. "So, you've made your choice."

There had never been a choice. But looking at the scarred man, I couldn't say that out loud. "Lucas," I started, but nothing else would come out.

He waited several seconds for me to continue, but when I didn't continue he sighed. "Did you tell him?" he asked in a low voice.

I swallowed the sudden lump in my throat and gave a jerky shake of the head. "You're not going to tell," I started, unable to complete my question.

Annoyance played out across Lucas's face. "It isn't my secret to tell," he said firmly. For a moment he looked at a loss for words, then those blue-green eyes met mine. "Did I ever have a chance with you?"

I closed my eyes briefly, unsure how to respond. As much as I wanted to forget, or rather go back and change, my choice to turn to him for comfort, it had happened. Lucas had, whether I wanted to admit it or not, given me the comfort and safety I'd needed. He deserved an answer, but I couldn't begin to process the question, not now. Not here.

His eyes trailed over my shoulder, then in the blink of an eye the smiling mask was back. "So no, sandstorms aren't normal for this time of the year, but isn't it just a great coincidence that one happens just as . . . Well, speak of the devil."

I blinked in confusion, then turned my head to see Jeremiah and Rashid duck into the small hall. Jeremiah gave his brother a frosty look then turned to me. His face softened but he didn't try to touch me, just stood close enough that his arm brushed my shoulder.

"Rashid, my old friend." Lucas's words seemed deliberate, the smile on his face forced. "I came for answers to questions, not a tour of this lovely desert. I thought you would have something for us by now."

"Alas my old friend, it is you who are mistaken." Rashid pulled an envelope out from under his arm and handed it over to Lucas, who took it gingerly. "Your task was not an easy one, nor was it cheap."

Lucas eyed the other man thoughtfully as he opened the yellow envelope and pulled out the contents. Frowning at the paper in his hands for a moment, he passed it over to Jeremiah. "Do you know him?"

I peered over Jeremiah's arm as the billionaire studied the photo. The picture was grainy, like it had been taken from far away and blown up. The single man pictured was wearing sunglasses, and could have been any other dark-haired, sunglass-wearing men in the world. Jeremiah gave a growling sigh. "This was the best you could do?"

"Hardly." Rashid favored the man beside me with a small smile. "I also got a name. *Alexander Rush.*"

Jeremiah shook his head. "Doesn't ring a bell."

"Well, it should. Apparently, he's your brother."

9

Neither Jeremiah or Lucas said anything for several long seconds, and then I couldn't keep my mouth shut.

"*Another* one?"

Both men turned to look at me, and I squared my shoulders, staring back. Two Hamilton men in this world were enough for my taste.

Jeremiah looked between Rashid and the photograph for a moment, then shared a glance with Lucas. "There have been several people over the years who claimed Rufus was their father," he said carefully, handing the photo back to Lucas. "How do we know he's who he says, and how do we know you're correct?"

Rashid shrugged. "Whether he is or is not related is of no concern to me. He believes he is, and that is enough."

"How did you find out about this?" Jeremiah persisted.

"Don't ask him that," Lucas interrupted before Rashid could answer. The arms dealer was peering intently at the photograph, appearing to ignore everyone else. "He gets all cryptic and shit, saying *he has his ways* or something."

Rashid flicked an annoyed glance at Lucas. "My cryptic bullshit may have uncovered the man out to murder you," he snapped.

Lucas grinned widely. "Hey, I didn't say you don't produce good results."

The exchanges made me wonder just how "friendly" the two men were. I remembered that, when we'd exited the helicopter at the hotel, neither man had shaken hands. Rashid might have owed Lucas a favor, but despite the assertions of friendship, neither man seemed to like the other much.

"I do not like to be mocked." Only slightly mollified, Rashid turned back to Jeremiah. "I have an extensive network of informants, but I must tell you this information was difficult to attain. Whoever Mr. Rush may be, he is exceedingly difficult to track or learn about."

"It's a start, and more information than we had previously. I'll get my people working on it as soon as we get back to the hotel."

"You're in contact with them?" I asked, surprised.

Jeremiah nodded, and pulled something from his pocket. "I picked it up from a retailer in the hotel the morning we left. Haven't been able to call out yet as there isn't much reception in the middle of the desert."

I stared at the small phone in his hand, a sick churning starting in my gut. Something told me that my time in this life was coming to a close, and there was nothing I could do about it. The best thing would be to reveal everything and get it over with but . . . I looked up in Jeremiah's beautiful face and felt the cracks in my heart grow wider.

"Lucy?"

I turned at my name to see Amyrah walking up behind her brother. She glanced around the throng of men, then back at me. "I was wondering if you'd like to ride back with me?"

Her offer was a godsend that I didn't deserve. Swallowing back my rising anxiety, I gave her a genuine smile. "I'd love to, thanks." Without looking at any of the men, I slid past them and followed the Arab girl out into the sun.

"What was that about?" she asked once we were out of earshot.

I shrugged. "Information exchange, testosterone fest, whatever you'd like to call it."

"Ah." She peered at me as we moved toward her vehicle. "Men being men, then?"

I laughed, cut short by a shaky breath. "I'm ready to go home."

Amyrah nodded. "We'll be back at the hotel in a couple hours."

The hotel wasn't the home I'd meant. I wanted, more than anything, to go back to who I was before, back to the life I'd lived before I even heard of Jeremiah Hamilton. My existence may not have been easy then, but the simplicity and straightforwardness of my situation had been easier to bear.

Now, I felt as trapped as I had when Jeremiah had offered me that contract.

"Is everything okay?"

Shaking my head, I gave Amyrah a small smile. "I'm just tired." I followed her into the vehicle, wondering what adventures lay ahead of me now.

And finding that I couldn't bring myself to care.

"I have something to show you."

I sat on the bed while the other girl busied herself in the large bathroom. Amyrah's suite was almost as large as mine and, as far as I could tell, seemed to be more like an apartment than a hotel room. Pictures of her brother and what I guessed were family lined the walls, and the closet that I had briefly seen was full of clothes. In a way it made sense; her brother owned a share of this hotel, perhaps they also lived here full time.

"You ready?"

I nodded, then realizing she couldn't see me called out, "Ready."

Still there was a pause, then finally the door opened and Amyrah stepped out. "What do you think?"

My mouth dropped open, and a genuine smile stretched across my lips. "You bought it!" I exclaimed, grinning up at the shy girl. The red dress looked as good now as it had in the store, and I could tell my pleasure made the other girl happy.

Amyrah blushed and bit her lip, but sashayed over to a full-length mirror in one corner of the room. She turned this way and that, admiring herself. "I've never owned anything like this," she said. "I don't know if I'd have the courage to wear it out of this room."

"Sure you can!"

The other girl rolled her eyes. "My brother will think I am crazy," she murmured, smiling at her reflection in the mirror.

"Screw your brother." The words were out of my mouth before I even considered how inappropriate they were. It was one thing to make fun of your own family, another thing for someone else to say such things.

But my comment just elicited a startled laugh from the other girl. "Screw my brother," she repeated, then giggled. "He would not like it if I told him that." She studied her reflection for a moment, then lifted her arms to shoulder level and began moving her body like the dancers from the previous night.

I clapped my hands as she twisted her hips, moving in a small circle and ending with one last hip bump. "I'll bet he wouldn't like that either."

Amyrah looked pleased with herself. "He is my brother," she said, as if that answered everything. Perhaps it did. "I know he will love me, even if I choose to become a dancer."

The idea of the conservative girl before me running off with the Bedouin camp to be a dancer should have been funny, but instead of laughter, I felt tears well up in my eyes. My breaths grew labored as I struggled against the sudden and inexplicable need to break down. No matter what I did however, I couldn't stop the shivering that began in my belly and spread throughout my body.

Amyrah caught my eye in the mirror and spun around. "Are you all right?" she exclaimed, kneeling down beside me on the bed.

I nodded my head repeatedly, but couldn't say anything. Finally, I shook my head. "No," I croaked.

"Lucy, what happened?"

The concern in her voice bolstered me enough to get myself back together, at least somewhat. "I made a mistake. A *huge* mistake, and I'm . . ." *Afraid.* God, I was so afraid. Not about what would happen to me, but what would happen to Jeremiah when he found out what I had done. I knew he loved me, knew it with every fiber of my being.

And I knew my betrayal had destroyed that forever.

Amyrah grabbed my hand, pulling me forward, and I collapsed sobbing onto her shoulder. Breathing was difficult but I didn't care. Anguish about what I knew I had to do coursed through me, spilling out in wrenching gasps and muffled cries. Soft arms wrapped around me, holding me tight like I hadn't been held since before my parents died. Guilt and agony poured out of me, and I clung to the woman before me.

Eventually, I realized I was blubbering all over a beautiful red gown, being held by a girl who had known me barely a couple days. I leaned back, scooting over on the bed, but Amyrah kept a tight grip on my hand. "What happened?" she asked again, enunciating every word.

"Have you ever made a mistake so big, it feels like you'll never get past it?"

Something about her concerned look gave me my answer,

that she was free of that burden. She still squeezed my hand, moving around so that she was in front of me. "Would you like me to call your men?" she asked, her tone serious.

I barked a laugh at her phrasing. "No," I said, the sudden humor too much right then. "No, I'm fine. This isn't because of them." A bold-faced lie, but it seemed to do the trick.

"You didn't kill somebody, did you?"

I turned startled eyes to Amyrah. "No," I said in a rush, and felt her relax.

"Then whatever is wrong can be fixed, right?"

But I was wrong, I realized. I might as well have killed love, at least when it came to Jeremiah Hamilton. Everything I knew about his history, the way he had looked at me the last few days, told me my news could shatter that inside him forever.

Closing my eyes, I covered my mouth and focused on breathing normally. It took several deep breaths to calm my quaking lungs. *Such a drama queen you are, Lucy Delacourt,* I admonished myself, mortification settling over me like a blanket. I certainly had a high opinion of myself, thinking I had that much control over another man's emotional well-being. Smoothing the hair from my face, I wiped my eyes hastily with the back of my hand and stood. "I'm sorry," I said, balancing precariously. "I don't know what came over me."

"Lucy," Amyrah called as I turned to go. Biting my lip, I turned to look at the other girl. Concern and anxiety was written all over her face, and her hands were clenched tightly in front of her body. "If you need any help," she said, "please let me know."

I gave a jerky nod, dashing away new tears that leaked from my eyes with one hand. "You do look gorgeous though," I murmured, attempting a smile. Apparently I didn't do a good job with the expression because the worry in her face deepened, but I couldn't stay there anymore. "I'll call you soon," I mumbled, then turned and left the room, heading straight for the front door.

I stood outside Jeremiah's front door for several minutes before I finally got the nerve to give it a light rap. Really, it was barely more than a whisper, and I forced myself to knock harder a minute later. I didn't want to be there and had no idea what I would say when the door opened, but was never given the chance to find out. The door remained closed, even after a third attempt, and the pressure around my heart decreased slightly as I turned toward my own room.

Light streamed through the open windows, as bright as the desert sands we'd gone through the previous afternoon. Somewhere in the room came the faint hum of a fan, and the gossamer curtains across the window swayed in the small breeze produced. I leaned back against my door for a moment, allowing the nervous shaking in my legs to ease a bit, before moving further into the room.

Reaching up, I pulled out the clip from my hair and let it fall in a tangle to my shoulders. A shower and nap sounded divine; my nerves could use the relief. I had already started unbuttoning my shirt, moving through the living room to the bathroom at the back of the suite, when I saw something nearby me move.

I gave a startled squeak, stumbling back against a nearby

chair as Jeremiah rose to his feet from the couch beside me. He'd been sitting there the entire time, and I'd been so pre-occupied that I hadn't seen him. My heart racing, I leaned against the chair and placed my hand over my chest as he crossed the room, pausing to look outside. "Jeremiah," I said breathlessly. "I was just . . ."

"When," he asked, his voice as cold as I'd ever heard, "were you going to tell me you *fucked* my brother?"

10

My team was able to locate Loki's boat," Jeremiah continued as I fumbled for the chair beside me, my legs suddenly weak as jelly. "I suppose once the job was over and the cargo was gone, there was no reason to hide its presence. Nobody was aboard, so they were able to do a search of the vessel. A *thorough* search. Any ideas on what they found?"

At that moment, I wanted nothing more than to run away, not have to face the anger and hatred of the man before me. My legs, however, were far too feeble to hold me up, let alone do anything as strenuous as running. I couldn't speak, could barely breathe. My lungs screamed for air but the pressure in my chest left me no room.

"Lucy, please elaborate as to why there were *condom wrappers* in the main cabin's bathroom."

His voice held that familiar commanding note, the one that had always sent me running to do his bidding before. *He expects me to do the same as I always did.* I closed my eyes, the sick churning in my gut turning into a fiery pit. "You left me."

He paused for a second, as if trying to figure out how my answer fit his question. "That isn't what I . . ."

"You *left* me." My voice was stronger than I felt inside, but I still couldn't look up at his face. "I said I loved you and had that thrown back in my face, then you told me I could leave. What was I supposed to think?"

"So you show that supposed emotion by jumping in bed with my brother?"

My head snapped up. Jeremiah was looking at me down his nose, head high and proud. I surged to my feet, determined to meet him head on. "What was I to you?" I demanded, staring up into his cold expression. "Was I just your whore, a toy to play with until something better came along?"

Something flickered across his eyes as I spoke, and then his brows came down. "Don't think you can turn this one back on me," he muttered darkly.

"This is *all* about you," I exclaimed, spreading my arms wide. "Oh, heaven forbid someone else makes a mistake, but let's jump all over that one so we can cover our own sins."

Rage spasmed across Jeremiah's face, then disappeared again beneath his mask. He leaned in close. "You. *Fucked.* My. Brother." he said, enunciating every word.

I stared up at him, some of the fire inside me draining away. My jaw started to tremble, and I clenched it tight, not allowing my gaze to leave his. "Yes."

He leaned back, and then gave a jerky nod. "You're fired."

My body went stiff with outrage, but I felt the cracks in my heart grow larger. Legs trembling, I put a hand on the back of the chair beside me to steady myself.

"As per the contract, all income is now forfeit and is owed back to me with interest." His voice was clinical and detached, as if he were talking about a financial report.

"Are you *serious*?" Anger suffused me, but I didn't know how to express myself. All I wanted to do was beat some sense into his stupid head, but I knew he'd twist anything I said. "This is about your goddamned *contract*? That digital piece of garbage would never hold up in court if I threatened to sue you for sexual harassment, and you know it!"

"Try it." An arrogant condescension entered his shuttered gaze as Jeremiah stared at me down his nose. "You'll find life very difficult with me as an enemy."

I stared up into his cold, implacable gaze. There was nothing I could do right now to redeem myself in his eyes, a part of me reasoned, so why try? Frustration welled up, and my fingernails dug into the plush upholstery of the chair. "Is that what I am to you now? An enemy?"

When I thought about it pragmatically, the loss of the money stung. I didn't want any part of it now anyway, however. I'd be back at square one . . . no, I amended, square *zero*. "So you'll ruin me," I said in a brittle voice, staring at the mantelpiece behind him.

He snorted derisively. "You're already ruined, it won't take much."

A black hole opened inside my heart, sucking at my remaining emotions. The enormity of my situation hit me like a train: I was stuck halfway across the world with no way home and no money to call my own. There wasn't a doubt in my mind he would drain my bank account; I saw it in his eyes. He wanted to hurt me, to make me suffer, and he had the clout to make that happen. "That was a low blow," I whispered, "even for you."

Across from me, I saw Jeremiah shift. "Lucy . . ."

I flinched away from his outreached hand. He froze, but I couldn't bear to look at him. "I was never anything but your paid whore." Except now I wasn't being paid, so what did that make me? The righteous anger that had sustained me was bleeding away, leaving an aching chasm where my heart once beat.

"You're an asshole, Jeremiah Hamilton," I murmured, and then turned away. My legs didn't feel capable to support me but I still managed to stagger out of the room. There was no dignity in my escape; I just needed to get away from him.

The moment I was around the corner I collapsed sideways against the wall. My limbs trembled and the growing emptiness in my chest threatened to consume me. All I wanted to do was fall down into a hole and stay there for a very long time, but I couldn't do it yet. I had to get away from Jeremiah; I couldn't bear to see the anger and hatred in his eyes.

Bracing myself, I pushed off the hard surface and made it to the door. Swinging it open, I started to exit then blinked at the figure that was already there.

"Hello, gorgeous," Lucas said in a cheerful voice. "Just wanted to see . . ."

A sob escaped me at the surprise. I couldn't take this, not now. His voice trailed off as I tried to push past, then he grabbed my elbow. "What's wrong?"

The upbeat tone was gone. There was a commanding

note to his voice, demanding an answer, and I was so tired of being told what to do. "Let me go, I need . . ."

I trailed off, trying to push past him, but Lucas didn't relent. He grabbed my shoulders and turned me so I faced him. "Lucy, what happened? What did he do?"

There was the wild expression in his eyes, concern for me in his voice, which broke something inside me. "He knows." The whispered words were ripped from me, and I swallowed back more emotion. He cut me loose and everything— everything I'd been through was for nothing. "I'm *fired*."

I spat out that last word. The instant after the words left my mouth, I wanted them back, but it was too late. Words had power; speaking them aloud cemented their meaning. I couldn't look at Lucas; to see the confirmation in his eyes would destroy me absolutely.

Behind me, I heard my name called again and cringed, desperate only for escape. Then Lucas pulled me away from the doorway and stepped between my former employer and me. "You son of a *bitch*."

At the same time he said that came the solid smack of flesh and bone meeting, and around Lucas's lean frame I saw Jeremiah stagger back. My hands flew to my mouth in shock as Lucas advanced on his brother. "Anya wasn't enough for you," the gunrunner snarled, delivering another blow to the side of Jeremiah's head. "You have to ruin another life . . ."

Jeremiah surged up to his feet, and Lucas fell back, landing hard on his side against the tile entryway. Jeremiah faced me, a raging bull looking to charge, but all his attention was on his brother. "You've taken everything from me," Jeremiah said in a low, tight voice, aiming a kick at his brother.

"*I've* taken everything?" Lucas absorbed the blow and grabbed his brother's lower leg, twisting and pulling sideways. "You ruined my life, you ruin everything you touch! You're no better than our father."

Both men scrabbled at one another as I stood in the hallway, watching in horror. I couldn't move, rooted to the spot, as the two men grappled. Jeremiah managed to put his brother into a chokehold from behind, but Lucas, still on his knees, brought his larger brother over and sideways. The small entryway table rattled as Jeremiah hit it, sending the decorative glass plates falling sideways to shatter on the tile.

They were on their feet immediately, and Lucas charged at Jeremiah. Gasping, I backpedaled into the hallway as the two men spilled out of the hotel room. They were locked together, slamming against the far wall and falling sideways to the floor. From beside me I heard a woman cry out in surprise, but I was too riveted by the scene to look. They were muttering low enough that I could only make out brief curses.

I thought Jeremiah would be able to take his brother down easily, but Lucas held his own and put up a hell of a fight. All the rage and pain from their shared pasts seemed focused in this one struggle. The two men grappled at one another as they rolled around on the ground, throwing punches and the occasional knee. They fought like little boys, not grown men; training was thrown out the window, all that was left was the anger.

"You turned Anya against me," Jeremiah grunted, "now you try and take Lucy . . ."

"Anya never betrayed you, you stupid son of a bitch."

There was a pause in the struggling, and Lucas took advantage of the moment. He delivered several blows to Jeremiah's torso before a fist sent the gunrunner tumbling sideways. Jeremiah rolled to his knees. "You're lying."

Lucas wiped the blood from his torn lip. "Sure, I approached her to spy for me, but she turned me down. So I got my information from elsewhere, toyed with your plans, and what did you do?" He lashed out, kicking his brother in the ribs. "Threw her out, did everything you could to discredit and wreck her life. I picked up the pieces because what happened was also my fault, but I'll be goddamned if I let you do it again!" He spat blood on the floor between them. "Father would be so proud of you."

Behind me, the elevator doors opened and several men in suits spilled out onto the floor. They flowed past me toward the two fighting brothers, who seemed to have exhausted their mutual rage, at least for the moment. Each was hauled to their feet by the suited guards, and at the same time both looked directly at me. I staggered back a step and stared between them, as if trying to decide which man to approach.

Screw them. The thought came unbidden to my mind. I moved away, unable, unwilling to listen to more. *Screw them both.*

Both men were restrained, giving me my chance for escape. I took it, backing into the still-open elevator and mashing the button for Amyrah's floor. When I heard my name called, I hid against the side of the car and didn't breathe until the elevator closed and began its descent. Even then, I only held myself together by a thread. The dead feeling inside me was a bleeding wound, crawling through my body like a slow poison. I thought for sure I was going to be sick, and held tight to the rail, struggling to not make a mess inside the elevator.

I knew immediately which room was Amyrah's when the doors opened onto her floor. Two men stood outside, staring directly at me. One man raised his hand to his mouth and murmured something. I stopped at the elevator threshold, suddenly unsure of what I was doing, and afraid of what reaction I'd get.

I clutched the elevator frame, looking around the dark hallway, when the room door was wrenched open. Amyrah's head appeared around the entrance. "Lucy? Is everything okay?"

In the other room, I listened to Amyrah arguing with her brother in Arabic. I couldn't understand what they were saying, but heard the heat in their voices.

Rashid had appeared at his sister's door less than ten minutes after I'd arrived. It was barely enough time for me to compose myself from the mess I'd become. Amyrah had laid a blanket over me and promised to be right back, then dragged her older brother outside the room. It hurt to think they were arguing over me, that I was the cause for yet more discord, but I couldn't do anything except lay there.

There's a clarity that comes with having all emotion drained away. I'd experienced something similar before, not long after my parents' death. In that bank office, listening to a lawyer explain the decisions my parents had made, a bleak future was laid out for me that I nevertheless eventually fought against. Back then, my world had revolved around saving my New York family home, shrinking until that was all I could think about. For nearly two years, I'd put my life on hold, struggling to achieve that one goal.

In the end, I'd ultimately lost it all.

The guilt of losing my family's home barely held a candle to that which I felt now. This time, there was no bank or evil entity fighting against me. I'd called the shots here, made all the wrong decisions. The blame for that part was entirely mine, and I'd have to live with my choices.

But I'd be damned if I'd feel any shame for what Jeremiah had done to me. He was blinded by his own arrogance. There had never been any real option except to sign his contract back in New York. I thought my eyes were wide open to what I was doing, and stupid me had fallen in love with an ass.

I felt like such a fool.

Finally the arguing stopped, or at least grew quieter. A few moments later, Rashid appeared through the door, followed by Amyrah, who came to stand beside me. She rested her hand on my shoulder, chin up and staring resolutely at her brother. I didn't know what they had been arguing about, but the Arab girl's support right then meant the world to me.

Rashid didn't appear to approve, but he had a defeated note in his eye when he glanced at Amyrah then back to me.

"You saved my sister's life, and for that I am forever in your debt."

For a moment, I put aside my own grief and asked, "Did you ever find out who it was that tried to take us?" If I'd once again been the reason for others getting hurt, I wasn't sure how I'd feel about it.

"A man in my position, someone who deals in information, makes enemies." His eyes flickered up to Amyrah, and while his lips pursed, I saw his position soften a bit. "I've dealt with those responsible, but I still have you to thank. Ask me for anything and I'll grant it."

"I want to go home." My voice was a croak, and I grimaced. "Back to New York," I added after clearing my throat. That would be a good start, just getting back to the States. Pride kept me from asking any more; I'd deal with that when I arrived back on home soil.

The silence stretched. Rashid's eyebrows rose slightly as if he was surprised that was my only request, but he nodded. "Done."

The door opened and another man in a dark suit entered quietly. He padded over to Rashid and whispered something in his ear. Rashid immediately went still, although his expression didn't change. "You'll have to excuse me, there is an urgent matter I must attend."

It wasn't until he left that I saw Amyrah deflate with a breath I hadn't realized she was holding. She murmured something in Arabic, and then smiled down at me. "I surprised my brother by arguing," she said, a small smile forming across her lips.

"Thank you." I grabbed her hand and, not caring about what traditions I might be breaking, kissed the knuckle in thanks.

"I wish you would tell me what happened," she said, kneeling down beside me. Genuine concern leaked from her eyes. "I am not as fragile as you might believe."

How I wished I could tell her, to spill my pain and let someone else help me. But it wasn't her problem, and I didn't want to risk any condemnation for my choices. There was enough of that inside me to last a lifetime.

When I didn't speak, Amyrah sighed and nodded. "Come," she said, holding out her hand to help me up, "let's go get your things."

One of the guards near the door slipped out, probably to make sure the coast was clear. It amazed me how normal this all was to the Arab girl beside me. She didn't seem to notice the bodyguards hovering around her, the added steps made to keep her protected. I got the impression this had been the story of her life and she'd grown to accept it long ago.

I'd barely tolerated two men hovering over me, let alone a small army. Overprotective brothers were obviously not always all that fun.

We were passing through one of the living rooms when a small crash came from ahead.

"Where is she?"

I fell back a step as Jeremiah's voice boomed from the entrance to the suite. Amyrah threw me a panicked look then said something to the guards beside her, who raced toward the sound of scuffling. I stood, frozen, as the sounds grew closer.

"Dammit, I know you're in here. *Lucy!*"

My chest constricted at his voice, but I stood rooted to the spot. From across the hallway, I saw the familiar figure of Jeremiah appear, then suddenly several other figures appeared around him. A "Look out!" died on my lips as he quietly and efficiently took them down. I knew the moment he spotted me because he sprinted the length of the corridor.

More figures appeared from openings on either side of the hall, and Amyrah tugged me back into her large bedroom. Before the door could close however, it was jammed open by a large arm, then Jeremiah pulled himself into the room. He dragged the two men attached to him into the open area and managed to fling one away by sheer brute force. He took another step into the room, but was taken down as more guards streamed through the doorway.

No. I didn't want this. Why was he even here? "Please, please don't hurt him," I moaned, moving forward, but Amyrah grabbed my arm and held me in place. Two men had firm grips on each arm, and as Jeremiah lifted his head to look at me, I saw my own pain and anguish reflected in his eyes.

Then another bodyguard moved forward, a small black object in his hand, and I realized what was about to happen.

"Don't hurt him!" Wrenching my arm out of Amyrah's hold, I launched myself at the guard holding the taser. Grabbing his arm, I spun him around and away from Jeremiah.

Then, like someone flipped a switch, every muscle in my body went rigid. My fingers dug into the other man's arm as my body bowed back. A silent scream formed across my lips but nothing would come out but a guttural exhale as the diaphragm spasms pushed the last of the air from my lungs. Aftershocks continued throughout my body, my muscles no longer under any voluntary control. Then as suddenly as it appeared, it was over, and I collapsed bonelessly to the floor.

From somewhere nearby I heard a roaring sound. At first I thought it was just another aftereffect of the taser until I heard a man's pained cry. I couldn't do anything but stare at the wall in front of me, struggling to breathe. Then hands pulled at me, lifting me off the ground and back around so that I was staring up into Jeremiah's face.

A tear slid out of my eye at the tortured look on his face, but I couldn't move my arms to touch him yet. His eyes darted up, a hard glare for someone across from us. I lolled my head sideways to see the guards standing back a few feet, as if afraid to move forward.

It took every ounce of willpower and strength I had at that moment, but I finally managed to move my hand onto his arm, then up to his shoulder. "I'm sorry," I tried to say, but my lips could only form the words. The words weren't enough—they would never be enough—and yet they were all I had.

"But why?"

I heard the plea in that one word, and what little emotion I had left tore at the remnants of my heart. It was the same question I'd asked him before, back on the ship. I'd deserved an answer then, and hadn't gotten one. He deserved an answer now . . . and I had nothing. "I thought you'd rejected me," I murmured, the words a whisper. It wasn't everything I wanted to say, but it was all there was.

He swallowed. "We're quite a pair, aren't we?" he murmured, pushing back the hair that was plastered to my face.

Lifting my shoulder slightly off the ground, I finally levered my hand up to touch his face. "You'll never be able to forgive me." My eyes closed as my hand fell back to my chest. "I'll never be able to forgive me."

"No." But I saw the truth in his eyes. My actions lay like an abyss between us, and I doubted either of us would ever be able, or willing to bridge it.

Foreign chatter surrounded me, and Jeremiah's grip on my body tightened. I looked up to see his gaze darting at several points, but I didn't take my eyes off him. "You deserve better," I murmured, and saw his stricken gaze fall back to me.

My strength had returned enough to push away from him, but I couldn't make myself do it. In his arms, I was safe for the first time in what felt like forever. My brain told me I needed to let go, leave and get on with my life, but my heart wasn't ready.

I wasn't sure if it would ever be ready.

The guards surrounded us again, pulling on Jeremiah. I rolled away, and as he released me I saw the fight finally leave his face. This time he didn't protest as the guards dragged him backwards and to his feet, but his gaze remained on me. I felt like there was something I should say, a final word before we parted forever, but my chest hurt too much to speak.

"Lucy . . ."

I couldn't bring myself to look at him. "Just go." I was tired, so very tired. Amyrah stepped forward and helped me up and into a nearby chair as Jeremiah was dragged out of the room. The front door slamming was like the final nail in my coffin. "I want to go home," I murmured, staring blankly at the ground.

There was a moment of silence, then Amyrah's arm went around my shoulders. "I can at least do that for you."

11

The Dubai Airport was an eclectic mixture of Arab and Western culture, but I was too interested in leaving to really pay much attention.

Amyrah and her bodyguards dropped me off, and the Muslim girl seemed reluctant to see me leave. "Please keep in touch, yes?" she said as we hugged goodbye outside the main entrance of the airport. "Perhaps someday I can come and see you."

I smiled and hugged her back but made no promises. As much as I was grateful for her help and support, I had a feeling I would never see Amyrah again. We came from and moved within very different circles. If not for Jeremiah, I would never have thought to visit Dubai, nor would I have likely been introduced to Rashid.

While parts of this experience had been magical, I didn't anticipate such things would ever happen to me again.

The airport was a decent size, but I'd been through far larger. Finding the gate was easy enough, and I sat down in the chairs to wait it out. Amyrah had offered to fly me home on her family's private jet, but I'd had enough of that lifestyle and opted for a commercial flight.

I sat watching the different people filing around the airport concourse. I think, had this been any other time, I would have enjoyed people watching. There was such a diverse and eclectic mix of inhabitants within the airport. I was watching an Arab family go past, the woman in a heavy black *abaya* and the children in decidedly Western garb, when an older gentleman sat down next to me. I ignored him, not really in the mood for chat. Dark thoughts still swirled around in my mind, but for the most part I was numb. Experience told me it wouldn't last long, but for now I was grateful for the dull flatness I felt.

"Pardon me, miss, do you have the time?"

The older man's had a very upper crust British accent. I just shook my head, not looking at him. I knew it was rude, but right then I wasn't up for any interactions with strangers.

"I thought you kids these days always had the latest gadgets."

Despite a need for peace, my mouth twitched in one corner. "Not all of us," I mumbled, turning over the passport in my hands. Amyrah had managed to retrieve that much for me, but I'd left everything else. Even this wasn't really my passport, just a fake Lucas had made so we could fly to the Emirate city.

I supposed as long as it got me home, I couldn't complain.

"Now where did I put that pocket watch of mine? Blast!"

Something about his voice made me blink. Frowning

slightly, I tilted my head sideways to watch the man pat his pockets. Everything about him was bushy, from his beard to his eyebrows. He was partially turned away so all I could see was a profile, and while part of my brain protested, something about him seemed familiar.

"Ah, here we go!" He clicked open an antique pocket watch. "Half past three. Later than I thought."

Abandoning any sense of propriety, I openly stared at the man beside me. His thick mustache stretched in what I assumed was a smile, except I couldn't see his mouth. He looked old, but something about the blue-green eyes staring out at me didn't seem . . .

I blinked again, and then looked away toward the concourse. It felt like I should be laughing at the absurdity, but all I could manage was a tired sigh. "What are you doing here, Lucas?"

He opened a newspaper casually on his lap and began flipping through the pages. "Accompanying you home, of course."

His words set off a small spark of indignation. "I can take care of myself, you know."

"Oh, I definitely know that. I saw what you did to Alexei on the ship. I just thought you might like some company."

The memory made me wince. I turned away, not wanting to make a scene. Everything that had happened over the last several days was still a raw wound that I didn't want to touch.

"So," Lucas asked a few minutes later after a long and protracted silence, "where are we going?"

I sighed. "*I'm* going home."

"And where is that exactly?"

"I don't know." It was a question I knew I'd have to answer soon. When I'd signed that contract and Jeremiah had whisked me away, I'd lost contact with everything about my previous life. I'd even lost my phone, and hadn't memorized my roommate's number. That wasn't going to be a fun visit, but hopefully she would let me get my stuff and, if I was really lucky, maybe let me keep staying there.

"Well, I forbid you to go."

The sudden arrogant tone fired me up. I'd had enough of such things from his brother and shot Lucas an annoyed look, only to see him waggle those bushy eyebrows at me. "I'm a big strong silent type that likes to order people around," he continued dramatically, dropping the accent in favor of mimicry. "I tell you what to do and you lick my boots in thanks. Oh yes, and watch me be broody. My jutting Neanderthal brow line should have its own zip code."

I gawked at him, and then covered my mouth. Dammit, I didn't want to laugh. Part of me wanted to hold on to my pain, wallow in my misery, but his impression of Jeremiah was perfect. Somehow, hearing Lucas speak made the whole situation seem ridiculous. The bushy eyebrows and beard with a pitch-perfect Jeremiah voice only added to the absurdity.

Shaking my head, I looked away at the crowd hurrying past to their respective planes. Where once upon a time I'd enjoyed people watching, now it gave me little joy. Right now I was in a foreign land, surrounded by the unfamiliar and exotic, and all I could think about was getting home. Perhaps in hindsight I would regret not taking advantage of my situation, but for now all I wanted was to escape.

"My brother doesn't deserve you."

Lucas had completely ditched the British accent and false joviality. He sounded angry, and I glanced at him briefly. In my heart, I didn't believe his words. Beneath the fake beard I saw the bruising and puffiness from his fight with Jeremiah. It hurt me to know I'd been the cause of more pain, and I looked back down at my hands.

"I'm sorry I caused this."

I shook my head. "It wasn't your fault. I made some of the decisions that got me here." I lifted one shoulder in a tired shrug. The sadness was creeping back, making me long for the numbness I'd felt before.

"No." My response seemed to fire him up because he squirmed in his seat before looking at me again. His eyes darkened as he leaned into me. "You deserve so much better than this, better than anything our fucked-up family can give you."

"Oh, Lucas." The self-recrimination in his words touched off something inside me. I brought my hands up to his face and turned his head so we were eye to eye. I stroked the bruised sliver of exposed skin on his cheek, the false beard prickly against my thumb. "Somebody once told me we all have choices, even if they aren't good ones. You're worth so much more than this life you lead right now."

The muscles beneath my palm clenched, and the sudden

yearning in his eyes nearly undid me. "Let me stay with you," he rasped, covering my hand with his own. "I'm a better man around you. I need . . ."

He trailed off as I shook my head sadly. "You're already a better man, Lucas."

A woman's voice echoed over the PA system, announcing the boarding for my flight. His fingers dug into the back of my hands as if to hold me in place, prevent me from leaving, then finally they slid down my arms and to his lap. I leaned forward and kiss his whiskered cheek. "I can't be your absolution," I whispered against his skin, wishing that there were some way to change that.

But I was done with the Hamilton family. I couldn't bring myself to tell him that, not now, but it was the truth. There was too much pain and history now to ever allow for a normal life if I chose to stay with either brother.

And I had only ever really wanted one.

"Goodbye, Lucas."

I stared as the bartender poured colorful drinks on the countertop, trying to decide if it was worth it to get wasted or if that would make things worse.

Winter storms had extended my layover in London's Heathrow, so I'd retreated to a nearby bar. The British airport was very different from the one in Dubai, but its inhabitants were no less varied. It felt much more normal to me, more western, but I missed the exoticness of the Arabian airport. Dubai was an experience I'd never thought I'd have and, while not every part was perfect, it was a memory I'd treasure.

But mostly, I missed Jeremiah. He was the one I wanted to forget, as well as the choices that had damned me to a dreary life.

It was tempting to try to forget but, somehow, I doubted alcohol would help there.

"Can I buy you something?"

I looked beside me as a man around my age sat down in the seat beside me. He was handsome in a normal way, wearing a light suit that complimented his dark hair. His expression was placid and friendly, but I gave him a wan smile and shook my head. "No, I'm good."

"You sure? Look like you could use a drink."

Great. Now strangers were commenting on my melancholy. *I must look like a wreck*, I thought, and shrugged. "I don't even know what to order."

He flagged down the bartender. "Two Midori sours," he said, and then turned to me. "So, where are you headed?"

"New York City."

"Ah, an east coast girl." He cocked his head sideways. "You have a faint accent though, French Canadian?"

My eyebrows shot up. Most people didn't notice; even Jeremiah, as astute as he was, had never mentioned it. "I was born in Quebec," I replied, more than a little impressed. "Moved to New York when I was ten." It had been the year my grandfather died, leaving us the house where my mother had been raised.

"That must have been tough for you."

I shrugged. "No little kid likes to move, I guess." He seemed nice enough, not as overbearing as Jeremiah or as wily as Lucas. He looked like any businessman, clean cut and well dressed, but I could tell from my brief time with Jeremiah that the man before me wasn't rich. His shoes weren't high-dollar, the suit not an expensive cut. He seemed normal, the kind of man I should end up with.

Once upon a time, I might have been attracted to someone like this. Now, he seemed so drab in comparison.

I took a deep breath, fighting against my own disappointment. *Would I always compare other men to Jeremiah?* "What about you?" I asked, forcing a friendly smile, "where are you heading?"

"Oh, I'm traveling to see family," he answered as the bartender arrived with our drinks. I sniffed the green liquid then took a sip, and was pleasantly surprised by the sweet taste. "So is anyone special waiting for you at home?"

His innocuous question destroyed my mood. I set the drink on the countertop, the syrupy liquor turning to ash in my mouth. It was difficult to tell if he was hitting on me or just making conversation. "I just got over a bad breakup," I answered, hoping he would get the hint.

"Ah yes, how is Jeremiah doing these days?"

At first, his response didn't register. I blinked, then looked back at him. "Excuse me?"

"You've had quite a rough time lately," he continued blithely, waving around his drink for emphasis before taking a sip. "Of course, that probably started more with when your parents were killed by that hit-and-run driver than when you were seduced in an elevator."

It was like someone had reached inside my chest and had a stranglehold on my lungs. I couldn't breathe, couldn't even move. In my hand, the plastic cup rattled against the wood bar, but no one around us seemed to notice my distress.

"I took a little visit to your family home in upstate New York," he continued, stirring the green drink with the little straw. "Very pretty, more so in person. The family inside it now hasn't kept up the place however, which is a shame."

"Who are you?" I whispered, the words squeezed out of me.

"But I suppose the sins of the parents are passed down to the next generation," he continued, seeming to ignore my question. "Your parents couldn't see past the moment, mismanaging their finances so that when they were killed in a silly accident, they ruined your life . . ."

Throwing my drink in his face wasn't a conscious decision. The sound of the ice cubes hitting the linoleum below shocked me, but the other man's expression didn't change. A few people looked over at us, but nobody seemed interested in joining our discussion.

He paused, then picked up a napkin from the counter and wiped his face. "I probably deserved that."

"Who are you?" I repeated, my voice shaky but louder this time. Inside I was a mess; that he knew so much about my life had me in a panic, but I had nowhere to go. I'd abandoned the only people who could help me, believing myself not involved in their problems. Now I was sitting alone, thousands of miles away, being told that I was now as big a part in this story as any Hamilton.

For a brief moment the stranger didn't respond, just stared at me. "What do we know about the Hamilton family tree?" he said finally, tilting his head sideway in thought. "Certainly a noble heritage going back several generations. Their money was made on the backs of others, trampling lesser men to achieve their ends. The current generation boasts an arms smuggler who's taken an untold number of lives, and a commando who is no better than his father with his own militia."

No better than his father. My adrenaline-fueled brain put together the pieces. "You're Alexander Rush."

"Ah, you've heard of me. Rufus Hamilton's bastard, one of many no doubt—is that how they described me? Loki's friend is very good at gathering information, but guess what?" He leaned forward. "I'm better."

The blithe tone as he spoke, the way he ticked off details of my own life to me, cut me to the quick. The danger I thought I was leaving, the deadly intrigue and drama, had followed me. I was being pulled into the snare as surely as any Hamilton, except I didn't know how to fight this. I didn't have military contacts, or a spy network, or an armed militia.

I didn't stand a chance.

"You're very lucky to have left when you did." Alexander looked at his watch. "I need to make my exit, but it was wonderful talking to you. I wanted to meet the woman who brought both Hamilton men to their knees."

Something about the way he said that made me tremble

harder. I couldn't open my mouth to deny it; my body was frozen in place. I sat there unmoving as he stood up, grabbed a jacket from the back of the seat, and walked past me. My brain played out scenarios on how I was about to die, but the seconds ticked past and nothing happened. I couldn't, however, make myself turn around to see where he'd gone.

My brain told me I was hyperventilating but I couldn't stop my racing heart. There was no way I could have imagined all that; the two glasses were still on the counter in front of me. For several seconds I sat there, trying to control my breathing. I had nowhere to go, nobody to call.

I was alone.

"Oi, can you turn the telly up?"

The loud question next to my head startled me. A quick glance around the bar confirmed that nobody was watching me, but I still felt horribly raw and violated. That stranger had known too much about me; to have my life be such an open book, to have him speak of my parents . . . I had to get out of here, and grabbed my thin sweater off the back of the chair as the bartender turned up the television broadcast.

Words like nails in a coffin filtered to my ears as I tried to slip out of the airport bar. ". . . bombing in a Dubai hotel . . ."

If I thought I'd already reached the end of my chain, those words shattered the links. I whipped around to see images of the Almasi Hotel on the small television behind the bar, smoke all but obscuring the tower.

No. Please God, no. The newscaster was saying something but I couldn't hear, through my jumbled thoughts. I covered my mouth in shock, then turned and stumbled out into the causeway.

I had to get a hold of myself. Danger seemed everywhere; the busy terminal had hundred of eyes, any of which my brain screamed could be deadly. Not knowing where to go, I staggered toward the nearest chair. The gate was all but empty; I shared the space with one other lady, but the rest of humanity poured through the narrow walkway. I felt trapped inside the tube; taking deep breaths wasn't helping.

Something vibrated in my pocket.

Startled by the sound, I jumped in my seat, then tentatively reached inside and pulled out an unfamiliar cell phone. It wasn't mine; in fact I had no idea where it had come from. Freed from my pocket, it rang loudly, the display showing a blocked number. Holding my breath, I pulled the clamshell open and pressed the green button with a shaky finger. "H-Hello?"

"What's up, gorgeous?" Exuberant tones spilled through the phone. "Miss me?"

"Lucas?" A cold wave of relief rolled over me, and I clutched the phone to my ear. "Where are you?"

"Well, funny story that. Still in Dubai, technically, although I'm not sure how international . . ."

"Someone was here." The words spilled out, the sobs I'd been holding down threatening to rise to the surface. "Somebody approached me at the bar. Lucas, he knew my name, he knew everything about me, talked about my parents' death . . ."

"Lucy, calm down." The jovial tone was gone, replaced

by a much needed calmness. "I need you to start from the beginning."

But I didn't care about that, I needed to know information. "The television said there was an explosion," I asked. "In Dubai, at the hotel. Lucas, the man said I was lucky to leave when I did, what happened? Is Jeremiah all right? What about Amyrah?"

"There was an explosion, but I need you to get to safety. Where are you right now?"

I looked quickly around. "I'm at gate B13. Lucas, is Jeremiah all right?" I had to know, and his pause after my question only made my heart race faster.

"Listen Lucy, I'm going to get you help. Right now however I'm a little bit tied up with . . ."

"*What about Jeremiah?*" I hadn't meant to shout the words, but it felt like my heart was going to burst from my chest. I ducked my head, covering my eyes with my hand to block out the swirl of people around me. "Please Lucas, tell me he's all right."

It was several long seconds before he finally spoke. "I'm sorry Lucy, but I—"

The line went dead.

"Lucas? *Lucas?*" I pulled the phone from my ear and stared at it. The call had been dropped with no way to reconnect.

I'm sorry Lucy. In my mind, that only meant one thing.

I wanted to throw up. Wrapping my arms around my stomach, I leaned forward until my head was between my knees. I kept my eyes tightly shut, struggling to breathe through the icy clamp around my heart.

No. No no no no. I could have lived my life without Jeremiah. It would have hurt knowing he was no longer mine, but I could have dealt with that. If he was dead however . . . Moans escaped me, and I put the back of my hand across my mouth.

I was holding my breath, and I forced myself to exhale, then take another breath. Another small moan came with the exhalation, and I felt tears spill over my hand.

I don't know how long I sat there, trying to get myself together, before I realized I had company. A deep, shaky breath later, I looked up to see three men in suits surrounding me.

"Ms. Lucy Delacourt?"

Two of them were in uniform and looked poised for action, their hands on their belts. I couldn't see any guns but had no doubt they were there. The third man stepped out in front of me, flipping up a badge. "I'm agent Atwater with Interpol. Ma'am, we need you to come with us."

12

When I was escorted out of the airport terminal and taken to a very stark interrogation room, I didn't imagine I'd be left alone long enough to get bored.

As time passed with nobody coming into the room or checking on me, the fear bled away into nervousness, then annoyance. I cast the large mirror on one wall questioning looks, not sure what to do with myself. They'd already confiscated the phone Lucas had slipped into my pocket but a simple clock on the wall ticked off the seconds as they passed. What I needed was answers, and the nothing I was getting made me anxious.

I stood up and paced the room, not knowing what else to do for myself. Several times I passed by the mirror, then finally knocked on the glass. "Hello? Are you going to question me or something?" I called, feeling foolish for talking to my own reflection. "Am I free to go?"

The door to the room clicked open, startling me. An older woman in a suit stepped inside, holding a notepad and several files under her arm. "Hello, Lucy," she said, her voice tinged with a French accent. "Sorry to keep you waiting."

I wasn't interested in idle chitchat. "Where's Jeremiah?" I blurted, not believing for an instant she didn't know to whom I was referring.

The woman's eyes narrowed, and she tilted her head to the side. "You're not a colleague of his brother Lucas Hamilton?"

So that was who got me in this mess. "I'm an acquaintance," I hedged, not sure how much I could tell her.

She cocked an eyebrow. "An intimate acquaintance?"

There was no way for me to stop the flush that rose over my cheeks, which of course gave me away. "I need to know what happened to *Jeremiah* Hamilton," I emphasized. "I saw the news but didn't get details before your men showed up. What happened at the Almasi Hotel?"

"Miss Delacourt, why don't you have a seat . . ."

"Dammit, stop pussyfooting around!" I was getting pissed off at the nothing that was being accomplished. "Some stranger bought me a drink in the bar, listed off intimate details of my life, and told me I was *lucky* to have left when I did."

"Do you know who this man was?"

She didn't seem at all fazed by my outburst. I pressed my lips together, not sure whether to answer any more questions. "Who are you anyway?"

The woman held out her hand. "I am Marie Gautier, an agent for Interpol. I've been in close contact with your friend Lucas, or Loki if you prefer."

I shook her hand cautiously, not knowing what to say.

Lucas had said he'd get me help, was this woman a contact of his? "I need to know what happened in the Almasi Hotel. Please," I added when her lips pursed, "I saw there was an explosion, and some people I knew were in there."

Marie nodded. "There was indeed an explosion, and several people were injured. I can get details if you'd like, but I'll need something from you."

"I'll tell you everything I know, work with a sketch artist, whatever you need. Just please get me some information about my friends."

Her gaze went to the mirror, as if silently communicating with whoever was behind there, and then she again indicated the table and chairs. "I'm eager to hear anything you have to say, Miss Delacourt."

Despite my assertion to tell them everything, I left off a few bits of information. Mostly it related to sex, the name of the boat we used in the Caribbean, and any mention of Matthews and Franks directly. But everything else I laid bare, glad to finally get a chance to unload everything I'd bottled up inside. If this woman or the people listening outside that mirror were at all untrustworthy, or decided to pin any blame on me, I'd be in a world of hurt.

"So you acted as a translator for the original deal, then were coerced onto the ship?"

The agent seemed very keen on discussing this, which made me nervous. By answering truthfully, I was also essentially incriminating myself, but I was so tired of secrets. "Lucas *kidnapped* me from his brother's estate, then brought me to that meeting. So yes, I participated, but it wasn't by choice."

The agent looked poised to ask me another question when there was a sharp rap on the mirror beside us. She glanced over, and then stood to her feet. "If you'll excuse me a moment."

Once again I was alone. This time I knew I was being watched so sat still, fiddling with the table, until Marie came back to the room. She didn't look happy by whatever news she'd been given, and sat back down at the table across from me. "Miss Delacourt," she said, pulling pictures out of one file and spreading them before me, "do you recognize any of these men from your time with Lucas?"

I studied the images, wracking my brains to place any of the faces. "Him," I said finally, pointing to a picture of an older gentleman. "Lucas called him Mr. Smith, I think the shipment was his. But I don't know any of the others."

If the agent was going to say anything else, she didn't get the chance before the door opened, and I looked over to see a man enter the room. He had a no-nonsense look on his face, and his eyes briefly flicked over to me before fixing on the other agent. "My name is Evan Rothschild and I will be representing Miss Delacourt in this matter."

I squinted up at the smaller man, not sure what was happening. His accent was American, and his round face was red as if he'd run here.

"I didn't know Lucy had retained a lawyer," Marie stated.

"I'm here on behalf of my employer, Jeremiah Hamilton."

That got my attention. "You've spoken to Jeremiah?" I asked.

The lawyer nodded at my question but kept his attention

on the agent as I reeled at that news. "I'd like a moment in private to address my client."

Marie looked like she was sucking on a lemon. "Your client has information on a potential terrorist," she started.

"And she has been cooperating fully with Interpol officials," the lawyer interjected. "Is she being charged with anything?"

"Does she need to be to make her stay?"

"Hey!" They were talking as if I wasn't right there in the room. I glared at the lawyer. "Can the client butt in for a moment? I'm here to help."

Marie glanced at me, then back at the lawyer. "She needs to work with a sketch artist," she said after a moment. "It isn't safe for her to leave . . ."

"My employer is taking care of that already, and would like Miss Delacourt to be released into his custody."

"Out of the question."

"Can I use the bathroom?" My bladder was fine, but I'd had enough of being talked over. I stood up. "It's through this door, right?"

The agent gave an exasperated sigh, and then nodded. I didn't wait but tried the knob, eager to leave the small room. The door was locked, but as I jiggled the handle it turned and opened out toward me. A large man in a dark suit similar to Marie's stepped aside, allowing me to pass back into the narrow hallway. He indicated a direction and I turned, and then stopped in my tracks.

Jeremiah stood not twenty feet away, a dark wall in the well-lit corridor. My feet were rooted to the linoleum as I drank in the sight of him, adrenaline coursing through my body.

Behind me, Marie and the lawyer stepped into the hall, continuing to bicker, but I only had eyes for Jeremiah. He stared back at me, silent as the grave, his face as closed as ever. Gone was the uncertainty I'd seen in him the last few days; he was back in familiar settings, once more in charge of his world.

What I'd give to have even an ounce of that strength right then.

He continued to stare at me, and with his continued silence the small kernel of hope in my heart died. The stress of the last several hours roared up suddenly, and I clapped a hand over my mouth to stifle a sob. I wasn't going to cry again, I wasn't, but seeing him so suddenly, thinking I'd lost him forever . . .

Across from me I heard Jeremiah curse, then arms stretched around my shoulders, pulling me into a solid embrace. I breathed in through my nose, let that familiar scent wash over me. The emotions I'd tried so hard to contain went spilling free. A sob escaped me, and I wrapped my arms around his torso, burying my face in his suit. "I thought you were dead," I whispered, and knew he heard me when his arms tightened around my shoulders.

There were so many things I wanted to say but all I could do was cry and cling to his solid frame. I didn't want to be the needy damsel in distress, it hurt my pride, but oh, it felt so good to have some help.

"If we're done here," I heard the lawyer say behind me.

"Not so fast." Marie's words were like a cracking whip. "I need answers. Both of you were at the scene of a bombing only hours before it happened. Do I really need to tell you how this looks?"

"We'll cooperate fully with your department," Jeremiah interrupted from above me. He didn't seem fazed in the slightest by her threats; his cool gaze never wavered.

His words however seemed to mollify the French agent. "Miss Delacourt? Can I count on your help identifying the man you claim you saw?"

A thin rivulet of anger snaked through me at her insinuation that I lied, but I nodded, too tired to fight. Clenching my fists, I let Jeremiah go and stepped away, turning to face the agent. "I'll help you, but I don't know myself what's going on."

"However you might think yourself innocent, you're tied to this." Her words reverberated through my brain as two more agents flanked us. Marie whispered to the man beside her, who disappeared through another door. "We'll need to know everything you saw and heard, anything he may have touched, whatever you remember."

"I'm here to help."

My mouth was dry, my body trembling from the stress, and then I felt hands slide down my arms. Jeremiah leaned down and whispered, "I won't leave your side."

Oh, how much I wanted to believe that.

We were there for another three hours, and when they finally released us it was very grudgingly.

I worked with a sketch artist to get a picture of Alexander, half-expecting someone to come in and say they have video of him from the airport monitors. From the way they were acting however, it didn't sound like they had any real images. I couldn't figure out why that would be—we'd been in a very public place that I knew had more than a few cameras— but they seemed very interested in getting as detailed a sketch as possible from me.

It was a face that was etched into my brain. I wouldn't forget it anytime soon. The deceptive innocence on his features, the calculated attempt at looking so normal as to be invisible. It made me wonder how much of what I saw was real, or if his appearance to me had been as much a costume as Lucas's.

Still, I faithfully recounted the high widow's peak, dark hair, and blue-green eyes that only in hindsight held Hamilton traits. My mind kept flashing to the horrific scenes from the Dubai hotel. It made me queasy to think he could have been sitting next to me on the airplane to London and I never would have known.

By the time we were done, I was feeling fuzzy and mentally drained. Jeremiah never left my side, even when I was doing the sketch, and his presence bewildered me. Even though he sat quietly, his presence was like an elephant in the room. My mind kept flashing back to our last conversations, the words that were spoken and secrets laid bare. It was distracting to say the least, and worry over what this meant made me nervous and jittery.

"We will be giving you a security detail and placing you into protective custody," Marie said as the artist packed up her pencils and exited quietly.

From behind me, Jeremiah spoke up for the first time. "That won't be necessary . . ."

"On this, I'm afraid I must insist." Marie turned back to me. "Ms. Delacourt, for whatever reason a potential terrorist has chosen to reveal himself to you. You've seen his face, and are therefore a liability."

Chills spread through me, but I frowned. "But he didn't seem to care that I saw him. In fact, he made himself as memorable as possible: why?"

"We'd like to know the same, which is why for now you'll be protected. And Mr. Hamilton?" When Jeremiah glanced at the Interpol agent, she added, "No more heroics this time. I've read your file, I know exactly what happened with you and your men in New York. Any armed 'guards' we see on British soil will immediately be detained and we'll separate you and Ms. Delacourt."

If the woman's threat had any effect on Jeremiah, he hid it well. He didn't answer however, just held the door open for me as we exited the small room. I was happy to leave, but didn't like the idea that we'd have an escort.

"I have reservations at the Carlton Tower . . ."

"Too public. My men will take you somewhere safe outside the city."

I wondered if she was doing that for our safety, or for the safety of any innocent bystanders. As far as we knew, the bombing in Dubai had been meant for the Hamilton brothers but had missed both, instead impacting guests of the hotel. Guilt skewered me and I glanced up at Jeremiah, but he was as unreadable as ever.

There were so many answers I needed to know, but they all boiled down to one question: *why?* Why was Jeremiah being targeted? Why was the billionaire helping me? And why was I being brought into the whole mess?

If I'd hoped to be riding in separate vehicles, I was sorely mistaken. We walked for a while before heading outside into the chill London air. A black car was waiting for us, and as we drew closer I realized it was a very different sort of cab. For a girl who'd grown used to the cabbies of New York City, the boxy vehicle was definitely outside my norm.

"This is your safest transport?"

Jeremiah's displeasure was obvious, but Marie just shrugged. "This will blend in with the rest of the city and hopefully throw off any others trying to track you."

The biting wind was leeching through my clothing, and I ducked into the vehicle. It was as spacious as it looked from the outside and I scooted to the far side of the vehicle. The car rocked slightly as Jeremiah stepped inside and paused, peering around the enclosed space. I stared out the window, refusing to look at him, but saw him pause for a moment before taking the seat furthest from me diagonally.

It was hypocritical of me, but the fact that he stayed far away from me hurt.

The drive out of town was a silent affair. I couldn't even enjoy the sights because his presence overshadowed everything. It would have been the perfect chance to ask my questions, except I was afraid of what I'd hear. There was no escape in that moving cab; I'd be trapped, forced to deal with whatever he said.

I was too much of a coward, so I kept my silence.

It wasn't until we got out into the British countryside that I started noticing our surroundings more. I had no idea how far we'd be going, but the scenes grew more pastoral and rustic as the cab ate up the miles. The sun poked through the dreary clouds only a few times before sinking below the horizon. Even in the fading light, I could see the green hills dotted with white sheep. As we drove further I felt a small smile lift one corner of my mouth. I'd been to London as a child, but never around the country itself. Stonework homes straight out of medieval times were interspersed with modern buildings and vehicles, creating a fascinating dichotomy.

"I thought you would like to know, Amyrah is okay."

My heart skipped at his words, and a burden I'd been carrying was lifted from my heart. I laid my head against the glass in relief, not trusting myself to speak for a moment. "How did it happen?" I finally asked

"I don't know, my plane was already in the air when my men sent me the news." He paused, then added in a softer tone, "I don't think Rashid made it."

My eyes fluttered closed, sadness for Amyrah's loss weighing on my mind. "Why is this happening?" I whispered.

I thought the question had been lost in the rumble of the cab's noise, but Jeremiah still answered after a moment of silence. "I don't know."

"Why does he hate you so much that he'd kill innocent people?" I looked away from the window back to Jeremiah.

"I think we're only an excuse for him, a way for him to kill people and lay the blame at another's feet."

"It's like Archangel all over again," I mumbled, remembering the assassin who'd been sent after Jeremiah. I'd foiled his plans, and barely survived my two encounters. Fear settled around me again. "I saw his face, now he's going to . . ."

I couldn't finish. A chill prickled my skin, permeating down to my bones, then there was a rustle of clothes and Jeremiah was beside me. "I'll keep you safe, I promise."

"Why?" I looked him square in the eye, too drained to feel shame or sorrow over the rift between us. "What am I to you anymore?" *What was I ever to you?*

"Because . . ." Jeremiah reached for me, then I saw his hand clench into a fist. "Because . . ."

I laid my fingers on his lips. "Never mind," I said softly, rubbing my thumb over his chin. Light stubble had already made it rough, and I dropped my hand to my lap and leaned into him. "Just hold me. Please."

His arms almost immediately went around me and I curled against his body, reveling in the feeling of being held.

13

It was close to the middle of the night when we finally stopped in front of a stone house. Rain had started to drizzle on the car at some point, but I'd been curled on the seat, passed out with my head in Jeremiah's lap. As I came back to consciousness, I noticed he laid his jacket over me. I appreciated the warmth and nuzzled his leg as our driver got out and went into the large house.

Jeremiah's crotch was just above my face. My brain still sleep befuddled, I reached out and stroked the bulge through the trousers. I felt his thigh muscles clench beneath me as Jeremiah let out a quick breath, but otherwise he didn't move. Under my hand he quickly grew, and I massaged his hard length with the heel of my hand.

Fingers clamped down on my wrist like a vise, holding me in place. I turned my head up to see Jeremiah staring down at me, his green eyes glinting in the faint light. Shame coursed through me and I rolled upright, trying to scoot away, but Jeremiah kept his hold on my wrist. "Let me go."

"Lucy . . ."

Beside me, the door opened, letting in a rush of chill air. I turned to see one of the agents, and felt the grip around my wrist lessen. Tearing my hand free, I quickly exited the car, moving sideways as Jeremiah followed. He didn't approach me however, and I realized when I saw his white shirt that I still wore his coat.

"This way," one of the other guards said, his British accent thick, and I followed him around the entrance as our cab drove away. A fog had seeped over the countryside, and the air remained wet and chilled. Despite myself, I burrowed into the coat, wrapping it around me to block out the cold. It smelled of Jeremiah, who trailed behind me, and my hands clenched around the thick fabric.

As we moved around the house, I realized it wasn't actually a home but a bed and breakfast. The open lot that I assumed was meant for parking was deserted; we seemed to be the only guests.

"We stay here for the night and move again tomorrow," the young blond agent told us, stopping in front of a green door. He knocked three times, then the door opened and another heavyset agent with dark hair stepped out. The other agent nodded, and the younger agent motioned us toward the door. "Through here."

The entryway led into a short hallway with rooms on either side. "These are your rooms for the night."

I turned the knob to the one closest to me and peeked inside. A small lamp was already lit, highlighting the floral wallpaper lining the walls. It was quaint, enough room for a

queen bed and a dresser. The bathroom was at the end of
the hall, apparently to be shared between our rooms.

"Get some sleep, we'll be heading out at first light."

"Where are we going?" Jeremiah asked. I turned back to
see the frown on his brow. "We were never told our destination."

"For now that's privileged information, but tonight I can
promise you'll stay safe." He looked at each of us in turn,
nodding his head. "Ms. Delacourt, Mr. Hamilton." Then
he stepped back and closed the door, leaving us alone in the
hallway.

My fingers curled around the doorway to the room I'd
chosen. To say I was nervous was an understatement, but
it felt rude to just close the door without saying good night.
All I wanted to do was run away

"Lucy, we should talk . . ."

"No." I held up a hand, shaking my head as I backed into
my room. "There's nothing more to talk about." I bit my
tongue to keep from saying anything else. I could apologize
every day from now to eternity, and it wouldn't erase what
I'd done. The CEO of Hamilton Industries never struck me
as the forgiving kind, and I knew I wouldn't survive any
punishment he intended to mete out.

One thick hand wedged itself between the door and frame.
Against my better judgment, I peeked outside. Jeremiah
stared down at me through that narrow sliver, more emotion
than I'd seen all day contorting his face. The knuckles on
his hand were white from his grip on the frame. "Lucy," he
started, but didn't seem to know what to say any more than

me. His stare was intense, almost pleading, but Jeremiah Hamilton didn't beg. Everyone knew this.

Frustration welled up inside of me. "What do we have to talk about?" I asked, my hand gripping the door handle tight. "You made your feelings clear in Dubai and I can't . . ." I took a shaky breath. "More happened on that ship you don't know about, but it doesn't matter. As you so eloquently put it, I f . . . fucked Lucas." I stumbled over the word, my knees trembling. "And I can't take that back."

This time, Jeremiah didn't flinch. "I should have kept you safe."

"Bullshit. This wasn't your fault." Exhaustion spread through me like a wave; I was too tired to argue any more. I closed my eyes, shutting his overwhelming presence out as best I could. "Good night, Jeremiah."

"Lucy . . ."

The one word was as broken a plea as I'd ever heard. I hid behind the door as tears pricked my eyes and I covered my mouth with one hand, unable to speak. Jeremiah's hand left the doorframe, and it took everything in me to put it shut those meager few inches.

Once more, I was alone.

And my heart had fallen to pieces all over again.

I couldn't sleep, too plagued by grief and worry. The safety net I'd had in Jeremiah was all but gone; there was no comfort to be had now. All I did was toss and turn all night until the sky outside grew light.

The small clock beside my bed barely registered five in

the morning when there came a sharp knock on my door and the agent's voice said, "We need to head out."

Groaning against the pillow, I rolled over and onto my feet. Rubbing the sleep, or lack thereof, from my eyes, I smoothed out my rumpled clothing and stumbled to the door. I hated that I was still in these clothes, and hoped I'd get some new ones soon. A shower also sounded lovely, but I didn't want to run into Jeremiah so bathroom breaks were quick.

I poked my head out the door and, seeing it was empty, stepped out into the hall. Unsure whether Jeremiah was still inside his room or not, I hurried out to the main part of the bed and breakfast. The low light of dawn shone through one window, and a few lamps were on inside the bigger room. Along one wall was a tray of pastries and packets of jam. Considering how rushed everyone seemed, I doubted there would be time for breakfast, so grabbed a couple scones and muffins for a quick snack.

There was a shuffle on the far end of the room and I saw the two agents from yesterday enter the room. The older man stepped forward. "Are you two ready to go?"

I started to nod, then watched in confusion as the younger blond agent picked up a decorative bottle and slammed it behind the other man's head. The older agent went down, crumpling in a heap on the ground. The blond man stepped over his partner, his face screwed up in regret.

My confusion turned to horror as he unstrapped his sidearm and pulled it free. "I'm so sorry about this," he told me, screwing on a long silencer, then raised the gun and pointed it at me.

A month ago, I would have died at that moment. My feet would have been rooted to the ground in shock, my brain unable to believe this could be happening. I would have stood my ground, and been shot to death by the agent.

It was amazing the difference a very scary month made in a girl's reaction times. I'd probably need therapy after this.

"Jeremiah," I screamed, dropping the pastries and bolting for the still-open hallway door toward our rooms. I heard the unmistakable pop of the weapon as I cleared the door, and a gouge appeared in the wall behind me, dangerously close to my shoulder. I shut the door and raced for my room, the agent in hot pursuit.

There was no escape from my room except the window and the door, and that second option wasn't really a choice. However, the small room afforded me nothing in the way of protection; if he started shooting through the door, he'd be certain to hit me. "Jeremiah," I wailed, kneeling into the far corner as something slammed against my door.

There was the sound of scuffling outside, then grunting noises from at least two individuals. I heard two more bullets splinter through the walls, then a truncated cry. Worried for Jeremiah's safety, I crept forward and pulled the door open a crack.

Jeremiah's head snapped toward me. "Stay inside, I don't know how many others there are."

I took a shaky breath when I saw the gun in his hand and not the agent's. The blond man was on the floor, both hands in the air and a grimace of pain on his face. "He knocked out his partner," I said, chills coursing through me at the sight of my assailant groaning on the floor. I hid behind the door, knowing it was a futile gesture if another gunman showed up. "Why did he attack us?"

"I don't know, and I don't care."

"He took my family."

I looked back down at the agent who was struggling upright. He paused when he saw his gun in Jeremiah's hand, the muzzle trained at the agent's head. One of his arms was cradled against his chest, but he looked desperate. "He said that I needed to . . ."

"We needed to die and your family would be released?"

The guilt on the other man's face answered Jeremiah's gruff question. The billionaire glared down at the man at his feet, then lifted the gun. "We're leaving," he said, and beckoned to me.

"No!"

There was a shuffle on the floor, and Jeremiah lowered the gun back to the other agent and calmly pulled the trigger. The agent gasped, and dropped the smaller weapon he had in his hand. It clunked against the ground as the agent panted, holding his leg with his one good hand.

"Give me your phone. Now."

It took several seconds but the agent sifted through his pockets then lifted up a bloody object, hands trembling. Jeremiah took the cellphone from the agent, then held his hand out to me. "Come on."

I wasn't sure it was safe yet but didn't want to stay here, so

I took his hand and stepped carefully over the prone agent. "I'm sorry about your family," I murmured as Jeremiah ushered me out and toward the exit.

Before we went out the main door, Jeremiah leaned down and checked the pulse of the older gent still slumped on the floor. "He's alive," he told me, then rummaged through the man's pockets for the car keys and dragged me outside.

It felt weird getting into the passenger seat on what my brain thought of as the driver's side. "Where are we going?" I asked as Jeremiah started up the black cab car.

"Don't know, but we can't stay here."

We'd barely gotten on the road when the cellphone in Jeremiah's pocket rang. We shared a look, then he answered the call, setting it on speakerphone.

"Status on the cargo?"

Marie's accented voice was easily recognizeable, but for whatever reason her words gave me chills. She wasn't in on this deal, was she?

"Still alive," Jeremiah growled, "This cargo is going to find its own way home."

There was a pause, and I could almost see the woman asking people around her to trace the call. "What have you done with my men?"

"Your agent was compromised and attacked us first, said a mysterious "he" had his family. I think we all know who he meant."

"Mr. Hamilton, just stay where you are. We will come and sort this out . . ."

"No." Jeremiah's answer was short and sweet. "We tried it your way, now it's my turn."

"Mr. Hamilton, if you try to bring your militia over here and start an international incident . . ."

"This already *is* international, Ms. Gautier, or have you forgotten Dubai? If I find anything, I'll let your office know immediately. Goodbye."

He shut off the speakerphone first but I could hear the strident tones of the Interpol agent before he ended the call. He rolled down the window and chucked the phone out, then sped up down the narrow road. "We need to find another vehicle and a phone."

"The red boxes are public phones I think; maybe the next town will have one."

"What else happened on that ship?"

His question surprised me. I glared at him. "You want to talk about this now?"

"Yes."

I sighed and stared out the window. "Your brother saved my life. Twice." I reached up and touched the nick on my throat. The wound hadn't even finished healing. "Once from another gunrunner who, um, wanted a go, and then from a saboteur with a knife to my throat."

We were silent for a while before he spoke again. "Is that why you slept with him?"

"No." My answer was instantaneous, but after I blurted out my answer I paused to think about it. I hadn't wanted to examine the situation until now, as the whole thing still confused me "Maybe. I'm sure that was part of it, in fact it might be a huge part." I sighed. "Yes, I know he kidnapped me, and yes I know he's nothing but trouble, but . . ."

I trailed off, trying to make sense of the whole situation. "When you walked out, it hurt. Like, soul-crushing kind of hurt. You called my love a "platitude" and disappeared, and at that moment I didn't know if you'd return. Then Lucas appears, gives me a choice to stay or go, and when I choose you I'm kidnapped—again!—and put on that ship."

"I'm sorry."

I blinked. To hear those words coming from Jeremiah's lips was more than slightly odd. "Sorry for what exactly?" I asked, not quite sure what to think about his apology.

"For not keeping you safe."

Eyes closing, I leaned my head back against the seat. "You really don't get it, do you?"

"Well, what would you have me say then?"

"What would I . . ." I let out a frustrated groan, crossing my arms. "I'd have you figure that out by yourself."

"Lucy . . ."

"I was almost raped, almost killed! Maybe you know how to deal with those kinds of situations, but I don't. I needed comfort, some sense of security, and I didn't know if you even cared that I was . . ."

The conversation was making me angry, dredging up emotions I hadn't yet dealt with. Letting out a shaky breath, I stared out the window, the bumps from the cobbled road beneath us rocking me gently.

"But you blame me for what happened."

I sighed. "No Jeremiah, I don't blame you."

"Then why . . ."

"Dammit, I don't know!" I wanted to tear my hair out at that moment. "Why are we even talking about this? You made it very clear from the beginning that I was no more than a dirty little secret, making me sign that contract."

"So you do think it is my fault."

"Oh my God." I covered my face with one hand. "Why am I even arguing with you?" It was like beating my head against the wall.

"I need to understand," he persisted. "One day, you say you love me . . ."

"Which you rejected."

"Lucy, I went for a drive."

"You told me no and then. You. Walked. Away."

"I looked everywhere for you," he exploded, pounding the steering wheel. "Dammit, when I got back to that fucking house and realized you'd been taken, I did *everything* I could to find you. Being without you, knowing you were somewhere dangerous and there was nothing I could do, hurt. I couldn't breathe, could barely function, because . . ." He trailed off, going completely still.

"Because why?" The anger had leached out of me with his rant, like his outburst had been my own catharsis. I didn't know why I was holding my breath, but I was. "Because you loved me?"

I'd meant to say the words sarcastically, but they came out as a whisper. He didn't answer for a long time, staring straight out the window and gripping the steering wheel tight. Then he peeled his left hand off the wheel and laid it across the dash, palm up, as if asking to hold my hand. "Maybe."

Dumbfounded, I stared at him, mouth open in shock. Emotion welled up in me suddenly, spilling over into anger. "You son of a bitch," I choked out, hammering my fist into his shoulder once, then again. There was no way for me to express myself in that moment; all I wanted to do was hit him for being such a, a *man*.

He didn't move a muscle, letting me vent my frustration and keeping his open hand between us. I hated the implacable calm, the patience with which he sat there. All I wanted in that moment was to beat him into submission, but I crossed my arms and sat there, stewing in my own juices. "You think holding hands is going to fix anything?" I muttered, glaring out the window.

"No, I don't. But it's a start."

My arms remained over my chest as the silence dragged on. Jeremiah continued to drive, stoic as ever, and finally with a huff I unfolded my arms and slapped one hand into his. He didn't acknowledge my annoyance, but laced his fingers through mine and squeezed tight.

"I hate you right now," I huffed, unwilling to let him know just how *right* it felt holding his hand like this. Gooseflesh prickled my arm as I looked away, out the window at the countryside, and tried to ignore the joy that wanted to burst.

He hasn't said anything, you're just holding his hand. Stop being such a ninny.

But when he squeezed my hand, a smile tugged unbidden at my lips. I made darned sure however that he didn't see it.

14

We switched cars a total of four times that day, and I felt worse with each theft. Jeremiah kept us well away from larger cities or any place with a hint of cameras, and I appreciated the paranoia. Still, I knew we were inconveniencing innocents with our deception and didn't like the idea of being or acting like a criminal.

Then again, I hated the idea of dying much more.

The day bled away with us running zigzags through the countryside. Jeremiah visited several different phone booths, never spending long before taking us back out on the road again. The second car we acquisitioned had about one hundred pounds stashed away inside the glove box, which Jeremiah pocketed.

"Tell me we're going to pay these people back eventually."

"We'll pay these people back eventually."

I believed him.

By the time the sun was starting to set, I was ready for a shower and bed. I'd slept very little the previous night and still wore the same clothing I'd left Dubai in, and so wasn't feeling all that sexy. So when we pulled into another little bed and breakfast, this one much more rural, I was done for the day.

Jeremiah had me book the room, another quaint bed-and-little-else, while he took care of the car. I wasn't sure what he meant, but by that time I didn't much care. At least this room had its own bathroom attached, and as soon as he disappeared again I stripped down and jumped in the shower.

The hot water lasted nearly forty-five minutes before rapidly going cold, and I relished every minute of it. By the end, I felt more refreshed than I had all day. I dried my hair and wrapped the towel around my body, my next load of business being washing my clothes. That done, I laid them to dry over the metal rails beside the sink and shower.

I'd barely stepped out of the bathroom when the room door opened and Jeremiah stepped inside. We both froze, staring at one another across the room. He had a hungry look in his eyes that made my nipples tighten beneath the terrycloth. I watched as he stepped inside and slowly closed the door behind him. The small *snick* of the lock made me tense.

I backed away into the dresser as he stalked close, towering above me but not touching. My hand gripped the terrycloth tight to my chest as I struggled for words. "Do you want to talk now?" I asked in a breathless voice.

"Fuck talking."

My breath seized in my chest. One large hand covered mine, prying it gently from the top of the towel. I swallowed, stomach muscles trembling as his rough skin grazed my chest. Slowly, as if unwrapping a gift, Jeremiah pulled the knot in the top of one breast open before opening each end of the towel like a box.

I shivered as the cool air hit my damp skin but kept my eyes on his. It was a struggle not to move, to cover myself, to run into the bathroom and lock the door behind me. I knew this was bad news; there was no way I should allow it to happen.

But, oh God, I wanted this with every fiber of my being.

His hands skimmed down my breasts, sensitive nipples tightening more against his palm. He didn't stop there, his hands trailing down my sides as he bent his knees, crouching lower. Those beautiful lips were inches from mine and I lifted my head as his hands moved around and cupped my backside.

I squealed in surprise as he lifted me up, my arms moving behind his shoulders to keep from falling backwards. Green eyes stared up at me, and as I wrapped my legs around his waist his gaze dipped to my breasts. "I've been thinking about these all day," he murmured, then tipped his head and grabbed one nipple between his teeth.

My head fell back, body trembling as I bit back a cry. Fingertips dug into my backside as he sucked, flicking the hard nub with his tongue. He moved to the other and I pressed myself again his mouth, fingers gripping his thick hair. "Jeremiah," I breathed, the word a benediction, and a shudder went through his body.

Still holding me up, his fingers crept to my backside, parting the globes and sliding lower. A choking cry was forced from my lips as he found my core, rough digits gliding through the slick folds. His thumb crept back, massaging another entrance point I knew he loved, foreshadowing no doubt for what was to come.

He stepped back and spun us around, then gently settled me onto the bed. I released him, leaning back against the frilly pillows. We hadn't pulled back the sheets yet so I was atop the quilted comforter, and it seemed that was exactly what Jeremiah wanted. "Grab the headboard with both hands," he said, "and don't let go unless I say so."

His hands kneaded my abdomen as, trembling, I did as he said. "If you let go," he murmured, "I'll be forced to spank you. Nod if you understand."

I swallowed and nodded as he sank to his knees beside the bed. "I've missed you like this," he said in a soft voice, tracing his fingers over my stomach and hips. "You won't move, won't make a sound as I play. Understand?"

Biting my lip, I nodded again, and squeezed my eyes shut as his hand immediately dipped between my legs. My whole body seized as he dragged one fingertip over the small pearl of my clit, and I fought not to push into his touch. The heel of his other hand smoothed over my belly and down to my mound, allowing me no chance to recover. A finger slid inside me, barely stretching the skin, and my heels dug into the bed as I rose up to meet it.

Almost immediately, his other hand landed against my backside in a sharp spank. I flinched and settled back onto the bed, swallowing hard as the knowledgeable hands began their onslaught anew.

If this was a punishment, it was pure, delicious torture. I had the headboard in a death grip and worried that I'd bend or break the metal posts from my straining, but they held firm. Any time I vocalized, I got a swat on my rump until the skin there burned. Holding everything inside however, forcing myself to lay still and endure, only heightened every touch, every caress.

I was a quivering mess by the time his hands left my body, so turned on it almost hurt. Jeremiah stood to his feet, fingers going to his belt. "Hands and knees on the edge of the bed."

There was pleasure in hearing the stoic commando's voice tremble as I did what he said. He rummaged through something, and I peeked around to see a paper bag in his hands.

"Eyes forward."

When I turned around and rolled my eyes he smacked my backside again. "No rolling your eyes."

There was no way he could have seen that. "Sadist," I muttered, and even though I'd been expecting it still jumped at the next spank.

"Maybe." Humor laced his voice, then his hands gripped my backside again, spreading the globes apart. I sucked in a breath as the cool air hit the slick flesh, fisting my hands into the blankets. Then he slid his thumbs up my crack, massaging my rear opening. The skin was still soft from the shower but the ring of muscle was tight as a board.

He leaned down over me. "I'm going to fuck your ass later tonight," he whispered in my ear, "but first, I need to hear you *scream*."

My breathing was uneven as he pulled back, then I felt him kneel beside the bed. I barely had time to press my face into the bed, gripping the comforter tight, before I felt Jeremiah's lips on me. He ran his tongue along the interior of my folds, and then started his sensual assault on my weeping entrance.

There was no stopping my cries this time, and I could only hope that whatever neighbors we had were forgiving. The bed muffled most of them, but Jeremiah wasn't satisfied until I was a trembling, mewling mess. By the time he pulled away I was a quivering wreck, mumbling my pleas into the comforter.

"What did you say?"

"Please. Jeremiah, please, I need . . ." I squeezed my eyes shut as something thick and blunt probed between my legs. There was no need for extra lubrication; he slid inside me, my quaking walls stretching to accommodate his girth. I gasped against a lace pillow, tilting my hips up for his next plunge.

"God, you feel so good," he grit out, swiveling his hips and surging inside again. I threw my head back and cried out, and Jeremiah grabbed my damp hair in one meaty fist. He didn't pull hard however, only held me in place as he pounded inside me, stretching and sliding against all the right spots.

The orgasm I'd been denied surged to the surface, but I stayed poised on the brink for an agonizing moment. Nearly crying from need, I pumped my hips in time with Jeremiah's, but it wasn't until his teeth grazed my shoulder that I tilted over the edge. The lace swallowed my wail as I came hard, and felt him shudder behind me.

Jeremiah collapsed over me, breathing hard. He laid a kiss to my ear, lips playing with the skin there, and then pulled himself out. I collapsed sideways on the bed and watched him clean up. I raised my eyebrows slightly, too tired to do much else. "You got condoms too?"

He winked at me. "Just in case."

The light-hearted gesture made my jaw drop. I watched, bemused, as he cleaned himself up. "You're really enjoying this, aren't you? Danger without having to deal with the family business."

Jeremiah didn't answer immediately, but I already knew the answer. The stoic man I'd come to know had been one burdened by the responsibility of the family business. I knew the story: his father's mechanizations and death had taken away the only life Jeremiah had wanted, forcing him into a mold he didn't want to fit. It wasn't until now however that I began to see more, and I cocked my head to study him. "You remind me of your brother."

Immediately I knew that wasn't the right thing to say when his shoulders stiffened. *Way too soon for comparisons,* I mentally noted. *But, in for a penny* . . . "Look," I said, sitting up in the pillows. "I get that you've had a hard life. I don't even know most of what happened, but what little I've seen was pretty crappy. But if you had a chance to do what you wanted, would you still be CEO of Hamilton Industries?"

"No." His answer was immediate, and very telling.

"Then why are you still there?"

Jeremiah's face shut down. "I have to be there, or everything will be liquidated. It was how my father set it up: if I leave, everything breaks apart."

"Then let them liquidate it. Or find a loophole." I snorted. "Too bad Lucas is a wanted felon, maybe he would've taken it back."

"It's not that easy."

"Of course it's not. But it's one option." I pulled the comforter around myself, then rolled over until I sat on the edge of the bed. The room was small so it didn't take me far to reach out and snag his hand. "You've played hero so much, it's as though everything in your life has been about saving people. But sometimes, you have to let go."

Someone knocked at the door.

I froze, holding the sheets to my chest. At that moment, I was in no condition to run; there was no way I could get a stitch on in time to escape if someone barged through that door. Jeremiah laid a finger to his lips as he tiptoed across the room and looked out the peephole, then opened the door a crack. "You weren't followed?"

"If I was, I lost them."

I knew that voice. Jeremiah opened the door wide to allow the other man inside. I snatched up more blankets to cover myself with as Ethan, Jeremiah's former head of security, came through the door. He stopped when he saw me, and I felt my face flame in embarrassment. His gaze was fleeting however, and he turned back to Jeremiah.

"I appreciate you coming. Did you have problems getting into the country?"

Ethan shook his head. "I'd had a plane ticket bought already, so it didn't seem suspicious. I have an interview for a security consultation job outside of London."

Something passed between the two men in the uncomfortable silence that followed. Ethan had been with Jeremiah in the Rangers, but the bald man's presence put me on edge. The last time I had seen him, he'd handed me over to a hired killer. In his defense, the killer had traded me for Ethan's wife, Celeste, but I couldn't look at him without remembering. Jeremiah had fired his former squadmate over that stunt, and I wasn't sure what legal issues he had over the incident, so it was definitely a surprise to see him here.

"I wouldn't have contacted you if I had any other options," Jeremiah said, his voice flat.

"And for that, I'm sorry," Ethan replied. "But I'm here now, and willing to help."

"Celeste?"

"She's still angry, but we're trying to work things out."

Jeremiah nodded, then turned to me. "Get some rest, I'll be back in a few minutes."

It was on the tip of my tongue to tell him I deserved to know what was going to happen too, but the fact we had company kept my lips sealed. Ethan quirked an eyebrow at me but his face didn't otherwise change, and I knew there was no hiding my status with Jeremiah now. My public persona had always been that of an executive assistant, a role that was discarded in private. Somehow, given how observant Ethan was trained to be, I doubted the lie had escaped his notice, but it was out in the open now.

I thought that, given the danger surrounding me, I'd find it difficult to sleep. The moment my head touched that pillow however, my body melted into the bed and I was out like a light.

Apparently, a life of crime in the British countryside agreed with me.

I didn't wake up when Jeremiah came into the room alone, nor did I stir when he crawled, naked, into bed with me. A small part of me must have been conscious however, because my dreams took on a sensual spin. I wasn't sure how long I was lost in that haze between sleep and the waking world, but I woke myself up with a moan as something pressed inside me.

Jeremiah's arm was under my head; I could smell his scent all around me. The weight of his body rolled me onto the bed, pressing my belly to the tangled sheets. Teeth nipped my ear as the head of his penis eased back, then pushed again at my forbidden entrance.

"God, you're so tight."

The strain in his voice made me smile into the pillow. He'd massaged lube generously to both himself and me while I slept, and moved with delicious slowness farther inside me. I tilted my hips up, silently allowing him the access he wanted, and he kissed my neck in gratitude. There was no frenzied rush to the finish, no need for anything except the contact. His movements were languid, his breathing heavy. He was turned on, and that knowledge brought out the same in me.

"I love having you like this," he murmured in my ear,

rotating his hips and pressing inside me. "Laid out under me, mine to do with as I please."

I love. It was the first time I'd ever heard him say those words like that. Part of my mind registered the significance but filed it away to ponder later, too tired and distracted right then to look too deeply. "Anything you want," I whispered back, then gasped as his hand slid beneath me and palmed my breast, brushing a hard nipple with his thumb.

"I have what I want right here."

Joy bloomed inside me, and I turned my head to look back at him. In the dark, all I could see was the reflection of his eyes. "I love you."

He didn't answer, and I hadn't expected any more. But the tempo of his thrusts changed, becoming more forceful, his breathing more ragged. I pushed my face into the pillow, glorying in the act of giving him pleasure. Small moans worked their way free from my lips as I felt him reach his peak.

"I love you, Jeremiah Hamilton," I whispered into the pillow as he came above me, the muscles of his abdomen vibrating against my back. One last dreamy sigh escaped me, and then I felt him pull out and curl up next to me. He pulled me tight against him, nuzzling my neck.

We stayed like that for several moments as I felt my limbs once again grow heavy. "I need to clean up," he said softly, kissing one cheek. "Go back to sleep."

Slumber had never been far from my consciousness. Jeremiah wrapped the blankets back around me as he stood off the bed, and I snuggled into the warm cocoon.

I had a brief memory of arms enfolding me and lips

whisper something in my ear soon after, but I was too far gone into sleep to remember what was said.

It wasn't yet light outside when there came another knock on the door. We were instantly awake, and Jeremiah crept silently to the door while I waited on the bed. The darkness made it difficult to see anything, which only heightened the uneasiness inside me.

Another knock sounded only seconds later, three soft taps followed by a dull scrape. Jeremiah crouched to the ground and opened the door a crack.

"We found something."

15

There were very few people in life to whom I took an instant disliking, but the odious little man standing across from me ticked me off the minute he grabbed my ass.

I thought Jeremiah was going to rip his head off, but Ethan stepped between him and the small man. "Easy. Let's not get into a fight before we get our information."

The informant gave a nasty laugh as he let himself in behind the bar. "Cute lass you got there, mate." He waggled his eyebrows at me. "Wanna trade up for a real man?"

The man's words made my skin crawl. He reminded me of the troll dolls my mother had decorated her office with when I was a kid. His ears and nose were overgrown to the point of absurdity, making his already beady eyes look even smaller. He had a perpetual smirk on his face, as if certain nobody would mess with him and he wasn't above using that to his advantage.

Two large guards stood beside us while odious little man poured himself a drink. I glanced between them and Jeremiah, who had already gotten himself back in control. "Digging at the bottom of the barrel, aren't we?" he murmured, low enough that only Ethan and I could hear him.

"He can help us," Ethan replied. "Ronny's a rat, but a well-connected one."

"Oy, I heard that!"

"You were meant to, jackass," Ethan muttered, glaring at the small man. The two bodyguards shifted, as if waiting for an order, but were waved off by their boss. "Jeremiah, this is Ronny Fitch. He says he has information on Alexander Rush."

Jeremiah was dubious, but he managed to hide any disdain. "Tell us what you know."

"Oh no, that's not how this works." Ronny waved his drink at us, grinning. "First, we discuss payment."

"How much?"

"One million."

"Done."

Ronny's eyebrows went up. "I'm talking cash, and up front before you get your information. And the price just jumped to ten million, since you *obviously* came unprepared."

Jeremiah growled, and I laid a hand on his arm. The tension in the room rose, but Ronny didn't seem to notice, pouring himself another drink and slamming it back. The pub we were meeting in hadn't yet opened; the sign out front said we still had three hours before lunch, which meant no witnesses. The bodyguards beside us were bigger than both Ethan and Jeremiah and had a combat-trained vibe about them.

Jeremiah's glare was fixed on the smug little man behind the counter. "I can get you your money, but we need the information first."

"Oh ho, you really think so?" He reached under the bar, and we all tensed until he pulled out a newspaper. He flipped through the pages, licking his fingers to grab the pages, then folded it back and laid it atop the counter. "Read it and weep, buddy."

Jeremiah stepped forward and picked up the paper carefully. I peeked over his shoulder and read the headline:

BILLIONAIRE MIA, ASSETS FROZEN PENDING INVESTIGATION

I looked over at Ethan, then up at Jeremiah. He was busy reading the article, but from the way his brow drew lower and lower I could tell it wasn't good. I chewed on the inside of my cheek, suddenly nervous but trying not to show it.

"You're shit outta luck, mate," Ronny crowed, saluting Jeremiah with his glass. "And since you can't pay my fee, our business is done."

"I thought you already knew about this," Ethan murmured as Jeremiah crushed the newspaper in his hand. "We can figure something else out."

"You really think he has information?" Jeremiah asked in a low voice.

Ethan looked between the self-satisfied ass behind the bar and Jeremiah. "I think he's our best shot."

"What's wrong with you lot, you deaf? I said scram!"

One of the large bodyguards stepped forward and made the mistake of grabbing Jeremiah's arm. He exploded into action, twisting around and pushing the bodyguard into the bar. The other guard went for Jeremiah and Ethan got in the way, engaging him as I skittered sideways away from the fighting. Chairs were overturned and tables toppled as the men went at it, and I moved away further toward the door.

Jeremiah managed to get his assailant onto the ground while both Ethan and the man he was grappling with fell to the floor. I winced at the sound of flesh meeting bone, but the loud crunch of bone breaking energized me. The way Ethan was cradling his left arm didn't look good. He still had his legs wrapped around his attacker's waist, however, blocking blows with his good arm. Grabbing a nearby chair, I waded into the fight, slamming it over the man above Ethan.

The chair barely fazed the burly man, who reached for me, but the distraction was enough for Ethan to get the upper hand. Even crippled, he managed to get several blows in before the guard went after Ethan's bad arm. The former Ranger grunted, body spasming in pain, then Jeremiah was there pulling the big guard off his friend.

Immediately switching his attention to the new target, the beefy man threw a roundhouse punch, but Jeremiah stepped inside and boxed the other man's ears. A swift kick to the other man's knee and instep had the burly guard toppling into a nearby table and onto the floor. Ethan snaked an arm around the big man's neck and pinned him to the floor in a chokehold. Jeremiah didn't waste any more time, but stalked back to the bar.

Ronny, seeming to just realize he was defenseless, cow-
ered against the back of the narrow bar. He took off sideways
toward the back exit but Jeremiah jumped forward over the
bar, grabbing the lapels of Ronny's brown jacket.

"C'mon mate, I didn't mean . . ."

Jeremiah slammed him down onto the countertop. Ronny
howled, the smirk long gone from his face. He grabbed his
bloody nose, eyes wide and gleaming with pain.

"You want to give me that information for free now?"
Jeremiah said, leaning down close to Ronny's terrified face.
"Mate?"

"Why do I feel like I've seen this movie before?"

The address Ronny had, after some *persuasion* from Jeremiah, turned out to be a solitary cabin out in the middle of
nowhere. We'd moved far from London, firmly entrenched
in the countryside. The house in question was down a long
winding road that was in full view of the house. No trees
dotted the landscape, although the grass could have hidden
a car in places.

"How can we be sure this isn't a trap?" I murmured.

"It's undoubtedly a trap."

Well, thanks for that pep talk. "Then why are we going there?"

"Because I have no other way to be absolutely certain this
is the place. And there is no *we* here, *I* will be going into that
house alone."

"Bullshit." Ethan's voice was low but fierce. "There's no
way I'm letting you take that on alone."

My eyes fell to Ethan's bandaged arm, and I wondered somewhat cynically how he could help us now. I'd found a first aid kit in the pub and managed to splint up Ethan's injured arm, but he really needed to go to the hospital to have it fixed. He didn't look inclined to leave though, clearly as eager to get into danger as Jeremiah.

"I need you to take Lucy someplace safe."

His words drew the bald man up short. "You want me to watch her after what I did the last time?"

Jeremiah looked his former squadmate and security chief in the eye. "Is there anything I should know right now that would prevent you from doing this?"

Ethan glanced down at his arm, then back up. "No."

"Are you being blackmailed by our target, or in any way colluding with him?"

"No."

Something warred in Jeremiah's eyes, and then he clapped a hand on Ethan's shoulder. "You ever do that again," he said, "and I'll kill you."

Beside me, Ethan chuckled. "I wouldn't expect any less."

I let out a frustrated breath. *Men.* "This is all very touching, but I'm not leaving Jeremiah's side."

"Yes, you are."

I rolled my eyes. "No, I'm not. Look," I hurried to say before he got too logical, "I'm already as much of a target as you; if that creepy meeting in the airport said anything, it's that I'm a part of this now. I'm safer with you than away."

"So he can hit two birds with one stone?"

"Well, would you rather I get killed in a car bomb while you were investigating the scary cabin over there?"

That silenced him for a moment, and I could see the wheels turning in his head. If I'd learned anything in my time with Jeremiah, it was patience, but the emotion was hard-won and difficult at that moment. I took his hand in mine. "Why get Ethan involved in this anyway?" I continued, trying to drive my point home. "He's still trying to reconcile with Celeste and, as far as we can tell, the authorities don't think he's connected. Do you want him or his wife targeted by Alexander?"

Beside me I saw Ethan shift. "I owe you," he said in a low voice, the words obviously meant for Jeremiah.

"Not this much." Jeremiah's lips were a hard line as he gestured to Ethan's splinted arm. "You need to take care of that quickly."

"I've had worse and you know it."

"You have," Jeremiah agreed. He jerked his chin toward the cabin. "I don't know what this is, but we have to check it out."

Ethan stared Jeremiah in the eye. "I can't let you go in there alone."

"I know, but I have to do it myself. Goodbye, Ethan."

The bald man's hands curled into fists, and he glared at the cabin. Then he sighed. "If you die in there, I'll never forgive you."

"Well, I forgive you, if that helps any."

Some of the tension left Ethan's shoulder. "Yeah," he muttered, "it kind of does." He looked at me, then back to Jeremiah. "Take care of yourselves. Should I leave the car?"

Jeremiah shook his head, and we watched as the bald man got into his vehicle and drove away. "The car would have been nice," I said wistfully, not looking forward to the long walk.

"A car would be seen by anyone in that cabin. There's a good chance they've already noticed us anyway."

I stared at the small cottage. "So what are we going to do," I asked, "walk right up to it?"

"Not quite. You stay here, and I'll go check it out."

I glared at him. "Like hell."

Jeremiah gave me a droll look. "Do you have training to sneak into an open location like this undetected?"

"Well, no, but . . . Why are we even here? If you know this is a trap, why are you playing right into it?"

"If we run, he'll chase us, keeping one step ahead, and we won't even know we're dead until it's too late. If we play into his little game, there's a chance he'll slip up and give us the chance to take him down."

"That is the stupidest . . ." I groaned loudly. As much as I didn't want to be left alone, I also didn't want to go into that cabin. "What am I supposed to do if someone comes down the road?" I asked in a sarcastic tone. "Hide in the grass? Maybe pretend I'm some kind of rock and hope they don't notice."

Jeremiah just stared at me for a moment and then, surprisingly, he wrapped me in his arms. "This is going to be okay."

I had no idea until I felt his arms around me how *scared* I was. Everything welled up suddenly: the fight earlier, the running and hiding and thievery to get where we were. I'd held myself together pretty well, but there on that English dirt road, I wanted nothing more than for this nightmare to end so I could have a good cry. The safety in his arms was an illusion, and I *hated* that.

No. I will not *break down out here.*

My breathing was shaky as I stepped away, out of Jeremiah's arms. I didn't want to admit it, but he was right: this exercise wasn't for me. "Fine," I said stiffly, "I'll stay here and try to keep out of sight." Easier said than done on a hill with no trees, but I figured that was a given.

He laid a kiss on my forehead. "I'll be right . . ."

A car sped around the corner suddenly, startling me. Jeremiah shoved me behind him as another came from the opposite direction, stopping just short of us. Several men and one woman stepped out of the vehicles. "Freeze!"

We stayed still as more cars swarmed around us. They approached us carefully, guns drawn. Jeremiah slowly put his hands on his head, and following his lead I did the same.

They cuffed Jeremiah first, making sure he was compliant and fully restrained before they turned to me. The cuffs bit into my wrists, and I winced as they shoved my arms up and pushed me against the side of one car. The door across from us open, and a familiar dark-haired agent exited.

"I told you I would find you, Mr. Hamilton."

"Agent Gautier, we need . . ."

"I don't want to hear it, Mr. Hamilton." To the agents behind us, Marie said, "Put them into the car and let Felix know we're coming in."

It seemed fate wanted me to see inside that little cottage after all. This, as it turned out, was neither as quaint nor as scary as I'd imagined.

Agents bustled around the modern interior; it was too many bodies for the small cabin, but nobody seemed to care. Jeremiah and I, still cuffed, were set down on the couch and left mostly alone. We stayed silent, not attracting any attention, but there was no escape from Marie when she finally confronted us.

"Do you leave a mess *everywhere* you go, Mr. Hamilton? You know what we found at your last location? One of my agents unconscious, the other having swallowed a bullet from his own gun."

I swallowed at the news, remembering the fear in the agent's eyes when he'd mentioned his family. Marie paced before us, her low heels clacking against the wood floors. "And we have yet," she added, clearly agitated, "to find his immediate family to inform them of his death."

A shard of ice went through me and I began to tremble. Jeremiah moved over, bumping his shoulder into mine, letting me know he was there.

"While you were gallivanting across the countryside playing your little games, we've been searching everywhere for a madman before he strikes again."

"His vendetta is against the Hamilton family."

"That may seem so to you, but so far as I can tell none of you are the ones who have been hurt." She clenched her fists and stopped pacing, glaring at us. "Yet here I have one agent dead and several more in Dubai. Who knows how many more innocents he will slaughter before he finally gets his supposed 'targets.'"

"I'm not asking for preferential treatment." Jeremiah tried to stand, but the agents behind us clapped their hands onto his shoulders, pushing him back to the couch. "Look, we know he's after us, we just need to get him into the open."

She waved her hand through the air. "All of this is irrelevant. How did you find this place? Who told you to look here?"

Jeremiah hesitated, and Marie jumped on it like a shark. "You received your information from somewhere, tell me who."

"We were told this was where to find Alexander."

Marie blinked, looking disturbed. "You were given these coordinates? But why . . . ?"

"Ah, my baby brother, here to rescue me from the utter mundanity of my current existence."

I swiveled around to see Lucas beaming at us, looking quite at home with the whole situation. The confusion on Jeremiah's face quickly melted to irritation as Lucas all but skipped into the main room. He stopped next to Marie and, ignoring her completely, opened his arms wide. "Welcome to hell!"

The French agent pursed her lips. "You're not supposed to be walking around, Loki."

"And this," Lucas stated with a tight smile, "is what I have to put up with every minute of every day. Seriously, gorgeous location—sucky roommates. It's like the vacation home I never wanted." He plopped down on the couch next to Jeremiah and put an arm around his brother's shoulders. "Please, tell me you brought takeout."

The cuffs were still on us both, which was probably a good thing for Lucas as Jeremiah looked ready to throttle his sibling. That didn't mean the man wasn't up for stirring the pot a bit. Grinning like a loon, he plopped down right between us, not caring that there wasn't room. He threw arms around us both, smiling at us in turn. "The whole family, back together again. Almost brings a tear to my eye."

Something about his words made goosebumps break out over my flesh. "Jeremiah," I murmured, "do you remember what you said before about hitting two birds with one stone?"

All heads swiveled to look at me, including Marie's. I looked at them, then back at Jeremiah. "We're all right here, in the exact same place, based on information that is supposedly from Alexander himself . . ."

I saw comprehension dawn first on Marie's face. The logic that my brain didn't want to grasp mobilized the agent. She began barking orders, and the group around us started tearing down their various setups. "Get their handcuffs off!"

A black agent threw a set of keys to Lucas, who quickly unlocked his brother's cuffs, then my own. Jeremiah surged to his feet, as did Lucas who pulled me up. "We need to get out of here now."

Then my world exploded.

16

Waking up was painful.

    I stayed in a fuzzy stupor for too long, my brain unable to deal with reality quite yet, before I finally came lucid. My whole body hurt, as if I'd been slammed to the ground repeatedly by a team of linebackers. I lay there for a moment, taking inventory of all the small pains, before daring to move so much as an inch.

Immediately I knew I was in trouble when my leg wouldn't budge. Something heavy lay atop it, but in the darkness I couldn't see what it was. I coughed, the air a mixture of smoke and dust. My brain didn't seem up for the challenge of thinking much beyond the discomfort, the act sending shards of pain through my skull.

Stuck in place, I lay back down on the uneven floor, closing my eyes and simply trying to breathe. My lungs felt tight, too full of particulates, but right then breathing was all I could manage. Anything else hurt too much, and when the coughing started, it brought sharp pains up the pinned leg.

Jeremiah. The memory was there, but distant. I saw a familiar man's face in my mind, green eyes staring down at me, but anything more hurt too much to think about. I squeezed my eyes shut, tears leaking out and drying almost instantly against the dust on my cheeks.

I reached out blindly with one hand, feeling out my surroundings, and felt something shift nearby. A groan echoed through the small space as someone else woke up. "Are you okay?" I managed to croak, my voice all but gone.

There was silence for a long moment. "Lucy?"

The voice put me in mind of a carefree, flippant personality. I closed my eyes. "Lucas. What happened?"

"Dunno." I heard him shift next to me, and then he gave a small groan. "Hang on."

Light from a cellphone illuminated the space, and I squinted as it was pointed directly at me. Shielding my eyes, I looked around the small area and saw thick pieces of wood holding up rubble less than a foot away. "I liked it better when I didn't know what was on me," I whispered faintly.

"No kidding, right?"

The silence had sharpened my hearing, and through the pain in my skull I thought I heard voices. Lucas must have as well because he said, "Help is on the way."

I squeezed my eyes tight, lethargy overwhelming me. "So tired," I murmured, only wanting to sleep.

"Hey!" The sharp voice reverberated inside the tiny space. "No sleeping until we're out. You might have a concussion."

The lethargy continued to spread however, and no matter

how I tried to keep awake my body demanded otherwise. I reached out a hand toward his voice. "Lucas."

I vaguely remember someone tugging at my arm and saying something in my ear, but nothing could keep me awake.

The next time I awoke was to bright lights being shone into my eyes. I batted at the hand feebly, the rays splitting through my head like nails, and the light disappeared. Voices echoed around me, and as I blinked the world into focus, they started to make sense.

"I'm tell you, we can't go back to your office."

"That is the only option I have at this point." Marie's heavily accented voice told me the Frenchwoman was under a lot of stress. "We are not equipped to deal with a situation like this."

"He expects us to do that, don't you see? We can't do what is expected or we'll walk right into another trap."

"I thought that's what you said we should do," I croaked in a hoarse voice, and both arguing parties paused to look at me.

Instantly Jeremiah was at my side, kneeling down and picking up my hand. "How are you feeling?" he asked softly, laying his fingers on my knuckle.

I waved a feeble hand in the air. "Meh." The movement hurt—hell, breathing itself hurt—but the gesture seemed to relax Jeremiah. I shifted my legs and sucked in a pained breath. "My ankle," I moaned, making myself go still.

"You were pinned under the main roof joist of the cabin. It took some time to get it off your foot."

"What about Lucas? Is he all right?"

"Present, and in one piece. Well, mostly."

I rolled my head back to see Lucas approach, hobbling slightly. He was clutching his midsection and moved slowly, but his smile still shone in the darkness. He waved off any concern, kneeling nearby. "How's the leg?"

Steeling myself, I wiggled my toes, and then flexed my foot the barest hint. I had no idea how long I'd been out but could tell it was stiff and swollen. The pain was still there but at least it wasn't such a surprise this time. "Been better, actually."

Lucas's grin widened. "That's my girl."

The arms around me tightened, and Lucas's eyes flicked to Jeremiah. I gave a frustrated groan, realizing the tension that statement brought up, but Lucas backed down. "Do you know what happened?" he asked Marie, who I noticed was also leaning heavily on a broken two by four. "RPG, hand grenade, bomb that was already placed?"

"I have people working on it, but most of our equipment was damaged in the blast." Marie's voice sounded hoarse, like she'd been breathing smoke or barking orders all night. "We don't have enough light to do a thorough sweep, plus we have our own wounded to tend."

"Well, we can't stay here."

"That much I know, Mr. Hamilton." Another man in a dirty suit came up and whispered to the French agent, and Marie hobbled away.

I lolled my head sideways against Jeremiah's arm. "What

happened?" I whispered, glad for the darkness. My headache was receding but not quickly enough for my peace
of mind. "I remember my cuffs coming off, then the explosion."

"There were three explosions actually," Jeremiah answered
in a gruff voice, "all perfectly targeted to bring down the
cabin. This wasn't directed at any one person, it was designed
to inflict as many casualties as possible."

I squeezed my eyes shut, swallowing. "Can I have some
water?"

"I'll get it," Lucas said before Jeremiah could answer. The
scarred man stood to his feet stiffly and shuffled away into
the darkness.

Between the pain in my ankle, the horrible headache,
and the stress of being targeted by a madman, all I wanted
to do was cry. "How are you doing?" I asked, squeezing his
hand.

"Decent. The couch landed on top of me, shielding me
from most of the blasts."

The image in my head made me smile. "You got attacked
by a couch?"

"Let's keep that little secret between us, shall we? It definitely took the brunt of the attack though, but when everything settled I couldn't find you."

His last few words were ragged, and a big lump settled at
the base of my throat. "I want this to be over," I mumbled,
clinging to Jeremiah's shirt.

He drew in a ragged breath, and then laid a hand on my

hair. "I've got you," he murmured, leaning down and kissing the top of my forehead.

I couldn't help but wonder if that would be enough to survive this.

"I need to contact my people."

"And I'm telling you right now, that could be a really bad idea."

Muffled voices woke me up for the third time. I was still in a dark area but nearby I could see lights illuminating a small area beside the ruin of the cabin. My bed was also no longer the grass outside but a cot, with a wadded-up jacket serving as a pillow. The pain in my skull had finally diminished, and I sat up carefully, testing out pain levels. I noticed someone had splinted my ankle, and left a single wood crutch on the ground next to me.

Swinging my legs over the side of the narrow cot, I sat there for a moment to make sure I was okay before trying to stand. The first attempt went badly; pain shot up from my injured ankle, and I cursed under my breath. The second time I kept my bad foot off the ground and twisted around, using the cot as leverage to get on my other foot. Picking up the crutch, I slipped it under my arm and hobbled toward the light.

I wasn't the only injury in the group. Several people, some of whom had bloody clothes and bandages, sat on cots up along the edge of the cabin wall. Around the edge of the light, I could see several covered figures lying on the ground.

As I watched, another figure was laid alongside the line, and I saw a pale hand roll out from beneath the cover.

They were the dead. I shuddered and averted my eyes.

The single light ahead of me, while bright, cast uneven shadows on the ground. I hobbled unsteadily across the ground toward the familiar voices, still arguing.

"Mr. Hamilton, while I respect your expertise in some matters, I need to get my men and your company to a safe location."

"And I'm telling you it's too dangerous to trust any communication you might receive. We need to figure out something free of any outside influence."

"Do we know what happened yet?"

My voice sounded hoarse as if I'd been sleeping a long time, but my question got their attention. Marie immediately dismissed my presence, turning to another agent who came up beside her, but Jeremiah rushed over to me. "How are you feeling?" he asked, the conversation with the Interpol agent forgotten.

"Tired. Like I have a broken ankle. It is broken, isn't it?"

"The skin was purple as I wrapped it, which isn't a good sign, but we won't know for sure until we get you to a hospital."

I groaned. I was completely helpless, *useless*, and the danger was far from over. "What are we going to do now?"

"We can't stay here. Nobody can tell how the explosion occurred, which means we don't know if it can be replicated. Right now we're sitting ducks. I don't trust any communication, any electrical equipment, because it can all be tracked.

Even the damned cars they drove here have GPS chips inside."

"My men are working now to remove those from two of the vehicles. The wounded will be taken back, while the third is repaired."

Jeremiah shook his head at Marie's words. "He can still track us from the skies. As far as I saw, there aren't any tunnels around here for us to use to hide from satellites, and we have to assume he's tapped into those, as well."

The older woman heaved a sigh. "Are we even sure this was Rush?

Jeremiah peered at her through narrowed eyes. "What do you mean? Who else could it be?"

Behind us, someone cleared his voice. "I *might* have made myself a few enemies over the last day or two."

I cocked my head sideways as Lucas shrugged, a jaunty smile spreading across his face. "After we parted ways at the airport, I made a slight spectacle of myself in order to attract the attention of the lovely agent here. Really darling," he added, glancing at Marie's tight-lipped face, "your lot took forever to notice me."

"You didn't have to hit that security guard," Marie said in a tight voice, ignoring Lucas's smirk and looking at me.

"But he was so rude to me when I was going through the security checkpoint," Lucas said, batting his eyes innocently.

"Loki here has been giving us information," Marie continued, ignoring the smirking man beside her. "The pictures I showed to you in the airport were part of that. He's helping us identify some of the key players in his arena."

I looked at Lucas. "Mr. Smith from the docks?" I remembered the well-dressed, calm older man from the docks in Jamaica. He hadn't looked dangerous but, remembering the fear in Niall's eyes, something told me he didn't take kindly to betrayal. "Do you think he knows already?"

A muscle ticked in Lucas's face although the smile never left his face. "I have no doubt he knows, hence why I'm not sure this is necessarily Rush."

"You're helping them?"

Lucas looked over at Jeremiah, raising an eyebrow at the dubious note in his brother's voice. "What, can't your big bro be a hero, too? Bet you thought you had the monopoly on that in our family."

"But we were directed here," I said, frustrated. "Whoever sent us must be the one who set it up."

"Unless one knew about the other and wanted to kill two birds with one stone." A voice called out to Marie. "If you'll excuse me," she said, and then faded away into the darkness.

Beside us, Lucas shifted. "I think I should probably go lie back down."

I hadn't realized until he said something how hunched over Lucas stood. "Are you all right?" I asked, moving toward him, but he waved me off.

"I'll be fine, I just need some rest." He glanced over at Jeremiah, the corner of his mouth tipping up. "See you in a few."

He definitely didn't look fine as he hobbled away back toward the cots, one arm around his belly. Part of me wanted to go make sure he was all right, but my throbbing ankle reminded me that nobody was really safe. My mind went back to the dead lying at the edge of the light, and I pushed myself deeper into Jeremiah's embrace.

Above me, Jeremiah was scowling into the darkness. "I don't trust them."

"Maybe not," I murmured, running a hand along his shoulder in a soothing gesture, "but what choice do we have?"

"None."

I laid my head against him, pressing up against the heat of his body. "Is this all Interpol?" I asked. What little I'd heard about the organization didn't seem to fit this scenario.

Jeremiah shook his head. "They've brought in the heavy guns, as well as local authorities. Britain's Crime Agency has a hand, and I've seen some NATO badges on men and equipment. I wouldn't be surprised if some of these people were CIA. Rush has made himself an international enemy, and we're stuck square in the middle."

Beneath me he was as hard as a rock, every muscle tight. Inside was a caged bull, searching for something, someone, to charge. At the moment however, no enemy was in sight, and unknown dangers lurked in the darkness. He was practically vibrating from the tension of holding himself back.

As I ran my hand through his hair, I felt some of that tension lessen. He looked down at me, then reached out and cupped my cheek with one hand. "I never would have hit you."

The abrupt change in subject confused me. I leaned away and stared up at him. "I know that." There were things I'd been afraid he'd do, but lay a hand on me was never a consideration.

"When we were at the hotel . . . When I reached for you and you flinched away." He broke off and looked out into the darkness. "My father . . ."

Given what little I knew about their family, any sentence prefaced with those two words never boded well. As gently as I could, I grabbed his chin and turned his face to me. The scowl was gone, but even in the dim light I could see the pain shining in his eyes. "Not once when we fought did I ever believe you would hurt me."

My words didn't seem to have much effect. "I could have," he murmured. "It would have been so easy."

"But you didn't." The vehemence in my voice finally got his attention. "You hurt me with your words, yes, but you were entitled to your pain. Even if you had carried out your threats . . ." I pursed my lips, realizing my wounds were too raw for me. The memory of his words still hurt, and I would have to deal with it eventually. "We both made mistakes, and forgiveness won't happen overnight."

"Perhaps."

"Jeremiah." I pulled his head sideways again, making sure we were eye to eye. "I don't know the specifics of your family life growing up, but I think I know the man you are now." I hobbled around with the crutch until we were standing face to face, and then entwined my arms around his neck. Jeremiah was watching me silently, but I knew I had his rapt attention. Inexplicably, tears formed in my eyes and I blinked them away as I continued. "You're incredible, and despite everything we've been through I'm so glad you were put in my life."

The silence stretched between us, but I didn't look away from his eyes. They glowed in the faint light, and while I couldn't tell what was going on inside his head I didn't care. Finally, he cleared his throat and looked away. "We should see how everyone else is faring."

If I'd expected a similar declaration from him, that would have been a disappointing response. As it was, I just snorted and rolled my eyes. *Men.* "Care to give a girl a hand?"

He turned slightly and held out his elbow toward me. Handing him my crutch, I wound my arm through his, squeezing close to him. There was so much more I wanted to tell him, but that would come later. Right then we had other problems to worry about, and with his help I hobbled back into the light toward the rest of our party.

17

"Do we have any idea where we're going?"

"Not a clue. But I think the general consensus is that we can't stay here."

I frowned over at Lucas standing beside me. "Are you all right?"

We were next to one of the large black vans sitting in front of what was left of the cabin. In the dim light, I could see a line of sweat running down Lucas's face. His pale skin glowed in the darkness, and he was leaning heavily against the hood of the van.

"Yup, I'm right as rain." He glanced at me. "At least I didn't turn into a gimp."

I flushed, fidgeting with my crutch. "Did you pull me out?" I asked, ignoring his sarcasm.

"As much as I could." With one hand, he gestured vaguely at my ankle. "Can you put any weight on it?"

I straightened up and slowly settled the foot flush to the ground. The pain was still there, but it was no longer excruciating like before. "A little," I replied, lifting it back up and resting on the crutches again.

"That's a good sign. Hopefully it's a sprain, or just bruising from that beam."

He fell silent, a condition I wasn't used to from him. "You really don't look good," I said, my brow furrowing in worry.

Lucas was saved from replying as Marie and Jeremiah returned. I leaned against Jeremiah as he glared at his brother. His grip around my shoulders was tight, and although I was thankful for his presence, the tension told me there was a lot we still had to work through.

"We have two cars ready to go," Marie said, opening the passenger door beside me. The agents had disabled the car interior lights to avoid detection, but she shone a flashlight around the interior as if doing one last sweep. "One of ours was damaged in the blast and my men are working on it now, but we need to get our wounded to safety."

"He'll be able to track us, no matter if we keep the lights off or not."

"It's a risk we have to take. I have injured men, and Lucy here might have a broken ankle. She certainly couldn't run in the event of another attack."

I bristled slightly, not appreciating having my condition be used to get Jeremiah's cooperation, but he nodded. "This van will be for the injured, we've already taken out the back seats."

Marie nodded and motioned toward the darkness. Several people came out, a few supporting others as they hobbled toward the vehicle. One by one they were loaded into the van, a silent affair except for the occasional gasp and stifled moan of pain. I leaned my head on Jeremiah's arm, but he stepped away and opened the passenger door. "Here, let's get you inside."

I let him help me onto the seat, and he lay the crutch up along my lap. "Are you driving?" I asked, pulling on my seat belt.

He didn't answer immediately, instead opening the sliding door on the side. "Come help me," he told his brother brusquely as people began filing toward the opening.

"Jeremiah," I said in a firm voice, "you're coming with us, aren't you?"

"Doesn't look like it," Lucas piped up, not moving from his spot against the hood. His teeth flashed in the darkness. "My guess is he's going to stay behind and play hero again."

No! I looked over at Jeremiah, but it was too dark to read his expression. "Is this true?" I asked, my voice tight.

When he still didn't answer, I reached out and grabbed his sleeve. "Are you staying here?"

"Only for a little while." The words sounded ripped from him, as if he hadn't meant to tell me. "I'll help with the third car and be right behind you."

"How long will that take?"

"It shouldn't be long. But there are more wounded who need to get to safety. I'll be right behind you."

I want to stay with you. The words stuck in my throat as my breathing grew ragged, anxiety threatening to overwhelm me. The idea of begging went against every aspect of my being, but right then it was the only option I could imagine. I kept my lips tight however, staring at him silently as he helped the last few people inside. "What about the other car?" I asked.

"It's too small to fit any more people, and is carrying most of the remaining equipment as well. Both vehicles will be taking different routes home in case you're being tracked, but you should reach it at the same time."

Something told me there was no changing his mind, and that made me want to hold onto him all the tighter. Lucas was right; Jeremiah looked as alive as I'd ever seen. He was in the middle of a disaster, helping people and being the hero.

He must have seen the indecision in my eyes because he leaned in toward me. "I need to know you're safe," he said in a hoarse voice, his gaze pleading with me in the faint light. "That's all that matters to me right now."

You matter to me. In his eyes however I saw the resolve, the burning desire to be useful. Swallowing my doubts, I laid a shaky hand against his cheek. "Be careful."

He grabbed my hand and kissed the palm. This close, I could see the approval and gratitude in his eyes, as if he were proud of my response. I ran my fingers along his face, memorizing the textures and shape, then reluctantly pulled my hand inside. I wanted to cry and argue, plead and beg, but it wouldn't do anything except make me look pathetic. Swallowing my fears, I pulled my hand in the car and sat back in the chair, biting the inside of my cheek to keep from crying.

"Come on, Lucas," Jeremiah said, signaling to his brother to follow.

Lucas shifted against the hood. "I'm . . ." He trailed off, his head turning to catch my eye through the windshield, and for the first time I noticed he was white as a sheet. "I don't think I can."

"What . . ."

I gave a strangled cry as Lucas slid sideways and collapsed in front of the wheel. Immediately, Jeremiah was at his side, and I craned my neck around the window to see what was happening. Lucas's breathing was shallow, and he gave a small moan when his brother's fingers pressed against his abdomen. Jeremiah jerked up the shirt and, even in the dim light, I could see the dark bruising along his belly.

"You arrogant ass," Jeremiah growled as Marie signaled over two other agents for help, "why didn't you tell anyone you were hurt? This looks like internal bleeding."

"Is that what it is?" Lucas asked faintly as the three men positioned themselves to lift him into the van. I couldn't tell whether it was a serious question, but his weak voice scared me.

He was lifted carefully into the van across the bench seat behind me, the only one left inside the van. I turned in my seat as far as my belt would allow and caught Lucas's eye. He gave me a wan smile and a small wave. "What's up, buttercup?"

Marie climbed into the driver's seat and started up the van. The doors slammed shut, and Jeremiah stepped back away from the van. Ahead of us, I saw the second car pull out into the driveway, quickly being swallowed up into the darkness.

Neither vehicle had their headlights on, and I wondered how the drivers would navigate until I saw Marie settle a pair of night-vision goggles over her eyes.

"Let's go."

I watched helplessly as the van drove away, pulling away quickly from the meager light by the cabin. Jeremiah's figure was all too quickly swallowed by the darkness, and I turned back around to face forward. My chest squeezed tight, and I swallowed back my tears.

Memories reared their ugly head of the day my parents died. The police called me several hours afterwards to tell me of the crash, and I had driven myself to the hospital to identify the bodies. There was no way I could do that again; I'd lose my mind if that happened with Jeremiah.

"So, you're originally from Canada?"

Marie's voice cut through the silence, dragging my attention back to the present. I glanced in her direction, then out into the dark nothingness spread out before me. "Quebec, actually," I mumbled, clearing my throat to get rid of the burr. "We moved down when my grandmother died and left us her house in New York."

"Ah, French Canadian. I have a sister in Montreal."

I knew she was trying to make small talk, but I wasn't in the mood. Turning slightly in my seat, I reached my arm back toward the seat behind me, feeling blindly for Lucas. When I found his elbow, I slid my hand up until I held his fingers. I gave them a little squeeze, and was gratified when he returned the gesture. "Why didn't you tell us you were hurt?"

"It was more fun seeing your face when I collapsed. Wish I'd had a camera."

I snorted. "If you didn't have internal injuries, I'd hit you."

"Go ahead, doubt it would make much difference now."

His words were strained, and I gripped his hand tighter. "Marie," I asked in a shaky voice, "how long is the drive?"

"We'll be there as quickly as I can move."

We drove in silence, the ride seeming to stretch on forever. Two other agents were in the back with broken bones; I could hear their pained grunts as we went over bumps in the road, but it was Lucas's wheezing that made my heart ache. Marie eventually took off her goggles and turned on the headlights as we hit the main highway. My throbbing ankle was a distant thought in my mind as I counted the miles until we stopped.

It was already bright outside when we pulled into a hospital near London. Medical personnel escorted by agents streamed out of the building, moving straight for our van. I pulled myself out, muscles stiff from the long ride. Shooing away a wheelchair, I watched as Lucas was laid on a gurney. I hobbled behind as doctors wheeled him inside, but was prevented from entering the elevator with him.

"He is going into surgery," Marie said as I tried to get past her. "Beyond here is only for doctors."

I subsided, watching helplessly as the doors slid shut. "Will he be okay?"

"Who can say, but these doctors will do the best they

can." She indicated my ankle. "You should have somebody check your leg."

To try and prove her wrong, I flexed my foot, laying it flat on the floor. It was stiff from the swelling, and while the pain was still high it was no longer excruciating. "I'm fine. What about Jeremiah and the other agents?"

"His group checked in thirty minutes ago that they were on the road heading this way."

My shoulders sagged, the breath I hadn't realized I held whooshing from my body. I wouldn't feel safe until Jeremiah had arrived, but it was good to know he was on his way.

"We were never able to talk fully about what happened to you after you left London. Perhaps we can catch up?"

The agent was being almost friendly, and I stared at her suspiciously. "We were cuffed and under guard the last time we talked."

"You had just shown up at a protected location, in the middle of a major operation. So we were understandably a bit suspicious."

Point taken. "I'll tell you everything you need to know," I said, and then sighed. "I'm more than a little tired of adventure at this point, ready for a boring life again."

"Be careful what you wish for, it might not be enough after what you've been through. While I certainly understand the sentiment, you've fallen in with company that may never give you peace like that."

"No kidding," I muttered, but one side of my lips tipped up. "You have someplace where I can prop up my foot?"

Marie didn't have a chance to answer before a young

agent hurried up to her. "We found them," he said in an urgent voice.

"Who?"

"Agent Sanders's family. His wife called from a pay phone less than a mile away, asking for her husband. We're bringing her in now."

Marie's lips tightened into a grim line. "At least some people came out of this unharmed," she murmured, and then turned to me. "I need to go, but still want to speak with you."

"Can I help somehow?" I asked, following after her on my crutches. "Maybe just listen to their story? If I can help with anything I'll let you know."

The Frenchwoman stopped and looked at me, then reluctantly shook her head. "I first need to inform them of Agent Sanders's death, then question them on anything they know. If they say anything you can help us identify, I'll let you know." She paused, and then cleared her throat. "I realize you were the wronged party, but prior to your, eh, altercation with Agent Sanders, he was a good family man and officer. Can I rely on your silence about his unwilling participation in this whole affair?"

"Of course." The desperation on the agent's face when he'd pulled his gun on me popped into my head. He'd been put into a no-win situation, forced to choose between his family and us. Despite everything, I could understand why he'd attacked us. I wouldn't transfer the burden of his action on any family, especially anyone who may have been held hostage by Alexander Rush. "Am I coming with you?"

"No, you stay here. As soon as someone checks you and

Lucas is well enough to move, we will take you both." Her lips thinned, and she scrutinized me closely. "What is he to you?"

I heard the insinuation clear in her voice, but I already knew my answer and tried not to take offense. "He's my good friend. Nothing less, nothing more."

Marie looked dubious but nodded. "I know you insist you are fine, but have a doctor look at your leg."

My lips twisted down but conceding the point, I nodded. As Marie walked away, a young doctor escorted by another agent approached me. "This way, ma'am," he said, and I followed him down the hall.

The doctor confirmed my suspicion of a sprain, and merely replaced the bandages. My foot was still swollen, but he explained the bruising was more external, likely from the trauma of the beam hitting my leg, and less from a break. He suggested x-rays, but conceded that if I had decent mobility and not too much pain, it was probably a sprain. The new bandaging reinforced the entire area, making it a tad easier to walk on although he cautioned against that for the time being.

Lucas was still behind the main doors, likely in surgery, when I'd finished my own examination. I wasn't sure how long I sat there, but despite everything that was going on, it allowed me a moment to rest my eyes. There had been too much running lately, too much danger; for this brief moment I felt secure, and I didn't want to give that up. The headache that had been subtly plaguing me since the explosion in the cabin had finally lifted, and I laid my head back against the wall and closed my eyes.

"Ms. Delacourt?"

A voice nearby shook me from my reverie. Next to me stood another doctor, this one a bit older, looking around expectantly. I had no idea how long I'd been napping, but saw that the same agents were still lined up along the hallway. "Yes?" I asked, sitting up.

The doctor looked at me and smiled slightly. "Your friend Lucas is asking about you."

That woke me up completely. I grabbed my crutch and pulled myself to my feet as the doctor continued. "His bleeding wasn't severe and we were able to get it under control with minimal surgery. He'll need to stay in bed for a little while." The last part seemed directed more at the agents than to me. One lady broke off from her post on the wall, pulling a cellphone from her pocket.

"Is he going to be all right?" I asked, pulling the doctor's attention to me. "Can I go see him?"

The doctor nodded. "He may be groggy for a while, but yes, I can take you to him."

"May I have a moment before you go in?"

I looked over to see one of the agents left behind at the hospital striding toward me. "Agent Anderson," she said as a curt introduction, giving me a swift handshake. She ignored the doctor and motioned for me to follow her. "Agent Gautier would like a word."

The new agent was an American, which I found interesting.

I followed her a few feet down the hall, stepping first inside the room she indicated. My experiences the last few weeks made me skittish to keep her behind me. Part of me wanted to trust her, but I had been through too much to be so cavalier about my safety. Even now, I was mentally cataloging everything, trying to figure out the quickest exit in an emergency.

I wondered if this was how Jeremiah felt all the time.

We stopped a few feet away, out of earshot of any nearby people, and the agent held out a cellphone toward me. I took it and held to my ear. "Yes?"

"I have a few questions to ask before you go see Lucas."

It felt like she was watching me; for all I knew, she was. "Sure."

"I've spoken with Agent Sanders's widow, and she has quite a tale to tell. However, I would like to hear your story as well."

"I'll help you how I can, but I'm not even sure what was happening. Jeremiah drove us around the countryside, switching cars as we went."

"Switching cars? No, never mind that. Did you stop anywhere? Meet with anyone?"

"Just one person," I lied, having already determined to keep Ethan out of it if possible. Jeremiah hadn't wanted his former teammate brought in, and I'd hold to his wishes. "We stopped at some pub and met a man named Ronny. He's the one who told us about Rush's supposed hideout, which turned out to be your cabin."

"Can you describe him?"

"Short, thin, annoying. Big ears, big nose, blond fuzzy hair like a troll doll. He was full of himself until Jeremiah took out the hired muscle and got the information. We met him at an old pub across from a grocer and a Laundromat, but I don't know the town. Jeremiah would be able to tell you; has he arrived yet?"

"One subject at a time. Did he have an accent?"

Even though she couldn't see me, I shrugged. "I'd describe it as Cockney, but I don't know how to be more specific than that. I could definitely pick him out of a lineup though."

"Thank you Ms. Delacourt, we can take it from here."

"But what about . . ." The line cut out in the middle of my sentence. ". . . Jeremiah?" Frustration welled up, and no small amount of fear. Swallowing hard, I handed the phone back to the agent. "Please let me know as soon as you can if they've heard from Jeremiah," I asked, my voice thick.

The redheaded woman nodded, and I drew in a ragged breath. Shoving my fears down, I lifted my chin and followed after the doctor into a nearby room.

Lucas lay in bed, and as I entered he rolled his head sideways. "Hey," I said, forcing my lips up into a smile. "You look terrible."

"Pot, meet kettle." Lucas gave me a tired smirk. "Glad to see you, too. Where are we?"

"Hospital. For the moment anyway." I sighed and sat down. "How are you feeling?"

"Ready to dance a jig." He shifted in the bed, pushing himself back and more upright, then winced. "Well, maybe just a waltz."

I stared at my hands, picking at my fingernails uncertainly as he got comfortable. "I want this to be over, Lucas," I murmured, wrapping my hands around the edge of his bed. "I want to go home and forget it ever happened."

"The world doesn't work that way, unfortunately. You can't escape your past, only face it and hope you survive the meeting."

The grim certainty in Lucas's voice told me that he'd been down this road before. Our situation was so uncertain, with too many unknown variables. My life felt like a warzone, even when I was on safe soil. Every sense was heightened, my emotions too close to the surface. There was no way of knowing when the hammer would fall next.

A small sound outside the door made me jump in my chair, and I cast a worried glance at the entrance. I glanced over at Lucas and saw him watching me, and dropped my eyes back down to my hands. Beside me, Lucas sighed. "I wish I could tell you it would be okay. That would be an easy lie, especially from me, right? But given all you know about the situation, could you believe me?"

No. Lies, no matter how well intentioned, would be pointless. The stakes were too high and too personal to gain any comfort from empty promises. I kept staring at my fingers, and the silence stretched between us. An inky darkness welled up inside me, threatening to drown every good memory I still carried.

"Lucy, look at me."

I dragged my gaze up reluctantly to see him watching me, head cocked to one side. The scar across his face stood out in stark relief to the pale skin, but his blue-green eyes were as alert as ever. The dark hair was no longer combed back, but shaggy and pasted to his face with sweat. Gone was the suave, sophisticated look I'd equated with the former smuggler; here was someone who looked every inch like they needed to be in a hospital.

He held out a hand, gesturing with his fingers toward me. Reluctantly, I raised my hand up to his and he covered it with both of his. "Lucy Delacourt," he said in as solemn a voice as I'd ever heard from his lips, "I promise that I will do everything I can to get you and my brother safe. Do you understand?"

You too. I couldn't bear the idea of losing the cocky, exasperating man before me. Unbidden, I leaned forward and, removing my hand from his, pushed the shaggy hair back behind one ear. Lucas's words faded to silence; his throat worked soundlessly at the gesture, those brilliant eyes boring holes into me. He looked ready to ask something, but someone knocked on the door behind me, startling us both.

Swallowing, I opened it a crack to peek outside. The lady agent who I'd spoken with earlier stood outside the entrance. "I thought you should know," she said softly, barely loud enough for me to hear. "I've received word from Agent Gautier. The team left at the cabin hasn't checked in for over an hour. We have no idea where they are."

18

They moved both Lucas and me out of the hospital within hours, probably for better security. Lucas was taken out in a wheelchair and transported by van, while I went in a car with the other agents.

They'd found Jeremiah's car an hour after I'd been told he was missing. There had been no traces of people at the scene—no bodies, nothing. The decision was made to pull everyone out of the public hospital only moments later. I didn't speak, just followed orders. Inside, I remained frozen, my body moving on autopilot.

An aching numbness consumed me, poisoning all hope and tainting any possibility of a good outcome. *Why had I let him go like that?* If I'd asked him to come, begged him to be *my* hero, he'd still be here at my side.

For the first time, it truly hit home that there might not be a happy ending. I or someone I loved might not walk out of the situation alive. The guilt and gnawing fear inside me was an iron weight, pulling me down and making even walking difficult.

The new location was very high security, a thoroughly modern building behind a thick gate. Guards were posted everywhere, weapons at the ready, as they hustled us inside. The agency hiding us was clearly ready for a war, and by all past indicators they'd likely get one.

I couldn't find it inside me to care any longer.

We shuffled down the lobby, past the security and up the elevator. Ultimately we ended up in another windowless corridor deep inside the building. Agent Anderson, who'd been by my side the whole time, led me into another room, and despite my mood I gave a sigh of relief when I saw Lucas. He was in a wheelchair, flanked by two agents, and looked like a king sitting on his throne. They bent to help him up and Lucas gave a grunt, as he was set carefully onto a nearby couch.

Lucas's eyes found me and, despite his pallor, a wide smile spread across his face. "Well, look at what the cat dragged in," he said, and then his eyes flickered to the agent by my side. "Ah, it's always nice to see a pretty face in these situations. Too much testosterone sometimes."

The redheaded agent flushed but otherwise ignored him. She signaled to the two other agents, who followed her out of the room. Lucas's eyes watched their departure, and then the smile slipped a bit. "Any news on Jeremiah?"

"Nothing." I sat down in the chair beside him, leaning my head back and staring at the ceiling. "They should have been here hours ago but there's no sign or word from that group."

"Bet they're wishing that car had the GPS now." When I gave him a dirty look, Lucas threw up his hands. "What do you want me to say? That I wish he were here? He's my brother, of course I do."

"I know." I drew in a shaky breath. "I hate being helpless."

"Ah, you're preaching to the choir." Lucas waved his hand over his body, laid out on the couch. "If the bad guys broke through that door right there, the best I could manage would be to shoo them away."

The imagery almost made me smile, but I wasn't in the mood for humor. "What's going to happen to you after all this is done?"

"No idea. If we manage to survive this lunatic half-brother of mine, I expect I'll get taken out by some other former acquaintance whose name I've turned over."

My gaze flicked to Lucas, then away. "We're a barrel of laughs, aren't we?"

Lucas's lips stretched into a grim smile. "Real comedians. Just what the situation demands."

"I don't know what to do about Jeremiah."

The words felt ripped from my chest, as if they were no longer able to stay trapped inside me. Almost immediately, I wanted to call them back, but kept my lips clamped shut. The irony of my situation, asking relationship advice from the "other man," was not lost on me. But I needed answers and, in spite of everything, I thought of Lucas as a friend and ally.

He gave a small shrug, his eyes looking off into the distance. "There's nothing you can do at this point," Lucas murmured. "He either forgives you or he doesn't."

"But . . ." I swallowed back the bitter gall in my throat, knowing he was right. "But how will I know if he's truly forgiven me?"

"You won't," Lucas said bluntly. "If what happened between us is so divisive, it'll take a leap of faith on both your parts. But it's no secret that you fell into bed with me on the rebound from my brother's stupidity, not for any love of me."

I flinched at the bitter note there, feeling my insides shrivel a bit. "I'm sorry," I murmured, feeling more wretched for having, however unintentionally, used him.

"Don't be." Lucas sighed. "Anya loved me. I knew this and manipulated her feelings to further my own goals, and sent her down a path of destruction. Plus, who knows how many others I've hurt with the smuggling. Believe me, I deserve much worse."

"But . . ." I trailed off as voices rose outside my door. Marie was back, and while I couldn't understand what she was saying I recognized her voice. Shooting out of my chair, I crossed the room as quickly as I could manage and wrenched open the door, peering frantically down the hall.

Agent Anderson was immediately by my side. "Ms. Delacourt, is anything wrong?"

"Did they find him?" I asked just as Marie walked past me.

The Frenchwoman frowned. "Ms. Delacourt, you should be resting . . ."

"Screw resting. We should be finding out where the group left behind's been taken. Did you find Jeremiah or Ronny?"

Marie pursed her lips together and shared a glance with

Anderson that spoke volumes. "Local law enforcement knew almost immediately who you had described," she said finally as an elevator at the end of the hall opened. "They helped us find him, now we need to see what he knows. As soon as I find out anything, I'll let you know."

They were empty words, as meaningless as air to me right then. My hands shook with a combination of rage and fear, and I gripped the doorframe to keep anyone from noticing. Marie was already looking down the hall, having dismissed my presence.

"Ronny's just going to stall," I murmured, trying and failing to contain my emotion. "We have to find them now."

"I'll let you know if they find anything," Anderson said, moving in front of me as I saw who was being escorted down the aisle.

Ronny noticed me quickly, and the sneer that split his face told his recognition. "Oi, love," he said, licking his lips lewdly, "ye couldn't get enough of me couldja? Fancy a roll now that yer bloke's out the picture?"

I shrank back, and as Ronny laughed, something inside me exploded. For too long I'd been running, and was done with being helpless. His words answered my own question: the slime knew something about Jeremiah's disappearance, but thought this all a game. He wouldn't tell; to him, it was more fun watching everyone else flop and flail aimlessly, right up until time ran out. His laughter rolled over me, echoing inside my skull, until there was nothing left for me to do but act.

Anderson stood between us, her attention on the snake in cuffs. I'd been observing her more surreptitiously than my conscious mind understood, and knew she had a gun. As she leaned forward, I actually saw it peek into the open for the first time, nestled securely against her hip.

Without thinking about the consequences, I dove for her weapon, unsnapped the holster and pulled it free. All eyes turned toward me in the commotion, and I knew I needed to act fast. Ignoring the pain in my ankle, I threw myself straight at Ronny, grabbing his clothing and held on, my momentum shoving us both back.

The hallway was narrow and we crashed into the far wall, a tangle of limbs and bodies. The two men holding Ronny were caught unprepared, and lost their grip on the hand-cuffed informant's arms. We collapsed to the ground, me atop the stunned man, the gun still in my hand and pointed toward his head. The sneer was gone from Ronny's face now, his eyes bugging out from surprise, but I didn't care.

Up close, he smelled even worse than I'd imagined. His lips were pulled back in shock, revealing brown teeth and foul breath that made me want to gag. The gun was loose against his chest, and I managed to get my wits about me fast enough to move it toward his face.

"Lucy, no!"

I ignored Marie's voice, bringing the gun up and under Ronny's chin. Around me I heard shouting and the other people with guns pulling them from their holsters, but my eyes didn't leave Ronny's face. The anger that set me down this path wasn't a sustainable resource. Dread of what the consequence would be bloomed inside my chest, making it difficult to breathe.

"She can't do this!" Beneath me, Ronny squirmed, unable to do much with his arms trapped beneath him.

His words triggered a memory in my head, and I looked down at the gun. Hands pulled at me, trying to separate me from Ronny. I pressed a small black tab right above the trigger, removing the safety, and yelled, "Hands off or he's dead."

I sounded like a bad cop movie, but the words worked. The hands let me go, and clicking off the safety ratcheted up the fear in Ronny's face. I pushed the gun up, my hand trembling with adrenaline. "Where did he take them?"

"How should I know?" Ronny was stiff as a board beneath me, his eyes wide and staring straight at my hand.

Could I actually shoot him? I wasn't sure. The gun shook in my hand, and I hoped he would think it was rage and not fear. All I could think about was Lucas with the doctors, and Jeremiah in danger.

But I knew if I saw that smirk on that little weasel's face again, pulling the trigger would be much easier.

"Lucy." Marie's calm voice came from somewhere behind me. "Let him go and put the gun down."

"You have to know something," I said, ignoring Marie's plea. "How did you get the information about that cabin?"

"He rang my mobile! I swear, I dunno where he or anyone else is!"

"What was the number?"

"Fuck if I know, but it was American!"

Never in my life had I imagined this kind of terror directed at me. Ronny seemed genuine, a veritable font of information now that his life was on the line. Nothing he'd said however was of any use in finding Jeremiah. Desperation was a choking blackness, and at that moment getting Jeremiah back was all I could focus on without going insane. "I'm going to count to three. One."

"Lucy, let him go *now*!"

"Two."

"Cúchulainn!"

I blinked, not understanding the word. "Who's that?"

"The Cúchulainn. It's a pub in London." Ronny was shaking now, great tremors that threatened to dislodge me. "That's the only time I met him in person. I know shit-all about your man but p-please, please don't kill me."

His pleas finally touched something inside me. I stared at the weapon in my hand, shame consuming me. I had the sudden and overwhelming urge to vomit as the gun slid out of my hand, dropping with a dull thud onto the linoleum. Hands once against grabbed me, tearing me away from Ronny and pushing me facedown onto the floor. Ronny's raised voice was part of the hubbub, but I was too caught up in my own despair to listen. Shouting continued above me as my arms were wrenched backwards and cuffs thrown on.

Great sobs built in my chest, leaving me gasping for air. I closed my eyes, my cheek against the chill flooring, and tried to forget the terror I'd seen in those brown eyes moments before. Guilt tore through me, and I wondered just how badly I'd messed up.

"You have to protect me." Ronny was babbling, fear still in his voice. "If he finds out I told you anything . . ."

"Take him to the interrogation room, I'll take care of the girl."

Marie's sharp voice cut through my dark thoughts. Two large men lifted me to my feet, an awkward proposition with the handcuffs and a throbbing ankle. As the adrenaline quickly wore off, the pain intensified. I struggled to balance on one foot, dreading the moment I'd have to walk.

"I can't have stunts like that, Ms. Delacourt."

I half expected to be hauled off into some jail, so it was a surprise when they steered me back toward my original room. Beside me, I saw Marie hand Anderson her gun again. "Try not to let this happen again," she said in a dry voice, and Anderson pursed her lips, flushing. "Report back to your agency," the Frenchwoman continued, "we'll take care of Ms. Delacourt."

The guards set me down on a chair. Nearby, Lucas was already on his feet, leaning heavily against a nearby table. "What did you do to her?" he demanded, moving toward me but finding his way blocked by the agents.

"Relax Loki, she's fine. The handcuffs are to keep her from doing anything else stupid."

I looked away, too ashamed to look at them. Ronny's face wouldn't get out of my head; the fear I'd seen in his eyes continued to haunt me. Misery poured through me and I fought back the tears. There had been too many lately and I had no right to self-pity in this situation.

Marie let herself out as Lucas settled himself beside me

tenderly. I kept my head turned away, unwilling to let him see my pain. He stayed silent far longer than I could have imagined before finally speaking. "I could get those cuffs off if you'd like."

I didn't answer, just stared at my knees. Beside me, Lucas took a deep breath. "Whatever you did out there wasn't your fault."

"Seriously?" I gave him a dirty look. "I stole Anderson's gun and held it on Ronny to get him to talk. How is that not my fault?"

One eyebrow quirked at my confession. "Kinky." When I said nothing to his quip, he sighed again. "Think about it, Lucy. Would you have ever done anything like that if Rush hadn't put you in this position?"

Rejecting his line of reasoning, I kept myself quiet. A moment ticked past, then Lucas asked, "Did he say anything?"

I shook my head and swallowed, my chest growing tight. "I'm scared."

The confession was like pulling a drain stopper; the tide of emotion swept over me and I hiccupped a sob. Lucas must have seen something in my face because he gathered me in his arms. There was no stopping it then; against Lucas's thin shirt, I gave way to the emotions and bawled my eyes out. Lucas held me, his arms around me as I cried and cried, unable to erase my uncertainty and Ronny's terrified face from my mind.

Agent Anderson never returned to my door. Marie returned nearly two hours later, accompanied by the two men who had moved me into the room. "Let me get those cuffs off you."

I stood carefully on my one good leg, one of the men holding my arm and helping me up. Marie unlocked the cuffs from behind my back, allowing me to stretch out my arms, but promptly locked my wrists together in front of me. I sighed but said nothing, wondering just how much trouble I was in.

"We have a few leads to pursue. A team has already been sent to search the pub Ronny mentioned. He clammed up after your little incident, demanding protection from his employer, so we're pursuing everything we have."

"Are you joining them?"

Marie shook her head. "Despite what you've seen, I'm not usually a field agent. But I'll know immediately if he pops up anywhere on the grid."

Lucas piped up. "And Agent Anderson?"

Marie gave him a suspicious look but replied, "She's with her own agency at the moment."

"She's not in any trouble, is she?" I hated to think I might have hurt her career.

"That's not for me to decide, but she'll be out in the field and you'll be here. No more stunts like that, Ms. Delacourt, or your next accommodations won't be as nice as this."

I jingled the cuffs around my wrist and sighed as the agents left the room. "I've dug myself in deep this time, haven't I?"

"Cheer up, Buttercup. We're still alive, right?"

"And Jeremiah?"

Lucas grew quiet at the mention of his brother. Depression darkened my heart, and I tried to change the subject. "What are you going to do after this is over?"

"Try not to die?" At my annoyed look, he shrugged. "That depends on whether the authorities like my information or not. It could range anything from jail to witness protection."

"A new life? It might give you a second chance at life."

Lucas snorted. "Witness protection would mean I'd have to be very boring and not attract attention. That would probably involve an office job in a cubicle." He shuddered. "I'd almost prefer prison to suburbia."

"It's not *that* bad. Maybe you'd like it."

"That thought scares me even more." He cocked his head sideways. "You really stole Anderson's gun?"

Amusement tipped his words, and I peered at him curiously. "Do you two know each other?"

"Oh, we met years ago but I doubt she remembers me. Yes, there's no history like old history."

"Now come on, you can't say something like that and not . . ." I trailed off as the lights shut off. "What's going on? Is the power out?"

Lucas shook his head. "The heater's still on. Go check the window."

I hobbled across the room and peered down. "I don't see anything happening down there."

"Check with the guards at the door, maybe they . . ." Lucas blinked. "Are you feeling suddenly tired?"

As a matter of fact, I was. My legs felt like they were filled with lead, like they were rooted to the spot. Struggling over to the couch, I picked up a crutch and used it to support me across the room to the door. Walking like this with cuffs on was difficult business, but I managed to open the door and peak outside.

Two men were already motionless on the floor, while another was trying weakly to crawl toward the bend in the hall. One guard was missing but the other one was slumped down beside the door, eyes closed. Heart thudding in my chest, I slammed the door shut. "Shit," I mumbled, my voice high and thin.

"Get back from there."

I tried to hobble across the room but the crutch caught against the edge of the desk, almost dumping me on the floor. Lucas's head was lolled back against the chair as if he couldn't keep it up anymore. "Fuck," he whispered, eyes wide and staring straight at me.

There were no latches on the window, no way to let fresh air inside. My arms felt weighed down but I still grabbed a nearby folding chair and swung it with all my might at the glass. It bounced back, the recoil tearing it out of my hands. I couldn't hold myself up anymore and crashed to the ground, pain shooting up my leg as I landed on the sprained ankle.

I tried rolling over, but my limbs no longer wanted to move from the ground. Lucas was similarly slumped in his chair, his eyes flickering open and closed as he tried to resist the toxin. Behind me I heard the door open, and footsteps as someone entered the room. A gloved hand grabbed my arm, and I was dragged over and sideways until I was face to face with a gas mask.

I felt a pinprick of fear, the last trace of my conscious mind, before darkness finally consumed me.

19

I woke up shivering against a bed of ice. My hands were no longer bound, but darkness surrounded me. Dawn put the clouds above me a dark blue, destined to get brighter but not quite enough light with which to navigate. Putting my hand on the ground near my head, I felt rough cobbles beneath my fingers, cold and damp in the winter frost.

"Ah, finally awake. I had wondered how much longer we'd drag this out."

That voice sent chills through me that had nothing to do with the night air. Trembling from far more than just the cold, I rolled onto my hands and knees to see Alexander Rush standing nearby. He watched me calmly, that still face showing me nothing.

As I pulled my legs under me, I felt something tug on my good ankle, some kind of restraint. In the darkness I couldn't see what it was, and reached out to find a thick chain coming from a shackle around my leg. The chain clanked against the cobbles as I tugged, expecting to find resistance, only to have something roll unsteadily toward me. An iron ball bigger than both my fists together lay there, fixed securely with the end of the chain connected to my leg. There was enough resistance that it held me in place, but not that I couldn't drag it if necessary.

This can't be good.

"The old ball and chain. Seemed rather fitting, don't you think?"

The relaxed voice grated on my nerves, giving me the edge I needed to shove aside the fear. "What do you want, Rush?"

"No pleading or begging for your life? Such a refreshing change." Rush walked toward me, his footsteps wet against the cobblestones, and then knelt down beside me. He didn't seem at all concerned about our proximity or that I could just about reach out and touch him. Then again, it took everything within me not to recoil from his presence.

We were on a road of some kind, although I couldn't tell where. Barriers along the sides made me think a bridge of some kind and somewhere nearby I could hear the distant sound of running water. Dark fog swallowed up most of the surrounding area except for one light shining to the right side of the road. I could see the glow of another light down the street but the slight rise of the road and my low position obscured its source from my view.

"I want something very simple for you, my dear. I want you to make a choice, that's all, then you are free to go."

Free to go? I stared suspiciously at Rush, but he didn't seem the least bit perturbed. "What kind of choice?"

There was a loud whimper nearby, as if someone was try-ing to speak past a gag. Annoyance flickered briefly across Rush's features before they smoothed out. "Excuse me a mo-ment," he said, his voice almost polite. Pushing himself to his feet, he moved back out toward the edge of the road.

I tracked his movements, and saw something across the road moving in the dim light. Rush reached down and hauled the hooded person to their feet, dragging them closer to my position beside of the road. The hooded figure had a chain attached to him that rattled softly with each movement. Grunts and muffled cries came from beneath the hood, and I noticed that whoever it was had their hands and feet tied together behind their back.

My heart squeezed with dread as Rush leaned against a large stone atop the bridge's ledge. I hadn't even noticed it before that moment, but it wobbled dangerously. Seemingly satisfied, he pulled off his prisoner's hood to reveal his pris-oner, and I felt a guilty mix of relief and horror to see our informant, Ronny.

"A familiar face, no?"

I covered my mouth with one hand, unable to speak. Even in the low light I could once again see the terror on the infor-mant's face as he tried desperately to speak through the gag. All that came out however were guttural cries, unintelligible around the fabric in his mouth.

"So what did he tell you? The location to my secret lair? A decoder ring, perhaps? Probably something mundane like a phone number to track. No matter, I suppose, a traitor is a traitor." Rush looked at the trembling man beside him, then shrugged. "It's so hard to find good help."

Oh God, no.

Ronny screamed around the rag in his mouth, desperate to be heard, but he had no chance. Raising one leg, Rush kicked the large stone over the bridge, giving Ronny the barest of shoves in the same direction. The slack pulled tight and Ronny's feet were jerked out from under him and up toward the ledge. With his hands tied behind his back, there was no way for him to grab any purchase; he rolled up and over the short wall, a muffled scream swallowed up by the darkness.

There was a brief silence, testament to our distance above the water, and then I heard a small splash from below. Rush peeked over the side then, apparently satisfied with what he saw, turned back around. "Who's next?"

Horror choked me, and I felt hysteria bubbling to the surface. Speech was impossible; I stared at the space Ronny had occupied only moments before, shocked by how quickly it had happened.

"Perhaps your lover, then? The middle child, always desperate for attention."

Paralyzed by fear, I watched as Rush moved toward an unmoving lump at one side of the bridge. Pleas died on my lips when I noticed the square silhouette perched on the ledge above. It looked slightly larger than the ball around my ankle and just as solid. In the rising light, I saw a chain leading down to the bundle of rags lying on the road.

"Yes, my big brother Jeremiah." Rush nudged the dark

lump with his toe. "He learned quickly to keep quiet while I talked, but it still took a few lessons." ·

The Jeremiah I knew would have already broken his brother's leg by now, so his stillness told me something bad had happened. I levered myself upright until I was standing, teetering on my good leg. Beyond the edge of the bridge I could see nothing; thick fog obscured everything such that I couldn't even see the ends of the bridge.

My whole body trembled as Rush's attention was again directed to me, and in the dim light he smiled. "The river here is shallow, not even ten feet beneath the bridge. More than enough however to do the trick. Shall I toss your beloved into the water's embrace next?"

The figure raised its head, and my strength gave out as I recognized Jeremiah's shattered profile. I tried to speak but all that came out was an anguished moan. Holding his head up seemed like more than he could manage, and his chin lolled back to his chest.

Attached to his leg was another chain, this one connected to an iron weight on the ledge. Trembling hard, I took a shaky breath and tried again to speak. "Rush, please . . ."

"So you're the bastard my father spoke about."

Rush stilled at Lucas's voice. I turned to see another figure unfold on the opposite side of the bridge, raising himself to a seated position against the ledge. Whereas a moment ago, he'd blended in perfectly with the dark stone of the bridge, now he sat apart, almost daring Rush to see him.

"Our mother found out about you, you know." Lucas's voice was strong, and if I hadn't known better I wouldn't think him injured. "She didn't care that we heard when she confronted father about it. He told her that he'd dealt with it, before beating her into silence again." Lucas cocked his head sideways. "I always wondered what he'd meant by that."

"My my, so you already knew about me. How interesting you never sought me out."

"I doubt you're the only bastard sibling we have. But if you think our 'legitimate' lives were any better than yours, you would be wrong. I'd say you were lucky not to be under the same roof as that motherfucker."

"Oh really," Rush murmured conversationally. "Did you watch him murder your mother, too?"

The ease with which he spoke the words stopped Lucas cold. The smuggler didn't speak for a long moment. "He what?"

"My mother was going to bring my existence to the press's attention. We were poor, and they would offer good money for a story like this." Rush shrugged. "My mother was determined that I see him, but hid me in a closet so he couldn't take me away. When he arrived, they argued and he hit her, which made her issue her ultimatum about the press." Rush shrugged, as if reporting a meaningless detail of his life. "So he strangled her."

There was a stunned pause, then Lucas cleared his throat. "He . . . killed her?"

Rush hitched one shoulder. "I was only seven years old and didn't know who he was until much later. By then, of course, it was far too late for revenge." Rush paused for a moment, as if lost in thought. "She was so pretty, dark hair and blue eyes. I kept her picture for several years until one of my foster families burned it in front of me."

The ease with which he recounted his life events was chilling. "I killed my first man when I was twelve. The justice system let me off because I'd been raped, sealed my records as a minor. I didn't know my father's real name for many years, but by then it didn't matter. By the time I was out of the system and gained that knowledge, the man was already dead."

Pity rose inside me, and I stamped it down mercilessly. Silence fell again, and then Lucas cleared his throat. "Well, okay," he said slowly, "when you put it that way, our lives were pretty damned rosy."

Ignoring their conversation, I turned my attention to Jeremiah. He stayed silent, unmoving, slumped against the low wall of the bridge. I couldn't tell if he was injured, couldn't even tell if he was alive except for brief movements of his head. The dawn sky lit the fog around us, not enough for me to see his features but so that I could make out his shape. Pale skin shone against the dark clothing, and I almost wept for joy when he looked up and our eyes met.

The bleakness I saw in his gaze broke my heart. He lifted a hand as if to reach for me, then Rush moved back between us. "We aren't here to reminisce about the past though, are we?" Dismissing Lucas, Rush turned to me. "You have a choice to make, my dear. Which will it be?"

I stared at him, trying to keep my roiling emotions in check. "Which what?" I whispered, deliberately misunderstanding in the hopes to buy some time.

Rush was nothing if not patient. "I'm giving you a choice. Two of you will walk off this bridge, allowed to live one more day. But you choose which one will die."

Words failed me again. My mouth moved as I struggled to speak, but there was nothing I could say that would make this situation any less hideous. "Just one?" I said breathlessly, unable to wrap my mind around the concept.

"One will walk—or in their case, stagger—off this bridge with you, and one will sink to the bottom of the Thames beneath this bridge. And don't you two gentlemen try and decide for her," Rush added, raising his voice so he would be heard by the brothers. "If either of you makes a decision to be a martyr, you all die. No, this choice is up to your mutual lady here."

"No."

The word was more a grunt than speech, but it was the first time I heard Jeremiah speak. I made a small mewl of distress as I saw him try to lever himself upright and slip on the wet cobbles. His hands were black in the low light, and something told me that dark stain pooled beneath him wasn't mud.

"Well, yes, actually," Rush said as if scolding a child. "Don't think I'll let the winning brother stay free for long, but you have another day of life depending on what Lucy here decides." Rush turned back to me. "My dear, both of your men are in dire need of medical attention. It would behoove you to choose quickly."

The face staring down at me couldn't be much older than I was, yet the evil I saw chilled me to the bone. Rush was close enough to me that it would only take a few steps for me to attack. The weight around my leg wouldn't normally be much of a problem, except that I'd be pushing off with my injured ankle. The offending joint pulsed with each heartbeat, swollen but not outright painful, but I couldn't trust it to hold me up.

After a moment of nothing, Rush sighed. "I see we need to give you added incentive." He moved to the center of the bridge and, reaching under his jacket, pulled out a long handgun and pointed it toward Jeremiah. "One."

Begging would change nothing, but I dropped to my knees anyway. The uneven cobbles dug into my shins, my ankle burning at the new position. None of that mattered however; I was about to lose everything no matter what I decided.

He swung the weapon toward Lucas. "Two."

"I choose myself."

Rush paused. "That wasn't one of my options."

"I'm serious. Think about it," I replied quickly, surprising myself by how strong my voice was. I licked my dry lips. "They both love me. You could still exact your revenge in the future but make them suffer in the meantime. They'd have to live knowing their lives came at the cost of mine."

Rush studied me for a moment, then his lips twitched up ever so slightly into what might have been a smile. "I like the way you think. Okay, then. Throw yourself off the bridge."

Everything inside me seized up. It was one thing to say you'd sacrifice yourself—it was something else completely to go through with it. "Do you promise," I asked in a shaky voice, "to let them both go if I do this?"

"No." His answer cut through the air like a knife. "But," he conceded after a moment's hesitation, as if savoring my panic, "you do make a compelling point."

"You won't kill them here on the bridge?" I repeated, my voice wavering. The chills that held me stiff with fear gave way to a quaking that threatened to shake me apart.

"I might." Rush shrugged. "You will get no guarantees from me, except that I will kill all of you now if you don't make a decision."

I looked at the large metal ball attached to my leg, sizing it up, and then slowly stood again. Grabbing the chain, I limped over to the nearest wall, pulling the heavy weight behind me. It was lighter than I thought, but still more than enough weight to keep me below the surface of the water.

There would be no swimming with this attached to my leg.

Out of the corner of my eye, I saw Jeremiah roll over. His arms weren't tied like I'd thought, and he feebly pulled himself toward me. "Lucy"

My face crumpled at his desperate plea. I didn't want to die, but somehow found the strength to cross the bridge and lift the leg weight onto the ledge. Carefully, I pulled myself up onto the stone barrier, but couldn't do anything more than squat there. The water below, still invisible through the fog, was much louder at this angle.

Jeremiah repeated my name, more forcefully this time. The chain rattled behind him, then pulled taut, halting his movement toward me.

From here, I could see the bruising on his face and body,

the puffiness around his jaw and eyes. Tears streamed down my face as our eyes met. *I love you,* I mouthed, and saw his stricken expression.

"Lucy, please . . . No."

Nearby, a seagull cried rang out, signaling the coming dawn. Still trembling, I stood up, blocking my ears to Jeremiah's pleas. I stared down over the ledge, trying to work up the courage to lean forward those couple inches.

Behind me, Rush made an annoyed sound. "Do you need some assistan . . ."

"FREEZE, POLICE!"

Lights shone on us from two directions, far enough away not to blind me but enough to illuminate the situation. Not ten feet from me lay Jeremiah, laid out on the street, his clothing and skin stained with too much blood. Shadows moved in the light, the cavalry advancing on our position.

Rush looked at both ends of the bridge, his lips compressing into a firm line. "I don't think so." He pulled something out of his pocket and pressed a switch. Twin explosions, one on either side of us, lit the night sky. Yellow flames rocketed into the air, shutting off the lights and making the old bridge shudder.

The blast shook the ledge beneath me, threatening to topple me down into the water below. I teetered on the edge, the stone in my hands wobbling uncertainly, before falling back hard on the cobblestone bridge. The air rushed from my body, my twisted ankle exploding anew in pain. Turning my head, I saw Rush move toward Jeremiah, his face twisted with rage.

I rolled sideways, still fighting for breath, and Rush's gaze swung my way. That instant felt like an eternity, his profile lit by the still-billowing flames and police lights. Somehow, I felt more than saw the evil smile that crossed his features.

Without a word, he lifted one booted foot and kicked the square weight attached to Jeremiah over the side of the bridge.

A hoarse cry tore through me. Jeremiah scrabbled weakly through the air, looking for something to grab but finding nothing. I screamed and, no longer caring about the pain, threw myself at him with everything I had left.

I landed half atop Jeremiah, my hip painfully impacting the corner of the stone railing. I barely managed to snag Jeremiah's shirt, wet with blood and stripped to rags, when the stone's weight jerked the chain. He rolled over the side feet first like Ronny, but my grip was enough to halt his momentum and allow him to grab onto the ledge.

I climbed up his body, grabbing everything I could touch to keep him from falling the rest of the way down. His skin was slick, making my job harder. Only his shoulders and arms remained atop the thick stone railing, and they strained to keep him from falling.

Above me, I heard the whooping of a helicopter approaching as Rush stepped in close beside me. I didn't dare look up, too focused on keeping my grip on the man in my arms, but Jeremiah stared past me at his brother.

"You were right, you know." Rush knelt beside us, mere inches away, and studied us dispassionately. The helicopter spotlight shone down on us, making dark shadows on his face and giving his already sinister smile a maniacal gleam. "Your death will hurt them so much more."

I heard the click of a gun and closed my eyes, then looked at Jeremiah. Blood and bruises covered his face, the damage at Rush's hands obscuring much of his beautiful face. But his green eyes shone bright, and in their helpless gaze I saw my death.

A chain rattled behind us, and Rush half-turned. "What . . ."

Something smacked into Rush, propelling him against the barrier wall beside us. I had a brief view of dark hair and a familiar scarred face, and then a gunshot split the air. Both men jerked and fell sideways, a second square iron weight teetering atop the ledge. The helicopter spotlight moved away, plunging us into sudden darkness, but I could hear the grappling right next to me.

My hands were full keeping Jeremiah aloft, but my eyes were riveted on the scene beside me. Rush and Lucas rose from the ground just as the helicopter made another sweep, silhouetting the two men against the light. Whether by design or accident, their struggles dislodged the remaining weight from the ledge, plunging it down toward the water.

I watched in silent horror as both figures rolled up and over, then plummeted down into the inky darkness below.

A wordless scream rose up from inside me at the heartbreaking loss. I clung desperately to Jeremiah as the wind picked up, shouts coming from nearby. I didn't look, unwilling to move so as not to drop the man in my arms. Suddenly there were more hands, holding and pulling at Jeremiah, dragging him up and over the barrier. I didn't release my grip, not even when I heard the metallic clang of the weight landing on the stone cobbles.

Gut-wrenching sobs shook my body, and someone pried me gently away from Jeremiah. I crawled backwards, enough to let the paramedics in to work, and watched as they swarmed over his unmoving body. It wasn't until somebody draped a blanket around me that I realized I was shivering, and not just from the cold.

The helicopter had landed nearby on the bridge, and a detached part of me recognized Marie jogging toward us. I barely acknowledged her as she stopped beside us, looking first at Jeremiah then me. "We need to get you someplace warm," she said finally, taking my hand and gently pulling me up.

Someone bundled me in another blanket, but I only had eyes for Jeremiah. I watched as they transferred him to a long board, strapping him down carefully.

"The blast destroyed a large section of the road," Marie said to my unspoken question. "Enough that we couldn't get vehicles in here, but not so much that we can't hike through."

"How did you find us?" I asked.

"Rush was good, but we're better. We managed to get past his hacks and access the street cameras, enough to follow him here. Fortunately, we seem to have arrived just in time."

My heart twisted. *Not in time for all of us,* I thought sadly, but didn't say anything as the French agent walked away.

Along one narrow wall of the bridge, I saw a lone figure

peering over the side. Agent Anderson stared down at the spot where Lucas and Rush had disappeared, and I hobbled over to stand beside her. "You knew him before this, didn't you?"

She was silent for a long moment, and then nodded. "Botched undercover operation three years back. He was there. Saved my life, made the bad guys pay. His information led to a lot of arrests, but he disappeared before I could thank him."

Anderson's face was covered by the darkness, but the still way she stood there staring down into the water spoke volumes. We stood there in shared silence for a moment. Lucas's face flashed through my mind, the big grin that was his mask, and a lump formed in my throat. "He was a good man," I murmured, swallowing hard.

"The very best."

Paramedics were carrying Jeremiah to a waiting ambulance, so reluctantly I turned away to follow. The crater and debris from Rush's explosion proved difficult for me to navigate, and in the end I was carried by one of the larger guards. I never lost sight of Jeremiah's still form as it was carried up to the street and toward the ambulance, making sure I remained beside him as the doors closed and we moved back toward the hospital.

20

The media went into a frenzy with the bridge story. Newspapers ran with all the bombings, conspiracy theorists debated online who actually did the bombing, but we were mercifully left out of it. The press were never told our identities, a blessing I didn't rightly appreciate at the time.

Jeremiah required two hundred eleven stitches to repair the damage he'd faced, both internally and externally. Rush had really worked him over, ensuring there would forever be scars to remember him by. Three days later, he still hadn't woken up, and I felt like I was slowly going insane. I stayed with him every day, appreciating the respite from the action but aching inside for his arms to hold me again.

Whatever issues we may have had with our passports and country-hopping was dealt with by lawyers and the international agencies. The red-faced man I'd seen in the London airport popped into the hospital twice with brief updates, which he gave to me in Jeremiah's stead. They retrieved my real passport, the US one this time, and said the way home was clear. But I held off on watching any news or listening to what was happening outside the hospital or my hotel room.

Now that the danger had passed, all I wanted to do was forget. That was easier said than done, however.

I stayed in a hotel next to the hospital the first couple nights. Nightmares kept me up, dark dreams that I never remembered. I would wake sweating, a scream on my lips, to the darkness of a lonely hotel room. The lack of sleep made my waking hours virtually unbearable, to the point where I wanted to run away from it all. Jeremiah's still form only made it worse, as if I'd lost my foundation. I didn't talk to anyone, just waited patiently for him to wake up.

On the third morning, Georgia Hamilton arrived at the London hospital. As she was his mother, I gave her room to be with her son, but I doubt I could have stopped her anyway. She ignored me completely but began interrogating nurses and hospital staff, demanding to know his progress. Georgia's face seemed more lined than I remembered, as if she'd aged a decade since I'd last seen her. She was as sour as I remembered however, but I supposed losing a son would do that to you.

She was out of the room, busy making plans for his immediate transfer, when the hand I held twitched, and then squeezed mine tight. I lifted my head off the bed and looked up, then began crying when I saw the blinking green eyes look at me. I didn't know what else to say, almost too overjoyed to speak, so I murmured, "Hey."

"Hey." His voice was rusty, face still tired and worn, but he was awake. I saw his mouth move and poured him some water, rising out of my chair to give him a drink. All I wanted to do was hug him close, but I'd seen his wounds and knew that would only give him pain. I did however caress my hand along his face, over the bandages on his cheeks and temple, happy to be touching him.

He squeezed my hand again, a tiny smile tipping one corner of his mouth, and then closed his eyes as I pressed the button calling the nurses.

The ride home was on the family plane, the same one I'd taken from New York to Paris less than two months prior. This trip was much more somber, plus carried more passengers to monitor Jeremiah's health. Georgia disapproved of my staying at his side, saying I was in the way and not even family.

"She stays." The two words, spoken in a rough voice tinged by pain, shut down Georgia's arguments. I could feel the anger from the woman directed at me but I didn't care, glad to not have to leave.

Being back on American soil wasn't quite the relief I'd imagined. They set Jeremiah up in his Manhattan apartment, deeming it closer to the hospital and medical staff than the Hamptons estate. As much as I disliked his mother, the woman was on top of everything. Maid service, hospital staff visits, in-home physical therapy; she arranged everything and insisted on staying to make sure it all worked. Georgia set me up in the guest room, on the opposite side of the penthouse suite, but I was in no state of mind to argue.

Two days after we arrived in New York, Marie paid us a visit at the apartment. When she arrived upstairs, I hurried to greet her. The Interpol agent seemed much more relaxed now that the danger was past; she actually smiled when we shook hands. "You've come a long way," I said, surprised by how glad I was to see her.

"A telephone is not enough for some news," she replied, looking around the spacious apartment. "Jeremiah is doing well I hope?"

"He is. Still confined to a bed which he hates, but better."

"And yourself?"

I paused, trying to decide on an answer, and then shrugged. "As well as can be expected, I suppose."

We stepped into the downstairs bedroom where Jeremiah lay, his thin computer sitting on a small breakfast tray over his lap. When he saw Marie he closed it and held out his hand in greeting. "I hadn't thought to see you again."

"I was in the US on business and thought I should bring you both the news news. Yesterday Rush's body was pulled from the Thames."

I sucked in a breath. "Are they sure?"

Marie nodded in Jeremiah's direction. "Preliminary DNA tests show a family relation to both you and your brother. As so little was known about him beforehand, we'll know more for certain in the next few weeks."

"And Lucas?" I asked. Out of the corner of my eye, I saw Jeremiah grow still.

"No sign yet, but I promise to keep you informed if we find anything." She paused, and then asked, "Do you remember if anything was . . . attached to Rush as he went over the side?"

The question seemed odd, and I looked at Jeremiah for confirmation. "No, there were just those weights on Lucas and Jeremiah. Why?"

"Apparently, Rush had a metal cuff around his wrist when he was found, although there was no weight attached like you described." She shrugged. "Either way, he is dead, and I wanted you to know."

"Would you like a drink?" I asked, realizing I was being a bad hostess, but Marie shook her head.

"I need to be back in Washington by this evening, so I should be going."

I thought briefly about hugging her, but held out my hand instead. "Thank you for coming all this way."

Her face softened a bit as she looked at me. "I'm glad you made it through this, Ms. Delacourt."

"Poor Lucas," I murmured after showing the French agent out. I sat down on the edge of the bed next to Jeremiah, taking his hand. "I hope he survived." Between his previous injuries and the two gunshots I'd heard just before they went over the side, the pragmatic part of me doubted the smuggler lived. The world seemed dimmer without his presence.

"Did you love him?"

I pulled back at the question, releasing Jeremiah's hand. There was no denying the bitterness in the phrasing, but his face was closed off, his tone a simple inquiry. A lump settled in my throat, and I shook my head. "He was my friend when I needed one, and now he's gone."

The answer seemed to satisfy Jeremiah, who laid back and closed his eyes. The dark bruising around his beautiful face made me want to weep. I had no idea what he'd gone through at Rush's hands, but I'd seen the wounds on Jeremiah's body. The sight hurt my soul and made me want to kill the bastard all over again.

Where do we go from here?

The stricken expression on Jeremiah's face on the bridge flashed through my mind again. He'd begged me not to jump, and although I'd ignored him at the time, I remembered his pleas. In that instant, something had bound us; I'd felt his desperation, seen the agony on his face. Now though, the cold mask was back, and I didn't know what to think. There was no talk of the future, no discussion of what would happen. Once again, I felt adrift in a scary world.

A strident voice rose from the living room and I suppressed a groan as Georgia entered the apartment. Within seconds she was inside the bedroom, accompanied by two ladies in nurses' scrubs.

"Ah, darling," she said, leaning down to kiss her son's cheek as if he was still a child. "The nurses are here to check on your progress, and I brought some help to clean up this pigsty. Really my dear, you make a terrible maid."

The last part was directed at me, and the accusation

pierced me to the quick. I looked away, self-esteem wilting under the biting accusation I knew was untrue, but that I hadn't the strength to fight. When I didn't move from my spot on the bed, Georgia finally deigned to look at me, distaste in her gaze. "Well, go on. Shoo, and let the professionals work."

"Mother, stop it," Jeremiah said in a dangerous voice, but I stood up quickly.

"No, let them look at you." I swallowed back the words I desperately wanted to say to Georgia Hamilton and, trying to keep my chin up, marched out the door. I thought I heard my name called but couldn't stay in there another minute. Tears were too close to the surface, and I'd be damned if I let either one of them see me cry.

Several maids bustled around the penthouse, cleaning and arranging things. My feelings of helplessness grew as I watched them tidy up everything that could have kept me busy, things that might have given me something to do. The apartment wasn't dirty; before we'd arrived, it had been thoroughly prepped for our arrival, probably by this same army of maids. I'd kept things as tidy as I could, and yet these ladies were busy enough for me to see I hadn't been thorough.

I'd never been one to take pride in my cleaning skills— honestly, I wasn't very "domestic" in the best of settings— but this was one more blow to my pride.

I was sitting on the couch, trying to just stay out of the way, when Georgia swept out of the bedroom. Immediately the ladies who'd been cleaning finished what they were doing and moved after her, already ready to leave. Georgia looked down her nose at me and rolled her eyes. "Surely you have something more useful to do than sit around my son's house doing nothing." She sniffed, walking toward the door. "I hate to think he would tie himself to a mooch like you."

Angry words rose and died on my lips. I wanted to defend myself, to make her feel as unworthy as she made me feel, but I was out of my league. If I had the chops to sling insults, maybe I would have stooped to her level, but the barbs left me too stunned to speak. *That couldn't be how I'm perceived in his house.*

Is it?

My breathing sped up, blood rushing to my head as my chest tightened. I stood up, suddenly needing to move, to *do* something, but despair crushed me into the floor. Covering my mouth with one hand, I dropped down beside the bar-stools, holding onto one as I tried to get control of my emotions again. I had to remember to breathe as I felt myself getting lightheaded, and gulped down several gasps of air.

A girl I'd gone to college with used to have panic attacks semi-regularly, and I recognized some of the symptoms. My heart squeezed tight, almost painfully, and I struggled not to be overwhelmed.

There was a light shuffling from nearby, and then I heard Jeremiah call my name. Hearing his voice gave me something to latch onto, a distraction from my sudden misery. I managed to get a deep breath into my constricted lungs, which helped. "Over here," I said, annoyed when my voice warbled. I stood up to see him frowning at me.

"What were you doing on the floor?"

"Stretching." I hated how easily the lie slid off my tongue, but I couldn't explain my problems to him. My heart continued to race, urging me to do something, so I moved into the kitchen. "Do you want me to make some lunch?"

"I'm good, but make yourself something if you're hungry."

It was my turn to frown as I studied him. "Should you be on your feet?"

"I'm tired of being kept helpless in that goddamn bed."

I winced at the bite in his words and tried not to read anything into it, but that was difficult given my state of mind. "I'm only trying to help," I said, unable to keep the brittle note out of my words. At least my back was to him so he couldn't see my face, which I was having trouble keeping composed.

Behind me, I heard him sigh. "I know that."

I would have given almost anything to feel his touch right then, hear him say everything would be all right, but he kept silent as he hobbled into the kitchen. I pulled out a box of brownies and set about searching the large kitchen for the necessary items. Oil, eggs and some walnuts were easy enough to find, but I couldn't find a pan. Crouching down, I rifled through the lower cabinets until I found some nested glass dishes that would work.

Jeremiah moved in beside me. "Let me help you with that."

"No, I've got it."

"Lucy, I can help you . . ."

"I said I've got it!"

The words came out sharper than I intended. Mortified by my outburst, I rose too quickly and clipped the edge of the glass dish on the countertop. It jerked from my hands, and I watched as it fell to the tile floor and fractured into several pieces.

"Shit!" I started to tremble as my anxiety peaked again. I cast around for a broom or dustpan but found nothing, so grabbed a roll of paper towels from the counter. "I'm so sorry," I murmured, tearing off several sheets and kneeling down to pick up the pieces.

"Lucy, stop, you're in bare feet."

"No, I need to clean this . . ."

"Lucy, *stop*."

Even now, his voice held the power to command me. But when I ceased movement, my emotions finally caught up with me, and a single sob escape my lips. "I can't do this anymore."

Silence filled the apartment at my words. There was no way I could look at Jeremiah in that moment; all I wanted to do was curl up in a ball and cry. The shaking hadn't stopped, but I hid my hands behind my back. I twisted my fingers around the paper towels, using them to relieve some of the stress.

"Can't do what?" Jeremiah asked after a long pause.

"This. Everything." I waved a hand around vaguely. "You don't even need me. I love you so much, and yet . . ."

I couldn't even say what I meant; everything was too jumbled in my mind. Jeremiah continued his silence and, taking a deep breath, I tried again. "I need to know where we are, where we stand. With our relationship." God, it was hard to say the words. I swallowed and continued when he didn't respond. "Now that the danger's passed, you won't even touch me. I'm useless here and it's killing . . ." I paused, realizing I was about to cry and hating myself for that weakness. "It's killing me to be beside you and not know if . . ."

If we even have a chance. My throat closed, unable to finish my sentence. I'd hit on the heart of the problem, and only realized it now that I'd said the words.

"This isn't easy for me either, you know." Jeremiah gestured to his body with one hand. He was practically humming with frustration, his face a dark cloud. "You're not the only one who feels helpless and trapped by their situation. You're going to leave me like this?"

I flinched at the bitterness there and felt a moment of shame, but a rising anger took hold of me. "If not now, then when? When will be the right time for me to go? A week, a year? Or am I supposed to sit around mooching off your wealth waiting for you to finally kick me out?"

"Lucy, you're not mooching."

"It feels that way to me. You have so much help already; I'm left with nothing to do, no part to play in your recovery. All I do in this apartment is sit around barely speaking with you, and I can't even tell if you want me here."

"Lucy." Jeremiah maneuvered himself in front of me. I wouldn't look him in the eye, even when he tilted my head back so I was looking upwards. "You're welcome to stay here for as long as you need."

He moved his hands up my arms and over my shoulders.

One palm cupped my cheek, and without thinking I leaned into his touch. "You don't need to go," he murmured, leaning down to touch my forehead to his. "Just say yes."

"Have you forgiven me for Lucas?" I asked instead, my voice barely above a whisper.

His hands stilled. Silence echoed through the large penthouse for too long. When he said nothing in reply, the last of my hopes drained away. I already knew the answer even before he spoke.

"I don't know."

The words seemed wrenched from him, as if he hadn't wanted to admit them aloud. His hand didn't release me, yet somehow I managed to find the courage to extricate myself. "Let me clean this up and I'll be on my way," I said, giving him a single nod.

The knot in my chest was wound tight, enough to keep my emotions from spilling free. The manic drive that had propelled me before was gone, and I carefully picked up the glass pieces and wiped the floor clean of any small shards. I lost sight momentarily of Jeremiah, but when I finally stepped out of the kitchen I saw him standing near the door.

If he'd asked me to stay, my resolve may have broken, but we both held our silence. I knew what this would look like to anyone else: I was leaving him at his lowest, like I couldn't take his injuries or how feeble he was. In truth, if he'd told me he forgave me, I would have stayed forever.

But he wasn't a man for lies, and his silence told me all I needed to know about his uncertainty.

He turned away from me, his movements jerky. "I'll call you a limo."

"Jeremiah." I laid my hand on his arm and he stopped. "I'm not your responsibility anymore." I gave him a wobbly smile, even though he wouldn't look at me. "This is Manhattan. I'm a big girl, I can hail a cab."

"Where will you go?"

"I don't know." In truth, I had no plan, and few options, but I did have a full bank account thanks to the man before me. Pulling out the cellphone he gave me, I started to lay it on the nearby entry table when he spoke.

"Keep it. Please."

I paused, and then put it back into my pocket. Part of me said to just walk out and not look back, but I couldn't do that. Too much had happened for me to leave as coldly as that.

I stepped in close and, pushing myself up onto my tip-toes, I leaned forward to kiss his cheek, except that at the last moment he turned his head toward me. Our lips met in a soft, almost chaste kiss. Tears squeezed out between my eyelashes as he cupped my face, his palms warm against my cheeks. I didn't want to let him go, didn't want to be the one to break the sweetest kiss I'd ever had, but as if by mutual decision, we finally parted.

"Goodbye," I whispered, unable to bear the bleakness in his eyes a moment longer, and made my way out of the suite.

I was wrong about hailing my own cab; the doorman to the building did it for me, which was something of a relief.

My limbs were stiff and heavy with each step I took away, but I still managed to get myself into the cab and direct him to any hotel outside of Manhattan. Traffic was as thick as ever, but the cabbie quickly realized I wasn't in the mood for small talk and silence reigned inside the car.

An aching numbness spread through me, but it was better than the pain. I stared resolutely ahead, watching the city shift around me, until we got to New Jersey. The cabbie was good; he found me a decent hotel with nice accommodations in Clifton.

I went up the stairs and into my room, lay facedown on the bed, and sobbed silently into my pillow until sleep overtook me.

21

The first bouquet of flowers came to my desk three months later.

"Looks like somebody has a secret admirer," Amanda teased as I stared at the arrangement in surprise.

"This is for me?"

"That's what the card says. So spill: who are you dating?"

I reached in and plucked out the tiny envelope. It did indeed say my name on it, and written on the tiny card inside was a four-word message that made my heart flutter:

I haven't forgotten you.

"Lucy? You look ready to cry. What did it say, was it that good? Can I see?"

I snatched the note away where she couldn't grab it, giving her a mock glare. "Aren't you supposed to be schmoozing the Canadians?"

"Well, that's what I came here to talk to you about.

They're from Quebec and speak more French than English, so I thought they might like it more if someone else did most of the talking." She elbowed me just for added emphasis.

"How did you know I speak French?"

"I saw you with that Haitian couple last month, plus I've read your file. You're even from Quebec, so you could totally be related to these folks. Or you could pretend you are— maybe you're their long lost sister or something!"

"Isn't that your job?" I asked, shaking my head and smiling. Amanda Reed helped run the fundraising arm of The Hope Doctors Network, which worked out of my small satellite office in Brooklyn. It was a smaller charity but it funded my friend Cherise, whose husband worked as a doctor in Borneo. When I'd emailed her asking for career options, she'd managed to find me an office job in the charity district. Apparently, I'd already met the charity's founder at a previous dinner where I'd helped raise money for Cherise, which helped grease the wheels and get me the job.

The first day I'd walked in, I knew I'd found my calling. I had paperwork up to my ears most days, but I'd never before taken such pride in my work.

"C'mon Lucy. Please, pretty please, I'd really appreciate the help!"

Amanda reminded me a lot of Cherise, constant bubbly animation that didn't know when to quit. She was young, barely out of college, with short red hair and freckles all over her face. Her face always had a smile and, I'd found out quickly, she was very difficult to turn down when she wanted something.

Perfect for someone whose job was soliciting donations for a charity.

"Okay, fine," I said finally, "twist my arm. I'll go with you, geez."

"You are a lifesaver, thank-you thank-you thank-you!" She peered over my shoulder again. "So, what does it say? Come on, it's not a state secret is it?"

I just gave her a wink and slipped it into my pocket. Her face immediately fell dramatically. "Aww, c'mon, please please please?"

"What are you, ten?"

She beamed at me. "Only on Fridays."

I rolled my eyes, but grabbed my jacket and followed her out.

The flowers continued to come regularly after that, sometimes large bouquets, sometimes single roses. Amanda continued to pester me about who they were from but I didn't tell her, mainly because I didn't want to get my hopes up. Work picked up as spring started to thaw the last of the snow, and the questions tapered off as she was out of the office more.

I saw no sign of Jeremiah himself, but the flowers continued to come, growing more beautiful as the summer approached. Even when my desk was full of color and wonderful smells, I couldn't take throwing any away until after they already wilted.

Then one day, a small packet with my name on it arrived with the flowers.

"Ooh, the secret admirer switches it up!" Amanda leaned over my chair. "Huh, a title company? How is that sexy?"

Frowning, I opened the envelope, pulling out what was inside. It was a thick stack of paperwork, clipped together with colored notes visible around the margins. A familiar address on the topmost page immediately caught my eye. The room around me began to spin, and I was glad to be sitting down.

Amanda leaned in close. She screwed up her face as she read over my shoulder. "What town's that?"

I covered my mouth in shock. "I'm getting my house back."

"What! Your secret admirer bought you a house?"

I leafed through the paperwork to see my name on nearly every page. Small sticky notes indicated the places I needed to sign, and paper clipped to the folder was a business card for a local title company. Rifling through, I came to a page that held pictures from the appraisal, and had to cover my mouth to keep from crying.

"Pretty house," Amanda said, leaning in close. "Holy cow. Is that really yours now?"

"How did this arrive?" It had never occurred to me to ask who delivered my packages each day.

Amanda seemed surprised by the question but shrugged. "Courier, I suppose. Hey, where are you going?"

I left the small office almost at a run, bypassing the elevator and heading straight for the stairs. It had been months since the bridge incident, but my ankle still ached as I sped down the three flights of stairs. I wasn't sure what I'd find, but when I got down to the street level I was disappointed to find nothing out of the ordinary. I peered both ways down the sidewalk, trying to pick out someone like Jeremiah's height and build. Few people were walking around this area of town, and none of those visible looked anything like the billionaire.

A hard lump settled in my throat. I pulled out my cell-phone and stared at it for a moment. Inside, nestled amidst the work contacts, was the phone number of the man who could answer all my questions. I was almost certain who had done this for me—who else did I know who could buy me a house?—but for whatever reason, he chose not to present himself. I considered finding the number and calling before slowly putting it away instead.

I still had my pride. It had taken a real beating recently, but I was slowly piecing my life back together. I knew I'd made mistakes, and part of me regretted the way I'd left Jeremiah in his Manhattan loft. There was no way for me to undo my choices at this point, only live with them. Wrapping my jacket around my chest, I took one last look around the area before heading back upstairs to my office.

A few days after receiving that envelope, I received an invitation in the mail at my apartment to the memorial services for one Lucas James Hamilton.

I stared at the gray sheet of paper for several minutes, then put it back inside the envelope and laid it carefully onto the counter. I looked around the apartment, blinking away the tears. My job barely paid for the rent here, but it was a quiet building in a decent neighborhood. Even if I hadn't taken this job, I could have stayed here for a year with what I had saved in the bank. After clawing and scratching so long to keep my head just above the surface, it felt good to have an emergency fund for just in case.

Services were set in four days time, and I knew I wouldn't miss them. I'd received no word since I left about the case, and had no idea where it stood. I hadn't heard from Marie or any other government office, so I wasn't sure if they'd found Lucas's body or if they'd merely given up the search.

I supposed, in four days, I'd find out.

The bright weather on the day of the services belied the somber occasion. Lucas, had he been there, would likely have had a witty quip about springtime in New York City. He probably would have appreciated this more than rain anyway, but it felt strange to mourn in such unusually sunny spring weather.

In typical Lucas fashion, even in death—if he really was dead—he kept everyone guessing.

As I expected, there was security at the entrance, and I showed them my invitation. They spent a while looking at the tablet I assumed had the guest list, and then the guard finally shook his head. "I don't see your name on here, Ms. Delacourt."

"She's with me."

Jeremiah strode up from inside the pavilion, and I took a deep breath, drinking in the sight of him. His hair was longer, not as clean cut as before, the tips brushing the top of his dress shirt. He looked good, but I could still see the faint pink lines on his face, scars left over from Rush's handiwork. A

cane extended from one hand, further proof of the continuing road to wellness.

"Sir, she's not on the list."

"You can take that up with my mother." He passed the two
men at the entrance, moving in beside me and offering his
arm. I hesitated only a moment before taking it, and allowed
myself to be escorted inside.

"I take it your mother removed my name?" My voice didn't
shake, which I counted as a small win.

"Despite what she thinks or does, you are my guest and
welcome here."

We walked slowly through a small hallway behind the entrance before emerging out into a veritable paradise. "Oh," I
said, breathless, as I looked out over the large area. Flowers
and large trees were almost artfully spaced out, and narrow
paved walkways wound through the areas leading to grassy
hills perfect for a picnic.

"It's a private area, used mainly for weddings and parties.
We used to go to come here when I was young. Despite my
father's best efforts otherwise, I still have good memories of
this place."

"It's beautiful." The trees here were in full bloom, a
month ahead of most others I'd seen in the city. Winter had
been long and it was good to see signs of its end. I bit my
lip, and then laid a hand on his arm. "How have you been
doing?"

"Getting better, despite what it looks like." He gestured with
the cane. "My mother thinks this is just so I can look more

suave and sophisticated." He set it on the ground and jerked his chin up, striking a pose. "Don't you agree?"

I couldn't believe I was having this conversation with Jeremiah, and smiled up at him. He seemed much more peaceful than I remembered, as if no longer weighed down by some unseen stress. "You've always been sophisticated," I said, bumping him with my shoulder. "But more like a bull in a china shop than suave."

"Duly noted."

While the garden here was a large area, only a small portion in the back was being used for the services and reception afterwards. Guests, none of whom I knew, mingled amongst one another, and I was glad when Jeremiah steered us around the various groups. I saw a thin woman in all black move into view, a hat perched atop her head with a delicate veil over her face. Even from twenty feet away, I could feel the disapproving gaze of Georgia Hamilton, but she didn't approach and I didn't care.

I was invited, I was here, and she would have to deal with it.

The service was short, with only a couple people standing up to say any words. Jeremiah spoke, speaking in general terms of when his brother was younger. I thought briefly of stepping up to the podium and saying something, but figured I hadn't known him long enough to eulogize or praise his virtues.

Something told me that I probably knew him better than several of the speakers.

Immediately afterwards, several people approached Jeremiah, clearly wishing to speak with him. He politely turned them all down and all but pulled me through the crowd. I remembered how, the last time I'd seen Georgia Hamilton, she'd faced accusations of selling access to her billionaire son. Surely she wouldn't do such a thing at her other son's funeral.

Then again, I wouldn't put it past the horrid woman.

"Walk with me?"

Arm in arm, we distanced ourselves from the group, moving further into the park. A stream lined with flowers flowed through the center, lazily meandering through the grassy knolls. As we moved further in, I heard the laughter of children nearby.

"This whole garden is part of a larger private park," Jeremiah said, as if answering my unspoken question, "but the entrance back there isn't the only way inside."

A jogger passed us, a dog on a short leash keeping pace. At the end of one small road was a playground, where I saw the laughter had come from. There were few people around us, giving a sense of privacy with so much space.

"Have I told you what an incredible woman you are?"

I swallowed and looked up at him. Piercing green eyes stared through me, and I cleared my throat. "No," I said, trying to keep my tone light, "but you can keep talking."

His chuckle warmed my heart, and I squeezed his arm briefly. "What have you been up to?" he asked as we continued to walk.

"Working mostly. I think you know where that is."

"Ah, so you've received my packages."

"If by packages, you mean flowers, then yes. They're beautiful." I cleared my throat again. "And I don't know how to thank you for the . . . bigger gift."

"Just tell me you're not going to turn it down."

That surprised a laugh out of me. "I don't have that much pride, I'll take it any way I can." I laid my head on his shoulder. "Thank you."

"Are you seeing anyone?"

It was a bold question, as direct as ever. I half expected it eventually however, and shook my head. "Not in the way you think, just a therapist every week. She's helped me a lot."

"Helped how?"

"Deal with the PTSD."

If the knowledge surprised him, he didn't show it. I didn't tell him about the panic attacks or the nightmares; now wasn't the time, and anyway they'd grown less frequent in the last few weeks. We walked in silence for a little while toward the bottom of one cobbled bridge. Here we stopped, near an old man feeding pigeons from a park bench and a family playing with a toddler on a blanket.

Jeremiah let my arm go, leaning against the fence nearby. "I miss my brother."

My throat closed up at the sentiment. "Me too."

"He could be a real dick sometimes but . . . Do you know he used to save me all the time from my father's anger? He was good at distracting Rufus, saying the wrong things at the right time and deflecting any punishment to him."

I moved in and wrapped my arms around him, pressing a kiss to his shoulder. "He loved you."

"I know. But I don't know if he realized I felt the same or how much."

"I think he did." I took one of Jeremiah's hands and tugged until he turned to face me. Reaching up, I tucked a dark strand of hair back from his cheek, brushing my thumb over the pink scar there. He reached up and held my wrist, pressing the back of my hand so it lay flat against his cheek.

"Do you know how much I love you?"

I let out a small gasp, feeling tears rush suddenly to my eyes. Dragging in a ragged breath around the emotion that threatened to choke me, I shook my head.

His other hand cupped my face, fingertips tracing the outline of my temple. "I do, you know," he murmured. "I knew it when I saw you step up on that ledge to jump, and before that even." One corner of his mouth tipped up. "I think I even knew when you were that girl on an elevator whose shy glances made me wild."

He wiped away a tear that leaked through my lashes, stepping closer to me. The cane, forgotten now, fell to the ground. He leaned in close and laid a kiss on my brow. "I always thought the words were unnecessary, trite even; if the feeling is there, why should you need to name it? But if losing Lucas taught me anything, it's that I need to say the words so I'm sure they know.

"So, Lucy Delacourt, let it be known that I am completely and utterly in love with you."

"Why?"

I could have kicked myself for such a silly question, but Jeremiah tipped his head back and laughed. I stared, realizing

I'd never seen him that happy before. He moved in close, caressing my face again, touching but not holding me. "Because you're strong, you're brave, and you put others first. Because you're beautiful both inside and out, and someone I consider my equal, and that I was stupid to ever let you walk out that door those months ago."

"And Lucas?"

My voice came out in a whisper, but Jeremiah only shook his head. "I'm not someone who can go casting stones on mistakes. As my brother proved, with how I dealt with Anya and himself, that I've made more than my fair share." He stroked my eyebrow with his thumb, and I leaned into his hand. "You're worth fighting for, and I'm sorry for letting you ever walk out of my door."

Tears streaked my face as I touched his face, mindful of the new still-healing scars there, then said in a choked voice, "Now that wasn't so hard, was it?"

Jeremiah laughed again, and then pulled me close. I wrapped my arms around him, burying my face in his dress jacket. "I love you," I murmured against him, and felt his arms tighten around me.

I felt something wet drop against my cheek, and for a moment thought it was a tear. When I felt another, then another on my hand, I pulled away and looked up. Since I'd arrived at the park, the skies above had grown cloudy again, and I felt a droplet of rain hit my cheek.

"Do you want to go back to the service?" Jeremiah asked as I put out a flat hand, testing the speed of the raindrops.

"I'd like to stay here, actually." The clouds hadn't yet blocked out the sun, although they were headed that direction. "I wish we'd brought an umbrella though, just in case it starts to pour."

"I'll be right back then."

"What? No, we can go back, your leg . . ."

"Lucy. Stay here." He lifted my chin until I faced him. "I'll be right back, won't be gone more than a minute or two."

I watched his lips move, listening but not really hearing his words. A familiar hunger swept over me, and I leaned forward those last few inches, pressing his lips to mine. Immediately he pressed me to him, his mouth taking control of the kiss, and I melted in his arms. I'd forgotten how well the man kissed; he set my body on fire, alternately nibbling on my bottom lip then teasing me with his tongue. When we finally separated, I was breathing hard, and not just from the lack of oxygen.

He tapped the tip of my nose with one finger. "Be right back."

Blowing out a breath, I hurried over to a nearby park bench and sat down. Beside me, an older gentleman spread out some seed for the birds before him. Pigeons mostly surrounded him, but there were a few starlings and sparrows in the mix.

"Would you like to try?"

The old man had a thick New England accent, but seemed decent enough. I stared at the bag dubiously, then shrugged and nodded. "Sure."

He poured some seed into my hand and we took turns tossing out bits to the birds pecking at the ground. "Seems like a nice young man you've got there," he said after a moment.

"I think he's a keeper." Gazing around the park, a smile settled on my lips. "The road up to this point wasn't easy."

"The best things in life rarely are. From that kiss, your beau seems to be quite enamored of you, too." He waggled his thick eyebrows suggestively, making me blush, and then looked at his watch. "Here," he said, handing me the bag of seed, "I think you can use this more than me. The birds are still hungry and I need to finish my walk."

"Thank you . . ." I trailed off as I met the old man's gaze. Blue-green eyes twinkled back at me, and for a brief moment I forgot to breathe.

"I heard what he said to you," the old man continued, looking out around the park as I struggled for words. "I'll bet his brother would have loved hearing that himself." He licked one finger and held it up like he was testing the weather. As if on cue, the rain began coming down progressively harder. I felt it start to drip down my scalp and onto my face, but couldn't break my stunned silence. He grinned at me with straight, white teeth. "Now this is more the weather for a funeral. Too sunny, and the dead are liable to rise up just to enjoy the day."

I watched, mouth ajar, as the old man stood up and stretched. "Great to meet you, missy," he said to me, winking. "Maybe we'll see one another again someday?"

No words would come, but as he started walking away I jumped to my feet. "Wait! Jeremiah, he would want . . ."

"He's a good man, and he adores you." The man looked away down the direction Jeremiah had disappeared only a minute prior. "Take care of my brother. And tell him . . ." He paused, and then grinned. "Tell him to stop being such a stick in the mud."

"He's getting better about that." The smile that lit my face couldn't be dimmed; my cheeks practically ached from the expression. "You'd be proud of him."

"Too late, I already am. Take care of yourself, Lucy." He stretched where he stood and shook out his hands, then his shoulders stooped suddenly as if with age. He looked for all the world like any older man walking away in a cardigan and golf pants. He started whistling a jaunty tune as he disappeared over the bridge and into a thick copse of trees.

I sat down again, unable to wipe the grin from my face. I threw a little seed to the birds as Jeremiah rounded the corner, the umbrella already open above him. "You look happy," he said, extending the umbrella to cover me. His eyes traveled to the paper bag in my hands and watched as I flicked some of its contents to the ground. "Bird seed?" he asked.

"You wouldn't believe me if I told you." I stuck my hand inside the bag for more seed and felt something large and heavy beneath the kernels. Frowning, I pulled it out and held it up to the light. It was a man's ring with a black stone and thick band. There was an inscription on the inside that was worn down with age.

"What . . . Let me see that."

I handed it to Jeremiah, and watched as he examined it

closely. "*Audentes fortuna iuvat.*" He looked from me to the birds. "The old man?"

When I nodded, Jeremiah looked around the park, but when he started to move away I grabbed his hand. "You won't find him."

Jeremiah stopped, his hands curling into fists. "Why didn't he tell me?"

"He just did." I tugged on his sleeve until Jeremiah finally looked down at me. "He also heard everything you said to me."

For a moment, I thought he would give chase anyway, try to follow after his brother. Finally however, Jeremiah sat down next to me, turning the ring over and over in his hands. I peered at it curiously. "Whose is it?"

"It belonged to our grandfather, but disappeared around the same time as Lucas. The inscription means *Fortune favors the bold.*" He stared at the ring for a little while, and then glanced at me. "He heard everything I said?"

When I nodded, a bemused smile came over Jeremiah's face. "Good." He slid the ring onto his finger then stood to his feet and held out his hand. "Let's go for a walk."

I wrapped my hand in his warm grip, standing up and leaning close to him. My head tilted over, laying it on his arm, and I watched as he twined his fingers through mine. Rain pattered against the thin material of the umbrella as people around us rushed for cover, but we just continued down the path, content in the moment no matter what the heavens threw at us.

22

So, am I finally going to meet this mystery man of yours? And, oh my gosh, can I just say again how *fabulous* you look in that dress?"

"Thank you, again, for the compliment." I shook my head at the redhead's exuberance. "And no, I told you it's a surprise."

"Oh, you are *so* mean. But did I tell you who I heard was coming tonight? Okay, picture it: handsome, rich, powerful, and yummy. I consider his attendance my *pièce de résistance.*"

"Jeremiah Hamilton?"

"Aw, I wanted it to be a surprise! I must have told you, didn't I? But I don't remember telling you though . . . did you really just guess that? Because that's one heck of a good guess."

"Amanda, how much coffee have you had today?"

"Only a few pots, why?"

The guests were starting to arrive, and I strained to get a look. Amanda and the recruitment crew had done a great job with this one, getting several A-list celebrities to hit the red carpet. The press was everywhere, covering the charity event from every angle. We were certain to be pasted all over celebrity blogs and newsstands in the morning, increasing awareness for our little charity. I couldn't have been prouder to be a part of organizing the event.

"Omigod, Cher made it! And that's Joan Rivers over there interviewing people and . . . holy crap, that's him, *that's him*! Tall, dark and sexy, twelve o'clock, twelve o'clock!"

I followed her pointing finger and let out a breath. *Sexy, indeed!*

Jeremiah stepped away from the limousine, ignoring the cameras as he ascended the stairs to the event. Beside me, Amanda was practically vibrating as he grew closer, but all I could see was the man I loved moving toward me. Between when I met him and now, he'd finally discarded that clean-cut look. Gone was the combed hair and stuffy demeanor, replaced by wavy, unkempt locks and a devil-may-care attitude. He wore all black tonight, a different style than the suits that surrounded us.

"Oh, he's looking this way. I'm going to *die* if he talks to us!"

When he stopped near us, I thought I heard a tiny *"squee"* from Amanda's corner, but Jeremiah had my full attention. He looked me up and down, and his lips turned up into an almost predatory smile. "You look tasty enough to eat."

I had to curl my hands into fists at my side to keep from running them through his hair. "You look just as breathtaking," I breathed, meaning every syllable.

He offered me his arm and, without looking at Amanda, I took it and fell into step beside him. Cameras nearby went off but I tried to ignore them, keeping my head high and making absolute certain I didn't fall down in these heels.

"Omigod, *jealous!*"

I stifled a laugh as Amanda's last shout echoed slightly through the entrance. There was no way I'd ever hear the last of this from anyone in the office.

The large ballroom of the hotel was packed, everyone mingling together as planned. Waiters in tuxedos passed around the hors d'oeuvres, keeping wine and champagne glasses filled for the guests. Near the center was a dance floor with several couple already there, while still more sat at the tables around the stage.

Jeremiah kept a possessive hand on my lower back as he steered me through the crowd. I didn't know what destination he had in mind, but was quite content when he twirled me into his arms on the dance floor. I spun around twice and then settled against him, leaning forward to breathe in his scent. *God he smelled good.*

"I see you chose a different dress than the one I had sent," Jeremiah said in my ear, his warm breath across my skin making me shiver. "I heartily approve."

"I didn't need your permission to choose what I wear," I said in a haughty voice, trying not to let myself feel too pleased by his praise. "Besides, this one was one-tenth the cost and looks just as good as anything high fashion."

"But I approve nonetheless."

The music changed to something slower, and Jeremiah

pulled me close. Something poked my belly and, eyebrows rising, I gave Jeremiah an amused look. "Really? Now?"

Jeremiah twirled me around the dance floor, looking very pleased with himself, while I battled between exasperation and raw need. Desire burst inside my belly, made brighter by the possessive gleam in his eye, and I struggled to keep myself under control. We'd made a mutual decision to take things slow, meeting for coffee or dinner, only to part ways afterwards with little more than a kiss.

Well, okay, a little groping and brief make out session in the back of his limo one night, but that was all.

Apparently, tonight Jeremiah was willing to chuck all our carefully laid plans out the window.

It was my turn to approve.

I wasn't watching where we were moving, too content to be this close to him, until the music ended. Jeremiah kept hold of my hand and led me behind the stage where the elevators hid. I suppressed a giggle as he pressed the button, biting my lip in anticipation. "You and elevators," I said, and then gave a squeak as he pressed me up against the steel doors.

"What can I say? I'm a creature of habit . . ." He dipped forward, capturing my lips, and I tilted my head to meet his assault. A sigh escaped me as I wound my arms around his neck, pressing my body against his. "You little minx," he murmured against my lips as his hands moved down to cover my backside. "You're not wearing underwear."

It was my turn to chuckle. "Brownie points for being prepared?"

The doors behind me dinged, and I clung to Jeremiah as he spun us into the elevator. His chest rumbled with laughter as he lifted me into the air, pressing me back against the elevator wall. I gave a small sigh as I felt his hardness press against my core, and tilted my head back to give him access.

"What will you give me?" he said, rolling his hips against me. His mouth dipped to my neck, sucking at the delicate skin there. "Your body? Your soul?"

"Anything," I breathed, my fingernails digging into his shoulders. I felt his head move down between our bodies, and gave a loud wail as he teased the sensitive nub between my thighs.

"Will you give me your love?"

"Always." I cupped his face with my hands, moving forward to kiss him softly. The need and desire I saw reflected there made the fire in my belly spread, but it was the tenderness that made my heart melt.

"I love you," he murmured, moving his hands up my sides to squeeze my breasts through the thin material of the dress. I wrapped my legs around his waist, giving him enough room to free himself from his pants before settling down over his hard shaft. He pressed the button for the topmost floor as I flexed my thigh muscles, lifting myself up and atop him. Given how slick I already was, I still gasped as he slid into me, my walls stretching to accommodate his girth.

"I love you," he repeated, surging into me and making me moan.

I stared down into his beautiful green eyes, smiling slightly as I rolled my hips and heard him gasp. He stared up at me, eyes wide and full of desire. "And what will you give me?" I murmured, clenching around him.

"Anything," he said, his voice thick with need.

I leaned down and brushed my lips to his. "All I want is your love."

"You have it," he breathed, tongue darting against mine. "You'll always have it."

Beloved.

bonus story

Exclusively for the *Castaway* novel, a bonus piece
continuing the story of Jeremiah and Lucy!

1

S o you're not going to tell me where we're going?"
"No."

"Not even the slightest clue? A hint?"

"No."

I let out a breath. "You know I'm not a big fan of surprises nowadays."

Jeremiah's green eyes glittered like emeralds in the darkness as his lips turned up slowly into a sexy smile. "I think you'll like this one."

Swallowing, I hid my body's reaction to his words by turning to look out the window of the limousine. Gone were the tall buildings and familiar New York City silhouettes I'd seen now for several months. Wherever this car was taking us was far outside the city limits. The countryside rose around us, spots of snow still dotting the landscape despite the warmer weather.

Jeremiah's hand smoothed down my leg, giving my knee a squeeze. "We're almost there."

Almost where? I bit my tongue, however, as the headlights shone onto a tall set of gates that opened as we rounded the corner. Trees lined the winding driveway, dense enough to block out the setting sun. It seemed like forever before the stifling trees open up into a large roundabout leading up to the biggest house I'd ever seen.

My mouth dropped as I stared up at the structure. Mansion didn't quite cut it: it looked more like a castle than a home. The building had at least four stories, with separate wings on each side. Stairs leading up to the door curved around the driveway, leading to large wood doors. The driver parked at the base and then opened our door as I continued to stare out.

"Would you like to see inside?"

The humor in Jeremiah's voice finally got my attention, and I turned to see him holding a hand out toward me. He was as handsome as ever in a black shirt and pants, his hair pushed back on his head. A few dark locks still framed the strong face that I'd grown to adore. Taking his hand, I stepped out onto the driveway, staring again up the giant structure. "And I thought your Hamptons home was large," I murmured.

Behind me, Jeremiah chuckled. "Wait until you see inside."

The Hamilton family mansion had always seemed to me like a fortress, but the house before me now was similar more to a palace. Everything about the home screamed old wealth. From the lush greenery and spring color everywhere, to the paver stones that made up the driveway. It wouldn't have

surprised me if a butler stood near the tall wood doors leading inside, awaiting any guests.

So I was only a bit taken aback when a redheaded woman
wearing a corset, heels, and very little else opened the door.
A delicate gold or brass chain was wrapped around her neck
like a collar. "My Master bids you welcome," she said, her
voice a sexy dulcet bell.

I stood there staring, too stunned to move, until Jeremiah's hand pressed against my back. "Shall we go inside?"

Snapping out of my stupor, I gave him a perplexed look
but walked through the heavy doors, followed by Jeremiah.
The interior was as grand as I'd imagined, opening into an
entryway framed by dark stairs, but it was the furniture that
immediately caught my attention. There were no guests milling about this area, but one willowy lady was seated nearby
on . . .

I squinted, and then blinked in surprise. She seemed to be
sitting on a man dressed only in a loincloth.

Another boy around my age knelt at her feet, his head
resting peacefully on her lap. Around his neck was a black
leather collar connected to a chain leash which was wrapped
around the woman's hand. The lady herself was dressed in a
suit that covered her entire body up to the neck, with spiked
heels that looked connected to the ensemble. Nearby, a
man appeared carrying a tray of hors d'oeuvres wearing
only a loincloth and a latex mask that completely covered
his face.

"Jeremiah," I murmured through stiff lips, the single word

loaded with questions. My eyes dropped to the waiter's naked ass until he disappeared from view.

"If you're not the least bit intrigued," he murmured in my ear, "we can leave now."

Intrigued? That was a mild word for how I felt at that moment. Whatever I'd been expecting, this wasn't quite it. "I thought we were going to a party."

"We are. Shall we go inside?"

I looked at him, and then back through the opening the waiter had just disappeared through. "I don't know," I replied in a low voice. "Are you setting me up for a heart attack?"

He chuckled again beside me, but didn't try to make me follow. "Gabriel is an old friend of mine. Our paths diverged after high school but we remained in touch."

"This is his house?" I felt rooted to the spot, trying not to stare as another group came inside, two men and a girl. She giggled as one of them swept her up in his arms as the other smacked her clothed backside. The men took the stairs two at a time before disappearing down one wing of the second floor. "And what kind of party is this again?" I asked in a faint voice.

"One for Gabriel's friends."

"So you've been to one these parties before?"

"Several."

Somehow, I couldn't quite picture Jeremiah on his hands and knees being used as a Dominatrix's seat. My thoughts went to the dominance he'd displayed in bed with me previously, and I cleared my throat. "I feel really over-dressed right now."

"You'll be fine. There's no need to participate unless you feel the urge."

Participate?

I clung to Jeremiah's arm as we walked in to the center of the house. Music with a heavy beat played inside. When we walked through the entryway my eyes were immediately drawn to several lit areas along the far wall. A woman dressed in thigh-high boots and a bright red corset was standing over a younger man who appeared to be groveling at her feet. I could hear her voice but not the words as she prodded him with the spiked heels. Even from this distance, despite the woman's actions, I saw the open adoration on the man's face.

Nearby beside him, a girl was suspended from the ceiling, covered almost completely in rope. Her eyes were shut and face serene as a bare-chested man beside her kept a silent vigil. For the most part however, people lounged around on leather furniture in the large area just chatting. It felt rude for me to stare, but my eyes grew big when a man walked past me, leading another girl bound in ropes. Her breasts were on display, surrounded and pushed up by the cord. The knots were almost artful in their placement, yet the girl's face showed an odd kind of blissful discomfort I didn't quite understand.

"So, ah," I asked, breathless, "you come to these parties often?"

"Not lately," Jeremiah said, the hand on the small of my back moving lower to cup my backside. "But I wanted to introduce you to Gabriel."

Despite my reservations, I sent a sly look up to him. "And

that's all you wanted to do?" Somehow, I doubted he'd take me someplace like this just to meet an old friend.

One corner of his mouth tipped up. "This lifestyle seems extreme, but its foundation lies in consent. I would never make you do something like this unless you allowed it."

"You better not," I said softly, bumping his arm with my shoulder, and then I swallowed again as his fingers pinched my ass.

"You would look delicious bound up for my own pleasure."

His words lit a fire in my belly, and I drew in a shaky breath. Jeremiah's hand on me was like a brand, claiming me as surely as any collar. When I looked around now through a haze of sensual delight, what I saw intrigued me. I wasn't sure I wanted to be bound as tightly as some of the women, or led around by a leash and collar like many we saw.

But it would be fun to find out what that felt like.

"Lucy Delacourt, I would like you to meet Gabriel Steele, one of my oldest friends and the Dom in charge of this home and party."

I extended my hand automatically, and then let out a ragged breath as I stared up at Jeremiah's friend. And up. Shirtless like this, he seemed even larger, more visceral and powerful. It wasn't just his sheer size that drew you—the man had to be close to seven feet tall—but the dominance he projected. Somehow, I managed to keep the first words that came to mind—*"You're big"*—from escaping my lips as his hand completely enveloped mine.

Gabriel must have read my mind anyway, because the

skin beside his eyes crinkled in apparent amusement. "Ah, Miss Delacourt," he said, bringing my hand up to his lips, "it's lovely to meet the man who tamed Remi here."

I snorted and rolled my eyes. "Tame is not how I would describe him."

Gabriel's eyes flickered to Jeremiah, and then back at me. "Perhaps not," he said, his mouth tipping up as he gestured toward me. "You look happy, old friend. Is the beautiful lady here that reason?"

Pleasure suffused me when Jeremiah nodded. "We may not be participating tonight," Jeremiah said, and Gabriel nodded.

"Let me know if you'd like a private room then." They shook hands. "It really is good seeing you again, Remi."

"A private room?" I whispered as Gabriel walked off. I watched as the large man crooked a finger at a subdued girl in a very revealing sailor outfit, who followed after him quietly as he ascended the stairs.

"Not everybody likes having their sexual encounters in public."

"Public?"

Cries from nearby made me turn my head toward the opposing wall. A girl, completely naked, was spread-eagled against the wall, straps on her ankles and wrists holding her in place. The man beside her held a short crop in his hand, and with a flick of the wrist he sent it smacking against her backside. The clap reverberated through the room, as did the girl's moan of pleasure.

My mouth dropped open, and I looked wide-eyed in the

darkness beside them to see another Dom seated on a couch. Between his knees knelt a naked blond man, his hands bound behind his back. There was no denying the bobbing motions he made with his head however. The Dom ran his fingers through the blond curls, encouraging the up and down motion.

Desire exploded through me. I felt a rush of heat between my legs, the muscles tightening with need. I couldn't tear my eyes away. My breathing quickened, goose bumps breaking out over my skin.

Jeremiah dipped his head close to my ear. "You like watching this, don't you?"

The dark promise in his voice made my voice catch. "How can you tell?" I asked, trying to sound nonchalant and failing miserably.

He made a pleased sound, lips like butterfly wings against the delicate skin of my ear as he answered me. "I can smell your desire."

The simple words electrified my body, setting me on fire. My legs felt like jelly, and I sagged against Jeremiah. The hand that had been cupping my backside wrapped around my waist, pulling me back against him. I gasped as I felt the familiar hard lump poking my back.

"I want to take you right now, over the bar right there." Jeremiah's voice was harsh, his grip implacable. "I want everyone to see that you are beautiful and *mine* to do with as I please."

My breaths were coming in pants, and I didn't protest as he pushed me back against a wall near the bar. A surprised cry exited my throat as he twisted his hand in my hair and jerked my head back so I faced him. Longing pierced my core and I clung to him as he bent down and nipped my neck. His hand slid up the inside of my pant leg, cupping my mound. "Should I take you here so you can watch, my little voyeur?"

Even with my mind clouded by desire, I still managed to be aware enough to realize we were in public. As much as I didn't want to disappoint him, I couldn't do what I wanted to do while surrounded by strangers. "I'm sorry," I whispered, kissing his palm and hoping he would understand.

He released my hair, and then swept me up into his arms. "Never apologize for saying what you feel," he said, moving cat-like across the room toward a set of nearby stairs. I held onto his neck as he moved up them swiftly, never pausing until we were inside a small, dark room. Only then did he set me down on my feet once again.

A thick piece of glass stretched out at an angle, with a panoramic view of the floor beneath us. I suddenly realized I'd never thought to look up; through the window, I had a better view than when I'd been down there. Behind me, I heard Jeremiah close the door and turn the lock.

"Nobody can see inside here. The glass is mirrored on the other side, giving us privacy."

The only light coming into the dark room was from the downstairs chamber. Jeremiah, still standing by the door, was lit only faintly, outlining the edges of his face and body. My heart sped up as he leaned against the wall. "Now," he said, his voice sharp with command, "strip."

I knew myself enough by now to realize the trembling in my fingers wasn't from fear. The fire in my belly burned brighter with each article of clothing I removed. Jeremiah said nothing as I unbuttoned my shirt and pants, laying them in a small pile beside my feet. When I got down to my bra and panties, I hesitated, until I heard his voice rumble, "Everything."

My bra didn't worry me too much, but I cast a quick look back as I hooked my underwear with my thumbs. "You sure nobody can see inside?"

"Are you disobeying me?"

The almost deadly calm in his voice made me shiver. "No, sir." Swallowing, I shimmied them down my legs, praying nobody could see my backside through the glass. The window behind me went out at an angle over the lower floor, such that I could almost lie atop it. I peeked back to see if anyone was looking up in our direction, and then gave a startled squeak when I turned back to see Jeremiah standing before me. I hadn't even heard him move.

The ex-Commando was sneaky that way.

Rough fingers trailed down my collarbone, between my breasts and across my belly. The surface muscles fluttered at his touch, trembling with anticipation. He continued his exploration down, but stopped just short of my mound. "Go to the window, bend down so your palms are on the glass, and spread your legs."

My breath hitched, but any protest I had died at the unyielding look on his face. Dropping my eyes, I turned around and did as he said, putting my hands on the glass. My breasts were in full view of everyone downstairs, should they think to look up and if the glass was at all see-through. I spread my legs and waited, watching what was happening downstairs.

Some of the action had changed downstairs. Two men, one blond and one with dark hair, were now chaining a woman to the wall. She was naked as well, petite beside the two men on either side of her. I couldn't see her facial expression, but my breathing sped up as the dark-haired man knelt before her and swung the girl's legs over his shoulders. The blond man grabbed her hair, jerking her head back into a rough kiss as the man on his knees settled his face between her thighs.

Fingers stroked my core, the sudden invasion eliciting a surprised cry from me. "You're so wet," Jeremiah murmured behind me, but when I turned to look at him he shook his head. "Watch what is happening downstairs."

The brunette writhed, her arms trapped by the restraints, as the man beside her dipped his mouth to play with her breasts. Her back was bowed from the pleasure, mouth wide in a cry I'm sure I'd have heard if not for the glass. The space between my own legs throbbed, desperate for touch. "Jeremiah," I moaned, making a small noise again when the other woman gave another cry of pleasure.

Fingers danced down my backside, lifting and separating the wet folds between my thighs. Then a hot breath was my only warning as Jeremiah's mouth clamped down on the aching bud. I gave a cry, my arms giving out. The window reverberated as my elbows hit. I laid my cheek against the glass, unable to hold myself up under the sensual onslaught.

My breasts pressed against the window, and I no longer cared who saw or heard my pleasure.

"Mm, I've missed tasting you like this," Jeremiah murmured against me. His tongue traced the edges of my quivering entrance and I gave another choked groan. "And I love hearing you cry out for me."

"Jeremiah." The word was a desperate sob, which he answered by plunging two fingers deep inside me. My gaze traveled back to the downstairs trio, who were all back on their feet. It was the blond man this time that moved around front, lifting the woman so that she straddled his naked hips. He thrust inside her, the muscles of his ass tight, hips pistoning himself in and out.

Jeremiah's fingers moved in time with the other man's thrusts, until I was a quivering mess. I heard the crinkle of the condom wrapper behind me as the dark-haired man below us released the woman's wrists. The blond man lowered himself to the floor, allowing the woman to straddle him. The dark man followed, positioning himself behind the woman, pushing her down so she was lying against the blond man's chest.

I panted in anticipation of my own as Jeremiah removed his fingers, positioning himself at my weeping opening. As the man below pressed himself into the other woman, Jeremiah slid inside me deliciously slow. I laid my forehead against the glass as he stretched me, the simple friction sending shards of pleasure dancing through my body.

"You're mine," he said in a soft, dangerous voice, as his hips began to rotate. With each thrust, I cried out, closing my eyes so it was only my own pleasure. I tilted my hips up, giving him more access, and he pushed inside me harder, his fingers digging into my hips.

Taking an unsteady breath, I levered myself back up onto my hands, bracing myself against his thrusts. The heel of one hand went to the small of my back and I bowed my spine, and was rewarded by a sharp intake of breath behind me. Smiling, I clamped down around him, squeezing first my belly muscles, then my butt muscles, and heard him groan.

"God, you're so tight."

Pleased with myself, I turned my attention back to the floor below, and gave a small cry of my own at the sight. The woman's head was tilted back, her mouth open in a cry, as behind and beneath her both men thrust into her body. Theirs was a perfect rhythm, a set pace so that all three were moving as one unit. The raw sensuality of their movements was its own turn-on: I couldn't take my eyes away.

Jeremiah's hands wrapped around each globe of my butt and pulled them apart, kneading the flesh as he thrust between. The hard breaths coming from him told me he was close, and frankly so was I. Tilting my hips back again, I matched his thrusts with my own, feeling my own orgasm rising quickly to the surface.

As if reading my mind, Jeremiah let go of me with one hand, reaching down and around my body. The first tiny flick of my hidden bud made my body jerk, sensation exploding throughout me. I gave a loud cry, and another as he did it again.

"I love hearing you come," he murmured in my ear, biting

the tender flesh as he massaged the small nub of my clit. The orgasm that had lingered in the background rose quickly to the surface, crashing into me with all the subtlety of a lightning bolt. My cry rang off the walls of that small room as my body shook, the pleasure breaking over me like a wave.

Behind me, Jeremiah gave a hoarse shout, his fingers biting into my waist, as he came inside me. His teeth briefly grabbed hold of the tender flesh of my shoulder, the bite almost painful, but only added to the carnal sensations of the moment. He kissed the spot and then laid his body over me, hands against the glass beside mine as we both struggled to regain our breath. I moved my right hand so that my fingers entwined with his, and he gave my hand a small squeeze.

Below, the trio of bodies was disentangling itself from one another, apparently having finished with their own pleasure. Several people around them were clapping, which I found odd. "Was that down there just a show?" I asked as Jeremiah pulled himself out of me.

"No, it was real. The other people are showing their appreciation for allowing them access." He laid a kiss to my shoulder. "Perhaps when we go down, you can also tell them how much you appreciated it."

My mouth dropped open and I felt my face heat up. "I can't do that." I peered down at the lower floor. "Are you sure they couldn't see us?"

"Would it have mattered if they could?"

I mulled over his words as I put my clothes on again. The thought of strangers watching us make love wasn't quite so repulsive suddenly, especially since I'd just gotten off to doing just that. In all the displays I'd seen tonight, there had been no interruption by outsiders, nobody who had tried to join in. That was my biggest fear, that someone would try and touch me, but something told me Jeremiah wouldn't allow that. Everyone at this party was being very respectful of others' boundaries, however. Indeed, despite the garish costumes and overt sexuality, I didn't feel at all uncomfortable around the people here.

My eyes having adjusted to the darkness, I looked around the room. "We couldn't even make it to the bed," I noted, and rolled my eyes at Jeremiah's wolfish grin.

"If the lady wants a go on the mattress," Jeremiah said, pulling me roughly into his arms, "I have no objections."

I swatted his shoulder, but tilted my head back as his lips descended onto mine. I moaned into his mouth, my body flaming again at his touch, as he molded my body against his.

The cellphone in his pants pocket chimed.

"Don't get that," I whispered, trailing my fingers down his muscled torso. My lips moved across his jaw and down his neck as I pressed the heel of my hand against the rising hardness I felt between his thighs.

The phone rang again, and Jeremiah stiffened. "I need to get this," he murmured. Kissing my head in an almost apology, he gently disengaged himself from my arms and pulled the phone from his pocket. Stepping away, he checked the screen, and then headed toward the doorway. "This is Jeremiah," I heard him say in a low voice before letting himself out, leaving me alone.

I stood there for several seconds, unsure how to feel about being summarily abandoned. Moments like this had grown more frequent over the last couple weeks, awkward situations where we'd be in the middle of something and he'd walk out of the room to take a call. Part of me tried not to take it personally—it was his business, and I didn't want to seem like I was snooping. But another more selfish part of me wanted to snatch the phone out of his hand every time and demand more attention.

I finished dressing, rearranging my hair to give him time to come back so we could hopefully finish our moment. When the seconds ticked past and he didn't reappear, I sighed and left the room, heading back downstairs alone.

2

O h my gosh, it's so good to see you again!"
    I hugged Cherise close, and then ushered her inside.
"When did you arrive in New York?" I asked as she stared
slack-jawed around the penthouse.

"Only last night. David wanted to come too, he's only been
to New York City itself a few times."

Cherise's phone call had been out of the blue and a pleasant surprise. "I would have loved to see him too. How are
you doing?"

"Never mind me. Girl, you've moved up in the world! Is
this where you're living now?"

"Mostly," I hedged, looking back at the spacious apartment. I still kept my small studio, but it was almost a formal-
ity at this point. My nights were spent much more often in
the Manhattan loft and in Jeremiah's arms. Somehow though,
it felt like I was bragging if I said that.

"Are you still working at the charity? You seemed to really
enjoy it."

I shook my head sadly. "It started getting weird for me once it got out I was dating one of the major contributors."

Cherise frowned at me. "They start pestering you for money or something?"

"No, not that. It was mainly just how I felt." I sighed, and then gave a humorless laugh. "You know where I come from, so I'm having a hard time adjusting to the fact I'm dating one of the wealthiest people in the world."

"Well, you'd better get used to it. I've seen the way that man looks at you." Cherise winked. "He freaking *adores* you."

"What about you?" I asked, distracting myself from my own thoughts. "Tell me everything about Borneo."

"It's the most fantastic feeling in the world. We finally managed to get an ultrasound machine for our clinic, thanks in part to the fundraiser you threw earlier this year. Now David wants to build a whole new section to the clinic, essentially doubling its size."

Cherise and her husband David, a doctor, ran a small charity clinic on the Indonesian island. I'd gone to college with both of them, and we'd unexpectedly reconnected last year while in Paris. She talked about the rainforest and the people they helped, and a lump slowly formed in my chest. My misery must have shown through because she stopped in the middle of a story. "What's wrong?"

I waved it off. "It's nothing."

"No, it's not nothing." She got up from her chair and crossed over to sit beside me on the couch. "Tell me what's wrong."

I shrugged, and then sighed. "I envy you. While I'm eating caviar and riding in limos, you're out saving the world

and splinting the broken legs of orphans. I just feel . . . useless here."

"Really? You eat caviar every day?"

A small smile tipped one corner. "Actually, not really, I
can't stomach eating that stuff."

"Girl, if you think caviar isn't palatable, you would *not*
want to hear about some of the things I've had to eat." Cherise's eyes twinkled, as if she were dying to tell me anyway.
"But why aren't you still working at the charity? Did Jeremiah
tell you to quit?"

"No, it's nothing like that." I hurried to defend him, shaking my head. "I feel like there's some mold I'm supposed to
fit, like I'm supposed to be wearing big hats and dress suits
now."

"Honey, he fell in love with *you*, not some high-society so-
cialite. I'm sure if he wanted that, there were tons throwing
themselves at him."

I sighed again. "It just feels weird whenever people bring
up his wealth in a conversation, and they do that a lot. Maybe
I'm just being sensitive, but sometimes it's as if that's all he is
to these people: a giant wallet."

"Yeah," Cherise murmured after a moment of silence, "I
can see how that would be a problem." She reached out and
took my hand. "Is that it though? You could talk to him
about this, see what he says."

I shook my head. "The last month or so, he's been really
pulling back. We had a nice night last night,"—I felt my face
flush at the memory—"but he's been out with work more
lately."

"You don't think that he's, well . . ."

"No, I really doubt it's that," I said quickly. "I don't think he's cheating, just working. But I haven't seen him much."

Cherise blew out a breath. "Silly goose," she chided, "you quit your job and expect him to entertain you?"

"Hey, you're supposed to make me feel better!" I gave a rueful laugh. "I've been an idiot, haven't I?"

"Well, if this doesn't work out, you can always come help us in Borneo."

I stilled, staring at Cherise. "Seriously?"

She shrugged. "We'd love to have you, and living expenses are pretty cheap. Frankly, I'd appreciate the company."

"That would be fun," I said after a moment, returning her smile. "I've been lonely lately too, and yes, don't say it, that's my own fault."

"I wouldn't say it's totally your fault. You should really talk to Jeremiah about this."

"If I ever see him."

"You said you went out last night?"

I flushed again. "Well, that was too fun to bring it up."

Cherise grinned, and I flushed harder. "Come on," she said, standing up, "show me around this place."

"I should take you to the house in the Hamptons," I said, "that place is huge."

She linked her arm in mine. "Of course you should. But for now I'm in an actual Manhattan penthouse, so I expect the royal tour."

I smiled back at her. "You're going to die when you see this kitchen."

"I've heard that the *foie gras* here is simply divine. Although you should probably skip that, dear, it has so much fat. Perhaps a salad for you?"

One of the downsides to dating billionaire Jeremiah Hamilton was dealing with his mother, Georgia. Lunches like this were more a chore and less a delight. Even now, seated at a table in a ridiculously expensive French restaurant, everything about her grated on my nerves. Making matters worse, Jeremiah had just stepped out to make a phone call, leaving me along with the odious woman.

Trying to ignore her, I focused on the menu. None of the items had prices, and I didn't recognize some of the names. The waiter stood patiently beside me, and I asked, "What do you recommend?"

"You can't even order for yourself?" Georgia gave a disdainful sniff. "Really, my dear, show a little backbone."

The edge of the menu crumpled in my fist. The waiter bit his lip, whether to hold in amusement or in sympathy, I couldn't tell. "The Kobe beef medallions in a wine reduction are very popular."

"That sounds good," I said, handing him my menu just as Jeremiah returned to the table.

"For you, sir?"

"I'll have the same."

I stared at the water glass in front of me, trying not to glare at Jeremiah. Being left alone with his mother wasn't my idea of romantic. Indeed, I'd had no idea she would be joining us, but she'd already been at our table when we arrived. There had been no chance to protest her presence without looking like a bitch myself, so I'd kept silent.

"I saw the Tiptons last week, darling. They asked after you which I thought was very nice. Apparently Francine saw you in the park while you still used that cane."

Jeremiah had only put away the walking aid permanently a few weeks back. The injuries inflicted by a madman had mostly healed, although the ex-Army Ranger still wasn't one hundred percent. I knew his condition was frustrating for him, and hated that Georgia would bring it up. Granted, she'd been by his side helping him heal through the rough days, something nobody had expected of her. It still grated, however, to give the abominable woman any excuse for her behavior.

"So, how is work?" I asked, sipping my water and trying to ignore the woman across from me.

"Busy."

Jeremiah's curt answer made me frown. I knew there was something on his mind and was about to ask, but Georgia was already talking again. "I brought in a decorator for the mansion. Deborah has some lovely ideas on how to spruce up the place, make it much more modern and not as drab as it is now. We'd have to get rid of the old furniture, of course. I always thought it was too dark in there anyway."

"That house belongs to Jeremiah." I couldn't keep the sharp, annoyed note out of my voice.

The infuriating smile on Georgia's lips widened into one of almost clownish proportions. "Why," she cooed, "he didn't tell you? We signed the papers yesterday afternoon transferring ownership to me."

My jaw dropped and I looked at Jeremiah, who had the good grace to look abashed. "I was going to tell you tonight," he murmured, but I still wouldn't look at him.

I tried unsuccessfully to hide my hurt, playing with the napkin in my lap. Georgia, the epitome of condescending grace, laid her hand on my arm. "I'm sure he had his reasons to keep this a secret from you, my dear. Then again, they are *his* responsibilities, not yours. Perhaps you overstepped the bounds of your relationship and he needed to . . ."

"Enough!"

The harsh, grating note in Jeremiah's voice cut off Georgia's gloat. Her lips tightened into a thin line, but Jeremiah continued before she could speak. "I've given you full ownership of the house Rufus left to me," he said in a low, angry voice. "Keep it, sell it, I don't care. Father treated you badly in his will, leaving you nothing. That is now fixed."

"Darling . . ."

"If I *ever* hear you bad-mouth Lucy in my presence again, I will make it clear to the world that any friends of yours are not friends of mine. I will cut you off, mother, as surely as Rufus ever did."

I blinked at Jeremiah. He had never defended me quite so brutally before; usually, he had a resigned tolerance for his mother's actions. Even Georgia seemed startled by his outburst, although she tried to gloss over his words. "I'm only looking out for your well-being," she said after a terse silence, rearranging the napkin in her lap. Her eyes darted around, as if to see who was watching. "Must you raise your voice to me in public?"

"This lunch was meant to be just for Lucy and I," Jeremiah continued. "I do not remember inviting you. I'll make certain to tell the host as much when I make reservations from now on."

Georgia went stiff, and then she threw her napkin onto the table. "I can tell when my presence is not wanted," she said in a voice like ice.

Yeah, right. I snorted but didn't say anything. Georgia leveled a glare at me, and then rested a cool expression on her son. "You choose this, this *girl* over your own family?"

"Good day, Mother."

Georgia's chin lifted high in the air. "Ungrateful little . . ." She trailed off, giving me one last glance that spoke daggers, and walked out of the restaurant.

I watched her until she disappeared, then reached over and covered Jeremiah's hand with mine. "Thank you for speaking up for me."

He squeezed my fingers. "I should have done it much sooner," he said, and then sighed. "I also should have told you that myself."

I bit my tongue on what I wanted to say. Despite everything we'd been through, I had no real say in what he did with his finances. It wasn't the fact that he gave the Hamptons house to his mother that galled, but the fact he didn't tell me about it beforehand. "We need to work on our communication."

Jeremiah sighed, and then nodded. The waiter arrived with our plates, setting down what was a tiny triangle of steak slices. I frowned, poking it with my fork. "Mind if we pick up something else on the way home?" I half-joked, and smiled a bit at Jeremiah's chuckle.

The steak was really good, if not altogether filling. I ordered dessert, which arrived quickly, a thin slice of deliciously rich cheesecake. "Now this is what I'm talking about," I moaned, offering a forkful to Jeremiah.

"I almost forgot, how was your meeting with you friend from Borneo?"

"Really good. She's up for just a week, so I'm hoping we can see each other again." I chewed another mouthful of sinful cheesecake. "She thinks I made a mistake in quitting the charity."

"Well, why don't you start your own?"

My mouth stopped moving. I stared at him, wide-eyed, as he sipped his wine glass. "I can't do that."

"Why not?"

"I'm not . . ." I stuttered into silence, and then tried again. "I wouldn't know where to begin."

"You did pretty well before," he said, and then finally took pity at my stunned expression. "Start it under my name if you'd prefer. You must still have contacts from your last job, I know they were sad to see you leave."

The group I'd been working with for several months had indeed been reluctant to let me go. I hadn't realized until it was too late just how much I would miss the job and the people in that office. It wasn't until I heard Cherise talk about

Borneo that I realized what a mistake I'd made. "You'd let me use your name? But what if I screwed everything up?"

He lifted my hand to his lips. "I believe in you," he said, squeezing my fingers. "I've seen you do remarkable things, Lucy, and I don't see why this would be any different."

A wide grin split my face. Grabbing his head, I pulled him in for a kiss, not caring if the public saw my exuberance. "Have I told you today that I loved you?" I murmured against his lips.

"Yes, but I can always stand to hear it again."

The cellphone on the table began vibrating.

I saw the change in his face immediately. My fingers tightened on his cheeks involuntarily. "Don't get it?" I asked softly, almost pleading.

He paused, body tense, as the phone vibrated several times, then went silent. I started to relax when it began to vibrate again, and Jeremiah sighed. "I need to get this."

I let him go, turning around in my seat as he picked up the phone, then stood and walked off toward the exit. Staring at the delicate orchid place setting in the center of the table, I woodenly placed my napkin on the table and stood up to follow him outside.

3

My apartment had always been tiny, but having grown used to Jeremiah's penthouse, it looked practically miniscule now.

I wasn't sure why I kept it at this point. Nearly all my nights were spent in Manhattan nowadays, falling asleep locked in Jeremiah's arms. There wasn't any place I'd rather be, so my insistence on keeping the tiny studio baffled both Jeremiah and myself. I'd barely even decorated, as if knowing my time here would be short, yet I couldn't quite give it up.

Sitting down on the large papasan chair, I picked up the photo closest to me. My parents had been married by my age; their smiling faces stared up at me, recognizable to me despite their youth. They'd been gone nearly four years now, and I was only just now finally moving past their deaths. Still, sometimes I would have given anything to see them again, or ask their advice on questions I needed answered.

I sighed and set the picture back on the small table, leaning back in the wide chair. If I was being perfectly honest with myself, I knew why I kept this apartment. Too often in the last few years I'd been set adrift, forced suddenly to make my own way in a harsh world. My parents' deaths had been the first blow; losing my family's home had sent me into yet another tailspin. Combine that with the rollercoaster ride that was my dealings with the Hamilton family . . .

There was a home waiting for me in northern New York, a gift I had never expected to get. Except for one trip after Jeremiah came back into my life, however, I hadn't gone to see it. Instead of giving me any joy, looking through the old house, which had been neglected by the previous tenants, had filled me with an aching sadness. I wasn't sure what I was expecting, but without my family there, it was only a structure. There were memories in every nook and cranny, but seeing it only brought back the pain of their loss all over again.

Someone knocked on the door, startling me out of my reverie. Levering myself up from the chair, I padded across the studio and looked through the peephole, and then opened the door.

"I thought I'd find you here."

I spread my arms wide. "Here I am."

Jeremiah stepped inside, and then surveyed the small apartment. His eyes fell on the round papasan chair, and he quirked an eyebrow. "A new acquisition?"

"It's comfortable." The papasan chair was big, with more than enough room for me to curl up into a ball or lay spread eagle across it. I'd already napped in it, and had grown to appreciate the unwieldy piece of furniture. To prove my words, I sat down in the wide cushion, spreading my arms across the top. "See?"

Jeremiah didn't take his eyes off me, but something in his gaze made me swallow. I squirmed as he walked over to me and, placing his arms on the wicker sides, leaned above me. "I can see some of its more entertaining uses," he murmured, and my body tensed with anticipation.

Not taking his eyes off mine, Jeremiah undid the clasp to my pants. In one fluid motion, he sank to his knees and lifted my legs, pulling the pants and underwear off and laying them beside the chair. The cool air hit my skin, but it wasn't the sudden chill that made me shiver as he spread my legs. "One taste of you is never enough."

My hands tangled in his hair as he set his mouth to me, my head falling back against the chair pad. Jeremiah licked and sucked, pulling the cries out from deep inside me. Fingers tightening around his hair, I tilted my hips up toward him, desperate for release.

"God, you're hot. All I can think about is you, how you taste when you come, how you feel around my cock."

He inserted one finger inside of me, then two, and I writhed at the stretching sensation. I arched my back as the pressure built, moving quickly to the surface. Moans blended with every panting breath, my body tightening with the rising orgasm.

"Come for me."

As if my body had been waiting for permission, the orgasm shook me at his words. I let out a strangled groan as

Jeremiah's hands squeezed my thighs. He gave my clit one last lick before lifting his head away from me. "You're so fucking sexy," he rumbled, and I heard the clink of his belt as he undid his own pants. "I want to feel every inch of your . . ."

The muffling ring of Jeremiah's phone filled the small space.

"Are you *freaking* kidding me?"

The words exploded unbidden from me, an expression of my frustration over the past month. I clapped a hand over my mouth, horrified by my outburst. Jeremiah laid his forehead against my belly, unmoving for a long moment. "I have to take this call."

"Don't go." I hated that I was begging for his time, hated it with every fiber of my being. My fingers ran through his soft hair, and it took everything I had not to grab on and not let go. There were things I wanted to say, but the words were too jumbled at that moment to escape my lips.

I felt the butterfly-soft touch of his eyelashes against my belly, and then he pulled back and stood up. "I'll be right back," he said, not really looking at me as he turned around and headed for the door.

My body went slack with disbelief, and then anger overcame me when he closed the door between us. I jumped to my feet, grabbing my pants and slinging them on quickly. Rushing to the door, I jerked it open to see Jeremiah standing in the hallway, talking in hushed tones on his phone.

He must have seen something in my face because he said,

"I'll call you back later." Hanging up and pocketing the phone, he faced me directly, hands behind his back and body straight as if I was a drill sergeant. "I need to go sign some paperwork."

He was bracing himself for anger. It was painfully obvious to me, and only added to my disappointment. Despite us dating, I had no hold over him. I'd always been careful not to impose myself on his life, make any decisions or grabs for his time that he might need elsewhere.

Perhaps I'd been too careful.

"I miss you." The words tumbled out as I finally spoke my mind for once. "All you ever do lately is work. Phone calls, interrupted dinners, interruptions with . . ." I trailed off, and then waved inside my apartment. "That." I raised my eyes up to his stoic face. "I miss you."

Whatever fight he'd been prepared for, I could see this wasn't it. Truthfully, I did want to rail at him, demand his attention, force him to finish what he started back there. I wanted to throw that blasted cellphone from the highest building in New York City. But I couldn't say that, because the real thing I wanted was *him.*

Jeremiah's hands clenched and relaxed, and he had the decency to look away. "I have one more thing to do with work, and then I'm all yours."

"Do you even know what today is?"

He leaned down and kissed my forehead. I closed my eyes, savoring the touch of his lips against my skin. "I'll be back here to pick you up tonight."

Deflated, I watched him walk away, toward the stairs. He hadn't even disappeared yet when his cellphone was back at his ear.

I pulled my own phone out of my pocket and dialed. "Cherise?" I said when a chipper voice answered, only further accentuating the glum note in my own. "Can you come pick me up?"

4

H e really just left after you said that?"
I laid my head against the car window, watching
the darkness of the city go past. "He had his phone out almost immediately too. I swear, that thing is practically grafted
to his head."

"Well, he is CEO for a powerful corporation." She rubbed
her hand over my arm. "I'm sorry hon."

"It isn't like I can demand his time," I continued deject-
edly. "He's his own person, deserves his space . . ."

"Says who?"

I looked at Cherise, who was frowning at the dark road
ahead. "It's not like we're married. We're just dating."

"You think marriage makes it easier?" She snorted. "Sometimes I have to corner David and practically tie him to the
bed just to get his attention."

I blinked owlishly at Cherise. "Seriously?"

"Well, maybe not quite so take-charge," she said, laughing, and then looked askance at me. "I always thought you

were more like that too, gung-ho and 'Rawr, I am woman hear me roar'!"

"Whatever gave you that idea?"

"Remember the charity gala last year? You were on fire, approaching any and everyone asking for donations."

"That was different, it was for you guys."

"Well? Pretend you're a charity case then. Or, something." She squeezed my shoulder. "You had it right before, you guys just need to learn to communicate."

"But what if this is how it is forever? Or worse, what if everything goes to pot?"

"Then you come down to Borneo and help us cure orphans and the sick."

Yes, there was always that. The more I thought about it, however, the more my mind rebelled. I had been through so much with Jeremiah, and even now the idea of leaving made me want to cry. As desperately as I wanted to help change the world, I couldn't give everything up so easily.

My pocket began to vibrate. Reaching in, I pulled out my phone and stared at Jeremiah's face on the front screen. Cherise glanced over to see what I was looking at. "He sure is handsome," she offered, and I smiled.

"He is."

I love him. The not-so-stunning revelation almost made me laugh. Here I was, contemplating moving to Borneo just because he was working too hard at a job I knew he hated. It was the height of selfishness to think of escaping when he really had no such choice himself.

Hamilton Industries was his family's business, but it had

never been what he wanted. His father, upon his death, had foisted it on Jeremiah as punishment for daring to rebel. Ever the hero, Jeremiah had stepped into a role he hated, just to save the many thousands of people whose jobs would have been eradicated. He was good at it too, but the position was a gilded cage; he didn't have the choice to run.

What reason did I have to leave him like that?

"Are you going to answer your phone?"

I looked at Cherise, my smile widening. The phone stopped vibrating with a missed call, but immediately started up again. Sliding the green bar across the screen, I pulled it up to my ear. "Hello, gorgeous."

The unusual greeting must have thrown him because he waited a full second before replying. "I'm at your apartment," he said in an almost cautious voice.

"I'm driving around the city with Cherise."

"Where are you now?"

"About a minute from your apartment," my friend answered, turning down a one-way street. At my look, she shrugged. "What? I had a feeling you'd change your mind on the whole Borneo thing."

"Borneo?"

Jeremiah's dubious tones made me smile even bigger. "Have I told you tonight that I love you?"

He didn't answer, and something told me that my cheery attitude was not the reaction he was expecting. That only made me want to laugh. "You ready for dinner?" I asked after a moment of silence.

"I had something else in mind."

Of course he did. I shook my head. "I'll see you in a minute."

"I'll be here. Lucy?"

I put the phone back to my head. "Yes?"

"I love you, too."

"That's a big smile you've got there," Cherise said as I pocketed the phone. "I take it you've patched up your difference and I lost out on a friend visiting me?"

"I'll come down and visit you one of these days, I promise." I laid my head on her shoulder unexpectedly. "Thanks for letting me rant and rave for a little bit."

"What are friends for?"

A long SUV limo was parked in front of my apartment building, but there was no sign of Jeremiah. I got out of Cherise's rental care and bent down. "Thanks again for the talk, I'll see you around."

"Yes, you will," she said with a smug smile. "Now, go kiss that hunky boy toy of yours."

The driver stood on the sidewalk beside the SUV, and as I approached he pointed toward the building. "He said he's waiting upstairs for you, Ms. Delacourt."

When I opened my door, the apartment was dark. I was just about to turn on the lights when a hand grabbed my wrist and pulled me inside, shutting the door behind me. I yelped in surprise as I was spun around, and then a thick body pressed me up against the wall.

"You didn't answer your phone." Jeremiah's voice flowed over me like a sensual storm, igniting my body. "How should I punish you for that?"

I gave a little sigh, not answering him but rotating my hips to rub my backside against the growing bulge I felt. The light stubble of his cheek scraped down the side of my neck as his lips blazed a trail along my hairline. Resting my head against the wall, I repeated the motion with my hips and was gratified when he pressed himself against me.

He pushed away from me, running his hands down the arch of my back and cupping my ass through the jeans. "I've been thinking about you all day," he murmured, moving his hands back up my body in a caress that left trails of fire in their wake.

"You left me," I murmured, and then squeaked a laugh as he spun me around and pulled me flush against his body.

"Not by choice."

I had no chance to say anything before his lips descended on mine, stealing away any more protests I might have raised. He swallowed my moan, strong hands gripping my backside and lifting me off the floor. I wrapped my legs around his hips, twining my arms around his neck as he pressed me back against the wall. His mouth alternately nibbled and sucked, and I sighed with enjoyment. He really was the most perfect kisser.

"I thought of a few more uses for that chair of yours," he murmured against my mouth, and I grinned into his lips. "But first, we need to get you out of these damned clothes."

"Anything you want," I murmured, and heard him chuckle.

He carried me almost effortlessly across the small room as I clung to him, pressed my body against his hard frame.

Settling me into the wide papasan chair, he tugged at my shirt. "Off."

I hurried to comply, removing the shirt and my jeans quickly. Light from the nearby street lamp streamed in through the window, outlining Jeremiah's perfect body as he pulled the button-up shirt over his head. I paused, enjoying the delicious view, until his hands landed on my bra. "This too."

With trembling fingers, I unhooked the strap of clothing and removed it from my arms, setting it beside the chair. I was naked except for my panties, laid out in that chair, and all I could think about was what we had done earlier with a similar position. Desire rumbled through me, my heart speeding up as he sank down on his heels.

I wanted to touch him, feel the chiseled planes of his body, but he caught my hands before I could reach him. Spreading them out, he smoothed my hands over the chair's metal edges. "Hold onto this, and don't let go unless I say."

My eyes squeezed shut as he leaned over my body, setting his mouth to the hollow between my breasts. A small moaning sigh escaped my throat, and then another as his lips moved sideways over my breasts. Teeth scraped the tender skin, but it was his tongue and lips that pulled the loud cry out of me as they twirled around my nipple. Rough nails scraped down my sides as his mouth dipped lower, hot breath trailing down my belly.

If he didn't approve of my underwear still being on, he said nothing as his fingers hooked through the elastic band. They'd barely left my skin before he set his mouth to my pubic bone, and my back arched off the chair. I lifted my feet, digging my heels into the frame of the chair, and I heard him chuckle.

"Good girl," he murmured, then moved that tiny bit lower, spreading my folds and running his fingers along my opening. Another groan erupted from my body, my breaths coming in pants now. He licked and pressed his fingers deep inside, but there was a desperation there that told me this wasn't all he wanted this time.

"Get on your knees in front of the chair."

I hurried to comply, my limbs like jelly from desire. Laying my cheek on the cushion, I reached out sideways to grab the frame on each side. Jeremiah's hands moved down my sides as if tracing my curves, and then I felt his naked member pressed against my butt. Gasping in need, I tilted my hips up to receive him, but that wasn't what he had in mind just yet.

Straps were fastened around my wrists, lashing my arms to the chair's frame. "Your apartment needs more toys," Jeremiah murmured in my ear as he tilted his hips, sliding himself between my wet folds. "Fortunately, I brought a few of my own tonight."

I heard the cap of a small lube container, and then hands lifted and parted my butt cheeks. The cool fluid slid across my back opening, fingers teasing the entrance. I knew the taboo aspect of this opening excited Jeremiah, so it didn't surprise me when I felt the butt plug slide up slowly inside me.

"For later," he promised, laying a kiss on the back of my neck. There was the familiar crinkle of the condom wrapper, and then his hand moved between my shoulder blades, pressing me down onto the cushion. The blunt tip of his erection probed my entrance, teasing the slick folds. Then, almost without warning, he jerked his hips forward, sheathing himself inside me.

I almost came right then and there. I didn't realize how worked up I still was from our truncated tryst earlier, but desire roared through my body at the almost brutal start. The straps on my wrists pulled tight as he began hammering in and out of my body. His arm wrapped around my belly, pulling me against his body as he laid his forehead against my shoulder.

This was what I'd been craving, the unforgiving harshness when he lost control. There was power in knowing that I had caused this, that it was my body, my actions, that took away the walls he always kept up. I loved it when he was this eager, when he took me as if his sanity depended on it.

Nails scored my sides, digging in to an almost painful degree. The small grunts I heard from him told me that he was close. My own orgasm was just below the surface, and I tilted my hips up to meet his thrusts. It only took a couple seconds of him rubbing just the right spot inside me, and then the pleasure rocketed through my body. I trembled, grabbing the chair frame for support, as behind me Jeremiah roared his own release.

His thrusts didn't stop immediately, as if he wanted to continue. Eventually however, they tapered off, and I smiled against the cushion as he laid a kiss on the back of my head.

I didn't move as he pulled free and stood up, giving myself

a moment to recover. When his hands finally released the restraints on my wrists, I allowed him to gather me into his arms. My apartment was tiny, so it was only a few steps to get to the bed at the far end.

"Couldn't you have at least gotten a queen-sized bed?"

I smiled sleepily. The twin bed was a thrift store find, and suited me perfectly. Trying to fit both Jeremiah and myself on it however was another story entirely. He fixed that however by laying me atop him so that I was staring down at his face. One hand brushed my damp hair behind my ear, his thumb caressing my cheek.

I laid a kiss on his palm, leaning into his hand. "You left something behind," I teased, shaking my butt that still had the plug inside me.

"I'm quitting Hamilton Enterprises."

The unexpected confession took my breath away. I stared, wide-eyed, down at his placid expression. He searched my face and cupped my cheek before continuing. "I've been torturing myself with this company for too long. It's time I lived my own life outside my father's shadow."

My discomfort momentarily forgotten, I levered myself up onto my hands. "You're really going to give it all up?"

Beneath me, Jeremiah nodded. "My father's will at the time of his death was ironclad: if I didn't take over, he would liquidate everything. His terms could have put thousands of people out of business, but it's been years now." He rubbed a stray lock of my blond hair through his fingers. "The lawyers are working on finding a way to mitigate the losses, but I don't care anymore."

The information still had me stunned. "So you won't be CEO anymore? Or are you giving up the money?"

Jeremiah shook his head. "The money outside the business is still mine, as is most of the real estate and items like the jet and cars. Much of my income went back into the business, but even if that remains tied up I'll remain wealthy."

"Are you sure you want this?"

He reached up to hold my head with both hands. "There's only one thing in this world that I've wanted more."

The grin that split my face made my cheeks ache, but I didn't care. Abandoning decorum, I wrapped my arms around his neck, pulling him close. "I'm so happy for you!"

He chuckled against my hair. "Life's about to get more interesting, that's for sure."

I beamed down at him. "You'll do great, whatever you decide."

"So, tell me: what was this about Borneo?"

It took me a moment to figure out what he was talking about. "Ah." Remembering my earlier outburst made me embarrassed. "Cherise, um, told me that if things didn't work out with us, I could help her and David out in their clinic."

Jeremiah didn't say anything for a long moment, and I bit my lip. "I was angry at you for walking away," I continued, a little desperate for him to understand. "You've been tied to your phone almost nonstop the last few weeks but wouldn't tell me why. I thought you were pulling away from me, making work more important."

"Silly woman." There was laughter in Jeremiah's voice as he shook his head. "You know I'd just follow you down there."

His words made my heart swell almost painfully, and I hiccupped a happy sob. "I was thinking, though," I continued, laying my hand against his chest. "About what you said on starting another charity. I'm not a doctor or a nurse so I probably couldn't help much in the field, but I'm really good at fundraising. I even enjoy doing it."

"You'd be really good, too." His fingers wandered over my body, down my thighs that straddled his hips. Between my legs, I could feel him stirring to life once again. He reached between my legs and pulled out the plug, but didn't try anything yet, enjoying our position now as much as I was.

"I love you." I couldn't say that enough to him. The words had been abused for him as a child, and getting him to realize they were more than mere platitudes hadn't been easy. Ultimately, it was getting him to realize what they meant to others, not just himself, that had changed his view. Jeremiah Hamilton loved fiercely, whether he'd known it before or not, and it constantly astonished me that he was mine.

His hands grasped my hips, pushing me upwards. I sat back, helping him maneuver me over his hard member pressed against my inner thigh. Leaning back, I placed my hands on his thighs as he pierced me slowly, pulling me implacably down around him. He stretched the tight muscles but it didn't hurt much thanks to his preparation beforehand.

I closed my eyes, allowing him this pleasure. His soft gasps echoed off the walls as I moved slowly, rolling my hips and pulling him in and out of me. The sensations of him being back there were enjoyable for me, but it was his pleasure that gave me satisfaction. His fingers dug into the soft flesh of my thighs as I rode him, and I could tell from the guttural sounds he made that he was close.

Leaning down over him, I laid a kiss on his neck, clenching briefly around him. "Come for me," I whispered, and smiled as, with a hoarse cry, he did as I commanded, his body shuddering beneath me.

Satisfied, I laid another soft kiss to his chest. "Are we staying here tonight?" I asked, already knowing the answer. When he shook his head, unable to speak, I lifted off him and moved to the floor. "Let me clean up then."

Fifteen minutes later I was ready to go. Jeremiah had already dressed, and he eyed the small bag in my hand curiously. "What are you bringing with you?"

"Everything I might need for your place." It was time for me to say goodbye to the apartment. Tomorrow morning, I'd give my thirty-day notice to the landlord. Jeremiah had been pressing me to make the move to his penthouse permanent, and I was finally ready to take that step. For somebody who always liked having a back-up plan, this was a huge leap of faith.

Something told me, however, that it was the right decision for me.

I hadn't realized when I'd seen him that Jeremiah was wearing jeans. That came as something of a shock; I was so used to seeing him in suits, not quite so informal. "A casual night out?" I said to mask my surprise, putting my arms around his waist and looking up into his face.

He laid a soft kiss on my lips. "Let's head down to the car."

My apartment wasn't too far from Manhattan Island, but traffic usually made it seem so much farther. We got lucky that night however, and fifteen minutes later pulled into the underground parking garage. I was laying my head on his shoulder, dozing, when he gently shook me awake. "We're here."

The penthouse floor had its own elevator access, but it still took a while to get upstairs. I stood next to Jeremiah, leaning against his arm, my fingers entwined with his. I was drowsy, my little plastic grocery bag of toiletries hanging beside me in my free hand. I'm not sure what I'd been hoping would happen tonight of all nights, but I was content right where I was at that moment.

The elevator opened into the dark penthouse. I'd barely stepped outside the doors however when every light in the large apartment flipped on at once.

"SURPRISE!"

5

I stared dumbly at the smiling faces before me, my brain not quite understanding their presence. It wasn't until they started the familiar refrains of "Happy Birthday" that the whole situation struck me. Clamping one hand over my mouth, I fought back against tears as everyone sang to me. Scanning the room, I saw faces that I hadn't seen in months, some of whom I'd never thought to see again.

"You have *no* idea how hard it was for me to keep this a secret!" Cherise moved forward and took my hands, drawing me further into the living room. "It's been on the tip of my tongue to tell you every single conversation we've had."

I turned to look at the man beside her. "David?" He gave me a sheepish smile and a wave as I looked at Cherise. "You told me he didn't come with you!"

"Correction," she said, prim as a school teacher. "I said he *wanted* to come, never that he hadn't."

Still too overwhelmed, I just hugged her, and then felt a slight tug on my sleeve. A girl with a dark scarf covering her hair smiled shyly at me, as if afraid I wouldn't recognize her. Ignoring any etiquette or cross-cultural boundaries I might be breaking, I pulled her into a hug. "Amyrah? Oh my gosh, I thought I'd never see you again!"

The Arabian girl just laughed, returning my hug. "It is so good to see you too."

When last I'd heard about Amyrah, she had only just awoken from a week-long coma to find out her brother had been killed in the explosion that sent her to the hospital. I'd known no way to get in contact with the girl and express my condolences, and now wasn't the right time. So I just hugged her close and whispered, "It's *so* good to see you again."

"So am I going to get a hug, too? I should warn you, I carry a gun for just such occasions."

I knew immediately to whom that French accent belonged, and let go of Amyrah. "Agent Gautier," I said, turning to the Interpol agent who had helped Jeremiah and I catch a madman a few months back.

The agent quirked an eyebrow at me, and then extended her hand. "You may call me Marie, now that our investigation is done."

"How did Jeremiah manage to get you here?"

"He has been setting this up a while and gave me enough time to ask for vacation." She slanted a look in Jeremiah's direction. "He also tried to purchase my ticket here to ensure my arrival, the acceptance of which is against agency policy."

"He means well," I replied in his defense, and Marie smiled.

"That's why I did not throw the tickets in his face."

A smiling redhead came up as Marie stepped back. "Happy birthday, hon."

"It's good to see you again, Celeste," I said, accepting a hug from her as well. I hadn't seen the former Hamilton Industries COO in months. While we hadn't really been close, the redhead understood more than most the dangerous ventures of late. She herself had been kidnapped by a hired killer and summarily rescued by her husband. The circumstances surrounding that event had sent her marriage into a tailspin, as I had been the one traded for her life. Celeste hadn't agreed with her husband's decision, but last I'd heard they were trying to work things out.

"Is Ethan here?" I asked, trying to be as delicate as possible. Last I'd heard, they were trying to repair their marriage. "Somehow I doubt he'd let you come here alone."

"Guilty as charged." He appeared beside his wife, reaching out to shake my hand. "Nice little party you have here."

Truthfully, there was little in the way of decorations, but against the back wall was a large round cake with what looked like too many candles. "Are you trying to make me feel old?" I murmured to Jeremiah as I went to look at it.

"Look on the bright side," he replied in a low voice, "you'll always be younger than me."

I beamed at him. "True."

Cherise lit them all quickly, and I blew them out with one breath, to cheers all around. Beside the cake was a small mountain of presents, but I ignored them and began cutting the cake.

"I can do that."

I gave the knife over to Cherise and stepped away as she began handing out slices. There were more people in the group but I only had eyes for one. Lacing my fingers through his, I pulled us sideways out of earshot of our guests, and then wrapped my arms around his neck. "So, was this the other reason for all those phone calls?"

"Perhaps." Jeremiah took my hand in his and laid a kiss on one knuckle. "You know that I love you, right?"

He was staring at me intently, as if trying to gauge my expression. I rubbed my hand down his arm, tilting my head to one side. "Of course I do." It was a silly question, but I wasn't about to tell him that.

"I'm not one for big showy gestures, and I tend to get it wrong when it comes to the romance department."

"I'd have to disagree with that assessment," I added, making a big deal of looking around the room and all our guests, but he wasn't finished.

"I can't imagine ever loving anyone as much as I love you, and there's nobody on this planet I'd rather spend my life with."

As Jeremiah slowly sank down to one knee and reached inside his pocket, I clapped my hands over my mouth. I couldn't tell if the guests had grown quiet, or if I'd just tuned them out. All I saw was the man I loved kneeling before me, opening a small white velvet box.

"Lucy Delacourt," Jeremiah said, presenting me with the largest diamond ring I'd seen in my life, "will you do me the honor of becoming my wife?"

I didn't realize I was holding my breath until I gasped for air. You could have heard a pin drop in that room; nobody so much as moved, but I doubt I'd have noticed anyway. Tears sprang to my eyes as I drew in a shaky breath, too stunned to move.

Beneath me, Jeremiah cleared his throat. "My knee's a little uncomfortable on this tile, Lucy . . ."

"Yes. Yes, you silly, wonderful man, *yes.*"

He surged up, wrapping me in his arms and lifting me of the ground. I laughed, unable to contain myself, as all around us cheers erupted from the crowd. Tears streaked down my face as I grabbed Jeremiah's head and laid a big, wet kiss on his mouth. I couldn't stop laughing though, but he didn't seem to mind. The biggest smile I'd ever seen was stretched across his face, and as he sat me down he picked up my left hand.

"My mother took my great-grandmother's wedding ring when my father proposed, but I wanted to start a new tradition." He spoke in a quiet voice, as if none of the people around us were listening in. Plucking the ring from the tiny box, he held it up to me. "I was given this diamond myself as a gift from an African client. It was uncut when I received it, so I don't believe he knew its true value."

Jeremiah slid the platinum band slowly onto my finger, continuing his story in a soft voice. "I was like that when you found me, as rough as any stone. You made me better, gave me the clarity I hadn't known I needed."

It was impossible to tell whether I was laughing or crying

by that point, but nobody seemed to care. Jeremiah laid a kiss on my hand again, just above the diamond, and I smiled at him through my tears. I finally became aware of the people standing nearby to wish us happiness, but I didn't want to give up my hold on Jeremiah.

"I love you," I whispered against his shirt, and felt his lips on my hair before I turned to show the ring to Cherise, who was nearly bouncing with excitement next to me.

Three hours later, I still couldn't stop staring at the ring on my finger.

"You know you'll go blind staring at that thing," Jeremiah said from nearby.

"It's so beautiful," I said softly for the hundredth time that evening. Lounging back on the leather couch, I held it up above my head. The lights above shone through the diamond as tiny rainbows wove through the facets.

"Wait until you see it in the sunlight, then."

Jeremiah settled himself on the couch just above my head, and I scooted over to lay my head in his lap. His fingertips stroked my shoulder and we sat there in silence, content to just touch. I put my hand beneath my head, careful not to scrape myself with the ring, and squeezed Jeremiah's leg. "So what happens now?"

I felt his body twist as he shrugged. "Marriage, I suppose. Kids. A house in the suburbs."

"We already have one of those, you know," I murmured,

thinking about my parents' home up north. After their deaths, I'd lost it to the creditors, until Jeremiah had somehow managed to get it back for me.

Something about the exhalation above told me he was amused. "So we do."

Somehow, though, I doubted Jeremiah would be happy with a boring existence. His and our future was wide open however; there were so many things we could do. The prospect was exciting and daunting at the same time.

We lapsed into silence again, his fingers still absently stroking my shoulder. "Have you told your mother?" I asked after a few moments.

"Not a word."

"How do you think she's going to take it?"

He snorted. "Probably like a screaming banshee."

I smiled at the images his words produced. "Think she'll get over it?"

"She'll probably forget it the first time we call her *grandma*."

The thought of children made my belly do flip-flops, but I kept my feelings to myself. "Somehow I doubt she'll take that transition gracefully." The very idea of watching *that* meltdown was enough to make me smile with anticipation.

"Her problem, not ours."

I thought of my own mother, imagining what she would have thought about grandchildren. My being an only child hadn't been by choice. I'd always known they wanted more, but that never stopped them from loving me to the fullest. A pang went through my heart. I wished they were here to see this.

Jeremiah must have known my thoughts were turning to melancholy because he gathered me up in his arms. I held onto his shoulders, straddling his hips on the couch so we were face-to-face. He smiled, stroking my cheek. "Mrs. Lucy Hamilton."

Everything inside me sang at the words, and I grinned wildly at him. My eyes fell to his full lips, and I caressed them with my fingers. Jeremiah pulled me close, revealing the hard bulge already growing again between his legs. "You're insatiable," I murmured, leaning down to kiss him.

"Only for you." He stood up with me still clinging to him. I moved to slide down to the ground, but he forestalled that by picking me up in his arms. "Allow me, madam."

He took the stairs two at a time, my extra weight apparently a non-issue. Still, I swatted his arm. "The doctor said you needed to be careful about that leg! Compound fractures like that can take longer than a few months to heal."

"I can deal."

He pulled me close into a kiss, effectively silencing further protests, as we entered the master bedroom. My jaw went slack as I took it in. The only light was candles, set all around the spacious room. On the bed, red rose petals were strewn across the comforter. I turned to stare at him, my eyes wide. "And you said you weren't romantic? Can I officially call BS now?"

"I'm afraid candles and roses are the end of my romantic ways." Jeremiah settled me on the bed, and then began stripping out of his clothes. "I want you now, to feel every inch of you against and around me."

I shivered at the dark promise in his voice, and hurriedly

shed my own garments. His fingers drew my underwear slowly down my legs as I removed my bra, and then he stalked up the bed toward me. The candlelight glittered off the marbled planes of his muscles and gave his beautiful face an almost feral glow. I loved it when he stalked me, all power and grace, but for tonight I wanted to try something different.

My hand seemed so small against his thick shoulder, but he gave way as I pressed him back and over. I followed his movements until I was above him, peering down at him in the low light. Straddling his thighs, I leaned down to kiss him, tangling my hands in his thick hair. He kissed me back, large hands gripping my waist as I trailed my lips down his neck, past his chest and down across washboard abs.

Jeremiah sucked in a breath as I wrapped my hand around his hard length. I gave it a few pumps, enjoying the hitch in his breath that told me he enjoyed it, and then set my mouth on the bulbous tip. Flicking the edges with my tongue, I sucked him in slowly, keeping one fist around the base. He was long but I moved at my own pace, enjoying the tiny thrusts of his hips toward my mouth. It was his turn to tangle his hands in my hair, guttural sounds wordlessly urging me to go faster.

I bobbed my head over him, alternately pressing my tongue against the base and flicking the tip, and then I removed my hand mid-stroke and took him deep. The tickle at the back of my throat made me gag, but my gesture was rewarded by a long groan.

"Fuck, your mouth," Jeremiah rasped, breathing too hard to speak. I repeated the move and got a similar response, which made me smile around him. Moving sideways on the bed until I was almost backwards, I tried again in the new position. Coming from it backwards, he went deep down my throat, and his hips came off the bed.

Hands grabbed my hips, pulling me sideways and back. A thrilled raced through me as I carefully straddled his head, my heart racing in anticipation. There was no preamble to his oral assault. He parted my folds and licked, and I cried out around his member.

Once he set to work on my pleasure, it became increasingly difficult to focus on the task at hand—or mouth, as it were. In very short order I was a quivering mess, moans of my own echoing off the wood floors. He used his tongue and fingers as a delicious torture, distracting me from what I'd been doing. Something told me he was ready to take over, but I wasn't quite finished yet.

Carefully, I turned back around so I was facing him again. I once more straddled his hips and lowered my body so my breasts pressed against his chest. His hands kneaded the flesh of my buttocks as I positioned myself above him.

"I'm too close to coming," he murmured as I laid my lips to his neck while rubbing the thick tip of his cock between my folds. "I should put a condom on before . . ."

He trailed off as I kissed him, lowering my lips and pulling him inside me. "I want to feel you come inside me," I whispered, and his body gave a small jerk. "Skin on skin, nothing between us."

Jeremiah looked as if he'd been given an unexpected gift. "You're sure?"

In answer, I pulled my hips up, and then settled down around him. Grabbing the headboard, I curled my hips up and around, moving above and on him in a sensual dance. The firelight glittered in his eyes as he groaned, fingers digging into my hips and urging me onward. His hands moved up my body, closing over my breasts and thumbing my nipples. It was my turn to cry out, pressing down hard with my hips to take him deep.

With a growl, Jeremiah threw me sideways down onto the bed, rolling over on top of me. Hands pushed my arms into the mattress as he thrust into me, all finesse gone. I cried out, wrapping my legs around his lean hips, urging him on, and tilting my hips to meet each thrust. He was an animal, taking me hard, and I reveled in every minute of it.

My own pleasure rose to the surface quickly, an endless wave that continued with each thrust. Jeremiah however came with a choked roar, his fingers digging into my shoulders as he shuddered above me. I felt him pulsing inside me and drew him down to lie on me as the last of his strength gave way. Little tremors shook his body, remnants of the hard orgasm, and I just smiled.

"I love you so fucking much," he murmured, hugging me close.

I gave a tired laugh. "Such a romantic statement. You should put that into a Valentines Day card."

"I don't give a damn what others think, just you. I love you, I love you . . ."

I just held him, his bulk crushing me onto the mattress, and closed my eyes. This was the happiest day I could remember so far in my life, and I was perfectly content right where I was at that moment. Stroking his hair, I looked again at the ring on my finger, the diamond shining gold in the firelight. "I love you too," I murmured, my heart singing as he hugged me close.

6

A h, my friend, it's good to see you again."

"Gabriel, you remember my fiancée Lucy?"

The Dom just smiled. "I had to read about it in the news-papers. You, my dear, are being hailed as a real-life Cin-derella."

I blushed but said nothing, looking around the interior of the mansion. Little had changed since the last time we'd vis-ited, but something felt different. Perhaps it was the fact that, this time, I knew what to expect. Maybe it was that I was now engaged to the love of my life.

Or perhaps it was the outfit I wore, chosen by Jeremiah, which gave me confidence.

"My home is yours for tonight," Gabriel stated, ushering us inside.

One of Gabriel's submissives approached me. "Can this one take your coat?" she asked, eyes cast down toward the floor.

"I'd like to do my own unveiling," Jeremiah said, laying

his hand against the small of my back. I smiled up at him as we entered the large room in the center of the mansion. Lusty cries came from the wall to one side, but Jeremiah steered me over beside the bar. Turning me to face him, he slowly unbuttoned the long trench coat, and then slid it off my shoulders.

Bereft of the cover, the cool air hit my nipples first, tightening them into hard buds. I didn't move otherwise however, keeping my gaze level with Jeremiah's. One side of his mouth tipped up as he ran his eyes down my body, his gaze like a sensual caress. "You look tasty enough to eat."

The corset was under-bust only, a deep red against my pale skin that was certain to attract attention. My breasts were uncovered, open to the room for anyone to see. The tiny strip of cloth that served as underwear barely covered anything, but it was what Jeremiah had chosen. Before we'd left, he had groomed me until I was smooth down there, with not a hint of hair showing around the tiny thong. It had been an interesting experience, one which he'd taken advantage of to wring an orgasm out of me.

Despite my resolutions, I still felt a faint flush creep up my shoulders and face. I didn't look around to see if anyone was watching however, just to see Jeremiah's reaction. He stepped away, laying the long coat over one barstool, and smiled. "Kneel."

I slowly sank to the floor, a move I'd practiced already many times in the tall heels I wore. There was a time when walking in shoes like this had made me cringe, certain I'd fall flat on my face or break an ankle. Even now, I only wore them when I was with Jeremiah, and he never left my side, ensuring I was allowed stability.

Of course, I rarely wore these shoes outside of the bedroom. They were usually up in the air, the thin heels pointed toward the ceiling as Jeremiah pumped furiously between my legs. But I'd grown used to them, and besides they seemed less shocking when I saw what some of the other Subs wore.

I looked up at Jeremiah, smiling as he caressed my head. His crotch was in front of me and, emboldened by the raw sensuality around me, I leaned forward to nuzzle him. Beneath my cheek, I felt him stir to life, and then his hand tightened in my hair, jerking my head back unexpectedly. "So you'd like to give our guests here a show?"

I focused on the lust, keeping my eyes on Jeremiah's face. "Yes, Sir," I breathed, silently telegraphing my desire.

His fingers traced down to the delicate collar I wore. It was something we'd discussed and researched as I grew to know more about the BDSM lifestyle. While there were couples that follow a Dom/Sub relationship all the time, I'd decided that it wasn't for me. I'd been surprised when Jeremiah approved, telling me he wanted me just the way I was.

That didn't mean, however, that such playing was kept out of the bedroom. Now, apparently, it would be in public as well.

Jeremiah stayed silent so I took the initiative, undoing his leather pants and reaching inside. I heard a tiny moan from above, my indication that I was doing well. Out of the corner of my eye, I saw people gather around as I leaned forward and laid a kiss along his shaft, but I only had eyes for Jeremiah.

"I love you," I murmured, barely loud enough to hear, but his hands tightened in my hair again in reply. I loved having him like this, and found that I loved showing him off. *You want a show?* I mentally challenged the onlookers, stroking his hard length. *Try and top this.*

Tracing my tongue around the tip, I twisted my head sideways and pulled him deep.